SUMM
CORNISH COVE

Kate Ryder

www.ariafiction.com

About *Summer in a Cornish Cove*

Set against the stunning backdrop of the glorious
Cornish Rivieria, this summer will change their lives
for ever!

Oliver Foxley is an acclaimed movie star, global
heartthrob and one half of Hollywood's golden
couple. But under the glare of the spotlight his
'perfect' life is slowly starting to crumble.

Cara Penhaligon is a struggling young Cornish artist, and widowed mother of two children. Life has been unbearably harsh to Cara, but meeting Oliver might just give her a second chance at the happiness she deserves. As each begins to heal the other, the pieces of Oliver's frustrating jigsaw puzzle effortlessly fall into place. But as the Cornish summer draws to a close, Oliver faces the toughest of choices, and no one emerges quite as they were at the start.

For my sisters,

who share my love of hidden Cornish coves

Imagine meeting
someone who understands
even the dustiest corners
of your mixed-up soul

Chapter One

Late September and the weather is on the turn, reminding the last remaining summer tourists the holiday season is finally over. Time to head home. With a threat of rain in the air people hurry along the streets, their collars turned up and heads bent low against the wind. The sea, the same colour as the sky, has no clearly defined horizon, merely a subtle merging of varying shades of grey. In the relative safety of the inner harbour fishing boats bob furiously, their rigging clanging in the strengthening wind. Beyond the outer harbour, huge waves smash against the rocks, sending plumes of spray rocketing skywards before plummeting to earth and cascading over the stonework of the pier. A group of reckless lads dare each other to face the force of the ocean, retreating at the last moment before edging their way, once again, to the end of the pier. Seagulls are buffeted sideways by gusts of wind and those that take to the wing are tossed about like puppets at the mercy of an inexperienced puppeteer.

Oliver stands at the edge of the slipway watching the drama unfold. This energy is what feeds his soul; his day-to-day existence is not enough. He glances at his wife standing beside him holding onto her waxed hat, her long dark hair flying madly. She was right to suggest they visit Cornwall at the end of the season. He feels invigorated and vitalised.

'Happy?' she asks, turning towards him, and he smiles. 'Let's find a café.' Not waiting for a response, she turns and walks along the harbour road.

Despite the deteriorating weather, the town is busy with people going about their business but several stop and stare as the couple pass by. At the entrance to a courtyard Oliver's wife halts. Swiftly she reads a display board listing the shops hidden within before leading her husband into its relative sanctuary.

*

It's been a quiet afternoon in the gallery. Engrossed in a book, listening to her favourite Moody Blues CD, Carol is pleased there have been so few customers as the book is a page-turner and she's almost at the end. Glancing out of the window, she sees a couple enter the empty courtyard and hopes they won't come in. Quickly she returns to the unfolding story, but a flurry of excitement outside diverts her attention. A gaggle of people have also entered the courtyard and her friend, Sheila, waves at her from the entrance. Flushed and excited, more so than usual, she points to the couple. As Carol peers

2

through the window to see what all the fuss is about, the bell above the door clangs. A slim, attractive, dark-haired woman enters and acknowledges Carol with a brief smile before turning to the man following.

'Look, darling, what wonderful paintings.' Her cut-glass accent fills the gallery. 'Isn't that the Minack?' She points to a canvas perched on the easel just inside the door.

By now, yet more people have entered the courtyard. Torn between finishing the novel, dealing with a potential sale and her desire to find out what's occurring outside, Carol places the book face down on the counter and turns her attention to the couple now studying the paintings displayed on the rear wall. The woman is in her late thirties or early forties. A strong, no-nonsense woman who knows exactly who she is, thinks Carol, before turning her attention to the man. Although he is facing away from her, she can sense his commanding presence. As the couple move slowly round the gallery, discussing the various paintings and examining the range of gifts on display, it's an interesting lesson in body language. The woman, with her all-commanding inner strength, appears to be in control, whereas the man, although possessing a strength of his own, seems to follow in her wake; not weakly but as an extension to his companion.

I wonder how Ken and I are perceived, Carol idly speculates, but as the man turns in her direction her eyes open wide and she breathes in sharply. He smiles a resigned smile; one of reluctant acceptance at her reaction to him.

'These paintings are superb,' he comments in a deep, distinctive voice. 'Do you know the artist?'

Carol can't find her voice and thank God she's sitting, as she seems to have lost the use of her legs. Summoning her fast-diminishing strength, she says in the smallest of voices, 'Yes, my daughter.'

The man's smile relaxes into one of sincerity, making his handsome face even more attractive.

'She has a wonderful talent.'

Intelligent, clear blue eyes.

Carol blushes and nods. She is so very proud of her lovely Cara.

As the woman calls over, he turns away. Knowing it's ridiculous at her age to be *so* affected in this way, Carol attempts to still her beating heart.

The noise in the courtyard has increased and she glances out of the window again. The enclosed space is full of people and Sheila, with her nose pressed flat against the glass, peers through the window.

That woman is so indiscreet, thinks Carol as she pulls a face at her dear old friend.

Lucky you, mouths Sheila.

With concerns about the heroine's fate now cast aside, Carol's attention focuses on the potential customers. They make a very attractive couple and appear to move as one, no doubt honed over years of being together. They dress similarly too. Both wear Barbour jackets and denim jeans; in the woman's case, tucked into a pair of Dubarry boots. The man's striped scarf gives him the appearance of a student, though he must be in his early forties, and there's the merest hint of silver at his temples on an otherwise full head of dark hair. But something doesn't quite fit and a small frown furrows Carol's brow. The woman has a straightforward clarity but there's something darker to the man, despite his dazzling smile. She's considering what that darkness might be when he turns and looks directly at her. Quickly Carol turns away, mortified he's caught her studying him.

'We love the way your daughter has captured the Minack Theatre under a clear night sky,' he says, and Carol knows he's being kind and putting her at her ease.

'Yes, it's a very different take,' she mutters, a range of emotions surging through her. With a deep breath she continues, 'So many artists paint it looking down at the amphitheatre and out to sea, but Cara's 'eye' visualises images in a very different way. This view, I think, has certainly caught the atmosphere of the place.'

'Indeed,' the man says. 'How much is it?'

'Seven hundred and fifty.'

He glances at his companion, an unspoken communication passing between them. 'We'll take it.'

'And I'll have these driftwood photo frames as well,' adds the woman. 'Samantha will love them.'

Concentrating hard on walking across the gallery, Carol lifts the canvas from the easel. She wraps it carefully, places it in a large, white bag on which 'The Art Shack' is printed in vibrant peacock blue and props it against the counter. Then, wrapping the driftwood frames in tissue paper, she places these in another bag.

'If you're still here next week you may be interested to know my daughter is having an exhibition in Truro starting on Monday,' Carol says, amazed that she's managed a complete sentence without stuttering. She slides the credit-card machine over the counter towards the man.

'Unfortunately we're leaving tomorrow,' the woman says.

'That's a shame. Have you been staying locally?'

The woman surveys her coolly. Instantly, Carol feels she's overstepped the mark, but why? She was only being friendly.

'Not far,' the woman replies in a noncommittal manner.

Carol hands the man his card and receipt.

'Please tell your daughter we will treasure this painting,' he says, bending to pick up the canvas. 'It's a wonderful memory of our visit.'

She promises to pass his message on.

He starts to walk away but turns back to her. 'I notice your daughter signs her paintings 'Cara P'. What is her name?'

'Cara Penhaligon.'

'A true Cornish name if ever there was one!' He smiles at Carol with a twinkle in his eyes. As her legs threaten to give way, Carol sits.

His companion is already at the door. As she opens it, the clamour of voices in the courtyard momentarily dips as the couple step out into the late afternoon air. Immediately people surge around and Carol notices how the man signs every scrap of paper presented to him with a quiet dignity, while the woman stands by proprietorially. He catches Carol watching him again and she blushes, embarrassed. He smiles. She can see he's trying hard to mask his resignation but the darkness she'd noticed earlier once more envelops him. Before Carol can contemplate this further, her friend charges through the door in a state of high excitement.

'Carol, can you believe it?' Sheila exclaims. 'Oh my God! Can you believe it? Here in little old Porthleven!'

Holding a piece of paper aloft, Sheila shimmies her way to the counter. Drawing the paper to her lips, she plants a firm kiss on the autograph. Carol laughs. Sheila is always a whirlwind of fun and enthusiasm, but her energy has extended beyond the norm this afternoon.

'No, Sheila, I wouldn't have believed it had I not witnessed it for myself.'

'Oh my God! Wait 'til Betty hears what she's missed.'

'She will be well fed up,' Carol says, looking out of the window at the now empty courtyard.

Bubbling with excitement, Sheila pulls Carol off the stool and spins her round. Both women giggle like schoolgirls.

'Grandma!'

Carol turns in the direction of the voice. Her grandson bounds across the shop towards her, dragging his school bag behind him, all cheeky smiles under a mop of blond hair. Momentarily her heart pinches at the image he represents of that other golden child she once knew.

'Sky, watch where you're going,' Cara calls from the entrance. Her daughter, Bethany, stands behind her.

Flinging himself at Carol, the young boy hugs her tightly, and she drops a kiss on the top of her precious grandson's head.

'Looks like you've been busy, Mum,' Cara says, glancing at the empty easel. 'Where's *The Minack* gone?'

But before Carol has a chance to respond, Sheila shrieks, 'Oh my God, Cara! You will never guess who your mother just sold your painting to. I can't believe it! Oh my God!' Aware that the boy stares at her, open-mouthed, she quickly adds, 'Pretend you didn't hear that, Sky.'

Cara looks from Sheila to her mother in bewilderment. Both women appear flushed with a feverish look in their eyes.

'Who?' she asks.

In unison the older women gush, 'Oliver Foxley!'

Chapter Two

Oliver leans over and switches on a side lamp, the glow from the fire no longer casting sufficient light to read the script lying open on his lap. He has been in his study for most of the day – in fact, the previous three days – but has yet to decide if the film is for him. His agent is right; it *is* a lucrative deal and the role is substantial. But, it will mean months away from the family on location. Can he face that again?

Despite Deanna and the kids being at home, it's quiet in the house and he knows they are giving him the space he needs. It's a well-honed strategy, perfected over twenty-plus years of marriage, and his children have never known anything different. It doesn't make it any easier to survive the 'grey mist', as they call it, but it does allow him time to assimilate and finally accept, to some degree, the despair and confusion that have plagued him since childhood.

Oliver sighs. Laying the script on the floor, he rises and places another log on the fire. It spits and sends sparks flying up the chimney. The study is his inner sanctum and this is where he spends a great deal of time. He wanders over to the French doors. There is still enough light to look out across the extensive, manicured lawns down to the lake at the edge of the woods that stretch as far as the eye can see. Most of it does not belong to him; the forestry is in the ownership of the National Trust. All is still, with no sign of the threatened snow the weather forecasters have predicted, and he watches as a wintry sun sets behind the North Downs rising beyond the tree line. It's a great house, Hunter's Moon, and one that has comfortably provided the space in which to raise a family away from prying eyes. Located down a long track leading only to a public car park in the woods, it is secluded and away from other properties yet close enough to be part of the wider community, should they so desire.

Oliver breathes in deeply.

His first major film role – the one that set him apart from other actors of his age and firmly established him as a player of note in the British film industry – presented itself only a year after leaving drama school. At the time, his parents worried he wouldn't be able to handle the fame and success so early in his career but Deanna was there for him. He smiles fondly as he remembers her arrival in the second year of his acting degree. She instantly stood out from the huddle of new students, the most attractive to him by far, not least because of her all-pervading, no-nonsense strength that filled the room, even then. She was not there to study acting but had enrolled on the stage management course. Nothing shallow about Deanna; she is his rock. Soon after the film's release they married in a small, private ceremony with only close friends and family present. However, almost immediately following their honeymoon, Hollywood came knocking. Relocating to Los Angeles for a couple of years, he worked the circuit and established himself as a leading man on both sides of the Atlantic. His chiselled looks, expressive eyes and ability to tackle characters with a sympathy and depth beyond his years stood him in good stead and only Deanna was aware of the pain that lurked behind the handsome mask.

With his Hollywood breakthrough came the money. Receiving sound advice from his accountant, he invested in a substantial house with accompanying land, set on the edge of an affluent village in the Surrey Hills, safe in the knowledge that wherever his career took him Hunter's Moon would be a lifetime home for his family. Close enough to London and the airports to enable him to continue his international career with ease, the property would also give the children, Deanna and he planned to have, the opportunity of experiencing as normal a life as possible; not one distorted by the excesses surrounding Oliver's chosen career, but a life grounded in the countryside. Over the following years they witnessed many of their friends' burnout and knew their decision during the early days of their marriage had been a good one.

Deanna loved the house as soon as she saw the sales particulars. Oliver recalls his wife's mounting excitement as they sat together one morning on the balcony of their LA rental apartment, the intense heat beating down and the relentless smog lingering on the horizon. He watched her devour the estate agent's particulars, amazed at his 'rock's' display of emotion. At the time, she was four months pregnant and prone to severe bouts of morning sickness. Ever stoic, she said nothing, but he knew she was desperate to return to the UK. The general emptiness of the people surrounding them in Los Angeles did not sit comfortably with his young wife and, being pregnant and unemployed, Deanna had plenty of time to think. As soon as filming wrapped they returned to the UK in time for Samantha to be born on British soil.

Oliver sighs deeply. He knows this memory process is cathartic. His therapist explained it was this act of counting his blessings that allowed him to emerge once more from the gloom and into the sun. But it's taking a long time, this time…

Gentle knocking at the door, and light pools into the room. 'Ollie, why are you standing in the dark?' Deanna flicks a switch by the door and four uplighters immediately throw some light upon the scene. 'How's the script?' she asks, not moving from the threshold.

'OK. Not sure I want it, though,' Oliver says, walking back to his chair.

'Why not?' she asks.

'It's a good role but I'd have to commit to several months away in the States and the Far East. Not sure I want to do that.'

Deanna moves slowly towards him. Perching on the arm of his chair, she places her hand lightly on his shoulder and asks, 'Darling, wouldn't a change be as good as a rest?'

Oliver glances at her. Not for the first time he wonders how she is always so sure of herself. In all that she undertakes Deanna is never at a loss, even when dealing with the children. If only he were half as confident then perhaps he could put his demons to rest once and for all. The only time he feels truly whole is in front of the cameras, deep in characterisation, but he knows it's these personal gremlins that make him so good at his craft. He is a first-rate actor.

Oliver shakes his head. 'I need to read more of the script before making a final decision.'

Squeezing her husband's shoulder, Deanna changes the subject. 'Are you ready to join us for supper tonight?'

Oliver would love to have supper in his study again, but can he really get away with it three nights in a row? His conscience tells him to pull himself together and embrace the world once more. Without realising, he sighs.

Deanna gets to her feet. 'Ollie, if you're not ready I can prepare a tray for you.'

'What time is it?' he asks.

'Approaching six.'

'I'll join you at seven,' he says.

She bends and kisses him lightly. 'Seven it is, then.'

As she turns to leave, Oliver catches her hand. 'I don't deserve you, Dee.'

'Oh, Ollie, of course you do! You're great at your job and a wonderful husband and father. You're the best.' He doesn't look convinced and she frowns. Softly she adds, 'And besides, I fancy you like mad… even now, after all these years.'

He wants to say, 'I am such a burden to your soaring eagle' but knows it will sound ridiculous, as though he's whining, even though it is how he feels. Instead, he pulls her into his lap and returns her kiss.

Briefly, Deanna closes her eyes. 'In an hour, Ollie,' she says, rising to her feet. 'Don't be late.'

At the door she turns back but her husband gazes into the fire, once more introspective and distant. Had he been looking, Oliver would have seen the briefest moment of assessment before Deanna quietly closes the door behind her. But Oliver Foxley is gripped by a melancholy that refuses to shift.

Why does he always feel so adrift and incomplete these days? He has so much going for him. To the outside world they are a successful, goal-driven, tight-knit family. His children are healthy, good-looking, high achievers with all the opportunities available to them that a comfortable upbringing affords. He has established a successful career for himself, is critically acclaimed and in demand; not simply typecast in all-action hero parts but often considered for roles demanding a more versatile actor. He no longer has to work and can pick and choose those projects that interest him. A number of blockbuster directors have all made themselves known to him, or he can choose to work with less mainstream professionals. Oliver Foxley is one lucky man. Then, why does he always feel as if part of him is missing?

He picks up the script again. It really is a good role but he doesn't respond to it. The film is certain to be a box office hit, but so what if it is? What difference does it make? Why put himself through it all again?

Oliver groans.

Glancing up, his eyes rest upon the painting displayed above the fireplace. In the flickering firelight the sea beyond the amphitheatre appears to come to life. Is it his imagination or is there a swell? Thinking back to that windswept day in September, when he and Deanna stumbled upon that little art gallery in Porthleven, he smiles at the memory of the pretty, flustered woman who proudly informed him how her talented daughter visualised images in a very different way and that the view she had captured across the Minack caught the atmosphere of the place.

'One hell of an artist to create moving waves on canvas!' he mutters.

Another knock at the door and Oliver wonders if the hour has passed already. He hopes not. As the door opens, hesitant blue eyes peer at him from under thick lashes.

'Hello, Jamie.'

'Is it OK to come in?' the boy asks cautiously.

'Of course!' Oliver pushes aside his gremlins and smiles at his youngest son. He opens his arms wide.

Running across the room, the boy climbs onto his dad's lap and snuggles against his chest.

'Are you having supper with us tonight?' Jamie asks.

'Yes.' Oliver's heart pinches; he is racked with guilt and full of remorse. He needs to look after his family… especially this son.

At nine years old, Jamie is quiet and prone to introspection. So like him at that age. His depression was already in evidence; although no one knew what it was in those days or even acknowledged it. He is determined his son will *not* follow in his footsteps. He will do all he can to prevent his youngest from falling prey to the debilitating mental condition that afflicts him. Oliver strokes Jamie's hair.

The boy looks up expectantly. 'Will you help us decorate the tree afterwards? Sammy's got the decs out and she's going through them now.'

Christmas Eve! How could he forget? Where has he been? If nothing else, this is a time for the kids.

'Of course! Come on, Jamie, let's join the others.'

*

It's late afternoon by the time the Christmas lunch is over. Ken and Barry, still wearing their Christmas cracker crowns, finish their annual washing-up ritual and wander into the living room to a round of applause.

'Well, that's given you a bit more practice, Bar,' says Sheila. 'Maybe you'll give it another go during the coming year?' Her husband laughs.

'Let's have a look and see what's on the box,' says Ken. He sits in the armchair and thumbs through the *Radio Times*. 'Missed the Queen's speech,' he mutters, and then more forcibly, 'You'd think they'd find something of interest to put on at this time of year, wouldn't you? Why rerun oldies year-on-year? Remind me why we pay our licence fee!'

'Quite right,' agrees Barry. Sheila rolls her eyes.

'Oh, hang on, here's one just about to start. A murder mystery. Always good subject matter for Christmas, don't you think, Barry? And, ladies, one for you too.' Ken grins at the women sitting on the couch. 'Starring that heart-throb who gets you all in a flutter!'

'Well, now, who could he possibly mean?' says Carol in mock indignation.

'You know,' Ken says, casting his wife an affectionate look, 'that actor who bought Cara's painting.'

Cara smiles. Yes, he's eminently watchable! She notices her mother and Sheila flush crimson.

Sitting cross-legged on the floor, Sky concentrates on weaving his remote-controlled Batmobile round the legs of the dining table. It's a Christmas present from his grandparents and he's been playing with it all day. He's getting quite expert at controlling its movements. Without breaking concentration, in a sing-song voice he says, 'Oliver Foxley.'

Chapter Three

Deanna studies her husband asleep beside her. He looks so serene; his features free from the stresses of the day and his demons stilled. A smile lingers on his lips. Even after all these years her heartbeat quickens at the sight of him – her beautiful husband – but little did she know what she was taking on the day she accepted his tentative offer of a first date. He was already well into his acting course when she arrived at the college to study stage management. He was instantly noticeable – the best-looking student. The other girls, and a number of the boys, watched in envy as he singled her out and showered her with his charm. And it worked. Her tough exterior melted under his adoring gaze. She would never consider herself beautiful, although she knows she possesses a certain attractiveness, but the young Deanna was aware enough to understand it was her strength of character and independence that Oliver liked most about her. He would be amazed if he knew how she truly felt about him at that time, but she was careful to maintain a cool persona and set herself the task of perfecting those qualities he liked in order to hold his attention. This strategy worked in her favour because, over the years, she has had to rely heavily on those character traits.

Deanna gazes up at the ceiling. She has slept fitfully and feels exhausted. Still uncomfortable, she turns onto her side and peers at the alarm clock. Should she get up or try for another hour's sleep?

Her movements disturb Oliver and his fingers find their way under her T-shirt. Gently he caresses her smooth, flat belly. 'Mmm… you feel good,' he says, nuzzling the back of her neck. 'Why are you awake?'

'Don't know.'

'I know what you need,' he says, gently rolling her onto her back.

As her body yields to him, Deanna momentarily casts aside the precision-like restraint by which she runs her life. Submitting to the sensations coursing through her, fleetingly she loses control and, moments later, with ragged breathing and muscles taut, Oliver finds his own release. Almost immediately Deanna moves restlessly beneath him, already thinking of her day ahead. Like yesterday, it is full of chores and expectations to fulfil.

Propping himself on one elbow, Oliver thoughtfully observes his wife.

'You always did know how to play me, Ollie,' Deanna says quietly, her eyes closed.

He smiles and gently runs a finger over her belly from one hip bone to the other.

'What time is it?' Deanna asks.

'Still early.' Oliver re-straightens her T-shirt and turns onto his back, one arm bent behind his head.

'Half an hour more, then.' Deanna turns away.

Oliver looks up at the ceiling, as his wife had only minutes before, as familiar disjointedness takes hold. Why does everything feel so discordant and hollow? Life has dealt him a pretty good hand. What more could he possibly want? It's as if there are no challenges left. He yearns for something but doesn't know what – just something more. Maybe it's his mid-life crisis. Possibly he should accept that film role. God knows, his agent is persistent enough!

Perhaps Deanna is right; a change would be as good as a rest.

But still he's unsure. Deep down he knows that accepting the role simply to take his mind off his disquiet is not the answer. It might have worked in the past, diverting him from his emotional battles for a short while, but his mind has grown wise to this avoidance technique.

Taking care not to disturb his wife, Oliver slips out of bed and pads silently across the room to the en-suite. Running the shower as hot as he can bear, he stands with water cascading over his head. This bout of melancholia has had him locked in its grip for a while now and he knows he needs to do something different to kick-start his lighter side. Deanna is always stoic regarding his mental disorder but sometimes it would be refreshing if she weren't so independent and, seemingly, indifferent.

Sometimes it would be nice to think she understood my inner demons and not simply ignored them. He shakes his head, trying to rid himself of the thought.

Standing with arms outstretched, palms flat against the cool tiles, Oliver closes his eyes and lets the full force of the water rain down upon the back of his neck.

When he first asked Deanna out it wasn't just because he found her attractive. It was as much to do with her confidence. She was a warrior of a young woman and his frightened, confused, inner self stilled in her presence. He was fascinated to understand what made her tick and what made her so different. She had none of his insecurities and he found the differences between them exhilarating. As they spent more time in each other's company they discovered they complemented each other well, and as soon as he graduated they found a flat together. Deanna continued her studies, while he ventured out into the competitive world of show business. Initially, it was his looks that drew attention and he was quickly snapped up for a controversial West End musical that broke new ground. It wasn't long before he came to the attention of the critics, and they loved him. His sensitive portrayal of the difficult role in which he was cast earned him critical acclaim and his looks were relegated to second place. His name was soon on the lips of people 'in the know' and there where whispers – ever-growing – that he was *the* young actor to watch. It would be a further eighteen months before he gained mass recognition and became a household name, and then life would never be the same again.

Water cascades over his shoulders and down his back. It should be soothing yet his mind gives him no rest. He has read through the whole script and it's a very good film with a strong, action-packed storyline providing an adrenalin rush for both actors and audience alike, but deep down he knows he doesn't want to be involved. He needs to do something, but what? Perhaps he should revisit Holy Isle. Rubbing shampoo into his hair, Oliver deliberates whether this is the answer and the more he thinks about it, the more the idea appeals. He could leave the world far behind for a while and indulge in his own spiritual needs. Then, maybe, this disquiet will be put to rest. Reaching for the bottle of shower gel, he squeezes a small amount onto the palm of his hand and rhythmically works it into his chest and stomach. As soon as he finishes showering he will check the website and make enquiries about the next course.

He's miles away and jumps when Deanna enters the bathroom. Dressed in a crisp white shirt and jeans, she gathers her hair into a ponytail as she walks across the room to the double basins.

'Do you want breakfast, Ollie?' she asks, turning on the cold tap.

'Please,' Oliver says, rubbing gel into his thigh and feeling the firm muscles beneath his fingertips.

'Scrambled egg and toast?' Deanna reaches for her toothbrush.

'Sounds good to me.' He will definitely find out about a course. His soul yearns for nourishment, to be lifted from the mundane.

As Deanna leans over the basin to brush her teeth, Oliver appraises her slender figure. He smiles at her wiggling bottom. He's always been fascinated how her slim body has stretched and expanded during four pregnancies, yet always returned to such firmness. At forty, she is toned and in very good shape. Whenever anyone comments on her physique Deanna always puts it down to having inherited good genes, but Oliver knows his wife exacts the same discipline and control over what she puts into her body as she does the running of the household.

Deanna spits into the basin, replaces the toothbrush in its holder and straightens up. In the mirror she catches Oliver's appreciative eye and smiles. 'I'm taking Sammy to the station this morning. She's going to Guildford with Rosie.' She turns to face her husband. 'Then I'm dropping Seb and Jamie at football practice. Is there anything you want while I'm in town?'

Peace of mind would be good.

'Nothing I can think of.' Oliver turns off the water. 'You have it all under control.'

Opening the shower door, he pulls a plump, Egyptian cotton bath towel from the heated rail and vigorously dries himself, as Deanna walks from the room. With a game plan in mind he feels stronger and the 'grey mist', temporarily suspended, flutters on the edge of his consciousness.

Securing the towel around his waist, Oliver walks to the basins and catches sight of himself in the mirror. His reflection always takes him by surprise. It's so different from how he sees himself. He, too, is in good shape – muscular and trim. At his age it's imperative not to lose his edge and allow younger actors the chance to knock him off the top spot before his time, and this means daily workouts. But he also knows this is not the only reason he puts himself under such pressure. It's as much to do with matching Deanna, like-for-like. He cannot fall behind. Looking at the handsome face staring back at him, once again Oliver is struck by the irony of his situation. No one would ever suspect the troubles he endures, the pain in his soul and the constant battle with himself.

Seeing what the world sees reflected back at him, Oliver looks himself in the eye and growls, 'Skin deep, Ollie. Skin deep.'

*

Cara is in her studio working on the latest painting. On the easel is a sweeping view of the cove with her bungalow, The Lookout, in the far distance. It is not going well. She is about to give up when her iPhone springs into life. Laying the paintbrush aside, she moves to the window and picks up the mobile propped on the sill.

'Cara, how's it going?'

Silently, she groans. 'Hi, Ben. I've got painter's block.'

'What you need is a change of scene. What are you doing Sunday evening?'

'Why?' she asks cautiously. As much as she likes Ben as a friend, she knows he wants more and it's getting increasingly difficult to keep him at arm's length.

'There's live music at Gylly Beach. Do you want to come?' Ben asks hopefully.

She's about to say there's no way she can get a babysitter in time, but hesitates. Maybe a night out is what she needs. It might give her the inspiration to crack on with this painting.

'The gang will be there,' Ben continues. 'Chilli and a pint for seven quid and the music's free. It'll be cool. Please, Cara.'

She looks out at the ocean; dark grey today under a bleak, colourless, January sky. Desolate, like her soul. She shivers. 'I'll just make a phone call and get right back.'

'Great. I'll be waiting.'

He sounds so hopeful. What *is* she going to do about him?

The wind whistles eerily and from deep within the bowels of the bungalow she can hear the children's voices above the sound of the television. Her mother answers on the third ring.

'Hi, Mum. How's it going?'

'Cara, darling, your father is driving me to distraction!'

Cara laughs. 'What's he done now?'

'He's only agreed to an exhibition of wildlife photography the very week I want to go to Madrid. He says I don't communicate with him so how is he supposed to know what plans I've made!'

'Have you already booked flights?' Cara asks.

'Well, no…' Carol's voice falters and then rises defensively '…but that's not the point! I wanted to go that particular week because of the fiesta. I've been talking about it for months, if not years! He's so damn maddening, your father.'

'But adorable, Mum,' Cara says, smiling at her mother's histrionics. Everyone knows Ken is the calming influence in that relationship.

'Oh yes, of course! He wouldn't be your father if he wasn't. Anyway, enough of me. How's everything with you, darling?'

Cara wonders what her mother would say if she told her the truth. Forcing a smile into her voice, she says, 'I've been asked out on Sunday night. Are you free to do a spot of babysitting?'

She knows her mother would like to see her settled with someone and senses, rather than hears, the sharp intake of breath.

'Of course. You know I love spending time with my grandchildren. What time do you want me over?'

As Cara gazes along the empty expanse of sand, she notices a vehicle pull up in the café's car park at the far end. A man gets out, swiftly followed by a springer spaniel.

Must be mad to be out in this!

She watches the man zip up his jacket and pause to look out to sea before walking down the steps onto the sand, his body bent into the wind. The dog is already on the beach, racing up to the water's edge and barking at the waves.

'Six should be fine. I'll do supper for the kids so you won't have to bother.'

'Don't worry about that, Cara. I'll rustle up Grandma's special. I'll even drag Grandpa out too and we can all spend some quality time together.'

'Thanks.' Knowing her mother is itching to discover who she's going out with, Cara holds her breath waiting for the inevitable question and is surprised when it doesn't come. 'Where's Dad's exhibition?' she asks.

'Eden. He's giving daily lectures as well so it's not as if he can just hang the pieces and leave!'

'But that's brilliant! There'll be other fiestas, Mum.'

Carol laughs. 'Hey, who is the mother here?'

'Me too, don't forget! But I don't like to think you feel you're missing out.'

'Never! But I would have liked to go to that fiesta,' Carol says with some regret. 'Anyway, Cara, I'm so pleased you're giving yourself a night off.'

'Bye, Mum, and thanks again.'

A sudden rain squall thrashes against the window panes, rattling the wooden frames. As the wind picks up, swirling under the eaves of the studio, an eerie sound like wailing women fills the air. Cara shivers.

It's cold, even with the heating on. Glancing up, she notices a stain spreading across the ceiling.

'Great! A leaking roof. That's all I need.'

Looking out at the turbulent sea, she sees white horses riding the crest of the waves. She never tires of this view, at any time of year. Every season has its merits. Even in January, when everything appears colourless and drab, the sweep of the bay is magical to her. She smiles at the memory of the first time she saw The Lookout. He was so unsure and worried she wouldn't like it. But she loved everything about it – from its quirky, unusual layout and dilapidated air, as if yearning for someone to care again, to the wildness of the surrounding cliff garden. Where others only saw its dangers, perilously perched above the beach, she saw the cliffs rising steeply behind as mighty protectors providing shelter from the bitter north-easterlies.

Cara's eyes follow the man who, undeterred by the weather, walks his dog along the beach. Behind him, the dark grey twist of road glistens in the rain, like a snake slithering through the countryside, making its way silently towards the sand before depositing visitors at the small car park serving the café. Her gaze follows the dirt track skirting the cove that gives access to the handful of properties hugging the cliffs. The Lookout is the last bungalow before the Atlantic and Cara likes the fact that its windows look out across the vast ocean towards Puerto Rico, some four thousand miles away. It is a relatively unknown cove and she likes that too, providing her with the privacy she needs to face her grief head-on and to find the strength to continue... for her little family.

Sighing deeply, she phones Ben. 'All organised,' Cara says, trying to muster some enthusiasm for the proposed outing.

'Hey, Cara, that's great! I'll pick you up at seven.' His excitement emanates through the ether and she removes the iPhone from her ear. 'See you, babe.'

Babe!

She watches the man approach her end of the beach; one of the more intrepid explorers who occasionally stumble upon the hidden cove. Turning his back to the wind and rain coming in off the sea, he glances up at the window and spies her observing him. He nods and Cara acknowledges him with a smile. He's older than she expected, but attractive and cloaked in an air of sophistication, as though he knows his worth. And he's definitely not local – she would have remembered him.

'Sorry, Ben,' she says quietly to herself.

Chapter Four

It's late afternoon and the house is quiet. Alone in his study, Oliver checks the Holy Isle website.

'Can I have a chat with you, Dad?' His eldest son is at the door.

'Of course. What's up?'

Charlie walks across the room and sits in the leather armchair in front of the fire. He's a good-looking lad, tall and sporty, with an easy-going nature and popular with both sexes. In fact, his social life astounds his parents.

Oliver waits for his son to speak. When he doesn't, Oliver uses their affectionate childhood name for him. 'Well, Charlie-Boy?'

Charlie glances up through thick brown eyelashes, a worried look clouding his eyes. He shifts uncomfortably but remains silent.

'I hear you've got a science project to finish before Monday,' Oliver says, diverting his son.

Charlie pulls a face. 'It's causing some problems, I can tell you, but Gary's working on it. Hopefully we'll have a solution by the end of the day.'

'It's a joint project, then?'

'Yeah. Nathan's also applying his humongous brain so, between us, we should be able to crack it.'

His son's newly acquired deep voice makes Oliver smile. Only last summer he was a young lad. Now he's almost a man.

'So, if you don't need your old man to apply his brain to your homework what do you want to talk to him about?'

Quickly Charlie looks away. It's unlike him to be so awkward and Oliver frowns. When he was Charlie's age he was in the grips of clinical depression with no one to talk to and nowhere to turn, but he knows this is not what afflicts his son.

'It's about...' Charlie shifts again, his fingers picking at the leather trim of the arm rest. Taking a deep breath, he looks at Oliver, wide-eyed and vulnerable. 'It's Penny, Nathan's sister.'

Ah! Fifteen and all those unharnessed hormones...

'I remember her from your party. Very pretty.'

'Yes, well…' Charlie flushes with embarrassment and the ensuing words come out in a rush. 'The thing is, she says she wants to go out with me but Karen's pretty too and I'm kind of dating her.'

Charles Foxley dating! Oliver attempts to hold back the smile.

'Can't be too bad having two babes chasing after you?'

'Dad, it's awful!' Charlie exclaims.

Oliver straightens up. How can that be awful?

'I like them both, although Karen is getting a bit heavy...' The sentence peters out.

There is so much time ahead for all this, thinks Oliver, but it's crucial he advises wisely. He sees the worry etched upon Charlie's usually carefree face, and his heart goes out to his eldest son. What would he do if he were in that situation? It's not a problem he has ever had to face. Deanna has been there for most of his adult life.

'Well, Charlie, you don't have to tie yourself to either girl,' Oliver says carefully. 'You're young and there will be many new experiences for you in the years to come. Just say you want to concentrate on getting good grades this year and then apportion your time between them.'

'But Karen and I have sort of been together for a year.'

Now it's Oliver's turn to look wide-eyed. He had no idea, and his son lives under the same roof! What else has escaped his attention?

'I really like Penny,' Charlie continues, 'but it will hurt Karen if I start seeing her best friend.' The boy sighs in exasperation.

'I don't have much experience in that field,' Oliver says honestly. 'Before I met your mother I had a couple of girlfriends, though it was nothing serious. I was too preoccupied with sorting out my own gremlins. But, if I was in your position I would ask myself if I really wanted to commit to just one person at such a young age.' Charlie listens intently. 'And if that relationship isn't all that it should be then I would remove myself from it and make myself more available to everybody. Not just Karen or Penny, but *everybody*. Enjoy your teenage years, experiment and experience things. Have some fun and don't get too bogged down before your time.' He smiles at his son. 'I hope that's of some help, Charlie.'

Deanna would have no problem dealing with this. She would know exactly how to handle it. Oddly, the thought depresses Oliver.

'Thanks, Dad. You've given me quite a bit to consider,' Charlie says, rising from the chair. 'I'd better get back to my homework.'

'Fancy joining me for a run later and getting some fresh air?' Oliver suggests. 'It's amazing how clear things can become then.'

'Yeah, catch you later.'

He watches his son walk from the room. The lad possesses an easy, athletic grace and Oliver wonders how many hearts Charlie will break before he finds his true path.

Turning his attention once again to the website, Oliver is immediately transported back to the island located off the west coast of Scotland where he spent a month the previous year. He was no stranger to the art of meditation; it was, however, the first time he encountered a special retreat devoted to Ngondro practice. His visit followed a particularly gruelling twenty months during which he worked back-to-back on two films – both box office hits – and it wasn't over once they were in the can. A punishing schedule of press interviews, chat shows and associated red-carpet events led up to the launch of each film. His bank balance benefited enormously, but his health did not and he emerged exhausted and battling depression. Is this the reason he is reluctant to commit to the latest role?

Oliver massages his temples. Even now he can feel the powerful serenity and sense of direction he experienced during that period of personal time-out. He smiles at the memory of the gentle, wise man who gave talks and teachings on Buddhist topics, conducted personal interviews and led walks around the beautiful island. The daily meditation involved periods of silence; an almost impossible undertaking since returning to *his* world. Suddenly Oliver craves it again. He checks the details but the website states the course is full. Hesitating momentarily, he picks up the phone. Almost immediately, a serene voice answers. Explaining who he is, Oliver enquires whether a place can be found for him. He is put on hold.

Feeling guilty at playing on his public status, Oliver is considering retracting his request when the serene voice returns. 'We wish you to know that you are held in the greatest respect, Oliver, and we are delighted you have chosen to further your studies with us.'

There and then, he books a two-week visit. Within a further ten minutes he has also booked a private helicopter to fly him to Holy Isle the following Saturday. For many years he has been unable to travel unrecognised in public and the pilots at the Hampshire-based flying company are used to landing their helicopters on the level paddocks behind Hunter's Moon.

*

Cara is somewhere between sleep and waking. Feeling warm and comfortable, she basks in the glow of a dream from which she hopes never to wake. However, the wailing women have started up again and refuse to keep quiet. Groaning, she attempts to block out the world and hold onto her dream. This is the most difficult and longest day of the year to get through and she has no desire to face it just yet. But sleep's sweet oblivion evades her and, reluctantly, she opens one eye. The room appears lighter than expected. Glancing at the alarm clock, she leaps out of bed and shouts to her children to get up. School starts within the next half-hour! As Cara runs from her bedroom into the hallway, the family's Labrador appears at the threshold to Sky's bedroom, excited by all the activity and noise.

'Beth, Sky! Get up! We're late!'

She peers into her son's bedroom. The room is in its usual mess but he is not there. Her daughter's room is also empty but, in contrast, tidy; the duvet straightened, clothes folded and toys neatly stacked.

'Barnaby, get out from under my feet!' Deftly sidestepping the dog, she bolts down the hallway into the living room.

Sitting at the dining table, dressed in their school uniforms, the children look up in surprise at her sudden entrance.

'Sky was hungry so I made him some toast,' Bethany explains, 'and I've given the animals their breakfasts too.'

Cara's heartbeat slows. Her daughter is so grown-up!

'You were hungry too,' says Sky indignantly, holding out a piece of toast to Barnaby.

Sitting obediently at the boy's feet, the dog gently takes the offering and swallows it whole.

'Sky, don't give Barnaby buttered toast,' Cara says. 'It's not good for him. I'm going to get dressed.'

She sprints to her bathroom, hurries through her ablutions and throws on the nearest clothes she can find. Running a brush through her hair, she glances in the mirror and then at her watch. It'll have to do! Charging back to the kitchen, she finds Barnaby licking the cat's bowl clean. Swishing his tail across the kitchen worktop, the cat directs a low, menacing growl at the large, yellow dog.

'Must everything go wrong today, of all days?' Cara groans.

'It's all right, Mum,' says Bethany. 'It'll be OK.'

She turns to see her daughter looking at her with such kindness in her eyes that it's almost her undoing. Cara swallows hard. When did that child become so adult? She rummages for car keys in the kitchen drawer and grabs her bag from the chair.

'Sky, if you don't get a move on we're going without you,' she calls in the direction of his bedroom.

'I'm coming!' The boy appears in the doorway, dragging a bulging school bag. Glancing at his sister, he rolls his eyes.

'Come on, then. And leave Barnaby here.'

'But he wants to come too,' whines Sky.

'Well, he can't,' snaps Cara, immediately overcome with remorse. 'I've got shopping to do after dropping you off at school,' she continues more softly.

Sky opens his mouth to speak but, catching Bethany's warning look, he closes it again. His sister whispers in his ear.

'OK, Mum, take us to school,' he says in a jokey-bossy voice and promptly marches across the living room towards the hallway.

As Bethany follows, she glances at her mother and mouths, Boys!

Cara wants to laugh, or cry; she's not sure which. Grabbing a jacket from the coat rack in the hall, she closes the porch door just in time to prevent Barnaby escaping through it.

'Sorry, Barns, won't be long. Then we'll go for a W_A_L_K,' she says, pressing the key fob and unlocking the doors to her car.

There's a threat of rain in the air and a cold wind blows in from the ocean. The choppy sea foams at the water's edge and the outgoing tide has left vast areas of shining, mirror-like sand, dull grey in colour, under a washed-out sky. All this Cara acknowledges as she follows her children to the car, and a modicum of peace comforts her stricken soul. She climbs in and quickly closes the door, shutting out the cold air, and glances in the rear-view mirror at her children already sitting in the back seat. Carefully reversing the car within the small turning space at the side of the bungalow, she heads up the dirt track and, ten minutes later, deposits her children at the gates of their primary school in Cury.

'Don't forget Janine's picking you up this afternoon,' she calls through the open window.

'We haven't forgotten,' Bethany says. Shifting the strap of her school bag to a more comfortable position on her shoulder, she waves with her free hand.

Sky, distracted by a friend calling to him, rushes into the school grounds without a backward glance.

Cara blows her daughter a kiss. Putting the car into gear, she drives to the supermarket on the outskirts of Helston, hoping it will have everything she needs. Taut, her senses stretched, she cannot let anything push her over the edge today. The car park is nearly full and she has trouble finding an empty parking bay, and there's only one trolley sitting forlornly at the entrance. Aware of another fast-approaching shopper, she quickens her pace and swiftly claims it. Methodically, Cara works the aisles. She's deliberating over the meat counter when she bumps into one of the other mums whose daughter is in the same class as Bethany.

'Hi, Barbara. How are things?'

'Oh, hi, Cara. Good, thanks. Nick's got a building contract with that new hotel in Penzance. It could be for up to a year.'

'Good for him,' says Cara, knowing only too well how challenging it can be to earn a living. 'Beth tells me Diana has been picked for the netball team.'

Barbara beams. 'Centre forward. She's thrilled!'

Cara nods politely. And then there's that familiar, uncomfortable pause. Will this ever pass?

'How's the gallery?' Barbara eventually asks.

'Oh, you know, Porthleven in January. But we're open most days and I have a few sales from the Internet, so can't grumble.'

Another awkward silence.

Barbara smiles nervously and stares at the contents of Cara's trolley. 'Looks like you're having a celebration!'

'Of sorts...' Cara says quietly.

Barbara glances at Cara with a questioning look. Suddenly she flushes crimson. Mumbling an apology, with studied determination she hurriedly pushes her trolley away. Cara grits her teeth. She can just imagine the woman's conversation later with her husband when she tells him that she bumped into Cara Penhaligon, today of all days...

Turning her attention to the meat counter again, Cara makes her selection before steering the rapidly filling trolley towards the drinks' aisle. Half an hour later she heads home. The tide is almost out and she decides to give Barnaby a run on the beach. As her car pulls up in front of the bungalow, the Labrador watches her every move, his nose pressed against the heavily smeared porch window. Struggling with shopping bags, Cara opens the stable door and

Barnaby rushes out to greet her, almost tripping her up as she makes her way to the kitchen.

'Good plan, Basil,' she says to the cat, positioned sensibly out of the way on the window sill amongst the pot plants.

Cara decants the contents of the bags into various cupboards and stacks the fresh food in the fridge. Finally, opening a drawer, she takes out a hairband and scoops her hair into a high ponytail.

'OK, Barns, let's go!'

As soon as the porch door is open the dog is out, rushing in circles and chasing his tail. Cara walks to the steps leading to the beach and the Labrador bolts past her. At the bottom he looks up and waits. As she steps onto the sand, he's away, running towards a flock of seagulls and scattering them into the wind. Cara laughs. There's an electric energy in the air and the sea roars in the distance. She feels her spirits lift. Walking to firmer sand, she turns towards Rick's Beach Hut and breaks into a jog, her ponytail bouncing from side to side. It's exhilarating being out here all alone on the empty beach with just her dog and the seagulls for company.

For the rest of the day she bakes and cooks. Although thankful to be busy preparing for the evening's gathering, she does so with a heavy heart. Her parents phone, which eases her mood a little, but she knows it's down to her to rise above the melancholy. Cara places an assortment of candles on the driftwood mantelpiece above the wood-burning stove and decorates the room with strings of lights. At around four o'clock a car pulls up. Instantly Barnaby rushes out to the porch, his tail wagging expectantly as the door flies open.

'Hi, Mum! We're just going to feed Bobkin.' Placing her school bag on the floor, Bethany pats the Labrador's soft, downy head.

'Hello, Mrs Penhaligon,' say the twins in unison.

'Hi, you two,' Cara says. Despite having known them since toddlers, it's still difficult to tell Janine's daughters apart. Barnaby bounces up at the girls. 'Just push him out of the way if he's bothering you.'

'It's OK,' responds Milly, or is it Molly? 'We know he's only playing.'

'Mum, I'm starving!' Sky says, dumping his school bag next to his sister's.

Cara laughs. 'You're *always* starving, Sky, but I'm sure I can find you something to eat before the others arrive.' She hands her daughter a colander of carrot peel. 'Beth, these are for Bobkin.'

'Hi, Cara. Delivered your little sunbeams home safe and sound,' announces her neighbour, a large woman with a big voice and a heart of pure twenty-four-carat gold. 'See you've been busy.' Janine moves aside as Bethany and the twins rush past.

'I thought Christmas lights would cheer the place.'

Marching across the room, Janine gives Cara a huge hug. Taken by surprise, Cara struggles to breathe.

'Darling, you and your little family cheer the place. It doesn't need further embellishment.' She releases Cara. 'But, be prepared. Sky has something to show you.'

Cara's heart lurches. What does she mean?

'It's a painting… for tonight.'

Sky and his paintings! Her son has inherited her talent.

'Thanks for the heads up.'

A flurry at the door makes them both turn and Barnaby rushes in, closely followed by Bethany holding her rabbit. Walking on either side, the twins enthusiastically stroke the lop-eared bunny.

'Come on, you two, time for tea. Let's leave poor Bobkin in peace.' Janine organises her children. Turning to Cara, she gives her a squeeze. 'Hope it all goes well.'

'Thanks, Janine, you're a good friend.'

'Anything, Cara. You know that. Now, come on, Mills and Molls, Mother says move!' Janine ushers her girls towards the porch.

A while later, Cara's guests start to arrive. It's a gathering of her closest friends. Tristan and his sister,

Morwenna, arrive first, roaring up the track on Tristan's motorbike. As soon as Sky hears the throaty roar he is at the porch door.

'Hi, Sky!' Tristan says, removing his helmet.

'Hi, Uncle Trist!' He's not officially their uncle but the children have known him since birth.

'Hey, Sky, do you like the motorbike?' Morwenna asks, as she dismounts. The boy nods. 'In the summer Tristan will take you for a ride down the track if you like.'

'Cool!'

'Thanks, Morwenna!' groans Cara, appearing in the hallway behind Sky. She pulls a face at her friend and then laughs. She knows Tristan cherishes her son and wouldn't let anything happen to him.

'Hello, gorgeous lady,' Tristan says, greeting Cara with a warm hug. 'A little something for the evening.' Fishing inside his leather jacket, he produces two bottles of red wine.

'These are for you too,' Morwenna says, holding out a bag. 'Tomato and olive loaves. Still warm, fresh from the oven, not from the bike's exhaust!'

'Thanks, guys.' Walking through to the kitchen, Cara deposits their offerings on the worktop.

'And who's this young beauty?' asks Tristan.

Cara turns. An animated Bethany has entered the living room. Her daughter smiles widely at Tristan. She's always loved him, even as a baby. Whenever

Cara had difficulty consoling her and was at her wits'
end, as soon as Tristan held Bethany she would settle
and gaze up at him with big, brown eyes.

In one bound Tristan sweeps the young girl into
his arms, lifting her high into the air.

'Uncle Trist, you're mad!' Bethany says, giggling.

'Mad for you, my darling girl.'

Bethany giggles louder. Whirling her around,
Tristan plants a smacker of a kiss on her cheek before
placing her safely back on the ground. Smiling with
embarrassment, Bethany glances shyly at her mother.
Excited by all the commotion, Barnaby starts to bark.
At the sound of a car pulling up, Cara looks out of
the window to see her remaining guests have arrived.
Martha and her husband, Stephen, and Sarah and
her boyfriend, Rob, decant in a heap from Martha's
old, beaten-up VW Beetle. Giggling, they dust
themselves off before entering the bungalow.
Instantly Barnaby is at the door again, getting caught
up in everybody's legs.

'Welcome to the madhouse!' Cara calls from the
kitchen where she's finding Tristan a corkscrew.
'Let's get some drinks on the go!'

The evening goes well. Although it's raining and
windy outside, the bungalow feels cosy and safe. The
living room is bathed in a subtle glow from the
candles and the Christmas lights adorning the walls.
Despite her initial hesitation, Cara knows that

marking the event again this year was the right thing to do. She looks around with satisfaction. It's been a good evening spent in relaxed company with plenty of laughter, despite the occasion. Bethany and Sky, astounded that it is past ten and they have yet to be sent to bed, loll on the sofa with Morwenna and Martha, while Stephen plays the guitar that has lain dormant against the wall for so long. With a sudden shock Cara realises it's *that* Coldplay song. Quickly, she rises. Crossing the room, she studies the photos her children have Blu-Tacked to the wall – a lifetime of events depicted in forty or so photographs – and propped on the ledge running above the wood panelling is Sky's painting. It really is very good. In an instant both her children are at her side.

'Do you like it, Mum?' asks her son.

'I love it, Sky,' she answers softly.

His painting is of a tanned, blond man riding the clouds on a surfboard the same colour as her life-sized one displayed on the wall above them. Tears prick her eyes.

Don't lose it… not now!

Suddenly Tristan stands. Pushing back his chair, he clears his throat. 'Um, I just want to say a few words.'

As one, she and the children turn in his direction. Immediately a hush descends, the mood shifting down a gear. Cara tenses.

'It's been two long years to the day since we lost Christo and never a day goes by that I don't think of my dear mate.' Bethany's fingers curl around her mother's hand. 'You left us way too soon.' Tristan's voice is oddly distorted and he swallows hard. 'I hope you're riding the biggest, never-ending, perfect wave. No wipe-outs, man, just dynamic barrels and getting tubed.'

A murmur of agreement fills the room.

Tristan clears his throat again. 'Christo, you're not to worry about anything down here, mate. Just look at this gorgeous, golden family of yours.' He smiles at the little family standing stoically beneath the surfboard depicting Christo as a young, sun-kissed surfer without a care in the world.

Feeling Bethany grow rigid beside her, Cara gives her daughter's hand a reassuring squeeze. Sky has backed into her and she places a comforting hand on his shoulder. Even Barnaby has joined them, sitting quietly at Sky's feet. As her guests wipe away silent tears, Cara steels herself against an overwhelming urge to join in.

'Nothing – and I mean *nothing* – will ever harm them.' Tristan's voice rises with emotion. 'We are all looking out for your Gwyneth, Beth and Sky... for you, Christo. The best mate a man could ever have.'

Chapter Five

Following an uneventful flight, Oliver steps out of the helicopter feeling refreshed. The weather, cold but clear, affords excellent visibility and it has been an enjoyable and interesting journey taking no more than three hours. The views have been spectacular, especially over the Lake District and Galloway Forest National Park. As the helicopter turned in over the Firth of Clyde on the final approach to Holy Isle, flying low over the island in preparation to land, the wild ponies, sheep and goats scattered.

For the first time in quite a while Oliver feels a small ray of hope pierce his dark mood. With head bent low against the downdraft, he walks quickly towards the awaiting party of monks, dressed in their saffron robes. They greet him warmly. He glances back at the metallic-blue AS355 Twin Squirrel sparkling in the crystal January sunshine and nods to Captain Mike Burrows. The pilot salutes him in return and, the next minute, the helicopter rises effortlessly from the ground before heading to the Scottish mainland and its refuelling destination.

'If you would like to follow me, I will show you to your room,' a gently spoken monk says as he takes Oliver's bag.

Walking with the monk in comfortable silence, Oliver breathes in the pure Scottish air and feels something buried deep within, shift. It's uplifting to know he will not be expected to 'deliver' during the next fourteen days. He can simply embrace the teachings and explore his spiritual understanding.

The island is as beautiful as he remembers and tranquillity and harmony permeate the air. Several people, seemingly oblivious to the cold, perform Tai Chai on the lawn in front of the blue and yellow Karmapa flag. Oliver recalls that the blue represents the sky (heaven), symbolising spiritual insight and vision, and the yellow the earth: the actual world of everyday experience. He also remembers that the symmetry of the wave pattern symbolises the Buddha's teachings, which flourish between the two and represents their inseparability. During his previous visit to the island this explanation resonated deeply with Oliver, who so often finds his own spirituality put to the test in the commercial world of show business.

As they approach the old farmhouse, a group of people turn in recognition and Oliver braces himself for the usual response. However, they politely acknowledge his presence without any further intrusion upon his privacy.

If only all humans had this respect for each other.

The monk stops and turns to face him. 'Your accommodation is here in the Harmony wing, which also houses the library.' Indicating another part of the building, the man continues, 'This is the Compassion wing where the kitchen and dining room can be found and this is the Wisdom wing, which houses mostly guest rooms.'

'Yes, I stayed in the Wisdom wing during my previous visit,' Oliver says.

The monk nods and enters the Harmony wing. Oliver follows. Ascending a staircase, they walk along a corridor and, halfway along, halt in front of a plain wooden door.

'This is your room, Oliver,' says the monk. 'You are welcome to enjoy the whole island, including the Mandala Garden. If there is anything you require during your stay please let me know. Lunch is served until two.' Standing back, he allows Oliver to enter the room.

Oliver glances round. Although basic, with the addition of a desk against one wall it is more luxurious than the room he'd been allocated the previous year. Immediately he walks to the window overlooking Lamlash Bay and drinks in the view. Turning to say thank you, he finds the monk has discreetly and silently withdrawn, leaving his luggage on the floor by the door. Oliver quickly unpacks, placing the few clothes he has brought with him in the one chest of drawers. He glances at his watch and, picking up his mobile, walks to the window again.

'Hi, Dee. I've arrived.'

'Good journey?'

'Yes, a very smooth flight in Mike's capable hands. Just to let you know that I'll be switching off the mobile and won't phone home during the next two weeks. If there's an emergency you can always contact me via the office here.'

'Don't worry about us, Ollie. Concentrate on unwinding and getting the most from your visit.'

Oliver looks out at the peaceful bay. 'Deanna...' He pauses, unsure of what he's trying to express to his independent, capable and practical wife.

'Don't think, darling,' she says. 'Just indulge yourself.'

Irritated, Oliver frowns. However, before he's had a chance to rationalise his feelings Deanna interrupts his thoughts.

'Must go, Ollie. There's someone at the door. Love you.'

'And you,' he responds automatically, but she's already gone.

Something uncomfortable lurks on the edge of Oliver's consciousness, teasing and refusing to take shape. Try as he might, he cannot bring it into focus. It feels important. Perhaps during his time at the retreat it will become clear. He switches off the mobile and places it in the drawer of the bedside cabinet, where it will remain for the duration of his two-week stay. There will be no communication with the outside world. Walking to the basin in the corner of the room, Oliver washes his hands and then heads down to the Compassion wing.

The dining room has a rustic charm with a collection of simple, communal, wooden tables around which half a dozen people sit. In the lounge area a fire has been lit in an open fireplace, and two women relax in comfortable chairs. From behind the food counter, another woman smiles at him. She makes no comment as he walks towards her; everyone is equal here. Describing the vegetarian meals on offer, she invites him to help himself. Oliver picks up a tray. Selecting a meal and a glass of apple juice, he turns to survey the room and heads towards a table where a young man with a ponytail sits scribbling in a notebook.

'Do you mind if I join you?' Oliver asks.

The man looks up. 'Feel free.'

'I'm Oliver, by the way.'

And so it begins. Throughout his stay on the island, everyone warms to the great-looking, famous actor who possesses not an ounce of arrogance. He touches them all in one way or another, and all leave the island with lasting memories of the spiritual man behind the public face.

For Oliver, it is a time of quiet reflection, understanding and acceptance of his place in the world and the days soon fall into a routine of Tibetan Buddhist chanting ritual, periods of silent meditation and walks around the island. At first, the other guests find it awkward when he helps out with basic tasks, such as making breakfast and simple cleaning duties, but his generous, unaffected nature soon puts them at their ease and, before long, they have forgotten his public image. He is simply a fellow human being on a quest for spiritual enlightenment.

On day three, Oliver makes his way to the Peace Hall: a spacious room with natural light streaming in from two sides of a high pyramidal ceiling. About twenty people are present, either sitting on mats or chatting in small groups. As he enters, the noise abates. Over the years Oliver has grown accustomed to the public's reaction to him but he still doesn't find it easy. Slowly, the talking starts up again. Sitting at the front of the room is a slim, middle-aged woman with startling green eyes, sharp cheekbones and short-cropped white hair. She smiles warmly and invites him to approach. Oliver is immediately struck by the gentle air of wisdom exuding from her.

'Welcome, Oliver. I am Francoise La Chance, your course leader,' she says in a soft French accent. 'We are delighted you have decided to join us again. Please help yourself to a mat and find a place in the room that feels comfortable to you.' She indicates several mats stacked up in the corner of the room. 'The majority of the people you see here have been on this course since the beginning of January though there are a few newcomers. I will ask you to introduce yourself and, perhaps, you would like to say something about your particular spiritual journey.'

Oliver nods and heads towards the mats. Picking one off the top of the pile, he surveys the room. To one side, near the back, two women sit in the lotus position with eyes closed. He walks towards them. As he places his mat on the floor, the younger of the two opens her eyes and immediately does a double-take.

'You don't mind if I sit next to you two ladies, do you?' Oliver asks.

'Err... um...' the woman stutters, looking like a startled rabbit caught in headlights.

The older woman opens her eyes. 'No, dear, you park yourself there.'

Oliver sits down. The younger one stares at him, her face growing ever redder. Mousey-haired with pale blue eyes, arching eyebrows and high cheekbones, she could be quite attractive but there's something about her as taut as a coiled spring.

'You look just like…' Her voice falters. 'Are you…?'

Oliver's lips form a thin smile. 'I'd like to say no but I'd be lying.'

The older woman glances at him with interest.

'Oliver Foxley,' he says, introducing himself.

At this, the younger woman breaks into a sweat, her chest heaving expansively as if unable to take in enough air.

'Gosh, it's warm in here,' she says, wiping her hand across her forehead. 'I know underfloor heating is a good idea, especially at this time of year, but honestly!'

She can't take her eyes off him and there's something wild and strange in the pale blue eyes that survey him.

'I'm Margaret,' says the older woman, 'and this is my niece, Sylvie.'

Oliver smiles politely.

At the front of the room Francoise rises from her mat and, instantly, a hush descends. All eyes are on her but for one pair. Acutely aware of the intense scrutiny coming his way, Oliver keeps his eyes fixed straight ahead.

'Welcome, friends, old and new, to the Ngondro Retreat on beautiful Holy Isle,' says their course leader, smiling at the group before her. 'Here you will gain a greater insight and understanding of your own particular spiritual journey. The retreat is run in accordance with the traditional way of practicing

Ngondro, as taught by Drupon Rinpoche. For those of you who have newly joined us, we focus on the four ways of changing the mind with teachings and guided practice. The four ordinary foundations include appreciating how rare this human life is and how fortunate we are to have the freedom and opportunity to practice the Dharma. We reflect on the impermanence of everything in this world, especially the human body, and resolve not to waste time but to practise the Dharma right now. We reflect on how our thoughts, words and deeds create consequences for ourselves and those around us, and resolve to commit to a virtuous lifestyle. We also reflect on the suffering inherent in conditioned existence, or samsara, and see how Dharma practice is the best way to make use of this life.'

As she talks, Oliver becomes increasingly aware of the inspiring acoustics in the room.

What a wonderful space to perform in!

Glancing to his right, he sees that the younger woman is still staring at him.

Francoise continues, 'I have spent over twelve years in retreat and specialise in the Vajrayana practices of Tibetan Buddhism, including the Ngondro.' She pauses and looks round the room. 'Perhaps our new participants would like to introduce themselves.' She turns to a young woman sitting at the side of the hall.

Momentarily startled, the woman takes a deep breath. 'Hello. My name is Jenny Harding. I'm a schoolteacher from Brighton.'

Francoise smiles encouragingly. 'And what has brought you to Holy Isle, Jenny?'

'Well, my boyfriend came here last year and his stories encouraged me to find out more for myself. We were hoping to come here together but he's away travelling in India.'

'Thank you for that, Jenny. Perhaps the fact that your boyfriend is currently in India indicates you are meant to start your spiritual journey alone.' Francoise turns to a middle-aged man sitting immediately in front of her. 'Perhaps you would like to tell us who you are and why you are here?'

There are four new participants in total. Finally it is Oliver's turn. As he starts speaking, the young woman to his right leans forward eagerly.

'My name is Oliver Foxley...' The room erupts into good-natured laughter. It's absurd for him to introduce himself; his is a household name. Oliver laughs too, comprehending the joke. 'I make a living by giving form to many words – someone else's words. I am expected to find and give meaning to these words, even when sometimes there is no meaning.'

The room is silent and Oliver wonders if he should stop there. What would the fall-out be if any of what he says finds its way into the press? Does he really care? He's not so sure he does. He takes a deep breath. 'As time goes by I find myself longing to hear and say words that mean something real, not just something I have to conjure up or create. Something bigger.'

The silence is a living being; pulsating, waiting…

'I understand that you have practised Ngondro before,' Francoise encourages softly.

'Yes. Last year I spent a month on Holy Isle during which time I practised Ngondro. That experience left me wanting to expand my knowledge but it's only now that I have found the time to do so.'

Francoise observes him with intelligent eyes. 'It must be difficult finding the balance between your existence in the wider world and your personal beliefs.'

'It can be,' Oliver responds, liking her compassionate understanding.

'Thank you for your honesty, Oliver. It can be difficult for all of us to keep spiritualism alive in a consumer-driven world, but it is achievable.'

Turning her attention to the other participants, Francoise says, 'For those of you who are not undertaking the full course but have already embarked on Ngondro practice, if you are only here for a short period of time you can continue with the practice you are doing. The daily routine will consist of periods of group practice with most of your time devoted to individual practice, together with periods of silence.'

The hours pass quickly. Aware that the 'grey mist' is quiet and still, Oliver wonders whether these teachings are threatening its existence and reducing it to a non-consequential entity at the very edge of the kingdom in which it has reigned supreme for more than thirty years.

At lunch, he finds himself seated at a table with Margaret and Sylvie.

'Is this your first visit to Holy Isle?' he asks, making conversation.

The older woman shakes her head. 'When I lived in Nottingham I used to attend every year, but I live in Vancouver now and it's more complicated to arrange. This is my first visit in three years.'

'And what about you, Sylvie?' asks Oliver.

Staring at him, she mumbles, 'My first visit.'

The young woman's demeanour is still intense, despite the morning's meditations. She has been close to him at every given opportunity and it occurs to Oliver that sharing a table is not mere coincidence. He listens politely as Sylvie informs him she is thirty-five, single, works in publishing and is a keen filmgoer. In fact, she discusses most of the films he has ever been in, regaling him with her knowledge of the actor. Wryly, Oliver thinks that if ever he needed a reminder of his filmography he would know who to ask. She seems pleasant enough, but needy, and each time they happen to bump into each other Oliver metaphorically rolls his eyes. At first, it's just in the dining room or the library but then it becomes a little too obvious. When he chooses to walk the island by himself and she appears, seemingly, out of thin air, he knows it's no coincidence.

'Sylvie, you never told me you enjoyed walking,' he teases, as he exits the Information Centre with leaflets in hand. God knows, she's told him everything else about herself!

'Oh, it's such a beautiful day I couldn't resist,' she says, falling into step beside him. 'You don't mind if I join you?'

With long experience of satisfying the expectations of fans, Oliver charmingly acquiesces. 'Please do, but I'm not doing the whole circuit, just going as far as the rock paintings.'

'Oh, but that's where I'm heading!'

Walking together, they pass an area of newly planted trees and climb past swathes of bracken and gorse, pausing to take in the beautiful view of Arran's mountains.

'This is so special,' Sylvie says turning towards him, her eyes shining.

Oliver acknowledges the truth in her statement, hoping it's the atmosphere of the place that's making her radiant and not some other misplaced emotion.

Following the western shore, they reach a sign indicating the cave where St Molaise lived. As Sylvie climbs the steps leading to the cave, Oliver opens a leaflet.

'What does it say?' she asks.

Oliver clenches his jaw. Why did he agree to share his walk with this woman?

'It says, "The cave is situated about ten metres above the high-water mark and consists of an overhanging sandstone rock with a sunken stone floor. It is thought that in Molaise's time much of the opening of the cave was closed up by a wall to keep the weather out."'

'Let's take a look!' Sylvie smiles down at him before disappearing inside the entrance.

Oliver sighs and follows. Carvings of simple crosses adorn the walls of the cave and an unusually designed cross is carved into the roof.

'Perhaps these were made by pilgrims?' suggests Sylvie.

Oliver glances at the leaflet again. 'That's what it says here. Apparently these are Norse runes and personal names.' He walks to one of the runes and runs his fingers over it.

As he studies the ancient carvings, Oliver becomes increasingly aware of Sylvie invading his personal space. A wave of claustrophobia consumes him.

Placing her hand on his arm, Sylvie purrs, 'What else does the leaflet say, Oliver?'

Every fibre in his body tells him to get the hell out of there, but Oliver steadies his nerves, hoping he's not about to have a panic attack.

'"In 1263, King Haakon of Norway brought a fleet of ships to the shelter of Lamlash Bay before fighting the Scots at the Battle of Largs. Vigleikr, one of his marshalls, went ashore at Holy Isle and cut runes with his name on the wall of St. Molaise's cave."'

Her fingers caress his arm and, swiftly, he steps away.

'There's a holy well a little further on I'd like to see,' Oliver says.

He can sense her disappointment. Quickly, he exits the cave and heads off towards the well at which, for centuries, people have come to drink its cold, crystal-clear water for the healing powers it is said to have. Sylvie catches up with him.

'What does the leaflet say about this?' she asks, the purr in evidence again.

This calming walk is turning out to be anything but!

Opening the leaflet once more, Oliver reads aloud. '"The Healing Well, or Holy Well, is thought to cure ills and bring blessings. In the eighteenth century it was recorded that the natives used to drink and bathe in the well for all lingering ailments. The same source describes the water as gushing out of a rock. At the beginning of the twentieth century apparently there was a cistern present, built of masonry with a stone spout, which delivered the water.'"

He glances up to find Sylvie staring at him with fanatical lust.

Oliver rapidly continues, 'It goes on to say, "The spring is overgrown now so you wouldn't get more than a footbath from it but the water is still cold and clear, albeit does not meet current EU standards for drinking water."'

The look in her eyes is feverish. She's going to pounce.

'So, Sylvie,' he says hastily, 'I trust you haven't got any lingering ailments that need addressing?'

'Wh-what?' she stammers.

'It's not safe to drink the water. We wouldn't want you to catch anything, now, would we?' he teases.

Sylvie laughs nervously and bites her lip.

When she loses her intensity she really is quite attractive.

'Come on, Sylvie,' Oliver continues more gently, 'let's find those rock paintings.'

Chapter Six

Stopping to talk to a couple of friends, Ben nods frantically at something they say and then, holding drinks aloft, continues his journey through the sea of people towards their table. Cara sits opposite Morwenna, Tristan and his new girlfriend, Jane, enjoying the Gylly chilli, which has lived up to its reputation. Several other friends have come along to listen to the band and she's relieved there are people around to dilute the intensity of Ben's attentions. She likes him and he's a good friend, but that's where it ends.

'What a crush!' Ben exclaims, sitting heavily on the seat beside her and handing her a glass of wine. 'Here you are, babe.'

Babe! Again…

With his arm draped casually round his girlfriend's shoulders, Tristan winks at Cara. She arches an eyebrow in response.

The popular band from St Ives is loud, and it's hard to be heard above the enthusiastic crowd. The music is a mix of jazz/blues with a rock element and the four lads have a loyal following, particularly in their home county. It's a good turnout and the café is packed.

As Ben bounces along the seat moving closer, Cara wonders why he always reminds her of an over-enthusiastic puppy.

'It's great you got a babysitter, Cara. You should try and get out more often. If you like, we could do this on a regular basis.'

'It's not that easy,' she says. 'I was lucky my mother could look after the kids at short notice.'

'I'll give you more notice next time, then you can plan ahead.' Ben grins at her.

Cara stares at him in dismay. He's either particularly thick-skinned or clueless. She looks up as a tall, young man with ginger hair approaches their table.

'Ben, didn't know you were here, mate!'

'Hey! When did you get back?' Ben asks enthusiastically.

The newcomer parks himself heavily next to Ben, causing the seat to bounce again and Cara to spill her drink. As everyone shuffles along to accommodate the extra body, Ben turns to his friend and Cara takes the opportunity to escape his suffocating attentions. It's short-lived. Putting his arm round her, Ben boisterously pulls Cara into the conversation, making her wine slop over the rim of the glass once again. Placing the glass carefully on the table, Cara shakes the liquid from her hand.

'Cara, this is Kev, an old university pal.'

She smiles politely.

Kev stares, open-mouthed. 'Ben, you old son of a gun, you never told me you had such a babe on your arm!'

'Cara's a good friend,' Ben says, reddening.

Raising his beer bottle in salute, Kev smirks. 'Well, here's to *good* friends.'

As Ben and his friend get into an earnest conversation about surfing, Cara switches off. She's heard all the discussions she could ever wish to hear about the best techniques and the various subtleties of waves, but that was in a previous life when she thought she had all the time in the world to indulge Christo's hobby. She wanted to be part of that scene… with him. Now, she has no wish to go near a surfboard ever again. It would feel like a betrayal knowing that her wonderful boy of the sea was no longer able to share the experience with her.

With the weight of Ben's arm on her shoulders, Cara is at the mercy of his expansive movements. Everything he does seems to be louder and bigger than necessary and she wonders what possessed her to accept his invitation. As she removes his hand from her shoulder, Ben briefly pauses in his enthusiastic debate to give her an inquisitive look, but the next minute Kev has diverted his attention. Cara glances across the table at Tristan and his girlfriend. They seem to be getting on well. She's met

Jane a few times before and likes her ready laugh and wicked sense of humour. Christo always despaired of Tristan's choice of girlfriend – mainly airhead surfer chicks – but she thinks he would have approved of this woman with backbone. Will this be the turning point for their friend?

'How are your children?' Jane asks, raising her voice and leaning across the table.

'Well, thanks. Beth has discovered a passion for ponies.'

'Ah yes, girls and their ponies tend to evolve into women and their horses. Once the joy of equus is discovered, boys and men tend not to get a look in, poor loves! What about Sky? What hobbies does he have?'

Cara smiles. 'Sky has such a sunny nature, he just loves being out on the beach with his dog. Keeping him entertained indoors during the winter months is quite a challenge but he's developed an interest in painting.'

'I think both your children are lovely, Cara,' Jane says sincerely. 'It's difficult to talk here. Perhaps you'd like to meet up for coffee sometime?'

'That would be great,' Cara responds warmly.

'Hey, come on, babe. Let's dance!' Ben interrupts their conversation. Without waiting for an answer, he grabs Cara's hand and pulls her along the seat. Jane laughs out loud.

Finding a space directly in front of the band, Ben jiggles wildly and Cara stifles a laugh. He's *so* enthusiastic in everything he does. Soon the beat of the music takes over and she rocks along with the crowd. For the first time in a very long time Cara feels an internal shift; a glimpse of happiness peeping through the crack of an opening door and a whisper of times to come. Suddenly she is unceremoniously spun around. On her second circuit, she catches sight of Tristan and Jane holding each other close, swaying to their own rhythm. And then Morwenna is beside her, successfully preventing Ben from spinning her a third time. Linking arms and smiling sweetly at Ben, together they dance; sisters united. He frowns, then, shrugging good-naturedly, joins in with the two women.

It's an enjoyable evening and when they finally spill out of the café into the cold night air, everyone is in good spirits. A strong, cold wind blows in off the sea and the sound of pounding surf speaks of an angry tide, fully in. Standing in a circle, stamping their feet and blowing on their hands, the friends hunch into their jackets.

'You know Ben's got the hots for you,' Tristan whispers to Cara as he wraps her in a warm hug.

'I know,' she groans.

'Don't do anything you don't want to!' He squeezes her tightly and she laughs, suddenly embarrassed.

'Don't forget coffee,' Jane says, raising an imaginary phone to her ear.

'Come on, you guys, it's freezing out here!' exclaims Ben, bouncing up and down.

The door to the café opens and a group of people exit, heading up the slope towards the road. Kev is amongst them and he calls out, 'Give me a bell sometime, Ben.'

'Yeah, will do. Right, that's it. I can't take much more of this wind. Let's go.' Grabbing Cara's hand, Ben marches her towards the street.

Tristan puts his arm round Jane and pulls her close. 'That lad's got a steep learning curve if he wants to win over Cara,' he says quietly.

At the top of the slope, Ben and Cara turn left and walk briskly towards his car, parked alongside the gardens commemorating the coronation of George V's wife, Queen Mary. Cara opens the passenger door, wishing she were already home with her children.

'What I'd give to follow the surf like Kev,' says Ben, getting in the driver's side and turning the heat on full.

'You'd miss us,' Cara says, waving at Jane and Tristan as they walk by.

'I'd miss you, Cara, not much else,' Ben replies, putting the car into first gear and pulling out into the road.

'That's just the drink talking. I think you'd miss much more than that. By the way, how much have you had?'

'Don't worry. Nothing I can't handle. Anyway, the Gylly chilli has soaked up most of it!' Ben turns onto Western Terrace. 'When's Rick's café opening full-time?'

'Easter, I think.'

'I don't understand him. Why settle for British weather when you could live in Australia?'

'Maybe he likes Cornwall,' Cara suggests.

'More likely got something to hide or running from something.'

'I don't know, Ben. I've never questioned his reasons for ending up in the cove. He's a great guy and that's good enough for me.'

'A great guy?' Ben glances at her.

'Yes! He's funny and generous, and great with the kids.'

'I could be great with your kids.'

She doesn't say anything and the silence weighs heavily between them. Staring out of the window at the passing countryside, Cara glances up at the night sky. No stars tonight. The only light comes from the few oncoming cars, their headlights assaulting her senses and intruding upon her dark, private cocoon. She wishes she could just close her eyes and float away to some other land where a golden, young man opens his arms to her and smiles…

'What do you think?' Ben's voice brings her back to the present.

'Sorry. What?'

'I was saying we could do this more often.'

Cara takes a deep breath. She doesn't want to hurt him. 'Life's pretty complicated at the moment.'

'But I could help make it less complicated.'

'I have so many things to sort out and little people to take care of. They come first. My life is secondary.'

'Cara, you cannot put yourself second forever,' Ben says grumpily.

'I can for the next twelve years or so.'

'Then I'll wait.'

'Oh, Ben!' Exasperated, she's also quite touched. 'I haven't got time to be involved with anyone. I like seeing you on a casual basis and if you're happy to run with that, then that's great. If you want something more, well… I'm sorry.'

Ben stares straight ahead, his knuckles turning white as he clutches the steering wheel. Never before has he voiced his hopes.

'I don't know if I can just see you on a casual basis,' he says eventually. 'You don't know what you do to me. A guy has needs, you know.'

This is *so* not what she wants.

Cara changes the subject. 'What does Kev do?'

Ben doesn't answer immediately. 'Don't know what he does now but he was a graphic designer. Talented too.'

'When did you last see him?'

'About three years ago. Why so interested? Would you like to see him on more than a casual basis?' he asks sulkily.

'Oh, Ben, now you're just being foolish.'

'Sorry, Cara.' He glances at her and places a hand on her knee. 'I'm so confused by all this.'

'Just get me home safely,' Cara says, removing his hand and placing it firmly on the steering wheel. 'This road can be lethal at night.'

They pass through the village of Gweek, skirting RNAS Culdrose, and turn onto the A3083. A few minutes later, just as the heavens open, Ben indicates right and switches on the windscreen wipers. On either side gnarled and wizened trees top the Cornish hedges. Some distance ahead, picked up in their lights, a fox slinks across the road. In one elegant bound it jumps onto the stone wall and looks back at the approaching car before disappearing into the night. The wet tarmac glistens in the beam of the headlights – like a road from a fairy tale leading to who knows where, but, for Cara, it's the way to the cove where she feels safe and protected from the outside world.

After a mile or so they reach Rick's Beach Hut. The building is in darkness and the car park empty. As Ben turns the car onto the track, its lights sweep across a tumultuous sea and Cara knows there will be rich beachcombing pickings to be had. In the distance, The Lookout's porch light winks at her – a reassuring beacon.

Quiet since turning off the main road, Ben now breaks his silence. 'Cara, I don't like this awkwardness between us.'

'Ben, I don't know what more I can say,' she says, wondering if he's going slowly on purpose to prolong their time together. Suddenly flustered, she knows there will be *that* moment before she can escape.

'Just don't say anything final,' he says, pulling up in front of the bungalow. He leaves the engine running. Intermittently, the wipers sweep the windscreen clear. 'I know it's hard for you, Christo was such a great guy, but I've sat back and waited patiently.'

What can she say? She's already told him...

'There's no pressure but I really would like to see you more,' Ben says beseechingly.

For a fleeting moment Cara feels as if she's the biggest bitch in the world but, without warning, Ben's hand encircles the back of her head. This is the moment she's been dreading. As he draws her towards him, Cara averts her face and Ben's lips connect with her cheek. Instantly, he releases his hold. The look of hurt on his face is almost too much for her to bear.

'Ben,' she says softly, 'I can't do this.'

'Can't you just give me some hope?' His eyes plead with her.

She cannot be all things to all people! She is too stretched as it is.

'Thanks for a great evening. It was very kind of you to ask me.'

'I'll phone,' he says disappointedly.

'Yes,' she says, and then wonders why she said it.

Opening the car door, Cara escapes through the rain. From the safety of the porch door she watches as he executes a three-point turn, carefully avoiding the other two cars parked in front of The Lookout.

Before heading up the track Ben glances at her, his face set in a grimace.

Chapter Seven

Casually dressed in sweatshirt and jogging pants, Oliver lies on the bed reading about Ngondro practice. The teachings are giving him plenty to consider.

Although it's late, he can't sleep and his mind is restless, despite hours of meditation. As he thinks back over his life, re-examining many of the choices he has made, there is the dawning realisation that those choices have not always been in his best interest. Depression settles around him like a thick blanket as his mind takes him back beyond the time when he found control of his destiny to his troubled and lonely childhood. Why he should have been the son with all the problems he still can't truly comprehend. Even the expensive therapy sessions didn't uncover the trigger point. Whereas his horizons appeared filled with unfathomable gathering storms, his three outgoing and older brothers easily sailed through childhood into adulthood, all finding successful careers in their chosen areas of expertise. He too, thankfully, fell into a fulfilling and highly successful career, one that has subsequently eclipsed those of his siblings, but this is where any similarity ends. Always the thinker and more introverted of the boys, Oliver struggled to make himself heard above his boisterous brothers. Even when he was heard, no one seemed to understand. On the rare occasions his mother would listen to the feelings he was trying to express, she would look at him aghast and either change the subject or turn away, which only compounded his fears and feelings of strangeness. Loneliness grabbed the young Oliver Foxley by the throat and turned his thoughts inwards; traits he is only too aware of in his youngest son. He will not let Jamie suffer as he did. As long as he has breath in his body, he will do all he can to show the boy there is a light on the horizon, despite the threatening thunder clouds.

Oliver buries his head in his hands. These severe bouts of depression are a physical pain, hard to bear.

Soft tapping at the door stirs him from his dark thoughts. His watch, lying on the bedside cabinet, tells him it's just after midnight. Tapping again. More insistent this time. There must be some crisis! Immediately, his thoughts turn to Jamie. Swinging his legs off the bed, Oliver strides across the room and opens the door. Standing on the threshold is Sylvie, looking a little lost and unsure, dressed in a baggy cardigan over pyjamas and a pair of slippers.

'Sylvie, do you know what time it is?' he says, his increased heart rate easing a little.

'I couldn't sleep,' she says, as if this is an acceptable answer. 'I thought I'd go for a walk and then saw your light was on.'

What's she doing in the Harmony wing at this time of night? He knows her room is in the Wisdom wing. She made a point of telling him.

Sylvie hesitates and Oliver watches dispassionately as she steels herself. 'Can I come in?'

He studies her carefully before standing back from the door but, as soon as she's in the room, realises his mistake. During the seven days he's known her, Sylvie's intensity has increased.

Whatever possessed me to let her in? My ridiculous, misplaced sense of compassion. I must be mad!

'Have a seat,' he says, indicating the only chair in the room.

Obediently, she sits in the wicker chair and looks up at him, her face displaying myriad emotions: fear; lust; anguish; love – he skirts over that one – but mainly loneliness.

'Why have you come here?' Oliver asks.

'To the retreat?'

He meant his room, but nods.

'I've been through a bad spell,' she says, plucking at the sleeve of her oversized cardigan.

Oliver groans inwardly. Sitting on the end of the bed, he rakes a hand through his hair.

'When Aunt Margaret said she was coming to the UK to visit Holy Isle I thought it would be good to join her,' Sylvie explains, looking at him uncertainly. 'To get away for a while.'

'And has it been?'

Her eyes grow large with raw emotion. 'I don't know,' she says in a small voice.

God, I'm no good at this! What would Deanna do? She'd be practical.

'Would you like some tea?' Oliver asks, rising to his feet. 'It might help you sleep.'

She nods.

He walks to the small table where a tray with a selection of hot drinks is laid out, all the while aware of Sylvie's hawk-like scrutiny.

'You told me you worked in publishing,' Oliver says, switching on the kettle and sorting out mugs and teabags. 'What do you do?'

'Editorial. I like words.'

'I like words too... which is just as well in my profession, I suppose,' he says with an ironic laugh.

'Words are my friends,' she says.

'Do you have many, Sylvie?' He glances at her. Seeing the shock on her face, compassion overwhelms him. 'A boyfriend?' he asks gently.

She shakes her head.

What am *I doing?*

As the kettle comes to the boil Oliver pours hot water into the mugs. It's only then he realises he's out of milk. He picks up the empty jug and turns to Sylvie, his skin prickling as she watches his every move.

'Just going to get some milk,' he says, waving the jug at her.

Is it safe to leave her alone in the room? Is there anything I don't want her to see?

He thinks he's overreacting. Sylvie's odd but she seems harmless enough. However, as soon as he steps out into the corridor, tension leaves his body.

The quicker this is over with, the better.

Hastily he makes his way down to the dining room. As he fumbles for the light switch, several energy-efficient lightbulbs cast a hesitant glow across the room and a dozen tables and chairs loom like marooned ships emerging through a sea of gloom. Oliver walks towards the small kitchen area and, opening the fridge door, quickly fills the jug from an open carton of milk. He heads back to his room deep in thought.

What causes one person to marry and have responsibilities that allow little room for anything else other than to get through each day at a time, and another to face four walls every evening with, maybe, a cat for company? It all comes down to choice.

Before entering the room, Oliver hesitates. It's important he take control. Sylvie will stay for one cup of tea and then he will escort her back to her wing. But as soon as he enters he's aware of a shift in atmosphere. The main light is no longer on and a side lamp casts a softer glow over the bed in which Sylvie now lies. Quickly scanning the room, he notices her clothes lying in a heap by the chair.

'What are you doing?' he asks sharply.

'Oliver, I need you,' she says, looking at him with vulnerable, saucer-like eyes.

'This is ridiculous, Sylvie. Get dressed.' He closes the door, walks across the room and places the jug on the table.

Sylvie sits up, the fleece blanket falling to her waist and exposing her small breasts. 'Oliver, I've loved you for so long. Please make love to me. No one need ever know.'

Incredulously, he stares at her.

If the press got hold of this…

'Love me? You don't even know me,' he says evenly. 'Cover yourself up.'

She kicks off the throw, exposing the full length of her body to him. She's thin but he can't help but notice her surprisingly shapely legs.

'Oliver, please,' she purrs. Little miss lonely knows how to play the minx. Seductively, she runs her hands over her breasts and trails her fingers across her belly, down to her inner thighs. Teasingly, she parts her legs.

'Sylvie, don't prostitute yourself in this way. You are worth more than this.'

She leans back on her elbows and arches her body towards him. 'Am I?'

'Of course you are!'

Moving towards the bed, Oliver picks up the throw and roughly covers her body. With a sudden movement, her fingers lock around his wrist and, before he has a chance to react, his hand is pulled down to her breast.

'Sylvie, stop!' he says, recoiling. 'I am not in the habit of bedding fans.'

Or deranged women!

'But I won't tell,' Sylvie purrs again.

'Get dressed.' Avoiding eye contact, Oliver picks up her clothes and dumps them on the bed.

'But, Oliver Foxley, I love you. Why won't you sleep with me?'

'You do not love me. You love an image in your head.'

'No! I LOVE YOU!' she shouts.

Shit! What if someone in the next room hears?

'Shhh... Sylvie.'

Sylvie sits up. Once again, the throw falls to her waist. 'What if I don't shush? What are you going to do then?'

Dear God!

'Don't play this game,' he says.

Suddenly she's on her feet, standing naked before him. 'Oliver, I need you!'

He steps away but Sylvie launches herself at him. Clinging on tightly, she wraps her legs around his waist. She's surprisingly strong and Oliver staggers back.

'Get off,' he says, trying to prise her fingers apart.

'No!' she screams. 'Love me!'

Bloody fool! Why the hell did I let her in?

'Sylvie, I'm just going to lay you on the bed.' Oliver speaks soothingly, as he would to an agitated, small child.

Perhaps, if she thinks I'm going to sleep with her she will lessen her grip.

Putting his arm around her waist, he stumbles across the room. As his knees come to rest against the end of the bed, Oliver leans forward but her weight takes them both.

'Oliver Foxley, I love you!' Sylvie says, immediately grinding her hips into his.

He tries to get off, but she increases her vice-like grip.

'Make love to me. I beg you,' she pleads.

'No, Sylvie, I won't. And do you know why?'

'Your wife,' she says sadly.

'No, not because of my wife. Because of you.'

She stills. 'What do you mean?'

'Let me sit up and I'll explain,' Oliver says, but her arms tighten around his neck. 'At least let me take my weight off you. I must be heavy.'

'I like you heavy on me,' she says, but her grip eases a little.

Looking down at her as he would a lover, the irony is not lost on Oliver. She looks a mess: dishevelled and desperate.

'Why are you doing this?' he asks kindly. 'You should have more respect for yourself.' He takes his weight on his elbows but her legs clamp around him. 'Sylvie, I have to breathe. Just let me get comfortable.'

'Promise not to go?'

'Promise.'

This is ridiculous!

Her grip is lighter now and Oliver shifts his weight. 'Wouldn't you be happier if I lay by your side?'

'No. Why won't you sleep with me?' she begs. 'Don't you find me attractive?'

Oliver considers his words carefully. He must not give her false hope. 'I think you are a lovely woman,' he says without emotion, 'but the Oliver Foxley you know exists only inside your head. I am not that man. There will be someone for you, Sylvie, believe me. I don't want you to look back at your time at the retreat and have any regrets. This is a turning point in your life. Embrace it and move towards a brighter future. You probably can't imagine it, but it will happen.'

Listening intently, Sylvie absorbs his words and silently weeps.

Oliver watches as the tears run unchecked down her cheeks. He recognises her pain and feels a surge of sympathy towards this strange woman. She's like a broken child and he wants to comfort her, but knows this will only make matters worse.

'Hush, Sylvie, don't cry. Life is not as dark as you think.'

Listen to me! Maybe something has rubbed off from that expensive therapist after all.

At last Sylvie unclenches her ankles. Oliver rolls off.

'Don't go,' she says in a small, cracked voice.

He lies at her side.

Thank God the paparazzi aren't here!

Turning towards him, Sylvie holds him tightly. As she rests her head on his chest, involuntarily Oliver's hand touches her hip bone. Her skin feels cold.

'If you won't put your clothes on at least let me cover you,' he says, grabbing the throw and pulling it over them both.

It is very intimate lying with Sylvie and Oliver is acutely aware of her nakedness. Little moaning noises emanate from her throat and he wonders at her mental state. It must be hard never having anyone to discuss things with, or not having someone with whom to share your life. In adulthood, he has never had to face that; Deanna has always been there. And then the children arrived and life, since, has been filled with noise, laughter and loving mayhem. But before then, throughout his late childhood and teenage years, it was very different, and it doesn't take much to remember what it was like.

Eventually, Sylvie stops moaning as she slips into sleep. With this troubled soul clinging to him and recognising only too well the haunted look in her eyes, unwittingly, Oliver is dragged back to his childhood. How dark life seemed then and how utterly helpless he felt. As the 'grey mist' descends with crushing intensity, laying waste to anything in its path, Oliver closes his eyes and succumbs to mental exhaustion.

*

Oh, it feels good! Warmth spreads through his body, filling the darkest recesses of his soul. Oliver groans. The 'grey mist' shrouds him, holding him in its throes, suffocating, but there's a golden light beckoning, enticing him to come forward to breathe its pure air. Higher and higher it asks him to travel and he quickens his pace, reaching ever more towards that beautiful golden light, longing to feel its warmth as it spills over, eradicating all pain and suffering. He groans again as he feels the hotness of her mouth on him, the tantalising flick of her tongue licking and swirling, up and down, prodding and probing – investigating.

Sylvie watches beneath hooded eyes. As Oliver emerges from deep sleep, in one swift movement she straddles him, her small breasts jiggling as she rides him hard.

What the...?

Oliver's eyes fly open; his hands on her hips in an instant. He tries to push her off, but her manic energy drives him on, higher and higher, towards not what is a glorious and forgiving, golden light. Feeling disgusted and dirty – and so angry at this betrayal – in that moment he hates her. Her moans have the edge of madness and Oliver bites down hard on his lip, refusing to give voice to his own. Unable to hold back, he reaches orgasm, and the full shame of his situation rains down upon him as the 'grey mist' claims him with a hollow laugh.

Looking at him with wild eyes, Sylvie unravels, spiralling down around him, possessing him and shouting out his name.

Shit! Someone must have heard that.

She falls forward onto his chest, breathing hard, and he can feel her heart beating rapidly as she repeats his name like a mantra. Forcefully, Oliver pushes her off. Rising from the bed, he pulls up his jogging pants. How the hell did she manage that without waking him? Looking down at Sylvie, all wanton and spent on his bed, he has never seen anything so hideous... nor has he ever felt so violated.

And in this special place, of all places...

Sylvie smiles; all warm and glowing inside. 'You know it's fate that brought us here under the same roof,' she says. 'You and me, we're destined to be together.'

Oliver stands with his back firmly against the far wall, desperate for a shower. He just wants her gone. 'Get out!' he says, his voice low and menacing.

He sees the hurt on her face. Ordinarily, his natural warmth and generosity would respond, but pity and understanding have crystallised into deep anger.

Confused, Sylvie frowns. 'But, I thought...'

Oliver cuts her short. 'Leave me alone,' he says, running a hand through his hair.

Sylvie gets off the bed. Misguidedly confident, she bends to pick up her clothes and crudely exposes herself to him. Slowly she pulls on her pyjamas.

Not waiting until she's fully dressed, Oliver picks up Sylvie's cardigan and slippers, grabs her by the arm and roughly marches her towards the door. Unceremoniously, he dumps her out into the corridor.

'Do not trouble me again,' he growls, shutting the door firmly in her face.

Sylvie stares open-mouthed at the closed door. Her arm smarts and she rubs it. Why is he being so rough, her love? Perhaps he likes it that way? He was *very* aroused. But, it's hardly surprising. After all, he's been her constant companion during many an evening in the lonely environs of her Twickenham flat and she's had years to fantasise and perfect that particular scenario. A smile curls Sylvie's lips. So this is the game he likes to play! One minute loving her, the next playing the distant, hard man. Yes, she can accommodate that, if that's what it takes. She likes the challenge he has set. She likes the chase.

Putting on her slippers, Sylvie picks up her cardigan and makes her way back to the Wisdom wing, humming to herself and playing the last half-hour over in her head, like a re-run of one of his movies.

Chapter Eight

Cara is still dissatisfied with her painting of the cove. To anyone else it would be considered brilliant but she thinks it doesn't possess her usual magic. Basil snoozes on the window ledge, having found a spot warmed by the rays of a weak February sun. Glancing out at the flat, grey sea, she wonders where her flair has gone. The tide, on its way out, has left great swathes of wet sand and the gulls have moved in, checking for any stranded small fish, crab or marine worm. There's no hint of a wind in the cove today – a still life in monotint.

'Argh!'

The cat flicks an ear.

In the background a radio presenter is having a lively discussion with his guest, an up-and-coming young actor who will be presenting one of the awards at the forthcoming Film and Television Awards Ceremony. Although Cara enjoys film and theatre, and likes to support Cornwall's performing arts, she feels so far removed from the glitz and glamour of award ceremonies that it's like listening to a discourse from another planet. Christo was always more of a music man. She smiles, recalling his obsession with Coldplay and Chris Martin and how, over the years, she gained the nickname Gwyneth. But that was then. The smile fades from her face. Placing her paintbrush on the palette, Cara descends the wooden stairs and enters the living room. Barnaby looks up expectantly from his dog bed.

'Don't get excited, I'm just making coffee.' She checks the water level in the kettle and switches it on, then immediately switches it off. 'OK, Barns, change of plan.'

The Labrador is up and out of his basket in an instant. Cara smiles. He has so much energy, he reminds her of Ben. Her smile fades again. What *is* she going to do about him?

Dumping her painting shirt on a chair, she grabs a fleece from the hallway and Barnaby's lead from its hook by the porch door, just in case. As soon as she opens the door, the Labrador rushes towards the steps leading down to the deserted beach. Cara follows. As she sets off at a steady jog towards Rick's Beach Hut with Barnaby racing around her in large circles, she feels something shift within; something stodgy that has been holding her back. Breathing evenly, Cara increases her pace, challenging herself not to stop until she's reached the café. She arrives at its steps red-faced, despite the cold, and doubles over to catch her breath.

'That was one serious run.' Rick's Australian accent is unmistakable. 'Been watching you all along the bay.'

She looks up and nods, unable to speak.

Scattering a flock of gulls at the water's edge, Barnaby races across the sand towards them.

'You deserve a cappuccino after that marathon,' Rick says.

'Good idea,' Cara says breathlessly and follows him inside.

The Labrador shoots through the open door and laps noisily at a water bowl placed conveniently in the entrance. Suddenly, from the rear of the café a springer spaniel appears. Barnaby turns to face it. Sniffing each other, tails wagging, with a couple of barks they tear away, play-chasing through the tables.

'Milo, here.'

Cara turns towards the voice. It's the man on the beach. An American!

'Hope my dog's not being a nuisance?' she says.

'Doesn't seem to be,' he responds with amusement in his tone.

'Cara, this is Greg,' Rick says from behind the counter. 'He and his wife are staying at the Marsdens' place for a few weeks.'

'Bet there are great views from up there,' Cara comments.

'That's for sure,' Greg agrees smoothly.

'Here you go.' Rick places a large cappuccino on the bar in front of her. A couple of Amaretti biscuits nestle on the saucer.

'Rick, you spoil me!' she says, hopping up onto a stool. 'At this rate I'll have no alternative but to run on my return journey!'

Rick smiles warmly. 'Hey, Greg, you're into art. You should check out Cara's paintings. She has a rare gift.'

Cara sips her coffee. It's hot and frothy, and just what she needs after her run.

'What's your style?' Greg asks.

She swivels in the direction of the man. Yes, her first impressions of him were correct: attractive, sophisticated and smooth.

'Mainly landscapes and seascapes.' She has the feeling he's filing away the information. 'The one I'm working on at the moment refuses to take shape, hence my exertions on the beach. I hope it may shake things up a bit.'

'Yes, that can work,' he says authoritatively.

Intrigued, Cara asks, 'Are you an artist?'

'Of sorts,' he says cryptically, and smiles.

Randomly, Cara wonders what his wife's like. Believing they are at the end of their discourse, she turns away.

'Do you have a website?' he asks.

She turns to him again. 'Yes, I have one for the gallery.'

'The gallery?'

She nods. 'I have a gallery in Porthleven. Perhaps you and your wife would like to visit while you're here?'

'I'd like that very much, though I doubt my wife will be up to it.' He doesn't elaborate. 'What's the name of this gallery?'

'The Art Shack. It's in the courtyard off Harbour Road.' Yes, he's definitely filing away the information. 'At this time of year we're open Tuesday to Saturday between eleven and three.'

The man nods. Conversation now over, Cara returns to her coffee.

Greg rises from his seat, the chair legs scraping noisily over the tiled floor and disturbing the dogs lying at his feet.

'Great English breakfast, Rick,' he says, walking towards the counter. He produces a soft leather wallet from his jacket pocket and hands Rick a twenty-pound note. 'Nice meeting you, Cara. I hope our paths cross again.'

'Me too,' she says, accepting the smooth, manicured handshake.

His grey eyes dance with amusement and something else, and Cara shifts awkwardly, caught out by a look that suggests 'a different time and place…'

Greg squeezes her hand. Pocketing his change, he turns towards the door. 'Milo, come.'

Cara places a restraining hand on Barnaby's neck as the spaniel peels away and considers *that* look. She didn't see it coming. She's so out of practice!

'Enjoy your walk,' Rick calls out after the American.

'Thanks. This cove is kinda special,' Greg says. He stands back from the door, allowing a middle-aged couple to enter.

As Rick fusses over the new customers, Cara finishes her coffee.

'What's wrong with Greg's wife?' she asks on his return.

Rick shakes his head. 'He said they're house-sitting for a couple of months while the Marsdens are in New Zealand, but I think it's more to do with his wife's recuperation. I don't know what's wrong with her.'

Of course, Milo belongs to the Marsdens.

She watches as Rick loads a tray with two cups of coffee, a plate of carrot cake and a hefty slice of Black Forest gateau.

'Well, this isn't getting anything done and you're tempting me with those scrummy cakes! I'd best be off. What do I owe you?'

'Nothing, my lovely. It's on the house.'

'Aw, Rick. Are you sure?'

He nods.

'Well, you're a mate, no doubt about that!' Cara hops off the bar stool and walks to the door, Barnaby at her heels. She turns and waves.

Rick smiles in return, his eyes following her as she walks along the boardwalk with her dog. It's not right that someone so lovely has been dealt such a raw deal. Life sure can suck! Sighing heavily, he picks up the tray and heads towards his customers.

Cara heads across the car park deep in thought. The cove attracts an interesting mix of people and Greg has intrigued her. He's certainly attractive, in that smooth, moneyed way American businessmen can have. She wonders what he does for a living. She doesn't have him down as an artist. And what's wrong with his wife? And that look! Maybe she has still got it. Feeling a few spots of rain, she breaks into a jog. Beside her, Barnaby matches her pace. As they near The Lookout she spies Greg and the spaniel way below on the beach, and the Labrador stops at the edge of the track to watch them.

'Barns, here,' she calls.

Hesitating for only the briefest of moments, the dog turns to follow his mistress.

Chapter Nine

Since returning from Holy Isle, Oliver is in the grip of debilitating depression. Despite daily meditation, he's unable to master the improving state of mind achieved before Sylvie's shocking visit. Why the hell did he allow her into his room and let things get so out of hand?

As a result of the critical examination of his life while staying at the retreat, a long-forgotten incident during his early career has resurfaced and now plays on his mind. One of his leading ladies – older than him and in her prime – not only encouraged the good-looking, vigorous, young actor to enjoy her company but positively demanded it. Subsequently, he found himself in a compromising position. But it's an unspoken rule on set that what occurs during filming stays amongst the cast and crew, and his marriage was not jeopardised. The actress in question – since recognised in the Queen's Honours List and now a Dame – was busy conquering the world and simply notching up yet another Hollywood 'rising star' to her list. However, in real life, when an obsessed fan meets his or her idol, how fine a line do those boundaries become? Oliver can only assume this is what happened to Sylvie. Meeting him so unexpectedly and finding him accessible must have tipped her over into fantasy land.

It's over a week since her visit to his room but Oliver still feels contaminated, and there's a lingering whiff of something terribly offensive. Thankfully, he didn't see her again until Captain Burrows arrived on the island two days later. A couple of the monks and several of his fellow attendees gathered to wave him off. As the helicopter effortlessly lifted from the helipad, he looked back to wave at the small gathering and saw her skulking around the side of the farmhouse watching him, her face as radiant as any lover's. His hand had frozen mid-wave and a deep sense of unease and nausea enveloped him as the unhinged element of her misplaced emotions rocketed through the air like a heat-seeking missile, hitting him deep in the solar plexus. Shaken, he was unable to forget the madness in her eyes all the way back to Surrey.

Oliver glances at the bedside clock – late morning. Deanna's perfume wafts from her pillow and fills his nostrils. They were finally intimate last night, the first time since his return, but the act seemed hollow and it took him a while to find his rhythm. Perhaps he was expecting too much, desperate to exorcise the memory of Sylvie. Disconcertingly, it was only when a vision of Sylvie straddling him, her small breasts jiggling, that his anger and disgust enabled him to satisfy his wife.

'Dad. Phone!' Samantha's shout carries along the hallway.

Oliver groans. Climbing out of bed, he pulls on jeans and a sweatshirt and is almost at the top of the stairs when his daughter turns the corner. The vision halts him in his tracks. Samantha wears low-rise skinny jeans and a skimpy T-shirt, and a good deal of bare flesh is on show. When he left for Holy Isle she was seventeen and a teenager. Now, less than a month later, she has transformed into a sexy, attractive, young woman; the splitting image of Deanna at that age.

What? she mouths, momentarily distracted by the look on his face. He shakes his head and smiles. 'It's Tas,' she says.

Taking the phone from her, Oliver kisses his daughter on the forehead and follows her downstairs. At the bottom of the stairs Samantha turns and sticks out her tongue, then smiles.

May look like a woman, but still a teenager at heart.

'Tas! How you doing?'

'Hello you old Fox. Long time no speak. What's up?'

'Family growing up too fast,' Oliver says, sitting on the stairs.

'Kids!' exclaims Tas. 'As if it's not bad enough having a back catalogue of films to remind you of the passing years.' Oliver laughs. 'How's that gorgeous god-daughter of mine? Sounds all grown-up.'

'I swear she's turned into a woman overnight.'

'They have a habit of doing that, so I've been told!' Tas says.

'Looks just like Deanna at that age.'

Tas lets out a long, low whistle. 'Think you might have your work cut out there, Mr Fox. Any spotty boyfriends hanging around?'

'Don't think so, at least not that I've been told.' Recalling his surprise at learning Charlie has been dating for over a year, Oliver now considers his daughter. 'Deanna might know differently but you know what these women are like, thick as thieves. I'd be the last to know!'

He and Tas go way back to drama school days. Simon Buckley – nicknamed 'Tas' because he originates from Tasmania – enrolled on the directors' course at the same time as Oliver studied acting. They met on the first day and struck up an immediate friendship. When Deanna joined the college the following year, the three of them hung out together and it was only natural that Tas was best man at their wedding.

'I tried you last week and spoke to Charlie,' says Tas. 'He said you were somewhere off the west coast of Scotland.'

'Yes, at the retreat.' Oliver blinks away an unwanted vision of a naked Sylvie bending over to pick up her clothes.

'How are things? Still got that damned albatross hanging round your neck?' Being a good friend, Tas is one of a handful of people who know about Oliver's mental imbalance.

I was on the point of releasing it when that crazy woman made sure it was still firmly in place…

'Yeah, 'fraid so.' Oliver turns as his family appears in the hallway. 'It's Tas,' he says to his wife.

Deanna takes the phone from her husband. 'Hi, darling, how are you?'

'All the better for hearing your voice.'

She smiles. 'Any sign of a Mrs Tas on the horizon?'

'You know me, Deanna. Just waiting for the day you finally realise that old Fox ain't no good for you!' Deanna laughs at the in-joke. 'No one compares to you,' Tas continues, 'although Ollie tells me Samantha is the splitting image of you at her age.'

Not recognising the compliment her husband has paid her, Deanna ignores Tas's comment about her daughter. 'At forty-four, Tas, you should be thinking of settling down,' she scolds, but there's a smile on her face.

'Forty-three, Mrs Fox! Give me a break!' he exclaims. She laughs again, and Oliver hears the lightness in it. 'Anyway, there are so many lovelies coming through the ranks why would I want to be tied down?'

Deanna shakes her head. 'You are shocking, Tas, but it's lovely to hear from you. Don't be a stranger. Come over for supper one evening. Now I must dash. I'm taxi driver to the kids today.'

'Will do, Deanna.'

'Bye, darling,' she says, making a kissing noise into the mouthpiece. She hands the phone back to Oliver and gives him an odd look. 'I'll be back, don't know when. I'm here, there and everywhere this morning. Tim's mum is dropping Jamie home from swimming later so help yourselves to lunch. There's plenty in the fridge.'

Oliver watches his family make their way out of the house towards the Range Rover parked on the driveway, Sebastian high-fiving him as he passes by.

'So what's new with you, Tas?' Oliver asks, contemplating the odd look Deanna has just given him.

'Been busy with the company. That's what I want to discuss with you. How's your schedule?'

'I've been sent a script, a box office hit for sure, but I just don't know… Can't muster up much enthusiasm.' Oliver drags a hand through his hair. 'Basically I'm procrastinating but my agent's on my back.'

'Well, listen up. I'm taking the company on tour to Cornwall this summer, visiting rural communities and performing in any building that will have us. Sports halls, chapels, village halls, pubs, that kind of thing. Then finishing off with a week-long stint at the Minack in September. It's a brilliant play by a talented, new writer.'

'Sounds good so far,' says Oliver. Having studied the painting of the Minack on his study wall many times, wondering what it would be like to perform on its stage, his interest is piqued.

'This is where you come in, Mr Fox. It will mean singing but I know that doesn't bother you. It needs someone with sensitivity, depth and a complex range of emotions and, well, as soon as I read the play I knew there was only one person I wanted as the lead. If I email you the script will you read it and let me know by Monday?'

'When does the tour kick off?'

'Easter. It's not strenuous, three shows a week at most. You could return home between performances. But think about it, Ollie, summer in Cornwall. All those cream teas and pasties! And if you fancy something a little more sophisticated, Rick Stein, Jamie Oliver, Nathan Outlaw... need I say more?'

Oliver laughs. This could be his reason to decline the movie.

'Email it over, Tas. I'll take a look and let you know by the end of the weekend.'

'I'll do it now. Hope you agree to do the play. It would be just like old times and a great break in a fabulous part of dear old Blighty!'

Replacing the phone in its cradle, Oliver walks to his study. While waiting for the computer to power up, he glances up at the canvas displayed above the mantelpiece, which is crammed with various awards, including one for the film that first put him in the A-list category. As he gazes at the painting, Oliver wonders about the artist who has so magically brought the Minack to life and created an atmosphere that fills his soul. It's as if he's actually there, looking out over the stage under a star-lit sky towards the Logan Rock. He studies the dark shapes of the cormorants perched on the rocky promontory jutting out into the calm, inky blue sea below the stage. A yellow glow from one of the beaches below Porthcurno suggests someone has discreetly set up camp for the night, and in the distance a bright white light shines from a tanker making its way across the horizon. The night sky is tinged with a streak of aquamarine, but the artist has mainly used dark colours: midnight blue, petrol blue, indigo, navy and grey, deepening to black. A colour palette that should be sombre, but the painting is peaceful and serene with the Milky Way hanging in all its glory in a vast sky above the spectacularly set amphitheatre.

The computer screen flickers into life and Oliver logs into his account. True to his word, Tas has emailed him.

Good to speak earlier. Attached is the play. Hope you see its merits. Subject matter starts off fairly heavy but stay with it – ultimately uplifting. Speak tomorrow. Tas.

Oliver opens the attachment. *Sorrows in the Sand* by Emily Miller.

Hmmm… Pretty gloomy title.

Settling into his leather captain's chair, Oliver starts reading. It's only when he hears the front door slam and Jamie call for his parents that he realises two hours have passed. The play is good – really good – original and dealing with tragedy in a sensitive, thought-provoking and intelligent way.

'Hi, Dad. Where's everybody?' His youngest son stands at the study door.

'Your mum's dropping them all off somewhere.' With a sudden shock Oliver realises he has no idea what his family are doing.

How can I be so disconnected from it all?

'What are you looking at?' Jamie asks, his hair still damp from swimming.

'It's a play Uncle Tas has sent me.'

'Is it good?'

'Yes, Jamie. It is.'

The play has excited him. The part Tas wants him to undertake is a complex one and it will be a challenge. At last, something he can get his teeth into. There and then, Oliver decides to decline the film.

'I'm starving. What's for lunch?' Jamie asks.

'Not sure. Let's go and find out.'

Jamie turns away. Shutting down the computer, Oliver follows his son from the room but pauses at the door to look back at the painting. Again, he marvels at how the artist has captured the atmosphere of the theatre under the stars. Feeling inextricably drawn to it, he knows he needs to go there and experience performing on its stage.

*

'Oh, come on, it's not even six months.' Oliver looks across the remnants of the evening meal at his wife nursing a glass of red wine. 'You're used to much longer stints. Anyway, it's not a gruelling schedule. I'll be home between performances.' He rakes a hand through his hair. 'I don't see the problem.'

Silently, Deanna looks back at him across the table, her face set and her eyes ice-cold steel. Not for the first time he wonders at his wife's self-control. Her strength still shocks him at times, reducing him to the 'little boy lost' he once was. But why is she being so stubborn about this?

'I would have liked to discuss this with you, Deanna. I really want to do this play.'

Deanna's lips compress as she swirls the ruby liquid around her glass, but still she does not speak.

Anger flares in him.

I don't need your approval, like one of the kids asking to go on a school trip!

'As you're obviously not going to discuss this with me I will tell you now that I am going to do this play, Deanna, whether you like it or not.'

'How bloody selfish! What sort of marriage is this?' Deanna explodes, her voice rising with emotion. Oliver flinches. 'I might as well be a single parent dealing with all the problems while you're away, God knows where! I support you through your illness and bite my tongue when you decide to take off at a moment's notice to that retreat of yours.' Deanna glares at him. She drains her glass. 'And what was all that about last night? Call that lovemaking?' Her eyes narrow. 'What happened in Scotland? And don't you dare tell me I'm imagining it. You haven't been the same since you got back.'

'Depression isn't a choice, Deanna,' Oliver says softly, lifting his gaze to hers. 'I accept you don't understand it.'

'You're right. I don't.' She spits out the words. 'One of us has to be strong for the children and apparently that's my role.'

Entering the kitchen, Samantha hesitates, immediately aware of tension in the air. She glances at her parents. 'Err, just getting a drink and then I'm off to bed.'

'OK, darling,' says Deanna, a little too brightly.

Avoiding eye contact, Samantha approaches the fridge and pours herself a drink. 'Night, Mum, Dad,' she says, walking swiftly from the room.

'Sleep well,' Oliver says.

A heavy silence descends.

The next minute Charlie appears in the doorway. 'You guys OK?'

'Fine thanks,' Deanna responds sharply, inviting no further comment.

Oliver raises an eyebrow, thinking that by tackling the problem head-on his fifteen-year-old son is showing more maturity than they are.

'By the way, I'm at Nathan's tomorrow so don't do lunch for me,' Charlie announces. 'I'll be back around seven.'

'OK, darling,' Deanna says.

'Goodnight, then.'

'Goodnight,' Deanna and Oliver say in unison.

They hear whispering the other side of the door, but it soon fades away.

'I don't know about you, but I've had enough of this,' Oliver says, rising from his chair. He starts to clear away the empty plates, stacking them in the dishwasher, and doesn't hear his wife leave the kitchen.

Wandering through to the TV room, Oliver flicks through the channels and watches a bland and meaningless film into the small hours. He is deeply saddened by the brick wall in their marriage. Although it was Deanna's inner strength and independent spirit that first attracted him, sometimes it feels like a mountain to climb. Eventually, he switches off the TV and makes his way up to their room. Deanna appears to be asleep and Oliver undresses quietly before climbing into bed. Not wanting to sleep with an argument hanging over them, he makes a move towards her.

'Don't even think about it,' she says in a cold, level voice.

Oliver turns away. There's no point in further discussions when Deanna is in this mood.

With their backs to each other, careful not to touch, eventually husband and wife fall asleep.

Chapter Ten

Brisk February winds whip across the beach as ice-white waves hurl themselves onto the pristine sands. Waiting for her children, Cara stands in the shelter of the porch looking out over the cove.

I will never tire of this view. Even on the chilliest days it's spectacularly beautiful.

'Mum, can Bobkin come with us?' Bethany asks excitedly.

'No. Grandma won't want a rabbit under her feet. Barnaby is enough.'

Her daughter purses her lips and turns on her heels.

'I can't find my trainer!' wails Sky.

'Look under your bed,' Cara suggests, without taking her eyes off the beach.

'It's not there!'

She sighs. 'I don't know how you manage to lose so many things!'

Sky frowns.

Turning back into the bungalow, Cara follows her son to his room. 'Oh, Sky, what a mess!' she exclaims. 'No wonder you can't find anything.'

Ten minutes later the search moves to the living room and the Labrador's basket.

'Oh, Barnaby, these are virtually new!' Cara cries, as she extracts a damp trainer with tell-tale teeth marks. She hands it to her son.

'Mum, have you seen my beret?' Bethany asks, appearing in the hall doorway.

Cara groans. 'No. When did you last see it?'

'Yesterday. It was hanging on my bed post.'

Cara starts towards her daughter's bedroom but then notices Barnaby lying on the sofa looking decidedly shifty. Pointing at the dog, she says, 'Try over there.'

Sitting on the floor, Sky inserts his foot into the damp trainer and squeals.

Cara sighs. 'Wear your brown leather shoes.'

'It's OK, Mum,' says Sky, overdoing the happy voice.

'No, Sky. Go and change.'

'I like these.'

She can't even control the dog so what makes her think she can control her children?

Rummaging amongst the cushions, Bethany finds her beret. 'Oh, Barnaby!' The dog wags its tail uncertainly. Studiously, the young girl checks the beret over. 'Phew! No damage.'

'Come on, kids. Ready now?' Grabbing the car keys, Cara ushers her children from the room. 'Come on, Barns. We won't leave you behind, even though you have been a little thief.'

The Labrador is off the sofa in an instant, following his mistress to the car. Suddenly Cara's mobile rings. Without checking, she answers.

'Hi Cara.'

'Hi, Ben,' she says, sliding into the driver's seat and pulling a face in the rear-view mirror at her children sitting in the back. Bethany giggles.

'Haven't heard from you for a while. Thought I'd give you a ring.'

'I've been frantically busy.'

'Wondered if you'd like to go for a drink?' Ben asks tentatively.

'I'm on my way out and haven't got my diary with me,' she says, cringing at how pathetically lame that must sound.

'No problem, babe. I'll phone tomorrow. We could do something with the kids at the weekend.'

She's about to put the car into gear but leaves it in neutral. Do something with the kids? They are not his to do something with! They are hers and Christo's. He has no right to think he can muscle in. Consumed by an irrational anger rapidly turning to despair, Cara grips the steering wheel and wills herself not to cry.

'Cara, are you still there?' She swallows deeply. 'Cara…?'

'Yes, I'm still here,' she says in a small voice, her eyes tightly shut and trying to block out the world.

'Are you OK?'

She takes a deep breath. 'Ben, we're late. Phone me tomorrow afternoon and we can talk about it then.'

'OK, babe. Bye, Ca...'

Oops! She didn't mean to cut him off.

Cara puts the car into gear. Twenty minutes later, she turns into her parents' driveway and parks behind Sheila and Barry's car. It's a happy afternoon and evening and Cara relaxes as her parents and their friends take over the children, allowing her a brief respite from her role as mother.

Later, as Carol and Cara stack the supper plates in the dishwasher, Carol turns to her daughter. 'Darling, are you all right?'

'Yes,' Cara answers a little too quickly. 'Just tired, Mum. I'm not sleeping well.'

Carol frowns. 'If you ever want a break we'd be happy to have the children for a few days.' Seeing the look of shock on her daughter's face, she swiftly adds, 'You know, if you want a weekend to yourself, or to go out with friends. Just to be a young, thirty something again. What about that young man you saw the other week? Perhaps you'd like to spend some time with him?'

Cara groans quietly to herself. The last thing she wants is to be left alone with Ben. She'd never be able to fend him off!

'Mum, that's really sweet but I'm OK.' She forces a smile.

'I just want you to be happy, Cara. We all do.'

Happy? She doubts she will ever be truly happy again.

'I know.'

'Who was that young man, by the way?' Carol asks.

'No one. Just a friend.' Her mother knows Ben, but she's not about to give him importance by naming him.

'Sometimes friends can turn into lovers, Cara, and often they're the best lovers to have.'

'Oh, Mum!' Cara laughs, suddenly transported back to her early teens when her mother felt it was time they had *that* talk.

'What?'

'You'll be telling me to take precautions next!'

Carol bursts out laughing. 'Well, just remember we're here if you ever want to relinquish your responsibilities for a while.' She watches the sadness return to her daughter's eyes.

'Anyone fancy a bit of glitz and glamour?' Sheila asks from the kitchen doorway.

'Always up for that!' says Carol, eager to lighten the mood.

'It's the Television and Film Awards,' Sheila says.

'Oh good. All those ridiculous, over-the-top speeches thanking everyone from the cleaner to the Pope and not forgetting darling babies and supportive other halves,' says Carol, leading the way into the living room.

'What's occurring?' calls Ken from the conservatory, as the women re-enter the living room.

'Hot-totty ogling for the next two hours!' remarks Sheila.

Lying on the floor with his dog, Sky quietly repeats, 'Hot-totty ogling.'

'Sky, you did *not* hear me say that!' Sheila cries, her hands flying to her mouth.

The boy looks up. 'I did,' he says innocently.

'Do you want to watch TV with us?' asks Carol to distract him.

'No, thank you, Grandma. I'm playing with Barnaby.'

Sorry, mouths Sheila to Cara.

Cara shrugs. What can she do? He's so bright and quick off the mark.

Carol picks up the remote control and joins her daughter and granddaughter on the couch. An image of the Award Ceremony host fills the screen. As verbose and witty as ever, he incorporates a couple of risqué gags into his opening monologue.

'Crikey, he's cheekier than normal,' remarks Sheila.

'It looks wonderfully glamorous at the Royal Opera House,' says Cara. 'How many times has he hosted it?'

Without hesitation, Sheila provides the answer and Carol nudges her daughter. Her friend loves anything to do with celebrity.

'Ever thought of appearing on *Mastermind*?' Ken comments, as he and Barry enter the room. Sheila snorts. 'What's everyone's poison?' Ken heads towards the drinks cabinet.

As the Awards Ceremony host entertains the audience with his rapier wit, typical wordplay and lovable silliness, Sheila's concentration is total. Ken barely manages to divert her attention when he hands her a gin and tonic.

'Must get a dictionary to hand for his particular style of hosting,' he says, nodding at the image on the screen.

'Now we come to the first award of the evening,' announces the host, 'Outstanding British Film.' The cameras pan across the audience, picking out a plethora of well-known faces.

As Carol and Sheila discuss the various actors and actresses, Cara feels her pent-up tension lift. Safe here, with her parents and their friends, she can block out the harsh realities of her life. Bethany snuggles closer and Cara gives her daughter a little squeeze.

A young, up-and-coming actor – the current Superman – reads out the nominations and, as the relevant clips are played, one particular actor catches Sheila's attention.

'Gosh, he's looking very dapper! Don't you think he just gets better with age, Carol?' Thoughtfully, she sips her drink.

'Oh, here we go!' says Barry, rolling his eyes.

'Shhh, Bar…' Sheila waves her hand to silence her husband, and Bethany giggles. Barry smiles at the young girl.

'And the award for Outstanding British Film goes to…' Superman pauses, milking the moment and keeping the audience on tenterhooks.

As the winner is announced, the audience inhales as one before erupting. Immediately the cameras sweep across the sea of faces, homing in on the winning team. Sitting in the row behind are Oliver and Deanna.

'Oh!' shrieks Sheila, spilling her drink down her front. 'Damn and blast!' Ineffectively, she dabs at her blouse, not once taking her eyes off the screen.

'That's his wife, Sheila,' says Carol.

'Yes, I remember,' says Sheila excitedly. 'Looks a bit of a hard nut to me. Now that I think of it she was rather aloof that day he was besieged by autograph hunters, poor love.'

Carol glances at her friend in amusement. She was one of those autograph hunters too!

'Who are you talking about?' asks Cara.

'Him!' Sheila cries, waving at the screen. 'Oliver Foxley!'

'As you say, Barry,' mutters Ken, 'here we go…'

Cara stares at the handsome actor who appears comfortable in the artificial surroundings of the Royal Opera House and assured of his standing within the elite gathering. Of course, he is stunning in his black tuxedo and bow tie, but she also thinks he looks genuine and honest.

'No one can be that good-looking,' she says under her breath.

'Oh, he is,' says Carol. 'Better actually.'

Cara smiles accommodatingly, not believing her for a moment. She glances at her mother and Sheila and is taken aback by the effect the actor is having on them. It must be because they've met him.

'Is he the man who bought your painting?' asks Bethany.

'Yes, *The Minack,*' Cara replies. 'Weird to think he's got one of my little old paintings.'

'Should have put another thousand on it,' comments Barry drily. 'He can afford it with the money he earns.'

*

Oliver looks across the banqueting hall of the Grosvenor House hotel and sees Deanna chatting to a smattering of A-listers including the seriously hot American movie star, Kyle Hemmings. Noticing how the Hollywood hunk listens attentively to her every word, Oliver feels a surge of pride that his wife is able to hold her own amongst them. With the award ceremony now over, they are at the glittering after party. It has been a night for deserved winners with several likeable, non-irritating acceptance speeches and, for once, Oliver feels he is in the right place at the right time; his equilibrium reinstated.

'Oliver, darling!' The actress, Dame Heather McMullen, glides up to him. Resting her hand lightly on his arm, she rises on tiptoe and gives him a peck on the cheek.

'Heather, you look wonderful,' he says sincerely. She's a good ten years older than him but he's always found her gamine looks highly attractive.

'And so do you, Oliver,' she says, smiling up at him with playful eyes.

'You flatter me.'

'Not at all. You were always wonderful but, like a fine wine, you are maturing nicely.'

Oliver smiles. 'Ian not here?' he asks, wondering if Heather's third husband and award-winning director is in attendance tonight.

She shakes her head. 'These award ceremonies are simply a bore to him. He's back home in San Francisco working on the next project.'

'I'm a great fan of his work.'

'As he is of yours.' Heather gazes up at Oliver, her eyes wide and innocent. A suggestive smile plays at the corners of her mouth. 'Is Deanna here?'

Oliver grins broadly. She is so wicked and *so* transparent.

'Yes, chatting up a major Hollywood star the last time I saw her.'

Heather mirrors his grin, but quickly tempers it as she turns towards an approaching figure. 'Catherine, how lovely to see you.'

'Heather, my dear. Love the hair!' Dame Catherine French, the legendary and world-renowned actress, air-kisses Heather, who pats her newly sleek, urchin cut.

Turning to Oliver, Catherine says, 'So nice to see you again, Oliver.'

'Likewise, Catherine,' he responds, kissing her on the cheek.

'I hear there are rumours of a new Bond film in the offing,' she says. 'I must say, I always believed you to be a strong contender for that role. Any thoughts in that direction?'

'It has never occurred to me,' says Oliver. 'In any case, the current incumbent is doing an excellent job and I doubt the powers that be are looking for a replacement just yet, are they?' He wonders if the actress has some insider knowledge but her face gives nothing away.

'Just checking,' she says, smiling sweetly.

'Besides, they'd be looking for a younger actor, someone like...' Oliver glances round the room '...that good-looking young man over there, for instance.'

The two actresses turn.

'Ah yes, Sooperman!' Heather says, suggestively accentuating the word.

Oliver laughs. He's always loved her wit. She could make a shopping list drip with innuendo.

'Well, if it isn't Dame Heather of McMullen and Dame Catherine of French!' says fellow actor, David Conan, as he approaches their group. He bows deeply to the two award-winning actresses, to which Heather bobs a cheeky curtsey in response. 'And Oliver Foxley. Good evening.' He nods respectfully to the actor.

They all slip into easy banter and, presently, the Master of Ceremonies calls for the gathering to take their seats. The room is spectacularly decked out, the tables dressed with props referencing each of the nominated films, and magnificent chandeliers glitter down upon the movers and shakers below.

Taking her leave of the Hollywood movie star, Deanna scans the room for her husband and Oliver watches as his wife makes her way through the throng. He thinks she looks every inch the star herself, adorned, as she is, in emerald and diamond jewellery. Having chosen a semi-goth look for the occasion, Deanna wears a Louis Vuitton black halter-neck dress with black Chantilly lace detailing adding a feminine touch, a deep slit teasingly exposing a flash of well-honed thigh. She takes her seat and grimaces.

'These heels are so high, my feet are killing me,' she says quietly to her husband.

'Slip your shoes off,' Oliver suggests.

'I might never get them back on again.'

He introduces Deanna to the others at the table, which includes a pretty young starlet bubbling over with excitement at having won Best Supporting Actress. She's met Heather and David before.

The evening is a complete success and the partygoers enjoy a sumptuous banquet along with first-class entertainment, followed by several hours of dancing. While busily chatting to David, Oliver spots the Hollywood hunk fast approaching their table.

'You don't mind if I borrow your wife, Oliver?' the American movie star drawls with a twinkle in his eye.

The next minute, Deanna finds herself whisked around the dance floor under the jealous gaze of the other women in the room. Wryly, Oliver notices his wife's heightened colour.

As soon as Deanna has vacated her seat, Heather is in it. 'Good old Kyle following my instructions,' she says mischievously. Oliver laughs. 'Care to give me a turn...' she pauses dramatically '...on the dance floor, Oliver?'

How can he resist? She's *so* skittish.

'My pleasure,' he says, pushing back his chair and gallantly offering his arm.

As soon as they join the other dancing couples, Heather is in his arms. She is as he remembers: pliant and lissom.

'Mmm, this feels good,' she says softly, as they move to the beat of the music. 'Do you remember, Oliver?' she asks, her eyes darkening with desire.

'I do, Heather.'

Slipping her hands beneath his tuxedo, slowly she slides them down his back, noting how well he has taken care of his body over the years. Her fingers come to rest on his firm buttocks.

'Oh, if only your wife wasn't here,' she murmurs in his ear, 'what fun we could have. Just like the old times...'

He smiles, memories stirring, but an image of Sylvie standing naked before him puts paid to any fleeting passion. Gently he removes her hands to his waist.

Heather looks up at him with a wistful look in her eyes. 'Yes, I suppose I had better behave myself, but you were always my favourite conquest.'

'Once again you flatter me, Heather.'

The actress shakes her head. 'No, Oliver, not flattery. It's true.'

Having been escorted back to the table, flushed and with a sparkle in her eye, Deanna casts around for her husband. When she sees him on the dance floor with Heather draped around him like a boa constrictor, she grits her teeth. She has always hated that woman! Over the years she's had to get used to Oliver being public property, often having to remind herself that it is she who has him for a lifetime and to graciously allow others their five minutes of contact, but it still galls her that women think they can walk all over her to get to him. It's three more dances before Oliver and Heather head back to join the others. Deanna can't be sure but, as they approach their table, she thinks the actress is covertly caressing her husband. Again, Deanna grits her teeth.

As Heather takes her seat on the opposite side of the table, she allows her gaze to meet Deanna's. For a long moment she regards Oliver's attractive wife and then, with the briefest of smiles, turns away to engage Catherine in conversation.

'Well, aren't you the belle of the ball!' teases Oliver, sitting down next to his wife.

Deanna smiles thinly, thinking about Heather's patronising look. She knows there's a connection between her husband and the actress. She's not stupid! It dates back to his breakthrough Hollywood film, when she was pregnant with Samantha. Suffering from severe morning sickness, she didn't want him anywhere near her, but it didn't prevent her from noticing how touchy-feely Heather was with her young, good-looking husband. What was particularly hurtful was it didn't seem to bother the older actress that Deanna and Oliver were expecting their first baby together. Heather simply acted as if Deanna didn't exist; she was merely an inconsequential appendage.

As always, Deanna rises above her emotions. Putting on a display of strength and independence – the very qualities that set her apart from other women in Oliver's eyes – she maintains a cool and level head throughout the evening. Several hours later, as the after party comes to a glittering end, they take their leave of fellow guests and head to their executive suite.

As soon as she enters the lift, Deanna removes her Jimmy Choo shoes and vigorously rubs her left foot.

'Painful?' asks Oliver. 'I'll give you a massage if you like.'

Glancing up, Deanna sees the promise in his eyes.

'That would be very nice, Ollie,' she says in a voice suggesting he has just won first prize.

He smiles at his wife; the mother of his children. So many of their friends' marriages have fallen by the wayside and he knows their success has a lot to do with Deanna's strength of character and purpose. God knows, women have offered themselves freely to him over the years and, had he chosen, he could have yielded to no end of temptation! Taking his wife in his arms, Oliver kisses her deeply. It has been a good evening and her response suggests it will continue to be for a while longer.

'Wow, Ollie!' says Deanna, drawing back for breath and sternly banishing any thoughts he may be thinking of Heather.

Oliver smiles again, thankful that the brick wall between them appears to be crumbling. Perhaps Deanna is thawing a little to his Cornish adventure with Tas after all. As he thinks of the summer months to come he is surprised by the excitement that takes hold deep in his belly.

*

Seven miles due west of the Grosvenor House hotel, Sylvie cannot sleep. Since returning to her flat two weeks previously, she has rushed home from work each day to watch Oliver's films. She has many to choose from; she owns a full catalogue of his works. Her flat is crammed with magazines and articles covering various aspects of his career, and numerous scrapbooks burst at the seams with newspaper cuttings, some even touching upon his home life. Sylvie Clark knows a lot about Oliver Foxley. She even knows what his wife and children look like.

Tonight she has been glued to the television, watching and recording the Awards Ceremony in the hope that Oliver might be there. Each time the cameras panned across the auditorium she frantically scanned the audience for a possible sighting. When she spotted him Sylvie's obsessive behaviour stilled and her breathing steadied, as she savoured every slight variation of his expression. But now, tossing and turning, her head is filled with his image as she recalls his voice, the handsome contours of his face and the feel of his body. How many times has she relived their time on Holy Isle? She can stand it no longer!

Throwing back the covers, Sylvie gets out of bed and crosses the room to a chest of drawers. Opening the top drawer, she removes a folded sheet of paper and walks through to the lounge. She switches on the television and sits on the floor in front of the screen and stares at the writing on the paper. How clever she was to have discovered it.

The day after her visit to Oliver's room at the retreat, she informed her aunt she was feeling unwell and would give that day's teachings a miss. However, once the first session started, and with her aunt safely out of the way, Sylvie headed for the office where a woman sat at a computer. She loitered in the corridor as inconspicuously as possible and pretended to study the noticeboard if anyone walked by. It was remarkably easy. When the woman left the room Sylvie slipped in and, being familiar with computers, almost immediately found the database of attendees. Checking the door every few seconds, she searched for Oliver's name and scribbled his details down on a notepad by the phone. Surrey – not too far away! Closing the database, Sylvie slipped out of the office unseen, leaving no trace of what she had done.

Throughout the night, Sylvie replays the recording of the Awards Ceremony, fast-forwarding and pausing on shots of Oliver. Obsessively rocking backwards and forwards, she hugs her knees and chews her lip. Dawn breaks over the Twickenham skyline and a frown furrows Sylvie's brow as she plots her next move.

Chapter Eleven

Walking along Harbour Road, Greg turns up his collar against the biting wind blowing in off the sea. Hunching into his jacket and quickening his pace, he heads towards the courtyard.

Carol is carefully dusting shelves, listening to her favourite Moody Blues CD, and doesn't hear the man enter. She's miles away, concentrating on Justin Hayward's mellow voice singing about the sun through the trees and a leaf on the breeze, and there's a faraway look in her eyes as she breaks into song.

Greg watches, amused. Eventually, he says, 'Justin might not be here, but I am!'

Carol spins around, rudely transported back to windy, overcast Porthleven. 'Oh, sorry! I didn't hear you enter.'

As the strains of 'Forever Autumn' fade and the more upbeat 'The Voice' fills the gallery, Carol studies the man before her. A smooth, attractive American; not the usual type found in Cornwall during February. She wonders what's blown him in.

'How can I help?'

'It's been suggested I should view Cara's paintings,' Greg says, looking around the gallery. 'I assume these are they?'

'Yes.'

As he stands back to examine the paintings adorning the walls, Greg experiences an intense emotion. Carol watches, fascinated. His clothes are stylish and expensive, and there's an air of money about him. Like her daughter, she wonders what he does for a living.

'Do you know much about the artist?' he asks.

Carol laughs. 'More than most!'

Greg drags his eyes away from the enticing canvases. 'I take it she is special to you?'

Carol smiles. 'Very.'

He frowns, his mouth twisting in annoyance, and Carol adds 'control freak' to her assessment. As Greg walks round the gallery, moving in closer to examine a painting before viewing it from afar, Carol wonders whether he is an art collector. Maybe Barry is right, Cara should add another thousand pounds to her paintings. The sound of the phone interrupts her musings.

'Good afternoon, The Art Shack.' Had she imagined it or did Greg sniff disdainfully?

'Hi, Mum. How's it going? Are you bored stiff? Any customers?'

'Darling! I've just finished dusting the ceramics,' Carol says loudly before turning her back on the man and whispering, 'and I'm currently being entertained by a rather refined American.'

'Greg?'

'I have no idea. We are not on first-name terms!'

'Richard Gere type, about five feet nine, slim build, salt and pepper hair with steely grey eyes,' Cara says.

Carol turns. The man is scrutinising the large canvas, which takes up a good proportion of the rear wall. Full of atmosphere, it portrays a wild sea at Portreath, the focal point a wave smashing against the end of the pier and pluming high above the stonework.

'Yes, I would say so.'

'He and his wife are in the UK while she recuperates from something,' Cara explains. 'Has he bought anything?'

'No.'

'Oh, I thought he might have,' Cara says disappointedly.

'Not yet anyway,' Carol says. As Greg glances across at her, she wonders if he knows they're discussing him. 'Darling, I'd better go.'

'OK, Mum, but try and sell him something. I'm sure he's loaded!'

As Carol replaces the phone, Greg asks, 'This artist who is so very special to you, is she a family member?'

'Ah, you've found us out.' Ignoring his patronising tone, Carol forces herself to warm to the man.

'A sister?' He seems amused by something, and his steely grey eyes toy with her. 'Or a daughter, perhaps?'

'Yes, Cara is my daughter,' Carol says, choosing not to rise to him.

Greg stares at her long and hard. 'Does she have an agent?'

'An agent?' Carol repeats.

'Yes, an agent!' he says, irritation registering in his crisp tone.

'No, she doesn't have an agent. Why do you ask?' Feeling threatened by his interest, Carol experiences an overpowering maternal instinct towards her daughter.

Greg raises his eyebrows. 'Your daughter has a rare and unique gift, that's why. I'd like to discuss it further with her.'

He takes a step towards her. Automatically, Carol steps back, thankful the counter is between them. Reaching into his inside jacket pocket, Greg produces a soft leather wallet and withdraws a business card. Neatly and purposefully, he places it on the counter in front of her.

'I'd like you to pass this to Cara and ask her to phone me.' It's an instruction, not a request.

Carol nods, unable to say a word. Her whole being screams at him to take his studied, cosmopolitan attitude back to whichever part of the States he's come from and leave them alone to get on with their lives.

Looking at her once more to ensure she has understood, Greg abruptly exits the gallery.

Carol glances down at the card. Slowly, she picks it up. Greg Latimer-Jones is Chief Art Director with *The New York Times*!

This could be a turning point for Cara. Carol knows she should be overjoyed that someone influential has recognised her daughter's talent, but she cannot ignore the niggling unease lurking in the pit of her stomach.

*

'Can you drop Sammy at the station, Ollie?' Deanna asks from the study doorway.

'When?' Oliver asks without looking up from the computer.

'Now. She and Rosie are going to Guildford again.'

Oliver is only half-listening. Tas says he will pick him up on Thursday for the pre-recce tour of Cornwall. It sounds like fun.

'Oliver?' Deanna's voice scythes through his concentration.

'Yes, Deanna, I'll take her.' Oliver logs off. He can visit the pharmacy at the same time and collect his medication.

Deanna turns away, her mind already on the next chore. Immediately, Jamie takes her place.

'Dad, can I come too?'

'Sure. Grab a coat.'

The boy turns and runs down the hallway. Oliver follows, scooping a set of car keys out of the wooden bowl on the hall table.

Samantha takes the last three stairs in one bound and lands at his feet. 'Thanks, Dad!' She gives him a peck on his cheek.

'Sammy, is that all you're wearing? It is only February!'

'Da-ad!' She draws out the word and gives him a withering look. 'Don't stress. This is cool!' She opens her hands expressively, showing off her outfit to him.

Oliver looks at his daughter standing there all fawn-like with her long, denim-clad legs, her T-shirt and short cardigan barely covering her midriff. 'Yes, and you'll be extremely *cool* if you don't wear something warmer.'

Samantha sighs. Walking to the lobby, she selects a thin, fitted, short jacket from the coat rack.

What can he do? Like her mother, she's her own woman.

Grabbing his jacket, Oliver calls down the hallway, 'I'm taking the Range Rover and Jamie's coming with me.'

'Pick up some milk, Ollie,' says Deanna, appearing in the kitchen doorway. 'We're running low.'

'Will do.'

As the Range Rover pulls out of the driveway onto the track, Jamie glances right. He notices a dark blue vehicle waiting at the entrance to the car park serving the walking trails through the forest. There's nothing unusual about this but its number plate displays his initials – JAF. Fifteen minutes later Oliver turns onto the station forecourt. Rosie is already there and the car has barely come to a halt before Samantha jumps out. Enthusiastically, she hugs her best friend.

Such expressive behaviour. You'd think they hadn't seen each other for months!

Oliver lowers the window. 'What time will you be home?'

'Not sure. Rosie's mum's dropping me off later.'

'OK, Sammy.' He smiles at the two teenagers. 'Have a good time.'

'If our plans change I'll give you a bell,' says Samantha, grabbing her friend's hand and walking briskly towards the ticket office.

Oliver glances in the rear-view mirror at his son sitting quietly in the back seat. 'How about we have a hot chocolate in that little café in Market Street?'

The boy's face lights up. Enthusiastically, he nods.

Ten minutes later, Oliver reverses the Range Rover into a parking bay in one of the town's three car parks. A dark blue car passes by. Jamie watches as it turns left beyond the next row of cars and slowly makes its way along the adjacent lane.

'Here you go.' Leaning over the seat, Oliver hands his son a few coins. 'An hour's ticket should be enough.'

The boy joins the queue for the ticket machine, keeping an eye on the dark blue car, which has pulled into a parking bay opposite the Range Rover, a double row of cars between. As the woman in front of him moves away, Jamie reaches up and inserts the coins into the slot. He listens to the change tumbling down inside the machine before pressing the yellow button. Taking the ticket, he walks directly up the aisle towards the dark blue car... JAF. He can't see who's in the driver's seat because he, or she, is reaching for something in the passenger footwell. Squeezing between the row of cars, Jamie walks towards the Range Rover and hands the ticket to his dad.

As they head towards the alleyway, Jamie lengthens his stride to keep up with Oliver and, soon, they emerge onto the high street. The locals are used to seeing Oliver out and about with his family and generally leave him alone. It's only strangers who stop and stare, not quite believing they've just seen *that* actor in *this* Surrey market town. Today, however, father and son make their way unencumbered through the morning shoppers towards The Bean. The café is heaving and there's only one free table. The friendly waitress has served them before and she welcomes them again. She's young and chatty and as she engages Jamie in conversation, Oliver watches his quiet, sensitive son grow in stature. Maybe his concerns are unfounded. Perhaps the boy won't face the same gremlins. He wouldn't wish that on anyone.

'Are you ready to order?' the waitress asks.

'Hot chocolate with marshmallows, please,' says Jamie.

'Oh, if only all my customers were as easy to please,' she says, giving him a wink.

'And a cappuccino for me,' says Oliver, opening a menu.

'She's nice,' the boy says, as soon as the waitress is out of earshot. Looking round, he spies a school friend at the entrance and waves. He turns back to Oliver. 'Dad, where are you and Uncle Tas going?'

'Cornwall,' Oliver says, looking up from the menu, 'checking out venues for the play.'

'Will you be away long?' Jamie bites his lip.

'About a week this time. From Easter I'll be away a bit more often until September.'

The boy looks crestfallen and Oliver feels wretched. His children are used to his absences and none are particularly affected, apart from Jamie.

'I'll be home between performances.' Oliver leans forward and affectionately chucks his son under the chin. 'Jamie, it's OK. I'll be back before you know it.'

The boy looks lost.

It's a look Oliver used to wear, although he never had the benefit of a parent's reassurance. It's hard enough when you're an adult but at nine years old, the same age as Jamie, he didn't realise what was happening to him. He was always over-thinking things, worrying about what others thought and if he'd hurt their feelings. He felt so tired, low and helpless most of the time, and was often on the verge of a panic attack. Sometimes he felt too scared to even go outside and his feelings of anxiety and suffocation could quickly get out of control, especially in crowded places. That's why, whenever he and Deanna have to be present at star-studded events, they make sure Jamie is kept well away from the spotlight.

'Here you go,' says the waitress, arriving at their table and presenting a welcome distraction. 'One cappuccino and a mug of hot chocolate.' She beams at Jamie.

Picking up a spoon, Jamie shovels cream and marshmallows into his mouth. To a casual onlooker he would seem like any other boy of his age simply enjoying time out with his dad.

Oliver stares at the chocolate-dusting stencilled leaf on the surface of his cappuccino, struggling with feelings of guilt sitting uncomfortably alongside the 'grey mist'. As soon as they've finished their drinks he will pick up his medication. He takes a mouthful.

With a cream moustache adorning his upper lip, Jamie looks in the direction of his friend now sitting at a table by the window. He notices a small, skinny woman enter the café and scan the room, her intense gaze settling on Oliver for a long while before shifting to him. There's a wild look in the eyes that hold his a fraction longer than is comfortable, and Jamie breathes in sharply.

Oliver glances up. Seeing the look of apprehension on his son's face, he turns in the direction of his gaze.

Shit! That looks like Sylvie.

He places his cup in its saucer and looks again, but the doorway is empty. The thought of her makes his stomach churn. As his heart starts to hammer, the café walls close in and he struggles to breathe.

Dear God! Not a panic attack.

'Jamie, I'm just stepping outside for a moment.'

The boy nods but says nothing.

Oliver quickly exits onto the street. The cold air offers some relief and his palpitations diminish with each deep intake of breath. Why is she still haunting him? It's been three weeks since he returned from the retreat. Exercise and daily meditation have helped but she still lurks in the dark, shadowy recesses of his mind. Oliver glances along the street one way and then the other.

She couldn't possibly be here, could she? Where did she say she lived? Was it somewhere in London?

He scans the high street again but there's no sign of Sylvie. He must have imagined it. Re-entering the café, Oliver settles up at the till and walks back to the table.

'Come on, Jamie, let's go.'

The boy smiles shyly at the waitress clearing away their empty cups and zips up his jacket before following his dad outside.

Oliver scans the high street once more. Paranoia is not something he wants to add to his list of failings. Holding his son's hand, he walks purposefully up the street towards the pharmacy and new stocks of his medication.

When they return to the car park and approach the Range Rover, a sheet of paper pinned under the windscreen wiper catches Oliver's eye. He extracts it and, with mounting apprehension, unfolds the note.

Oliver,

Phone me. 07908 317892.

I will be expecting your call.

Sylvie x

A sliver of fear uncoils in the pit of his stomach and his eyes sweep over the car park. He glances down at his son. The quicker they're out of here, the better.

Jamie is quieter than usual on the homeward journey. Not that Oliver notices, preoccupied, as he is, with all manner of scenarios playing out in his head. As the Range Rover turns into the driveway for Hunter's Moon, Jamie peers down the track, but there's no sign of the dark blue car.

Pulling up in front of the house, Oliver's senses are on high alert. What was Sylvie doing in town and how did she know this was his car? This is a secluded spot, well off the beaten track, and their phone number is ex-directory, but just how easy would it be for her to discover where he lives? He rubs the hairs standing erect on the back of his neck.

Jamie is already through the front door and hanging his jacket in the lobby when Oliver enters the house.

'Did you get the milk?' Deanna asks, appearing in the hallway.

Damn! That was the last thing on his mind.

'Oh, Oliver. I ask only one thing of you!'

Startled by his mother's harsh tone, Jamie stares at his parents. As Deanna marches towards them, Oliver takes a step back.

'Why is it always me who has to sort out this family?' she hisses, grabbing the keys out of his hand.

'Deanna, let me get the milk,' Oliver says, quickly following her out to the car.

'Oliver, you've already been to get it once!' Deanna says, repositioning the driver's seat. 'As usual, I'm the one who has to cope with everything around here. Aargh!' She thumps the steering wheel, takes a deep breath and steadies herself. When she speaks again her voice is calm. 'Just go to Cornwall.'

Oliver stares at her. 'OK, Deanna, I'll do just that,' he says, his voice equally calm.

Briefly, Deanna hesitates. The next minute she slams her foot down hard on the accelerator, sending the back wheels into a spin. As a shower of gravel flies towards him, Oliver jumps out of the way.

Frowning, he watches the Range Rover skid out of the drive. How can two people share the same life and yet be so separate? He so wants to share his fears and concerns with her.

Oliver stamps the gravel back into place as an iron fist squeezes his heart and depression takes hold.

Chapter Twelve

Ben's body fills the gallery doorway, all shaggy hair and bouncy attitude. Cara hopes his wagging tail doesn't sweep any of the items off the shelves. She smiles at the analogy.

'Hey, Cara. How's it going?'

'Good. I've had several sales this afternoon.'

'Hey, babe, that's great,' he says, bounding towards her.

Babe... again!

'Are you going to be much longer?'

'I'll close at three unless someone comes in,' says Cara, opening the drawer beneath the counter. What's this? She picks up Greg's business card and turns pale.

'You OK?' Ben asks.

'What?' Cara says, startled, having momentarily forgotten he was there. 'I just need to make a call.' She picks up the phone and punches in her mother's mobile number. After the third ring Carol answers. 'Mum, I've just found Greg's card in the drawer.'

Carol's heart sinks. 'Oh, yes, darling, I forgot to mention it.'

Cara frowns. It's unlike her mother to forget something as momentous as this. She watches Ben pick up a ceramic bowl and peer at the initials on the base.

'What did he say?' Cara asks. 'Do you know what he wants?'

Carol takes a deep breath. 'He wanted to know whether you had an agent. He also wants you to contact him.'

'Did he say why?'

'Darling, quite rightly he acknowledges that you have a rare and unique gift.'

'Oh, Mum!' Cara cries, suddenly overcome with emotion. Her parents have always supported her in her artistic endeavours and they fully encouraged her when she first talked about opening the gallery, but to describe her talent in such words… She glances at Ben, now handling a metal and semi-precious stone mobile. He's like a bull in a china shop and she wishes he would just stand still. 'I'll ring Greg tonight. By the way, are you still OK to look after the kids on Saturday?'

'Of course. Good weather is forecast. We'll take them out somewhere.'

'Thanks. I don't know what I'd do without you,' Cara says, suddenly overwhelmed by the events that have taken over her life.

Immediately picking up on the subtle shift in vibration, Carol says gently, 'You are the strongest person I know. God only knows where you get it from, certainly not me! And, as you know, your dad can be charmingly vague at the best of times, so it's certainly not from him either. Wherever life takes you, Cara, you will be OK.' She swallows the lump in her throat.

'I guess so,' Cara responds, forlornly.

Lurking by the door, Ben raises his eyebrows at her. She knows he's itching for her to finish the call.

'Bye, Mum. See you Saturday.' Cara pockets Greg's business card and switches on the answerphone.

An evening with Ben! Why did she agree to it? What a shame Janine was free to look after Beth and Sky. The gods are truly against her...

Switching off the lights, Cara steps outside and locks the door, surprised to be thinking how much she loves her life in Cornwall. Without waiting a moment longer, Ben grabs her hand and marches her out of the courtyard.

There's a hint of early spring on the breeze. The seagulls' raucous cries fill the air as they swoop around the fishing boats entering the inner harbour. Rising up the harbour wall, a huge swell follows Ben and Cara as they make their way towards the pub. Ben pushes open the door and enters with Cara in his wake.

'Hi, Cara,' the landlord says, as they approach the bar. 'How was your day?'

'A few more customers than normal. How about you?'

'Wednesday in early March? Can't complain!'

'Where shall we sit?' asks Ben, glancing around. Although several tables are occupied, there's still plenty of choice.

'How about by the window?' suggests Cara.

'OK. Choose something to eat and go grab a table,' Ben instructs, oblivious to the landlord's eyebrows shooting skywards.

'What's the special today?' Cara asks.

'Fish pie. Couldn't be fresher. Straight from Patrick's haul this morning.'

'Sounds good to me. And I'll have half a cider please.'

Walking towards the window table, Cara acknowledges a couple that visited the gallery earlier in the afternoon. As she pulls out a chair she looks out at the familiar view of houses and restaurants on the far side of the harbour and feels an uncharacteristic melancholy, as if all she has ever known is slipping away. Get a grip! Can't be all soppy around Ben. She looks up and smiles as he approaches with the drinks.

'Bottoms up!' Ben clinks her glass and takes a hefty swig of Doom Bar. Placing his glass heavily on the table, he smacks his lips together and lets out a loud and satisfied, 'Ah!'

Why is everything about him so big? So different from Greg. She fingers the business card in her pocket. Chief Art Director with *The New York Times*! Cara frowns. Why did her mother squirrel it away in the drawer?

'So, babe, have you given us any more thought?' Ben asks hopefully.

Cara sighs. She wants to give him an abrupt 'no' but knows this is way too harsh. 'Ben, one day at a time.'

Ben groans. 'I know you've needed time to grieve but don't you think you've done that by now?'

Cara reels in shock and then seethes with anger.

'Shouldn't you let someone new into your life?' Ben leans across the table and traps her hand beneath his. 'Christo would want that.'

'Drop it, Ben,' she says quietly. Swiftly, she removes her hand.

'Argh!' He leans back heavily in his chair. 'You can be so trying at times!'

So this is how it's to be, is it?

'Ben, you have no idea,' Cara says evenly.

The tense atmosphere is broken by the waitress arriving with their food. Cara doesn't recognise the girl. She must be a new recruit, at the start of the season.

'Who's having the fish pie?' the waitress asks and Cara nods. 'And you must be having the steak.' The girl flashes Ben a broad smile.

As they busy themselves sorting cutlery and condiments, Ben picks up the thread of their conversation.

'And neither do you, Cara,' he says sulkily.

'Neither do I what?'

'Have any idea.'

Inwardly Cara groans. She can't be all things to all people. She has her children to think of. She knows what he wants but if he can't chill and just accept her as a friend, she will have to stop seeing him completely. She looks round as the pub door opens. In walks Tristan and she has never been so thankful to see him.

Approaching their table, Tristan kisses Cara on the cheek and acknowledges Ben with a nod. 'That looks good,' he says, eyeing up Ben's steak. 'Think I'll order one myself.'

Ben sighs. Now Tristan is going to cramp his style.

'How's that studio ceiling holding up?' Tristan asks, pulling out a chair.

'So far so good, though I've got a couple of buckets in place.'

'What if Rob and I come over one day and make good? Would that do or does the whole roof need replacing?'

'Don't know really, Trist,' says Cara. 'Christo built the studio about six years ago so I guess we'll find out once we peel back the layers.'

'Leave it to me. I'll get it sorted,' Tristan says, rising to his feet and fishing out the ringing mobile from his jeans' pocket. 'Hi, Jane. Where are you, honey?'

Cara smiles to herself. It's good to see Tristan in love.

Within half an hour Tristan's girlfriend joins them and, distracted by the easy banter, Cara finds Ben's company acceptable. At seven, they leave Tristan and Jane in the pub. Ben insists on walking her to the car.

As she opens the driver's door he restrains her. 'Cara, I need to say something. I don't care how long it takes but I have plans for you and me. I am prepared to wait but you need to know how I feel about you,' he says, the words tumbling out of his mouth; his eyes imploring.

'Ben, just chill and enjoy the moment.' Cara attempts to get in the car but he blocks her way. She looks up at him enquiringly.

'Just one kiss, Cara, please.'

His need of her is sweet, but it's so not what she wants.

Taking advantage of Cara's hesitation, Ben moves in closer and wraps his arms around her. It's so unexpected he can hardly control himself and the ensuing kiss is wet and sloppy. Cara draws back.

'I won't push it, I promise,' he says, 'but I have needs.'

And then he's gone, walking out of the traders' car park and heading towards the town's main car park, whistling to himself.

Cara climbs in the car feeling numb. How could she be so stupid? Now he will never be able to keep his hands off her! She removes Ben's slippery wetness from her lips with her sleeve and rests her forehead against the steering wheel. Suddenly she remembers Greg's business card. Intrigued, she removes it from her pocket and punches the number into her mobile. She counts the number of rings and is just about to switch off when Greg answers.

'Er, hello, Greg,' she says, suddenly uncertain. 'It's Cara Penhaligon.'

'Cara!' He sounds delighted, but also amused.

'My mother said you called by the gallery and asked me to phone.'

'Correct on both accounts,' he responds in his smooth American accent. 'I very much liked what I saw. We wondered if you would come up to the house tomorrow evening with your portfolio?'

'I don't have a portfolio, just the website.' She hears the sharp intake of breath and knows he's thinking, what artist doesn't have a portfolio? She feels flustered, and it has nothing to do with the incident with Ben. 'It was destroyed in a flood a few years back,' she hurriedly explains.

'Well, perhaps you could bring a couple of your canvases with you, particularly the large one of the wave at Portreath.'

'Of course. What time shall I call by?'

'After eight. You know where we are?'

'Yes, I know,' she says, feeling ridiculed. Was their conversation the other day of such little consequence?

'We look forward to seeing you.'

'Bye.' Cara ends the call. Well, she's done it now! There's no looking back.

*

Oliver packs his bag. He and Tas expect to be away for a week and he wonders what the weather will have in store. He is deliberating over jumpers, T-shirts or fleeces when a flash on the periphery of his vision catches his attention. He looks out of the bedroom window towards the edge of the woods. It's a crisp, clear day and the sun, though weak, shines brightly. The manicured lawns stretch down to the lake and he sees the call ducks swimming undisturbed amongst the grasses at the water's edge. It's a beautiful vista and, not for the first time, he thanks his accountant for having given him such good advice all those years ago. Another flash… to the right of the lake. What *is* that? Perhaps it's glass? If so, he needs to clear it up before he departs. It wouldn't do for the kids to hurt themselves.

Knowing Deanna has just taken the children to school, Oliver finishes packing. Things have been frosty between them since the milk incident. Well, he thinks so. It seems to him that it doesn't bother Deanna whether they're getting on or not; she always copes. Again, he wonders about his standing within the family. Perhaps every father feels this way but it's playing on his mind more and more these days. Deanna is so capable. The thought depresses him. Briskly, he zips up the bag and carries it downstairs. Tas will be here within the hour. His friend is good, intelligent company and it's been a long time since they last shared an adventure. It will be fun to be on the road with him again. Placing the bag in the entrance lobby and grabbing a jacket, he walks to the kitchen. As he opens the back door there's another flash. Oliver steps down from the stone terrace and sets out across the lawns.

Sylvie lowers her binoculars and ducks behind a tree. Pressing her back firmly against its bark, she wills it to swallow her up. This won't do. She can't let him find her spying on him. But, damn him, he hasn't phoned! What should she do? He'll discover her in seconds. Quickly she darts through the foliage towards the main trail and by the time Oliver arrives at the edge of the woods, the trees have closed in around her.

Oliver studies the ground but there's no glass lying around. Funny, because he's sure this was where the flash came from. He thought he saw a movement through the trees but it could have been a deer. They have plenty around here. Oliver searches amongst the undergrowth and finding no obvious sharp implements, returns to the house.

Arriving at her car, parked at the entrance to the forest trails, Sylvie climbs in and tries to regulate her breathing. That was close! She desperately wants to see him, but not under such circumstances. As her heart beats a rapid dance against her rib cage she wonders what to do next. An hour ago she watched his family leave the house. Should she just brazen it out, walk up to the house and ask him why he hasn't phoned? No, he likes to play hard to get. Maybe if she teases him and suggests she won't be around for much longer, it will stir him into action.

In the rear-view mirror she notices a vehicle driving down the track. Picking up the binoculars, she turns in her seat. A big, masculine, bearded man is at the wheel of a 'look at me big bollocks' black Jeep. Childishly, she giggles at her description as she watches the vehicle turn into the driveway. What's going on here, then? Sylvie starts the car and turns it to face in the direction of the road, leaving the engine ticking over. Five minutes later she switches off. She is contemplating making her way back through the woods to spy on the house again when the Jeep pulls out onto the track and heads back towards the road. As she peers through the binoculars, Sylvie sees Oliver sitting in the passenger seat. Frantically, she turns the key in the ignition and aggressively puts the car into first gear. In her panic it stalls.

'Crap!'

She turns the key again and, grinding her way through the gears, drives up the track towards the road. She cannot lose them now, though the Jeep will be easy to pick out in the traffic. However, as she rounds the corner, the Jeep is stationary some twenty yards ahead with the Range Rover alongside. She can see Oliver's wife chatting to the man in the driver's seat. Double crap!

'Like Piccadilly Circus here today,' comments Tas, looking in the side mirror.

Oliver turns in his seat and looks over his shoulder. Sylvie ducks. She's quite a distance away but she sure as hell doesn't want to be recognised.

'Better move on,' Deanna says. 'Have a good journey.'

'I'll phone tonight,' Oliver says to his wife through the open window as the Jeep pulls away.

Deanna nods once and drives towards the entrance gates, keeping an eye on the dark blue car slowly approaching. As she turns into the driveway it speeds past, narrowly missing the Range Rover by a few inches.

*

'So what's with the wheels?' Oliver asks Tas.

'You know me and American Jeeps!' his friend says with a grin. 'Ever since I saw that first episode of *M*A*S*H* I knew there was no other vehicle for me. It's also a bit of a babe magnet.' His grin broadens.

Oliver laughs. Being so masculine and larger than life, Tas is quite a babe magnet without any props. 'When did you get it?'

'A couple of months back. Special order. Waited a while for it to come through, but it was worth it.' Tas slows at the roundabout before easing out into the traffic. 'Hey, Mr Fox, you and me hitting the open road again!'

'Brilliant,' says Oliver, conscious of the sudden excitement deep in his belly. 'So, who's this guy we're staying with?'

'An old mate from way back,' explains Tas. 'Rick had a bit of a wrangle with the law back home and found his way over here. He's been in Cornwall, all respectable-like, for the past four years. Runs a café in some out-of-the-way cove. Says he feels safe there!'

'Sounds like a storyline for a play.'

'Hey, you could be onto something.'

Falling into companionable banter, soon they are driving over the Hogs Back, leaving behind comfortable, commuter-belt Surrey and heading towards the Hampshire countryside. A couple of hours later they stop for petrol outside Ilminster. As neither want to run the gauntlet of interested stares from diners in the Little Chef, Tas visits the shop for sandwiches. On his way back to the Jeep he spots a dark blue car parked discreetly, but simply thinks it odd that once you've noticed a particular model of car you tend to notice it all the time.

Rejoining the A303, they head west once more: Destination Cornwall.

Chapter Thirteen

Lights blaze from Rick's Beach Hut as Cara drives by. She notices two cars in the car park: Rick's beaten-up old Land Rover and a big, black, American Jeep.

He's staying late. Wonder what he's up to?

As she follows the steep, narrow lane leading out of the cove, headlights ahead dip into darkness. Cara drives past a car parked in the only passing place on the lane.

What madness to stop there, and in darkness too! She could easily have ploughed into it.

At the brow of the hill she turns into the Marsdens' driveway and pulls up in front of the white house positioned high above the cove. She switches off the engine and sits for a moment. Why *is* she so nervous? Taking a deep breath, Cara gets out of the car and walks across the stone-chipped driveway. As she approaches the steps leading to the front door she considers walking away but, before she has the chance to bail out, she rings the doorbell. There's no getting out of it now. Cheery chimes sound from deep within the house. Backing down the steps, she stands on the driveway and grimaces, recalling the last hour during which she has tried on numerous outfits. Her bed is now littered with rejected clothes. Suddenly Greg's figure appears behind the obscure-glazed door. Too late to turn and run now. As the door opens she smiles nervously at him.

'Cara, so good of you to come at such short notice.'

She accepts his firm handshake, again noting the smooth, manicured hand.

Greg is dressed in a thick knit jumper, tan corduroy trousers and shiny brown leather shoes, and Cara is instantly struck by the outfit's studied casualness. It's as if he's just stepped out of a Barbour catalogue, which makes her feel even more insecure about her choice of outfit. Preferring comfortable clothes – mainly baggy jumpers, leggings and Ugg boots – this evening she has made an effort and has chosen a tunic over leggings with a pair of long suede boots.

'Thank you for inviting me.'

'Do you have the canvases with you?'

She looks towards the car. 'Yes, I've brought three, including the Portreath painting you asked for.'

'Good. I'll help you bring them in.'

Why does she feel as if she's about to hand over her life?

He follows her to the car. As Cara opens the boot and leans in, she knows her tunic will rise up, but she can't do anything about that. She pulls the large Portreath canvas towards her and passes it to Greg before removing the two smaller canvases. Holding one in each hand, she closes the boot with her elbow and glances at him inquisitively. She knows he's been checking her out.

Greg smiles, but his face gives nothing away. 'Marietta is looking forward to meeting you.'

Marietta… How exotic!

Cara follows him to the house. She's never been inside before and, on entering, debates whether to remove her boots. Feeling unaccustomedly clumsy, she wonders if the surroundings make her feel this way or whether it is Greg himself. Always so immaculate, he seems quietly amused. Greg strides down the hallway and Cara follows, entering a spacious, open-plan living room straight off the pages of an interior design magazine. She should definitely have taken off her boots; the shag-pile carpet is pale cream. The furniture and decor are tasteful and the room leads directly out into a Victorian-style conservatory filled with plants. As Greg props the large Portreath painting against the wall and relieves Cara of her canvases, she glances around. A large marble fireplace dominates one wall, its mantelpiece crammed with photographs of the Marsdens and various people, no doubt family.

'Darling, Cara has arrived,' Greg calls through to the conservatory.

There's movement amongst the plants and Cara finds herself face-to-face with a striking, middle-aged woman with the highest and sharpest of cheekbones. Meticulously made-up, she is dressed in a colourful caftan with matching turban. There is something extraordinarily aristocratic about Marietta Latimer-Jones and Cara feels hopelessly inadequate, despite the fact that the woman is in a wheelchair. She shakes Marietta's hand, which, like her husband's, is smooth and manicured. Unlike her husband's, however, her handshake is limp. Perfectly shaped, crimson nails add to the sense of the exotic, but – despite her overall appearance – there's no masking the illness in Marietta's watery, pale blue eyes.

'So pleased to meet you, Cara. Do come and sit with me. Greg, darling, would you be a dear and make some tea, or would you like something stronger?' Marietta looks questioningly at Cara.

She'd kill for something stronger but she must keep her wits about her. 'Tea would be fine.'

'Earl Grey?'

'Thank you.'

As Greg leaves the room, Marietta repositions her wheelchair amongst the plants.

'Do take a seat,' she says, motioning to a wicker chair. Cara sits as instructed, feeling insignificant by comparison to this exotic being. 'Greg tells me you are an artist.' Marietta's American accent is tempered with something else, which Cara struggles to identify.

'Yes.'

'Successful?'

Wow! Straight to the point! No messing with this woman.

'To a degree.'

As Marietta's pale blue eyes scrutinise her, Cara has the uncomfortable feeling this woman has the power to expose her to the core.

'And to what degree is that success?'

'Um…' Cara's mind has gone blank. Why does she get the feeling she's being interviewed? But for what? Think! 'Local press coverage, exhibitions in the South West, Internet presence.' It must sound so cosy to this cosmopolitan and sophisticated woman. 'And, of course, the gallery.'

Cara shifts in her seat. It's so hot in the conservatory.

A sudden noise at the door and the Marsdens' springer spaniel enters the room, closely followed by Greg holding a laden tea tray. The dog trots up to Cara and she pats his head, silently thanking him for the welcome distraction.

'Milo, good boy. Come.' Marietta taps the side of her chair and the spaniel obliges, lying down against its wheel. 'He's missing Veronica and John, I fear, but we will just have to do for a few weeks yet.'

Placing the tray on a Victorian cast-iron table, Greg picks up the silver teapot and pours tea into a bone-china cup. With a pair of silver tongs, he selects a slice of lemon from a small, dainty dish and adds this before passing the cup to Marietta. Cara watches transfixed. Everything about this couple is so studied; it makes her fearful to move in case she makes a fool of herself.

'I don't know about you, Cara – we always have lemon with Earl Grey,' says Greg, 'but there's milk if you prefer?'

'Milk, please.'

'Do you add the milk last?' he asks.

It feels like a test and Cara wants to laugh. Is it important? If so, she's fallen at the first hurdle by having milk with Earl Grey instead of lemon! As it happens, she does add the milk last but there's no room in her life for what she perceives as such pretentiousness. However, she's not about to start discussing the finer points of tea etiquette now. She nods, unsure how she might sound if she speaks.

'Weak or strong?' he asks.

There's no getting away from it, she's going to have to speak. 'Not too strong, thank you.'

Greg pours the tea. Again, she is mesmerised by his smooth, refined movements. It's as if it's a ritual.

As he hands the cup to her she concentrates hard on not spilling a drop. It would be just too humiliating to be on her hands and knees cleaning up in front of this couple.

'So, Cara, do tell us a bit about yourself,' Marietta says.

Cara takes a deep breath. She is definitely being interviewed. 'Well, I was born in St Ives. At a very young age I was introduced to the world of art and dabbled in oil paints and charcoal, freely exploring the possibilities of their application. I spent three years at Falmouth School of Art doing a Fine Art degree and, soon after graduating, fell pregnant with Bethany. I was lucky because my husband was very hands-on and he supported me in all my artistic endeavours, which gave me the time to emotionally and creatively focus on my art. Then I fell pregnant again and when my son was about a year old I opened the gallery in Porthleven, which has enabled me to display my work from another platform.' Cara pauses, wondering if this is what they want. Both Greg and Marietta listen intently. 'I work in both acrylics and oils, but as time goes by I find I prefer working in oils. I exhibit throughout Cornwall and have been interviewed by the local press, and the county magazines have published articles about my art.'

'And how do you feel during the creative process?' Marietta asks.

Cara considers her question. 'Excited. It's like going on a journey. It's having a conversation. I use photographs a lot and when I'm in the location I want to paint, I drink in its atmosphere and absorb it in my bones. It needs to hit at a cellular level. I'm grabbed by aesthetics: light against dark; the colours of green in the sea; the darkness of the wet sand. I see beauty in everything. I get excited by what I see – shape; texture; colour; the feel of the waves. I get caught up in it. When I look at the images back in my studio, my emotions connect with what I'm seeing and then it plays out in front of me. Although I'm making decisions throughout the process, there's a place of stillness deep inside where everything just makes sense. There's an absolute clarity.'

For a long moment, neither husband nor wife says a word.

Greg is the first to break the silence. 'And what is your inspiration, Cara?'

Feeling as if she's in the middle of the most intense examination, Cara shifts in her seat again. She didn't realise she'd have to sell her soul.

'As I mentioned previously, Greg…' Should she call him that in front of his wife, or Mr Latimer-Jones? 'My inspiration comes from the ever-changing landscape and sense of peace that Cornwall provides.

Each work I find is a culmination of emotions and memories utilising the beautiful landscape surrounding me. I spend as much time as possible painting in my studio and use the dynamic sea and heathland walks around me to gain creative clarity.'

Cara is astounded by the seriousness with which Greg and Marietta reflect upon her words.

'I feel I was born to be an artist. It was written in the stars,' she says. 'I get so lost in what I'm doing. It is an absolute knowing.'

Silence hangs in the air.

'And where do you see yourself in five years?' Marietta eventually asks.

'Oh, I don't have a game plan, as such. I have two young children to consider and it's enough for me to paint, run the gallery and provide for them. There are such things as school timetables to adhere to!'

She catches the swift look that passes between husband and wife and wonders what she has said to pique their interest.

'And do you have help with that?' Marietta enquires.

'Yes, my parents. And I'm surrounded by good friends.' Cara takes a sip of tea. It's hot and scalds her mouth. Willing herself not to spill a drop, very carefully she places the cup and saucer back on the table.

For some reason, she feels the need to qualify what she has said. 'I live very simply, Marietta. I love Cornwall and the cove is enough for me. It's my home. I've known little else and I'm not sure I would want to either.'

Marietta glances at her husband again. 'May we have a look at your paintings?'

Rising from his chair, Greg brings Cara's canvases into the conservatory. Marietta leans down and gently pushes Milo away before turning the wheels of her chair, expertly manoeuvring it into position. She examines each canvas carefully as Greg holds them up for his wife to view. Cara frowns; perplexed. She thought Greg was the art director. Pulling at the neck of her tunic, she shifts uncomfortably in her seat, feeling as if she's having the interview of her life. Suddenly Marietta looks at her husband and smiles, a hidden communication passing between them. Propping the canvases against the living room wall, Greg, once again, sits in the wicker chair opposite Cara.

'Cara, I'd like to keep hold of these three paintings,' Greg says, leaning forward. Placing his elbows on his knees, he presses his hands together to form a steeple, the tips of his fingers supporting his chin. 'I have contacts in London that I would like to show your work to.'

Cara considers her canvases and hesitates.

'There are competitions I feel your work should be entered for,' Greg continues.

Although aware of these competitions, Cara believes they have nothing to do with her everyday life. In any case, she's never had any spare money for the entrance fees. She's about to say so but then thinks it's a little churlish on her part. After all, Greg has taken the trouble to look over her work and, being Chief Art Director at *The New York Times*, he obviously knows what he's talking about. But, before she has a chance to respond, Marietta speaks again.

'Cara, life is very precious and opportunities like this do not often come along. You are young and carefree but, believe me; I know how finite life is. You don't think I wear this turban from some bohemian fashion sense, do you? No, I'm battling cancer and don't have the opportunity to consider what I'll be doing in five years' time. Grab all the opportunities that come your way with both hands while you have the chance.'

Cancer. How awful! But why should Marietta assume she is carefree? Again, Cara feels the need to explain.

'I'm so sorry to hear of your illness, Marietta, and I truly hope you overcome it, but I am not carefree, as you think. My husband died two years ago.' She does not elaborate.

Greg's attention is absolute.

'Then you, too, have first-hand experience of how precious life is,' Marietta says without compassion. It's simply a statement of fact. 'We are merely skin and bone and death will eventually come to us all. What is important is how we spend our time while we have breath in our bodies.'

Wow! Heavy for a Thursday night. Glancing from husband to wife, Cara has a sudden, urgent need to be home with her children. 'OK. Show the paintings to your London contacts.'

Marietta smiles weakly.

'Good girl,' says Greg. 'I will give you a receipt but, rest assured, I will take the utmost care.' He rises from his chair.

'I had better go,' says Cara, getting to her feet. 'It's past the children's bedtime and they have school tomorrow.' She fights the urge to curtsey, so strong is the feeling she's in the presence of royalty. 'It was nice meeting you, Marietta.'

'And you, Cara,' Marietta says. Leaning back heavily in the wheelchair, she watches Cara walk from the conservatory.

'What value have you given your paintings?' Greg asks, sitting at a desk in the corner of the living room.

Cara glances at the canvases. '*The Wave at Portreath* has a price tag of one thousand pounds, *Kynance Cove* four hundred and *The Men-an-Tol* is two hundred and fifty.' Suddenly embarrassed, she wonders if she has overvalued her work.

Greg jots something down on a piece of paper. Placing the pen on the desk, he folds the note and walks to the door. As Cara follows, she glances back at Marietta. The woman looks exhausted; her eyes tightly closed. Cara closes the living room door quietly behind her.

At the front door, Greg turns to her. 'Here's the receipt, Cara.'

'I'm so sorry about your wife,' she says, taking it from him.

'It's something we've lived with for a while. Marietta doesn't always use the wheelchair. Hopefully, with the new drugs she's taking she will be able to make long-term plans, despite what she says. But we live from day to day.' Cara easily empathises with the sadness in his eyes. 'I'm going to London at the weekend and will contact you once I have some news.'

Cara nods. She holds out her hand, but Greg steps forward and chastely kisses her on the lips. Astonished, she wonders if this is how polite New York society conducts itself. But, chaste or not, it's such an intimate thing to do when they're hardly more than strangers!

'Goodnight, Cara.' She watches amusement briefly replace the sadness as he opens the door.

Cara walks purposefully towards her car, trying to make sense of that kiss. And why does he always find her so amusing? Opening the car door, she glances back at the house, but Greg is no longer there. She climbs in, switches on the interior light and looks in the mirror. She's so hot and there's an unflattering, high blush to her cheeks. Lowering the window, she breathes in the cool sea air. Then, she unfolds the receipt.

No way! Surely he's made a mistake?

*

'Well, what do you think?' asks Greg, entering the living room.

'You are right.' Marietta turns towards her husband. 'An undiscovered talent and future major player.'

'I know they're still grossly undervalued but I added three thousand pounds to each painting,' he says.

Marietta nods once. A heavy silence fills the room.

'And that other thing?' Greg knows he shouldn't, but he cannot resist asking.

Marietta hesitates before answering. 'Raw and unsophisticated, but simply lovely.'

His eyebrow twitches with emotion. Abruptly, Greg turns away from his wife. It would be just too cruel for her to witness his smile.

*

Rick switches off the café lights and pulls the door to. It's a clear, cold night and a full moon illuminates the way to the car park. A few feet away from the boardwalk the high tide quivers, as if the mighty ocean, too, feels the chill. Oliver glances towards the horizon. The night sky is filled with the Milky Way. It's never as clear as this in Surrey. The air is too polluted, what with London and Heathrow in one direction and Gatwick in the other.

'My place is a couple of miles further down the coast,' Rick informs Tas.

It is so silent. The only sound is the gentle whoosh of waves on sand, and the tranquillity speaks to something deep within Oliver. Hunching into his jacket, he takes one last look out to sea.

'Up the hill, turn left, follow the road for about a mile and turn left again. I'm sure you'll keep up. Your driving skills can't have gone off that much!' Rick gives Tas a friendly punch on the shoulder, and the Tasmanian lays one on his Aussie friend in return.

Oliver climbs into the Jeep. Soon, they are inching their way up the steep lane leading out of the cove. It's narrow but they only pass one car halfway up, parked in darkness against the hedge. Turning right, they follow the cliff road as the full moon casts an eerie light across the Cornish landscape. They see no other cars.

'I know Rick doesn't want to be found but where the hell are we going?' mutters Tas.

They follow the Land Rover across open heathland, an occasional stunted and twisted tree hinting at the extreme weather the peninsula can sometimes experience. After a further mile Rick indicates right and turns onto a rough track, full of potholes.

'Obviously of the hermit persuasion,' comments Oliver.

'Never used to be. The life and soul, was Rick. Wonder if he's shacked up with anyone at the moment? Bit of a free-spirit is our Rick.'

'Guess you get a lot of those down here,' says Oliver, thinking how nice it would be to be one.

'Yeah, guess so. Here we go. Looks like we've arrived.'

Turning between two large granite posts, Tas parks the Jeep alongside the Land Rover. Before them is a traditional Cornish farmhouse.

'Home sweet home,' Rick announces, as they get out of the Jeep and retrieve their bags.

A lone car passes by.

'Don't often get vehicles down here. The lane doesn't lead anywhere,' Rick says, watching the car's disappearing tail lights. 'Probably a couple looking for a quiet spot!' He laughs and walks towards the farmhouse. Pushing open the heavy front door, mimicking an American drawl, he calls out, 'Hi, honey, I'm home!'

'Guess he is shacked up with someone, then,' comments Tas.

They enter a stone-flagged entrance hall and follow Rick through to a large and inviting sitting room, simply furnished with white-washed walls, exposed beams and a slate flagstone floor covered with scatter rugs. At the far end is an enormous inglenook fireplace in which a roaring log fire has been lit.

'Make yourselves comfortable,' Rick says, indicating several comfortable settees. 'Hi, honey. Look who's arrived.'

A tall, striking blonde stands in the doorway. Wearing a sweatshirt and tight skinny jeans, which only accentuate the length of her legs, she leans casually against the door jamb.

'I don't believe it,' says Tas, dropping his bag onto the stone floor. 'Tania Alexander! Well, would you credit it?' Marching across the room, he sweeps the woman off her feet and plants a dramatic kiss on her lips.

'Tas, put me down! Gawd, you haven't changed,' she says with a laugh. There's no mistaking the Australian twang.

Tas stands back to appraise her, as does Oliver. There's definitely something about Australian women.

'Looking good, Tan! How long has it been?'

'The Millennium, I think,' she says.

'Surely not? Wait a moment. Yes! The last time I saw you was at Niall's party in that incredible pad of his overlooking Harbour Bridge.'

'Yeah, that was a great night. Amazing fireworks.' She smiles at some memory and Oliver has the distinct impression she's not talking about Sydney's pyrotechnic display.

'So, are you two an item, then?' Tas asks, glancing from Rick to Tania.

'Kind of.' She smiles broadly.

'Rick, you never said anything, you secretive son of a gun!' exclaims Tas.

'Didn't I?' says Rick.

'You know you didn't.'

'Guess I've become a bit more selective what I tell folk in my old age.' Rick turns his attention to Oliver. 'Honey, this is Tas's friend, Oliver.'

Tania glances at Oliver for the first time and gasps.

'Don't worry, Tan,' sympathises Tas. 'Oliver is well used to rendering intelligent, grown women speechless!'

Rick looks on in amusement. His woman is *never* short of words.

'Are you really him?' Tania splutters.

Oliver laughs. 'Yes, I'm really him.'

She strides across the room and hugs him. 'Then welcome to our humble abode, Oliver Foxley.' She looks him squarely in the eye and there's no mistaking the interest lurking there.

'Thank you, Tania Alexander,' he responds courteously and she colours slightly.

'OK, introductions over. Let me show you your rooms,' Rick says, heading off down the hallway.

As Oliver and Tas pick up their bags to follow, Oliver knows that if he looks back Tania will be watching him. He resists. Sometimes life can be so predictable and he has come to Cornwall to have a break from all that.

'These are our B&B rooms. Both have en-suite showers,' explains Rick, opening the doors to two simply furnished rooms. Decorated in a similar style, each has whitewashed walls, exposed wooden floorboards, shabby chic furniture and king-size cast-iron beds. 'I'll leave you to get settled in. When you're ready, come back to the sitting room. Tan has prepared supper for us.'

*

Sylvie drives past the farmhouse and spots Oliver and the big, hairy man taking bags out of the Jeep. What are they doing in Cornwall? Little did she know this morning she'd be in the south-west by evening. It's late and she has no idea where she is. She follows the lane until it comes to an abrupt end. Two five-barred gates lead into fields. Switching off the engine, she climbs out. The night sky is inky black and full of stars and a huge silver moon is suspended high. It's so still but she can hear the muffled sound of waves not too far away, and she can smell the sea.

Sylvie turns and looks in each direction. The only light for miles is from the farmhouse. Oliver must be staying the night and she wonders how long he intends to be here. She starts to shiver and climbs back in the car. What's she going to do? About a mile back she noticed a sign for Mullion. She will go there, get something to eat, and then she'll come back to the lane and park up in the gateway for the night. It's been cold camping out in the car for the past few nights outside Oliver's house, as the spring temperatures plummeted. Although she cursed at the time, she's pleased she made the effort to return to her flat and grab a change of clothes and some moisturiser and toothpaste, unsure how long Oliver would keep her surveilling his comings and goings. She also has a sleeping bag and as long as she wears her beanie and keeps her face covered, it isn't too bad. Anyway, it's worth it. Oliver likes to play hard to get and she is getting an incredible thrill from the chase he has set her. The more difficult and frustrating it is, the more real it seems to her, and if this is what it takes to be close to him then this is what she is prepared to do.

Chapter Fourteen

Cara hits the 'on' button and waits for the computer to spring to life. Two days have passed since she visited Greg and his wife and she still can't make sense of Marietta's probing questions. She's eager to discover more about the woman.

It's quiet in the gallery, although there are more people about in Porthleven than there have been for several weeks. Early spring visitors. Cara searches for 'Marietta Latimer-Jones' and suddenly the screen is full of information. She clicks on a link which opens with a photograph of Marietta in her early thirties. It's a wedding photo. Dressed in a white silk outfit with fur-lined cuffs and neckline, she wears a matching fur headband with a diamond-encrusted white lace veil. The beautiful blonde with the highest of cheekbones and baby blue eyes looks adoringly into the eyes of the man at her side.

Wow! You were one attractive man!

Greg is dressed in a sharp, black suit and crisp, white shirt under a silver/grey waistcoat. At his neck is a silver textured tie. His hair is luxuriously thick and dark and he gazes lovingly at his new bride. Cara reads the caption below the photograph.

A winter wonderland wedding for the highly regarded New York art critic, Greg Latimer-Jones (34) and Marietta Von Baranski (32), artist and socialite daughter of Polish aristocrat, Baron Tomasz Von Baranski.

No wonder she felt she was in the presence of royalty! Cara checks the wedding date and makes a quick calculation. So, Greg and Marietta are in their early fifties. She devours the accompanying article, which informs her that Marietta is a figurative artist who has exhibited all over the world, her trademark being strong, flamboyant brushstrokes full of *joie de vivre*. Cara also learns that Greg first met Marietta in her native Poland when she was a talented, but undiscovered, artist. Swiftly she became his protégée and he encouraged her to move to America to further her career. At the time Greg was married, though that marriage crumbled fairly quickly, and he and Marietta became the darlings of New York society, fêted wherever they went. Not long after Greg's divorce, they married. However, although both husband and wife achieved great personal success, they never had children. When quizzed about her childless state, Marietta always responds, *'Art is my life's work. My paintings are my children.'*

Cara looks up from the computer screen as two middle-aged women enter the gallery.

'Oh, just look at all these divine paintings,' says a small, plump brunette. She looks across the gallery and smiles at Cara.

'If you need any help just ask,' Cara says before quickly returning to the screen. Learning about Greg and Marietta is fascinating.

So Greg was married before! She's not surprised. He's so refined and sophisticated and was so attractive. Still is… in an older man sort of way. He could have – and obviously has had – anyone he's ever wanted. No wonder he finds her so amusing! She must seem very hick and provincial. Cara glances up at the canvases adorning the gallery walls.

'Don't belittle yourself, Gwyneth.' Christo's voice fills her head. *'I always believed in you and look where you are now.'*

The two women are discussing her painting of St Michael's Mount, which she portrayed against a stunning sunset of vermillion and crimson, blending to deep violet and fuchsia pink. Always keen to stretch people's imaginations, she painted the causeway taking up the width of the canvas before swiftly reducing and leading the eye to the fortress sitting atop the granite outcrop.

'Oh, this is just fab,' says the small, plump brunette. 'Do you think Himself would appreciate it?'

'Does that matter?' asks her friend with a laugh.

'Not a lot!'

The women stand back from the canvas before moving to another, *The Crown Mines at Botallack*; the former tin mines dramatically perched on the cliffs above St Just. Cara has captured the landscape in the late afternoon sun with a grey, ominous sky hanging over a deep blue sea, the white surf crashing onto the rocks in the foreground. Full of atmosphere, it is an altogether earthier piece.

'Oh, I just can't make up my mind!' the brunette says in exasperation.

'Well, both paintings have drama but you'd have difficulty not noticing St Michael's Mount,' says her friend. 'If you want Himself to be forever reminded what a heel he's been choosing work over coming to Cornwall with you this weekend, well, this would definitely do the trick.'

The plump woman regards her friend for a moment before erupting into laughter. 'St Michael's Mount it is!' Looking over at Cara, she asks, 'You do take cards?'

Cara nods. She walks across the gallery and carefully removes the canvas from the wall. She painted it the summer before Christo fell ill, when both were blissfully unaware of the cruel twist of fate awaiting them only a few months later. They were happy and joyful, spending long, leisurely days on the beach with their young family, and she can see that joy reflected in her easy brushstrokes.

Unlike the painting of the cove. Will that ever take shape?

Wrapping the canvas in Bubble Wrap, Cara then packages it in brown paper before finally tying it off with string.

'I hope you don't mind carrying it like this? I don't have any bags large enough.'

'That's fine, dear,' says the small, plump brunette.

As Cara props the canvas against the counter, the gallery's phone rings.

'The Art Shack,' she announces. Wedging the phone between her shoulder and chin, she processes the woman's payment.

'Cara, hi. Tristan.'

'Hi, Trist. How's it going?' She hands the woman her receipt.

'Good, thanks. Just a thought – Rob's free tomorrow and it looks like we're in for a fine day. We could fix your roof, if you like.'

'Great! It will be a relief to have the studio finally sorted. What time?' Cara watches the women exit the gallery.

'Around ten. Jane said she'd like to come as well.'

'Oh, good. I like your girlfriend.'

Tristan chuckles. 'Yeah, me too!'

Cara smiles. 'I'll do lunch.'

'Great stuff, Cara. See you then.'

'Bye, Trist.'

She punches in her home telephone number. 'Hi, Mum. Everyone behaving themselves?'

'Like little lambs. How are things in Porthleven?'

'I've sold a few small items and two paintings, including the large St Michael's Mount. I'll bring in more canvases on Monday. By the way, how are you fixed for time tonight?'

'We're only going over to Sheila and Barry's for supper. Why?'

'Tristan and co are coming over for lunch tomorrow and I'd like to call into the farm shop on the way home.'

'That's fine, darling. It's such a lovely sunny afternoon I thought we'd all go for a walk on the beach.'

'Good idea. See you around five.'

*

It's a glorious afternoon and the unexpected appearance of the yellow orb in the sky has brought out not only the inhabitants of the cove but also visitors from further afield. The beach is alive with activity. Oliver sits on the decking to Rick's Beach Hut enjoying the warmth of the late afternoon sun. During the previous two days, he and Tas have visited several venues booked for the forthcoming tour and the variety of buildings they will be performing in has surprised him, each presenting its own challenges and particular atmosphere. It seems fitting to Oliver that the opening performance will be at Sterts Open Air Theatre on the eastern slopes of Bodmin Moor, with the closing performances in early September at that other open-air theatre in the west of the county, the Minack.

Earlier in the day they visited Blisland Inn on Bodmin Moor. 'A real pub where real men drink real ale,' Tas informed him. With seven real ales to choose from they were spoilt for choice but, following the landlord's suggestion, decided on a pint of King Buddha Special and the dark and malty Blisland Bulldog to go with their rump steaks in baps. The landlord, hale and hearty, regaled them with tales of his days serving the Royal Navy but, all too soon, the brief break in their schedule came to an end. Before heading off to the village hall to meet the caretaker and firm up their booking, Tas promised the landlord they would visit the inn again, only this time with the rest of the cast and crew in tow.

Oliver sips his coffee. Wispy white clouds dot a clear blue sky that merges with the sea, making it difficult to separate the one from the other. Half a dozen sail boats tack across the bay and a couple of canoeists drift leisurely in the shallows. Windbreaks and beach shelters have sprung up along the sand, giving the impression of a pop-up village. From Rick's decking the view encompasses the full length of the cove, as far as the flat-topped rock jutting out of the water about a hundred yards offshore. As Oliver glances up at the half-dozen assorted properties hugging the cove, the cliffs rising dramatically behind them, he wonders about the people lucky enough to live here with the beach as their playground. Two of the houses appear to be in immaculate condition, but a slight air of dilapidation hangs over the others. It's a peaceful, tranquil scene and, with the sun beating down, it could be anywhere in the world. Oliver breathes in the salty sea air and stretches his legs. The decked area is sheltered from any breeze by partial glass walls and he is alone but for a young couple sitting in the far corner, holding hands and talking earnestly.

How lucky they are to have their whole lives ahead of them.

The thought depresses him and he tries to shake off the feeling. The 'grey mist' has been absent until now, though he knows it is forever waiting to pounce in an unguarded moment. Oliver considers upping his medication.

A movement at the far end of the beach distracts him. A red Frisbee arcs through the air towards the sea, closely followed by a yellow streak that leaps, halts its flight, then disappears beneath the waves. Resurfacing a few yards further out, the dog paddles back to shore with its head held high, the red disc in its mouth. A blond lad, dressed in shorts and a striped T-shirt, stands at the water's edge. Oliver watches as the Labrador emerges from the sea, shakes itself and deposits the Frisbee at the boy's feet. Then, taking a few steps back, it waits expectantly. Again, the Frisbee is thrown into the air and the yellow dog streaks up the beach, never once taking its eyes off the target. Suddenly it leaps into the air, expertly catching the red disc in its mouth.

Such freedom. Lucky lad.

'Hey, Ollie, Rick's invited a few people over for supper tonight.' Tas pulls out a chair and sits down opposite him, a glass of beer in his hand. 'Tan wants to try out some new dish on us all. Apparently, cooking's her latest hobby.'

'Well, if the meal the other night is anything to go by we're in for a treat,' Oliver says generously.

Tas grunts. 'Yeah, Tania knows her way to a man's heart... one way or another!'

Oliver raises an eyebrow. 'Voice of experience?'

'You could say that!' The Tasmanian smiles wickedly.

Looking along the beach again, Oliver notices a woman and a young blonde girl have now joined the boy. As they walk in the direction of the café, the boy continues his game with the dog, which never misses a catch.

At least those two will sleep well tonight.

Silently, Oliver laughs at himself. Always the father!

There's something fascinating about this little group. The boy's natural exuberance speaks to Oliver's greyer, more cautious nature and the girl reminds him of a young Samantha. Come to think of it, the woman seems familiar.

'Could get used to this life,' says Tas, leaning back in his chair and turning his face to the sun.

'Yes. Great not to have a care in the world.'

Tas squints at his friend. 'Hasn't got any better over time, then?'

Taken by surprise, Oliver realises he's spoken the thought out loud. 'Not a lot. I know how to handle it better, but it's never far away.'

Tas shakes his head. 'The world has no idea.'

'And I wouldn't want it to,' says Oliver.

'No. But everyone thinks you lead such a charmed existence, Mr Fox.'

'I'm not an actor for nothing,' Oliver says drily.

Tas observes his friend a while longer. Rising from his chair, he asks, 'Do you want something to eat, Ollie?'

'No, thanks. I'll save myself for Tania's delights.'

'Ah yes, Tania's delights! Once sampled, never forgotten.' Tas laughs and walks inside the café.

Oliver sips his coffee. Suddenly the girl in the corner lets out a shriek. Glancing up, he sees the red Frisbee flying towards him. As it lands, skimming across the wooden boards, he puts out a foot and halts its progress just as the Labrador arrives at the edge of the decking. It looks at him inquisitively, then back at the young boy charging across the beach.

'Sorry, the wind caught it,' pants Sky.

Oliver looks into a face full of character, cheeky and charming, and something stirs within his soul. He bends to pick up the Frisbee.

'Did it hit you?' asks Sky.

'No.' He smiles at the lad. 'I've been watching you two on the beach. Your dog has very good eye to mouth co-ordination.'

'It's his favourite game,' says Sky, affectionately rubbing the Labrador's head. 'Barnaby and me, we can do this for hours.'

Rising to his feet, Oliver walks to the edge of the decking and hands the Frisbee back to the boy.

'I'm Oliver,' he says, wondering why he feels it's important to introduce himself.

'Pleased to meet you,' Sky says in as adult a voice as he can muster, which makes Oliver smile. 'I'm Sky and that's my sister, Beth.' He points behind him.

The approaching girl has an angelic face, different from her brother's and not quite so open, but still full of light and promise.

'Hello, Beth,' Oliver says.

Bethany stops and smiles shyly, then frowns. Turning away, she looks anxiously in the direction of her grandma, who is still some way behind chatting to Janine and the twins.

Oliver follows her gaze. He never forgets a face and instantly recognises the woman from the gallery in Porthleven. As Carol approaches, he watches the healthy glow to her cheeks increase and remembers how flustered she was that day he'd bought the painting.

'Well, hello again,' he says in a friendly manner.

'Hello,' says Carol, her mind in a spin. Fighting to gain control of her emotions, she draws her granddaughter to her for protection. Sky studies his grandma with interest.

'Do these delightful children belong to you?' asks Oliver.

'Yes, my grandchildren.'

Aware that Sky laps up their interplay, Oliver glances down at the boy, now casually leaning against the glass and grinning from ear to ear.

He's certainly going to break some hearts.

'Surely not? Surely they're your children!'

From anyone else, thinks Carol – like that smooth American – the comment would sound really crass, but from him, well... What a compliment!

'You are too kind, Oliver.' Speaking his name, as if he's an old friend, helps Carol assert a modicum of control over the situation and regain some composure.

'I'm sorry but I don't think I ever knew your name,' says Oliver, 'though I'd never forget your face.'

'Carol,' she says, flushing again.

'How do you know Grandma?' asks Sky.

Oliver smiles at the boy. 'I bought a painting from your grandma last year. A wonderful painting that I enjoy every day.'

Sky nods. *'The Minack.'*

'Yes, that's right,' Oliver says in surprise.

'Mum loved painting that,' Bethany says in a quiet, serious voice. 'The cormorants flap their wings when no one is looking.'

Sky gives his sister a withering look.

'Did you know the waves move too?' Oliver says in as serious a voice as the girl's.

Carol laughs. How charming!

Wide-eyed, Bethany looks up at Oliver. He winks. Quickly she dips her head but not before he's caught her shy smile.

'It may seem unbelievable, but I have studied that painting at length and I swear your daughter has given it life,' Oliver says to Carol.

Carol smiles and weakens her grip on her granddaughter's shoulder.

Walking from the interior of the café, Tas sees that Oliver has attracted a bit of a crowd – a pretty, older woman, typically flustered, and a cute, young blonde girl, gazing spellbound. However, the boy leaning against the glass with the Labrador at his feet seems to be taking it all in his stride. Tas approaches the little group.

'Tas, this is Carol, mother of the artist Cara Penhaligon,' Oliver says, standing aside to include his friend. 'This, here, is young Sky and his dog, Barnaby, and, last but not least, this is the delightful Beth.' He smiles warmly at the young girl.

'Hello, one and all,' says Tas, sweeping into a deep, theatrical bow to which Sky laughs, Bethany giggles and Carol smiles. 'I hope you will come and see our production when we're in the county next month.'

'What are you performing?' asks Carol.

'A drama. The Tasmanian Devil Theatre Company's production of *Sorrows in the Sand* and Oliver is the leading man,' Tas says, knowing this will pull in the ladies and put bums on seats.

'The Tasmanian Devil Theatre Company,' repeats Sky quietly, trying out the words.

'I'll certainly come along and bring some friends,' promises Carol.

'That would be a great start!' says Tas with a chuckle. 'I look forward to seeing you there.'

'So,' says Oliver, 'I've met the family Penhaligon and yet I have still to meet the artist herself.'

'If you're in the cove you're bound to meet Mum,' says Sky.

'Oh, why's that, then?' asks Oliver playfully. 'Does she also hang out at Rick's Beach Hut?'

'Sometimes, but we live over there.' Sky points to the cliffs at the far end of the beach.

'Talking of which,' says Carol, 'I must get you home before she gets back.' She doesn't have to but, for some reason, feels the need to halt the course of this conversation. She holds out her hand to Sky.

'Nice to meet you, Oliver Foxley,' Sky says, pushing himself off the glass. Calling to Barnaby, he walks towards his grandma.

'And very nice to meet you too, Sky Penhaligon.' Oliver smiles in amusement. It's only then that he wonders how the boy knows his full name.

Carol bids the men farewell.

Oliver and Tas watch the little family as they make their way along the beach. Sky, once again, throws the Frisbee for his dog. About thirty yards away, Bethany looks back and seeing Oliver still watching, breaks into a shy smile and waves. With his heart surprisingly pinching, Oliver returns her wave. Why does this little family group fascinate him so?

'Even the young, Mr Fox,' comments Tas. 'No one leaves untouched…'

*

It's dark in the lane and Sylvie switches on the small torch. She's already turned her ankle once. Loud rustling in the hedgerow a few feet away makes her jump. With her heart thumping wildly, she shines the torch in the direction of the sound and flashes the light up and over the hedge. All is still. Turning back to the task in hand she continues up the lane towards the farmhouse, avoiding the deep ruts.

Sylvie has spent the day following the Jeep from village to village. When it finally pulled up at the café on the beach, she waited until Oliver and the driver were inside before parking at the rear of the car park. Not knowing how long they'd be there, she walked along the beach and sat on the warm sand some distance away. For the next hour, or so, she kept her binoculars trained on the café. When she witnessed a woman and two children stop and talk to Oliver she vented her frustration with an angry shout. Why should this woman so easily approach him?

Sylvie trips and twists her ankle. 'Bloody road!'

Stopping to rub the offending leg, she freezes. Is that a car? Frantically she looks around, but there's no obvious escape. Ignoring the pain in her ankle, Sylvie scrambles up the bank, switches off her torch and presses herself tightly into a prickly blackthorn in early bloom. Headlights appear in the near distance before sweeping in through the granite entrance pillars. Doors open and close and voices briefly fill the air. Then silence. Gingerly, Sylvie clambers down the bank, rubbing her arms and pulling out several thorns. Should she abandon her plan and go back to the car? No, she's so close now.

There are five cars parked in front of the farmhouse. From two downstairs windows, light illuminates part way into the garden. Stepping out from behind one of the granite pillars and keeping close to the garden wall on her right, Sylvie makes her way stealthily towards an outhouse a short distance away. As she slips undercover of the lean-to she can see figures moving from one room to another. It's a clear night and the moon, though on the wane, shines its silvery light as she creeps across the lawn towards the farmhouse. Suddenly a figure appears at a window. She freezes. It's the driver of the Jeep. Sylvie holds her breath. If he looks out now he is sure to see her.

But Tas doesn't look out. His attention is elsewhere as he roughly closes the curtains, leaving a narrow gap. Sylvie lets out a long breath. It would be too embarrassing if she was caught wandering about in the garden. What would Oliver think of her then? She starts walking towards the farmhouse again. Peering through the gap in the curtains, she can see a large inglenook fireplace in which a fire has been lit. A man and a woman sit on a couch, their faces rosy from the heat. In front of them, a large coffee table is littered with several open bottles of wine and a number of glasses.

The lawns lead directly up to the farmhouse and Sylvie makes her way across the grass to the next window. Here, the gap in the curtains is wider, allowing a better view, and as she looks through she catches her breath. Sitting in a wingback armchair is Oliver, looking relaxed in an open-necked shirt and denim jeans. He is so damned gorgeous! She watches as he smiles at someone approaching. All at once, a tall, blonde woman walks into view, wearing tight-fitting jeans, a wide leather belt and a silky, loose, strappy top. She bends forward to hand Oliver a glass, at the same time giving him an eyeful of cleavage.

Sylvie's eyes narrow. What a bitch, openly flaunting herself like that! Watching carefully, she observes the look in the woman's eyes as she speaks to Oliver. He says something that makes her laugh and she flicks her hair over her shoulders, not once taking her smouldering eyes off him. Sylvie fumes. So near and yet so far. Why is he being so cruel, keeping her waiting? What is she going to do about it? Her mind is in turmoil. There are no clear answers and she must get back to her job… if she wants to keep it.

As she watches Tania perch playfully on the arm of Oliver's chair and flirt with him, Sylvie's jealousy grows until she is white with rage. She wants to throw a brick through the window, or, better still, smash the woman's head against a rock. How she'd love to feel the warm, sticky ooze of blood seeping through her fingers as the bitch's life drains away.

Sylvie turns away. She cannot watch any longer. Walking towards the corner of the farmhouse, she peers through the windows but all are in darkness, apart from the kitchen. The driver of the Jeep and another man sit at a table, drinking. A television in the background displays the news. It must be past ten. Sylvie carries on round the property, which is larger than it looks from the front. As she turns the corner, a door suddenly opens and an oblong of light pools out across the lawn. A burst of laughter and two figures step out into the garden. It's Oliver and the bitch. Shrinking into the shadows, Sylvie watches as the woman turns to the actor.

'So, Oliver, how about it, then? You and me,' Tania says, confident of her sexual prowess.

'I've told you, I'm a married man.'

'Bet that's never stopped you before.' Oliver laughs. 'Go on,' she coaxes, 'I just know we'd make sweet music together.'

Moving towards him, she puts her arms around his neck and presses her body against his. He can feel her breasts against his chest and the large buckle of her belt digs into his belly. Teasingly she sways against him. Placing his hands firmly on her hips, Oliver holds her still. Flattering as it is, he doesn't want this. He doesn't know what, but he has come to Cornwall for something else.

'Tania, it's not that I don't find you attractive,' he says, not wanting to offend her. 'You are a stunning woman and I am only human…'

'So what's the problem?' Tania purrs, ignoring Oliver's firm hold and swaying against him once again.

'As I said, I'm married.' Oliver tightens his grip. 'And you are with Rick.'

'So?' Tania challenges. 'Rick wouldn't mind. He's cool.' She steps away from him, out into the oblong of light so he can see her more clearly.

Knowing she's in danger of being discovered, Sylvie shrinks further into the shadows.

Tania raises her hands high above her head. Her skimpy top rides up to expose a flat, firm stomach and the cool night air teases her nipples erect under the silky material. She starts to sway, dipping and rising, not once breaking eye contact with Oliver. There's something deeply primal about her moves – a private, erotic dance just for him. Oliver swallows hard. She sure is one sexy lady.

'Just let it happen, Oliver,' Tania says in a husky whisper. Moving closer again, she rocks her body against his and draws him into a kiss.

Briefly, Oliver closes his eyes. She's sensuous, hot and tastes of whisky.

'Argh, Tania. Stop!' he groans, pulling away. 'You are one very naughty lady.'

Tania gazes up at him, disappointment reflected in her eyes. 'She must be pretty special, this wife of yours. One helluva pistol-packing woman.'

'She is.'

'Oh, well, I won't hold that against you.' She laughs hollowly at her small joke and swallows her desire. 'But you can't stop me flirting with you, Oliver Foxley.'

Laughing softly, Oliver shakes his head.

'Come on then, we'd better join the others,' Tania says. 'They'll be wondering where we've got to.' Reluctantly, she turns back into the farmhouse.

Sylvie's eyes have narrowed to mere slits as she lurks in the darkness. Sick with jealousy, she clenches her fists, her fingernails digging into the palms of her hands. She's so confused. He won't phone her but he'll fool around with that Australian harlot. Why? She thought he liked to play hard to get, but, apart from that lame excuse about being married, he wasn't exactly unavailable to that woman. The bitch! How dare she? He belongs to her! She will have to remind him of that.

Sylvie contemplates her next move and it might just have to involve that pistol-packing wife of his.

Chapter Fifteen

True to their word, Tristan and Rob fix the leaking studio roof, making good until Cara can afford a more permanent repair. Jane accompanies them and Cara delights in her company. The feeling is mutual, and the companionable, easy day quickly slips into evening. When she eventually gets to her bedroom, Cara sits on the edge of the bed and picks up the photo frame on her bedside table. It's her favourite picture of Christo, taken on the day she told him she was pregnant with Sky. His eyes are warm and full of love for his best friend who just so happens to be his wife. Their little family will soon be complete and life is good. They are not financially well off, nevertheless they want for nothing.

'Oh, Christo. Why?'

It's a heart-rending plea and Cara's eyes mist over. The hurt is as keen as ever. Time has not lessened the pain, merely masked it. Ominous, dark clouds obliterate her usually sunny outlook. Holding his photo tightly to her chest, she curls up into a ball as a hot, wet tear slides down the side of her face.

'Why?' The word is on her lips as she falls asleep.

Cara wakes several hours later in the same position, her face puffy and blotchy. Replacing the photo frame on the bedside table, she glances at the clock – 4.30 a.m. As she makes her way down the hallway and checks on her children, Barnaby appears at the living-room door.

'It's OK, Barns,' she whispers. The dog cocks its head to one side; it's unusual for a human to be up at this time.

Returning to her bedroom with Barnaby at her heels, Cara swiftly undresses and hops under the duvet. She closes her eyes against her reality, the enormity of which is overwhelming at this early hour, and when the dog jumps onto the bed she doesn't have the strength to send him away. As Barnaby lies down beside her, Cara draws his body to her for comfort. Eventually she falls into a fitful sleep.

A blond, teenage boy with mischief in his eyes coaxes her to climb the cliffs. They know they shouldn't. They've been warned against the crumbling cliff face many times, but they are young and invincible and defying their parents. The young Christo reaches down to her with outstretched hand and she extends her arm, yearning for his touch. But, just as his hand closes upon hers, the scene alters and here is Christo in his early twenties, happy and carefree. Lying on a towel on the sand, her body hot from a summer's sun, Cara watches him ride the waves; at one with the ocean. This is when the joyful, young man is at his happiest. Hearing his laughter, she senses his exhilaration. Suddenly he's running up the beach. Standing over her, he blocks out the warmth of the sun and shakes his head, showering her with cold droplets. Cara yelps. Once again, he holds out his hand, this time persuading her to come into the sea with him. Eagerly she reaches for him but as soon as she feels his tender, loving touch, he is gone…

Cara wakes, exhausted, and engages with the day a ghost of her normal self. Janine arrives to collect Bethany and Sky for the school run and her larger than life presence and booming voice make Cara wilt under the assault. Once the children depart, she slumps onto the sofa with head in hands.

Come on, Gwyneth, this won't do. Christo's voice fills her head.

She looks up, startled. There's no one there, of course, and she glances up at the surfboard dominating the living room wall with his characterful face smiling down at her.

'It's all very well you saying that,' she moans. 'You don't know how you teased me last night.' She can hear his joyful laugh. 'Christo, why are you doing this to me?'

Silence. She lies back and closes her eyes. Then, taking a deep breath, she steels herself and rises from the sofa.

Good girl, Gwynnie.

Is this what it's like to go mad, hearing voices? No, that's talking to yourself – she hasn't got there yet...

She makes a coffee and decides to tackle the painting of the cove again. As she climbs the stairs to her studio, Barnaby's nails tap-tap on the wooden treads behind her. Padding over to the corner of the room, the dog flops down against the radiator. Basil is already settled on the window sill. Cara switches on the radio and places the canvas on the easel. She stands for a while critically examining the painting, then picks up the paintbrush. Two hours later she lets out an exasperated sigh. The painting *still* evades her. She is unhappy with its composition and her brushstrokes feel all wrong. She glances out at the beach – a subtle mix of grey with heavy mizzle diffusing the light. How fitting! In an attempt to shake herself out of the sombre mood threatening to derail her, she puts the painting aside and starts on something completely different. Suddenly Barnaby is on his feet.

'What's up, Barns?'

The dog cocks its head and then trots to the top of the stairs. Barking once, he tap-taps his way down the wooden treads as Cara hears a knock.

As she descends the stairs into the hallway, Cara sees Greg standing at the porch door, huddled into his jacket with collar turned up and his hat set at a jaunty angle, offering some protection from the rain. Even in a bedraggled state he looks refined. He smiles at her through the glass.

'Hello, Greg. Come in,' she says, opening the door and wondering what she must look like. She hopes the bungalow is not too untidy, and then remembers the mountain of washing-up in the sink.

'Cara,' Greg says, planting a kiss on her lips.

Once again, Cara is taken aback. Why does he think he can do that? Not that she particularly minds. It just seems odd.

'You surely haven't walked here?'

'Only from the car park,' Greg says, turning to shake the rain from his jacket out of the door.

'Would you like coffee? I was just about to make one.'

'Please.' Greg hangs his jacket on the coat rack and places his hat on the shelf above.

As Cara walks into the living room, she critically glances around. It's passable but she definitely doesn't want him to see the state of the kitchen. 'Have a seat. How do you like your coffee?'

'Black, no sugar.' Greg sits on the sofa and looks round the room, taking it all in. His eyes settle on the art on the walls.

Quickly, Cara prepares the drinks.

'How was London?' she asks, entering the room. She hands him a mug of coffee and sits in the opposite chair.

'Very good.' Greg takes a sip and then places the mug on the floor.

The room fills with silence and Cara squirms.

'While I was there I met up with friends and colleagues who are this year's selectors for the Threadneedle Prize.' Greg pauses. 'You do know of the Threadneedle Prize?' Arrogantly, he arches an eyebrow.

Cara flushes, instantly transported back to her schooldays when she would panic before an exam. 'I do know of it,' she says, making sure to keep any emotion out of her voice.

'Well, as you know, the Threadneedle Prize is one of the most valuable art prizes in Europe and registration is now open. Up to six works may be submitted, which must not have been entered or selected for any other prize or competition in the UK or Europe. Do we qualify?'

Cara almost chokes. When did they become *we*?

'Yes. I have several works that haven't been entered for competitions.'

'You are aware of the enormity of this prize?' Greg continues. 'If you win, besides being awarded twenty thousand pounds in prize money you will be granted a solo exhibition. It would put you on the map.'

Twenty thousand pounds! She could have the studio roof properly repaired, take Beth and Sky on holiday *and* replace the car.

'Yes, I am aware.'

Greg laughs. 'Cara, you astound me. You are so cool.'

She smiles, but then frowns. If he thinks she's cool, then why does he seem to find her so amusing?

'Anyway, back to business. The exhibition runs from the thirty first of January to the seventeenth of February next year at the Mall Galleries, in central London. We need to register and submit your works online for pre-selection. Only if your works are pre-selected will they go forward to the final selection process.'

'What does that involve?' Cara asks.

'You will be invited to hand in your pre-selected works for a distinguished panel of selectors to decide whether or not to select them for the exhibition.'

'And if my paintings are selected, what then?'

'You will be asked to provide some biographical information for the exhibition catalogue together with a portrait photograph.' Greg smiles at Cara. 'All shortlisted artists are expected to attend a special awards dinner when the winner of the Threadneedle Prize is announced.'

Cara looks out of the window at the rain-lashed beach. Until now, her life has been Cornwall and she is happy with that. She has never questioned it. Although aware of the larger art world, she is content to remain on its periphery.

But life changed forever two years ago…

Perhaps that's what last night's dream meant. The past no longer exists. Perhaps Christo was guiding her to be open to new opportunities. Cara turns back to find Greg studying her.

'So, Cara, what do you say?'

She doesn't know what to say. She's still grappling with the finality of Christo.

But Greg doesn't wait for Cara to answer. 'If I go through your catalogue of works I can select six paintings that I think will be acceptable to the judges.'

She gazes up at the face on the surfboard. You no longer exist…

'Are all your paintings displayed on the gallery website, Cara?'

'Most of them,' she says, dragging her attention back to the present. 'There are a few in the studio that haven't been included.'

'Well, shall we take a look?'

Cara finds herself leading Greg into her inner sanctum and, over the next hour, they discuss her paintings. Having made his selection, Greg instructs Cara to photograph and email them to him.

'And now I must depart,' he says, glancing at his watch.

Following her downstairs, he retrieves his jacket from the coat rack and turns to Cara. She looks exhausted.

'Cara, I realise this is a lot to take in but your talent deserves to be seen on a wider stage. Your brushstrokes possess a brilliance and depth of emotion similar to the Old Masters. It's unfair of you to hide your light under a stone.'

Unfair?

'Trust me; I know what I'm talking about. You do trust me, don't you?'

She nods, unsure whether he's talking about his experience in the art world or something else.

'I will take you to places you haven't even dreamed of, and, Cara…' his eyes hold her gaze for a long moment '…I promise to never let you down.'

All at once the hallway feels too small. As Greg takes a step towards her Cara thinks he's going to kiss her again but, as if reading her mind, he simply reaches above her to retrieve his hat off the shelf. She looks out at the bay and tries to draw some comfort from the familiar scene. Things are moving too fast.

'I'll phone you once I've studied the gallery website and then we can discuss my final selection,'

Greg says. Seeing the look on her face, he swiftly adds, 'To see if it fits in with *your* ideas too, you understand. Goodbye, Cara.'

'Bye, Greg.' She watches as he, once again, places the hat on his head at a jaunty angle. Opening the porch door, without further ado, he walks briskly away through the heavy mizzle.

Greg confuses, yet excites, with his constant teasing of the world he inhabits. She knows he understands and appreciates her art in a way no one else does, but he also makes her feel inadequate and out of her depth, only to then retrieve the situation by offering support and guidance. It's just too much to analyse. She's exhausted by him.

Cara shuts the door on the world according to Greg.

*

Oliver rolls over. The digital alarm clock displays 04:05. Why the hell is the phone ringing at this early hour? It must be some emergency! Brutally wide awake, he throws off the bed covers.

Deanna stirs. 'What is it?' she asks, peering at the clock.

'The phone. All the kids are in, aren't they?'

'Yes.'

Dear God, not the parents!

Oliver switches on the bedside light and gets out of bed. Grabbing a dressing gown from the back of the door, he quickly makes his way downstairs, aware of the flicker of fear in the pit of his stomach. His father lives alone in the north of England and Deanna's parents are in deepest, darkest Norfolk. Switching on the hall light, he answers the phone, noting the caller has withheld their number, and braces himself for the worst. Silence. He speaks again. The silence is oppressive but he can sense someone listening. What the hell are they playing at?

'Speak now or hang up and give us all some peace,' Oliver says angrily. He waits. 'OK, this is how we're going to do this. If you have something to say, say it now or I will end the call. What's it to be?' Oliver's stomach is in knots. 'You've had your chance.'

He waits for a response. Nothing. Firmly, he presses the 'off' button. How did they obtain this number? Maybe it's just some drunken crank with nothing better to do at four in the morning than phone random numbers and annoy total strangers. Oliver waits a while longer then turns towards the stairs, the warmth of his bed calling. He's reached the half-landing when the phone rings again. Bounding down the stairs, two at a time, he snatches the phone from its cradle. Frenzied breathing, followed by silence. Creepy. His scalp crawls as he remembers the last time he experienced such powerful, tumultuous disquiet directed at him. After what seems an eternity, Oliver replaces the phone.

'Who was it?' Deanna asks, leaning over the banister.

'Don't worry. There's no emergency.'

'But who was it, Ollie?'

'Don't know. Probably just some crank.' Rattled, he adds, 'Why you refuse to have a phone in the bedroom is beyond me.'

Deanna frowns, but chooses not to respond. 'Should we call the police?'

Shit! No! If his suspicions are correct that would open a can of worms.

'I think that's being a bit overdramatic, Dee,' Oliver says, glancing up at his wife and hoping he sounds calmer than he feels.

'Come back to bed,' Deanna says.

'In a moment. I just want to check something.'

'Well, don't be long.' Deanna regards her husband a while longer before turning away.

It's quiet and peaceful in the hallway, but Oliver is no longer at peace. This solid and substantial eighteenth century lodge house has always represented a place of sanctuary, away from the eyes of a prying world, but now it doesn't feel quite so secure. The maelstrom on the other end of the telephone makes Oliver appraise his surroundings with fresh eyes. If the caller is who he thinks it is, just how secure is the house? How safe is his family? And how did she get his number? He walks from room to room, switching on lights, checking windows and external doors, making sure they are locked. Maybe they should get a dog. Even though Deanna has always baulked at the suggestion of pets, believing they contribute little to their lives, perhaps a guard dog would be a good idea. Having checked the ground floor, Oliver enters his study and sits at his desk just as the phone rings again. He snatches it up.

'Sylvie?'

A sharp intake of breath. Then silence.

'Sylvie, don't do this.' Opening the top drawer of his desk, Oliver removes her note. He should have phoned her. 'Why are you awake at this hour?' he asks, his voice as soothing as a lover's. 'You must be tired. Why don't you try and get some sleep? You will feel so much better in the morning.'

'I will if you promise to come to me,' Sylvie says, marvelling at her bravery.

It is her! Oliver pinches the bridge of his nose and closes his eyes as a piercing headache takes hold. 'Where are you?'

'My flat.'

'And where is that? You only gave me your mobile number.'

'My address is…' Sylvie stops. Is he trying to outsmart her? What if he sends someone else like the big, hairy driver of that Jeep? She wouldn't want *him* to visit. 'Oh, very clever, Oliver. I don't want the other man. I want you!'

Oliver's eyes fly open. 'What other man?' he asks, bemused.

'The driver,' she says.

'What driver?'

'The driver of that big bollocks black Jeep.' She giggles at her description.

Good God, she's talking about Tas!

Oliver's heart pounds. Taking a deep breath, he keeps his voice steady. 'How do you know about him?'

'You'd be surprised what I know,' she says, breaking into manic laughter.

Oliver glances up at the painting above the mantelpiece and something in its brushstrokes soothes his soul. He remembers the adorable young girl who told him how the cormorants flapped their wings when no one was looking and he studies them now, but their wings are still.

Oh, to be on that beach in Cornwall with those kids.

Surprised at where his thoughts have taken him, Oliver drags himself back to the immediate predicament. 'Sylvie, the driver's not here. I'm not going to send him to you.'

'Will you come to me?' she purrs.

'No. What passed between us in Scotland should never have happened.'

'But it did.'

'It was wrong,' he says, his stomach churning at the memory.

'I love you!'

'Sylvie, you don't even know me.'

'But I want to,' she shouts.

How's he going to get rid of her? If he doesn't get back to bed soon Deanna will come looking for him and if she hears him talking to Sylvie like this… That doesn't even bear thinking about!

'I have a hectic work schedule coming up and I won't be around very much,' Oliver says. 'What if I give you a ring from time to time?'

Perhaps this will fob her off.

Oh, how he loves to keep her on the brink! A thrill of excitement courses through Sylvie. If they only talk on the phone, maybe he will grow tired of the distance between them and come to her more quickly of his own free will. Yes, they will talk on the phone. She can wait a little longer. After all, she's waited all her life.

'All right,' she says submissively.

Oliver lets out a long, silent breath. 'Then goodnight, Sylvie.'

'Goodnight, Oliver Foxley. I love you.'

He waits until he hears her disconnect before replacing the handset. First thing in the morning he will have the number changed. But, if she's managed to get that, what else has she discovered? She said, herself, he'd be surprised to learn what she knows. Does that mean she knows where he lives? She must do! Her note was left on his car in town. He thought it was just a dreadful coincidence but after this latest development he's not so sure. And she knows about Tas.

'Shit!'

A wave of nausea hits him. She's obviously mentally unhinged. Just what is she capable of? When the 'grey mist' claims him his thoughts become very dark, and if Sylvie's mental illness is anything like that... Oliver shivers. Perhaps he should contact the woman who accompanied her to Holy Isle. But if he does that what else will come out? Hell! Every which way he turns, he's caught.

Oliver glances up at the painting of the Minack. Once again, it soothes his troubled mind. Something about it draws him in and it's not just that he will soon be performing on its stage. His thoughts turn to the cheeky, blond boy with the Labrador and his sister with the angelic face, and their pretty grandma who gets so flustered whenever they meet. Such different lives. It could be a world away. It *is* a world away. Momentarily Oliver forgets his troubles. He will soon be there – for the whole of the summer – and there it is again, that fluttering, all-consuming excitement building slowly and deeply within. He thinks of Tania and laughs. She's so obvious and brazen. No fudged areas there!

Oliver destroys the note - it wouldn't do for Deanna to find it - but not before he's transferred Sylvie's number to his mobile. Just in case…

Chapter Sixteen

The view across Mount's Bay in the early morning light is breathtaking. A sun-kissed, shimmering St Michael's Mount rises out of a sparkling sea; just like the magical Isle of Avalon rising from the mists. Should she paint the Mount in a similarly mystical fashion, representing it as something from the Arthurian legend?

'Mum!' Sky's voice from the back of the car brings Cara back to earth. 'You've missed Grandma and Grandpa's road.'

Damn! She's driven straight past the turning; such is the draw of that magnificent view. Cara pulls into a gateway and waits for a couple of cars to pass before executing a U-turn. As she drives towards the lane on the brow of the hill, the glittering, tidal island beckons to her in the rear-view mirror. Yes, she will definitely paint it with a mystical feel.

After a seemingly endless winter the countryside is, at last, coming to life and the Cornish hedgerows are a patchwork of yellow. The celandine and primroses are wonderful this year and clusters of daffodils sway in the breeze, shouting from the hedge tops. Cara smiles. There's a hint of a promise in the air. She follows the lane for half a mile and, as fields give way to housing, turns into a driveway. Her father stands at the open front door. As soon as the car comes to a halt, Sky rushes up to his grandpa and gives him a hug, and then runs back to the car to let Barnaby out of the boot. In the rear-view mirror Cara catches her daughter roll her eyes.

'Come on, Beth, let's go and see Grandpa. Go gently with the eggs.'

Bethany climbs out of the car, carefully holding a wicker basket packed with some of Bobkin's straw. Nestled in the centre are a dozen painted eggs. As an Easter present for her grandparents she has blown the eggs and decorated them in varying pastel shades, adorning each with flowers, birds, dots, circles and swirls. They are so pretty Cara thinks she could easily sell them in the gallery, though she doubts she could survive the complete take-over of her kitchen and the general mayhem that ensued while her daughter created her masterpieces.

'Happy Easter, Dad,' Cara calls out, as they walk towards him.

'And what have you got there, young Beth?' Ken asks. He gives his daughter and granddaughter a kiss.

'An Easter present for you and Grandma.' Proudly, Bethany holds out the basket. 'I painted them myself.'

'Well then, you'd best go and find your grandma,' Ken says, smiling affectionately at the young girl.

Cara hugs her daughter, taking care not to upset the basket. 'Enjoy yourself with Grandma and Grandpa and make sure Sky behaves himself! I'll join you tomorrow for lunch.'

'Bye, Mum,' Bethany says, entering the cottage.

Gruffly, Ken clears his throat. 'Have a good evening and don't worry about your children.' Noting the catch in his voice, Cara glances at her father, touched by his show of emotion. 'Your mother has planned a full day in addition to the Easter egg hunt. I only hope I can keep up!'

Cara laughs. 'Thanks for having them.'

'My dear girl, no thanks are necessary. It's an absolute pleasure. And I shall look forward to getting some exercise with that dog of yours.'

Cara checks her watch – almost time to open the gallery. She peers through the open doorway but there's no sign of her mother.

'Bye, Dad.' She hugs Ken and walks towards the car but, hearing an upstairs window opening, turns back to the cottage.

'Cara, darling, have fun tonight.' Her mother and Sky lean out of the window. With his paws on the window sill, Barnaby looks out of the fixed pane next to them. Cara laughs.

'Dad, just look at that dog. I swear he thinks he's one of my children!'

Glancing up at the bedroom window, Ken's heart swells. This is what he loves best; days with family.

'Happy Easter, Mum,' Cara calls, 'and, Sky, try not to be too cheeky. Be helpful.'

The young boy gives her a wide, disarming smile and Cara falters. Quickly, she turns away and heads towards her car. Having reversed out of the driveway, she glances back at the cottage. Her mother is no longer at the window but Sky is still there. He waves and Cara smiles at her son – the embodiment of Christo at that age.

*

Late afternoon, Easter Saturday, and Tas looks across the line of actors as they take their final bow. The Tasmanian Devil Theatre Company has pulled off its opening performance to an appreciative audience, unusually swelled by the huge London and local press interest present. The car park is overflowing and the pub over the road thriving from the additional custom. Tas silently congratulates himself on having brought together a multifarious troupe of performers. He knows his casting is inspired, and Oliver is no exception. He likes to spring surprises and is more than satisfied with the audience's reaction when Oliver first breaks into song. Accustomed to him playing the romantic lead or strong action man, few people have any idea of Oliver's pitch-perfect, baritone singing voice. A collective intake of breath reverberated around the theatre.

As Oliver comes off stage Tas slaps him on the back. 'A fine performance, Mr Fox. If you carry on like this, by the time we get to the Minack you may be word perfect!'

Oliver laughs. 'Stranger things have happened, my friend.'

It's exhilarating being on stage again. He'd forgotten the intimacy and immediacy of performing in front of a live audience. He likes the interaction. A couple of the cast stop to chat, pleased that the performance is out of the way and 'first night' nerves put to bed.

Clambering onto a chair, Tas clears his throat. 'Well done, everybody.' His voice booms out across the auditorium. 'A great opening performance at the start of what I feel is going to be a terrific run. I suggest you all go off and enjoy yourselves tonight and I'll see you all at Blisland village hall on Monday. Five thirty sharp. Don't be late. No excuses about narrow lanes, lack of signposts or being waylaid by the Beast of Bodmin Moor! If anyone has any questions I'm available on mobile but, for the most part, just enjoy the beautiful environs and get some clear Cornish air into your lungs before the long haul. Happy Easter!'

Oliver glances around the open-air theatre and recognises a number of journalists who have bravely ventured forth from the safety of the city to the wilds of Bodmin Moor. As they surge forward to interview the star of the show, he braces himself for the onslaught. *Sorrows in the Sand* is a thought-provoking play and a number of the audience stand in small groups discussing the message it has delivered.

'Excuse me.'

Oliver turns. An older lady, dressed in a colourful smock, peers up at him, a pen in one hand and a programme in the other. A small and immaculately suited gentleman stands at her side.

'I wonder if you would autograph this programme for my daughter. She did so want to come and see your performance tonight but she's rather poorly.'

'I would be delighted to.' Oliver smiles at the elderly couple. 'What a shame your daughter couldn't make it, but I hope you enjoyed the play.'

'Oh yes, indeed. A very powerful message.' A smile plays on the woman's lips. 'And you, young man, have a wonderful singing voice.'

'Thank you.' Oliver accepts her compliment as he takes the pen. 'What's your daughter's name?'

'Mandy.'

Several reporters jostle around Oliver and the elderly couple, eagerly noting everything being said.

'This is a wonderful theatre,' Oliver says, writing some words to the poorly Mandy. 'What a bonus for this part of Cornwall.' He hands the autographed programme back.

'Yes, indeed,' says the elderly man in a strong Cornish accent. 'We farm locally, lived here all our lives and wouldn't want to live anywhere else. We were very happy when the Sturrocks created Sterts.'

'When was that?' Oliver politely asks, listening to the variety of the man's tone as much as the meaning of his words.

'Second of June, nineteen ninety. We attended the opening production of *Othello*, directed by Ewart Sturrock himself,' the man says with pride.

Utilising the natural contours of a dip in a field, a classic, terraced amphitheatre has been created with a sail-like, all-weather canopy providing protection from the elements.

'How lucky you are to have this on your doorstep,' says Oliver.

'We've supported Sterts from the start,' explains the woman, taking over from her husband. 'We like the feeling of involvement you get sitting in the audience. It's not the same at Plymouth's Theatre Royal or the Hall for Cornwall in Truro.'

'It's a wonderful space with a unique atmosphere and I've certainly enjoyed performing here,' says Oliver. 'We need more people with the vision to turn old buildings and unusual spaces into theatre venues. That way, people around the country, like you, will be encouraged to support theatre and the arts.'

The elderly lady smiles warmly at Oliver. 'Are you in Cornwall for long?' she asks.

'The whole of the summer. This is our opening performance. Hopefully, once your daughter is well again she will catch one of our other performances.'

'Yes, I'm sure she will.' Her eyes twinkle at the actor. 'And I may accompany her!'

Oliver smiles. 'The box office has leaflets listing where we are performing. Hope to see you again.' Graciously, Oliver attempts to take his leave of the couple.

'Oliver, let's get a couple of photos with the old couple,' says a journalist he recognises from *The Telegraph*.

'Our Mandy will be so disappointed not to have her picture taken with you,' the elderly lady says, as Oliver stands between her and her husband. He smiles for the cameras.

'Thanks, that's great,' says the journalist.

'So, Oliver, what do you think about appearing on stage in Cornwall?' asks a reporter from *The West Briton*.

Suddenly Oliver is overrun by newshounds, all eager to learn his reasons for accepting a role in a play by an unknown writer, touring a far-flung region of the country.

Presently, Tas joins him. 'I can see a few more hacks lining up to interview you. Don't suppose there's any chance of us getting out of here quickly?'

Oliver grins. 'It wouldn't make good press if the director and his lead were seen hot-footing it from the theatre!'

'No-o-o, don't suppose it would.'

For the next hour, Oliver and Tas make themselves available to answer questions. Both men know how to play the media but, at last, they are ready to leave. In the late afternoon sun, director and actor walk companionably towards the car park.

As they approach the Jeep, Tas turns to Oliver. 'OK, Mr Fox. Time to party!'

*

Dusk descends upon the cove, softly cloaking it in subtle shades and hues. A few stragglers remain on the beach enjoying the calm of the evening.

'Tan, switch on the fairy lights, will you?' Rick calls to his girlfriend from the decking.

Looking up from the counter, Tania wipes her hands on her apron. 'OK, boss!'

She flicks a switch and suddenly the café takes on a magical appearance as strings of twinkling white lights play across the ceiling beams and out onto the decked area.

'Lookin' good, Tan, and I'm not talking about the café.'

Tania laughs throatily. 'How many bowls of salad do you want?'

'Use all the large ones.'

Peering at the open shelves beneath the counter, she counts eight. This is the first party of the season and it's been a brilliant day. A passable impression of summer. Hopefully, the weather will hold.

As Rick hauls on a rope, a large white sailcloth rises up at an angle across the decking. Tying it off, he stands back and appraises the outside space. 'Hope it won't rain, but just in case…'

'Rick, don't tempt fate!' Tania says. She looks up from chopping salad. 'What?'

She's so sexy, even in that apron!

'You… in the kitchen,' Rick says, 'just where I like you.'

'Excuse me!' Tania puts the knife down and picks up a juicy, ripe tomato. 'Just wait 'til I catch you…' Emerging from behind the counter, she runs through the café and out onto the decking.

Rick quickly jumps down onto the sand and backs away, hands up in surrender with a grin on his face. Tania lobs the tomato at him.

'Mind the chinos, Tan,' he shouts, neatly sidestepping the missile.

'Anyway, thought you liked me in the bedroom.'

'Yeah, there too!'

'Men!' Tania exclaims, grinning.

The first of the evening's guests arrive just as Rick lights up the three large barbeques positioned on the beach. Amongst the early arrivals are not only residents of the cove but also a family staying in the area for the Easter break.

'See Tania for the booze element,' Rick instructs, 'and once the coals are good and hot we'll get the barbies on the go.'

'We've been lucky so far with the weather,' comments the man of the family. 'Hope the rain keeps away.'

'Oh, don't you know? We're a rain-free zone here in the cove!' Rick responds, and the man laughs as he follows his wife and children into the café.

Rick loves to entertain – he's good at it – and Tania loves to party. Networking is her thing. Soon, strangers and friends intermingle as if they've known each other for years and as the party gets under way, a varied soundtrack booms out across the sand.

*

In the deepening dusk, Cara, Tristan and Morwenna pick their way along the track towards the illuminated fairy grotto at the far end of the beach.

'Rick hasn't lost his eclectic taste in music,' comments Tristan. 'By the way, Cara, I saw Ben at the garage earlier. Did you know Rick's invited him?'

Cara groans.

'Don't worry. We'll keep him at arm's length!' Morwenna promises, glancing across her brother at Cara.

'Much appreciated.'

Morwenna laughs.

'He's always so enthusiastic,' Cara says. 'I feel such a heel.'

'Be true to yourself, Cara. Christo wouldn't want it any other way.' Tristan smiles down at her.

Cara nods, but it's getting harder by the day to find excuses.

Stepping off the track and onto the sand, they make their way towards the party. Several people sit along the edge of the boardwalk and a red-hot glow radiates from the barbeque drums.

'There's Martha and Stephen,' Morwenna says, pointing towards the decked area. She shouts a welcome to their friends.

'It sure is revving up in there,' says Stephen, approaching with a bottle of beer in his hand. 'Quite a queue forming. I suggest you get your drinks sooner rather than later.'

'What do you two want?' Tristan asks, turning to Cara and Morwenna. They decide on lager and he heads towards the bar.

'Looks like we're in for a good night,' Stephen says. 'Tania's running the bar and you know what she's like once she's had a few!'

'Yeah, the drinks will be on Rick,' comments Martha.

Another shout of greeting and they turn in the direction of the car park. Ben, Rob and his girlfriend, Sarah, walk along the boardwalk towards them. As Ben makes eye contact with Cara he breaks into a huge grin and waves madly. Cara sighs.

'And so it starts!' Morwenna comments quietly in her ear.

'Don't!'

'I promise not to leave you two alone,' Morwenna says, giving Cara a quick squeeze.

As the moon rises in the night sky, rapidly cooling air consigns the unexpected warmth of the April day to memory. With denim jeans tucked into ubiquitous Ugg boots, Cara has layered a strappy French blue tunic over a long-sleeved white T-shirt, but she's thankful she remembered her cardigan.

'Hi, Cara!' Ben bounds up to her and plants a sloppy kiss on her cheek. 'Do you want a drink?'

'Tristan's on the case.'

'Hi, Ben.' Morwenna steps forward.

'Hi, Mo. Didn't notice you there.' Glancing around, Ben spies more friends in the café. 'Just going to get a drink and say hello to Jim and Danny. Won't be long.'

'Take as long as you want,' Cara says, waving him away, and Morwenna stifles a snort. Ben gallops towards the café.

'That lad!' Morwenna says, planting herself next to Cara on one of the strategically placed logs on the beach. 'Can you imagine him as a toddler? I bet he was into everything. His poor mum.'

Cara laughs. 'If you could bottle that enthusiasm you'd be well sorted.'

'Is Jane coming tonight?' asks Sarah, joining them on the log.

'Yes, later,' answers Morwenna.

Holding three bottles aloft, Tristan steps down from the crowded decked area onto the sand. 'Quite a battle in there,' he says, handing a bottle of lager each to Cara and his sister. 'Tania's well on the way to being pissed. She forgot to charge me for these.'

'That'll please Rick when he discovers his takings aren't quite as expected,' comments Stephen.

Tristan laughs. 'Hey, Steve, Rick's asked me to man one of the barbeques. Fancy giving me a hand?'

'Sure.'

Cara turns in the direction of the ocean. Although she cannot see it, she's aware of its mighty presence. The tide is on its way out and she can hear waves breaking gently on the shore some way beyond the illuminated area of sand. It still feels odd socialising without Christo. Will she ever get used to it? In her quiet acknowledgement of the power of the sea, Cara feels Christo at her side and is comforted.

'Hey, Cara, fancy a dance?' Ben stands in front of her, a ball of energy cutting straight through the private and introspective moment with her late husband. As Ben grabs her hand and pulls her to her feet, Cara is sure she can hear Christo's laughter.

'Hang on, Ben!' Placing her bottle firmly in the sand, Cara gives Morwenna a meaningful look.

They join several other people dancing to the music and, soon, Ben's enthusiasm begins to rub off. As the distinctive sound of Supertramp's 'Dreamer' drifts across the cove, Sarah and Rob join them and, all at once, the evening begins to feel like fun.

*

Tania spots Oliver as soon as he enters the café. She waves and is rewarded with a smile.

'What can I get you two fine men?' she asks.

They order Doom Bar.

'Had a little too much of the amber liquid, Tan?' teases Tas, as she sways towards the chiller cabinet.

She laughs her throaty laugh. 'Why, can you tell?'

'Just a tad!'

'How did it go today?' she asks, flipping the metal tops and handing over two bottles of cold beer.

'Oliver wowed them, especially the ladies.' Tas takes a swig of beer.

Tania nods expansively. Losing her balance, she falls against Oliver. 'Oops! Now how did I get here?' she asks flirtatiously.

Oliver puts his arm round her waist to balance her.

Tas laughs. 'Yeah, wonder how!' Looking around, he spies Rick tending the barbeques. 'Just going to say hello. Sure you'll be safe with her, Ollie?'

'Think I can manage,' Oliver responds.

Raising an eyebrow, Tas disappears into the crowd.

Nestling against Oliver's chest and breathing in his masculine aroma, Tania closes her eyes.

'You OK?' Oliver asks.

'Oh yes!'

'You've got customers,' he says, removing his arm, but Tania holds on tightly. 'Tania?'

'Oh, please don't send me back to work!'

He laughs. 'But you have customers.'

'They can go hang.' She looks up at Oliver, her eyes swimming with drunken desire.

'Tania, behave yourself,' he says quietly.

'But I don't want to behave myself. I want to be naughty. In fact, I want to be *very* naughty with you.'

'Sorry, not possible,' Oliver says.

'So you've said,' says Tania, sulkily. Pouting, she pushes herself away from him and sways back to the bar.

Oliver shakes his head. She certainly doesn't give up easily. Making his way through the crowd, aware of the numerous double-takes, he emerges onto the covered decking. Rick's music is an interesting mix spanning decades and he can hear Duffy's voice ringing out loud and clear. Wryly, he thinks it's a good job Tania is occupied with the bar otherwise she'd probably be dancing her special dance for him right here!

Glancing up from tending the barbeque, Rick catches sight of Oliver standing under the sailcloth. He nods to him in welcome. 'Good-looking bugger, isn't he?' he comments to Tas standing beside him.

'Who?' Tas asks, giving the sausages a prod. He looks up and follows Rick's gaze. 'Oh yeah, but the funny thing is Ollie doesn't see it. He's more concerned with the internal landscape.' Methodically he turns the sausages, neatly lining them up to expose their pink sides to the hot coals.

'Probably just as well,' Rick says.

Standing on the edge of the decking, Oliver looks up at the clear night sky. Free of pollution, the heavens are putting on a magnificent display of twinkling stars and planets. He breathes in deeply. It's a heady mix: the reflection of the moon on the water; the smell of the sea mingled with tantalising aromas wafting from the barbeques; the cool taste of beer; and Duffy's sexy voice. Letting the sensations wash over him, Oliver closes his eyes. It's been a good day and he feels balanced and at peace.

The sound of singing brings him back to the moment and he looks out over the beach. A group of people dance on the sand, carefree and happy. It looks like fun. A floppy-haired young man dances madly around a couple of women singing along to the music. Oliver takes a swig of beer and is about to swallow when his breath catches in his throat and his heart stalls. As noises become muffled and all around him blurs, every nerve in his body is suddenly on high alert as he focuses on this one thing. Eventually he swallows. Finally he breathes.

Cara laughs at Ben's mad dancing. Encouraged, he increases his tomfoolery.

'If Duffy could see us now she'd be well freaked!' shouts Morwenna above the singer's distinctive sound.

'Because we're fierce competition or crucifying her song?' Cara shouts back, mimicking the singer's studied moves.

Morwenna laughs. Suddenly Ben grabs Cara's hands. Singing loudly, he drops to his knees and pleads for mercy. Cara shoots Morwenna a wry look.

Morwenna laughs again. 'Steady on, Ben!'

Oliver is transfixed. He has never seen anything so exquisite in his life. Unable to take his eyes off the beautiful woman with the long blonde hair, he notes every little detail about her. Deep within, bubbling excitement takes hold.

Who is she?

As Duffy's song ends, the haunting sounds of Coldplay's 'Fix You' take over.

Tending one of the barbeques a few feet from Oliver, a sandy-haired man calls out, 'Hey, Gwyneth, this one's for you!' Turning to Rick, he says, 'Be back in a minute, mate.'

Abandoning their duties, Tristan and Stephen join the others on the beach. As if performing a ritual, the friends clasp hands and encircle Cara, each singing along to Chris Martin's thought-provoking words.

There's a look on Cara's face that Oliver doesn't understand, but he's profoundly moved by all that's unfolding. He watches as she joins in the dance, swaying in the centre, surrounded by her friends. Alone – but not alone. Oh, how he wants to be in that circle with her. Oliver shakes his head.

What the hell's happening?

'Hey, Mr Fox, want another beer?' Tas calls up to Oliver. Getting no response, he looks in the direction of Oliver's gaze and sees a group of people dancing around a gorgeous blonde. He glances back at Oliver then steps up onto the decking beside his friend. 'You OK, Ollie?'

Tas's voice shatters Oliver's paralysis. Blinking rapidly, as if coming out of a deep trance, he mumbles something about enjoying the beautiful view.

Tas glances at Cara again. She's stunning all right. 'Yeah, a real babe!' He nods at the bottle in Oliver's hand. 'Want another?'

Chapter Seventeen

Feeling an intense gaze upon her, Cara believes Christo watches over her as she dances to one of his favourite Coldplay songs. He used to play this all the time on that guitar of his. It's painful being here in the centre of the circle on her own, but she knows she's surrounded by good friends who care deeply for Christo's family. As Chris Martin's voice fades away into the cool night air, Ben enters the circle and draws her to him. Reality…

'Ben, I need to breathe!'

'Sorry, babe,' he says, lessening his hold but not releasing her.

'The barbie's almost ready,' Tristan announces. 'Who wants something to eat?'

Oliver watches. He doesn't have a choice.

Who's she with? She can't be on her own, someone like her!

He doesn't think it's that floppy-haired, bumbling, young man. His eyes follow her as she heads towards the barbeque, the feeling in the pit of his stomach intensifying. She's *so* lovely. Slowly he finishes his beer.

'What do you say to some grub?' suggests Tas, slapping him heartily on the back.

'Sounds like a good idea.' Joining the end of the queue, Oliver notices Cara is six people in front.

'Meat or fish?' asks Tas. 'I'm having both.'

Neither. Oliver has completely lost his appetite.

As they help themselves to plates from a stack on a table, Tas instructs Tristan to pile steak, chicken wings, sausages, burgers and mackerel onto his plate.

'What would you like?' Tristan asks Oliver.

'The steak looks good.'

'Is that it?' asks Tas incredulously.

'That's it, my friend.'

When the two men step up onto the decking, Tristan turns to Stephen. 'Do you recognise him?'

'Seems familiar,' Stephen says, piling meat onto a plate of the girl next in line.

'He's that actor, Oliver Foxley.'

'Really? He's a favourite of Martha's. If she spots him I won't see her for dust!'

Tristan laughs and turns back to the next person in the queue.

Oliver watches Cara work her way along the food tables. The bumbling young man is still at her side, but to his relief she doesn't seem to be with him. She appears to be part of a larger group. He watches as the young man says something to her and moves away to the top table. He is so busy observing Cara that Oliver doesn't notice Tas take a step back until too late.

'Sorry, Ollie,' says Tas, as they collide, 'but this lovely young lady needs to get to the bread.'

Oliver looks over his friend's shoulder. A tall, curvy woman stares at Tas, a blush spreading across her cheeks.

'Didn't mean to push in, I'm sure.' Morwenna's Cornish accent rings out loud and clear.

'Darling, you can push in any time.' Tas gives a small bow and Morwenna's blush deepens. 'Perhaps you'd like some of that wonderful-looking cheese over there to go with your bread?'

For once, Morwenna is at a loss, her usual witty repartee abandoning her. Oliver smiles to himself. He's seen it all before and this woman is very much Tas's type.

'And what sort of a cheese girl are you?' asks Tas, appraising her full figure. 'Maybe a strong Stilton, no?'

Morwenna stares; a rabbit caught in headlights.

'What about a Cornish Yarg, dark and mysterious on the outside yet concealing a creamy centre?' Tas says mischievously. 'Or how about a soft, yielding Camembert? Yes, I think that's what you are, soft and yielding.' Before Morwenna can respond, Tas guides her to the end of the table where the various cheeses are laid out.

Suddenly, there is only one person separating them and Oliver's mouth turns dry. He watches as

Cara stretches across the table and, picking up a pair of metal tongs, helps herself to salad. As her tunic rises up to reveal the neatest backside, Oliver's stomach muscles contract.

This is ridiculous! Get a grip!

The man standing in front of him steps out of the queue and moves further up the line. Now there is no one between them and Oliver can hardly breathe. Cara straightens up with her back to him. She's not as tall as he first thought. They are so close; she must surely hear his hammering heart. Her long, blonde hair glistens in the fairy lights and he fights the urge to reach out and stroke it. She has delectable curves in all the right places and she certainly looks good in jeans. Instantly, Oliver wonders what she looks like out of them. He closes his eyes, trying to clear the vision from his mind. When he opens them again she's turning to face him. Bathed in a wonderful golden light, she is the most beautiful woman he has ever seen, but there is deep sadness ingrained in the dark brown eyes that look up into his. Oliver recoils, appalled that this gorgeous girl is capable of displaying such hurt.

Aware of an intense presence behind her, Cara turns. After the initial shock of recognising him, the first thing she thinks is that her mother was right. He is even better looking in the flesh. As Oliver opens his eyes, Cara is amazed to find that the blue eyes gazing down at her speak of love, but then the moment is shattered as he recoils. Why did he do that? Does she have three eyes and a pointy head?

As they face each other, neither saying a word, Oliver struggles to make sense of his feelings. He has to say something, but what? Oh, *now* he understands. At once he has sympathy for all those women rendered inarticulate in his company.

'So, is that all you're having, Oliver Foxley?'

She has him at a disadvantage. She knows who he is. Oliver glances down at the lone steak sitting on his plate. He cannot speak, so all-consuming are his feelings.

'Why don't you have some surf to go with that turf?' Cara points to the plates of lobster halves nestling amongst the bowls of salad. 'This lobster was probably still in the sea this morning. I expect Rick picked them up from Patrick's catch first thing.'

Her voice is like music to his ears. Oliver concentrates on breathing.

Think, man! You have to say something.

'So, you're Gwyneth?' he says, amazed at how normal he sounds.

Now it's Cara's turn to recoil; the sadness in her eyes deepening.

Shit! What has he said? He wants to take away the hurt, not increase it.

Cara laughs sadly and he can tell his words have taken her momentarily elsewhere.

'A nickname,' she says eventually. 'My name is Cara.'

A beautiful name for a beautiful girl.

But now what? There's so much he wants to say but what *can* he say?

'What about some crab if you're not interested in the lobster?' Cara asks, giving him an odd look.

He's not interested in food. In fact, Oliver can't imagine ever regaining his appetite.

'Here, I'll choose something for you,' she says, taking his plate.

She leans across the table again and Oliver can't help himself; he has never seen anyone wear jeans so well. Eagerly, he drinks in her body.

By the time Cara turns to face him *that* look has returned and she catches her breath, as a sliding, liquefying sensation takes hold. No wonder he's such a believable actor if he can do this! She hands him the plate now laden with tasty morsels.

'Hopefully there's something amongst this to tempt you.'

It does look tempting but Oliver wonders if he will choke on the first mouthful.

Come on, man. Don't be mute!

'Thank you, Cara, for organising me.'

Is that it? Oliver groans inwardly, hoping he didn't sound sarcastic.

Again Cara and Oliver stand facing each other, neither saying a word. From out of the corner of his eye, Oliver watches the bumbling young man approach.

'Hey, Cara, Rick's lighting the bonfire,' Ben says, giving Oliver a questioning look. 'Come and see.' He grabs hold of her arm.

Swallowing her irritation, Cara pulls her arm free. 'I'll join you in a minute.'

Ben hesitates, then shrugs and lopes off towards the beach.

Cara turns to Oliver. He's still watching her and she's about to say something flippant when some deeper intuition tells her to resist. Instead, she smiles up at him, confused and a little off kilter… and then she's gone.

Terrific! You handled that well.

'Hey, Ollie. Over here.' Tas's voice cuts across the noise of the party.

Making his way through the crowd, Oliver steps down onto the sand and joins Tas and Morwenna on one of the logs. It's cool in the night air but the bonfire, crackling and spitting, gives off a fair amount of heat. Oliver sits down next to Tas. He notices Cara and Ben sitting with their friends on the other side of the fire. Is it the flickering blaze giving the impression of a golden glow around her? She looks magnificent. He could sit all night just gazing at her and enjoying her beauty, but he must interact.

'Ollie, this is Morwenna,' Tas says.

'Hi,' she says in a strangled voice, having immediately recognised him.

'Hi, Morwenna.' Oliver smiles. 'You all seem to have beautiful names in Cornwall.'

'Err, really?' she says lamely, knowing she's wearing her 'rabbit in headlights' look again.

Instantly Oliver finds his equilibrium. 'Yes, Morwenna is a lovely name.'

'I suppose so,' she mumbles. 'Morwenna is the patron saint of Morwenstow.'

'Where's that?' asks Oliver.

'On the north coast… almost in Devon!'

Oliver laughs. It's the way she says it, as if the neighbouring county is, somehow, inferior.

'Hey, Tan, come and join us,' Tas calls over Oliver's shoulder.

Standing on the edge of the decking with a plate of food in her hand, Tania turns at the sound of Tas's voice. She makes a beeline for Oliver.

'So, what do you think of the party so far?' she asks, as Oliver makes a space for her on the log.

'Great, Tan. Like the music,' says Tas, as the distinctive sounds of 'Riders on the Storm' drift across the sands.

With its real sound effects of thunder and electric piano playing emulating the sound of rain, there's something highly evocative and atmospheric about the music. There's also something deeply primal and Oliver's gaze slides over to the other side of the fire. Cara's earlier irritation with Ben makes him closely monitor their body language and it's clear they're not together. The bumbling young man appears happy to accept any crumb she may care to throw. Oliver is astounded at the profound relief he feels.

For God's sake, get a grip!

'I see Rick's still got his impeccable taste in music,' comments Tas.

Tania smiles lazily. 'Yeah, he knows how to create a good playlist.' Turning her attention to Oliver, in a low, seductive voice she asks, 'So, Ollie, is the music moving you too?'

'You could say that,' he says, not taking his eyes off the golden girl on the far side of the fire.

'How about we find somewhere quiet to enjoy it, just you and me?' she suggests hopefully.

Oliver drags his eyes away from Cara. 'Tania, you never give up, do you?'

'Well, you can't blame a girl for trying!'

'No, but you may have noticed that Rick is standing over there and we're surrounded by his friends,' he says, more harshly than he intended.

Taking a swig of lager, Tania almost topples off the log. With lightning-quick reactions, Oliver grabs her arm.

'Oops!' She giggles, regaining her balance.

Irritated by Tania, Oliver finds himself, once again, gazing through the flames at Cara. The tall, sandy-haired man who served him earlier sits on her other side. Could he be her partner? They seem at ease in each other's company and make a more believable couple than the bumbling young man. What the hell is he going to do? She's perfect! Oliver abandons trying to eat. Placing his plate on the sand, he watches as the sandy-haired man casually puts his arm around Cara and she immediately rests her head on his shoulder. Oliver reels at the level of jealousy coursing through him.

Beyond the fire, Tristan hugs Cara and says quietly, 'I think you've got an admirer.'

Cara groans. 'What *am* I going to do about Ben?'

'Not Ben. I'm talking about that actor over there. He can't take his eyes off you.'

Raising her head, Cara gazes across the sand towards the decking. Sure enough, Oliver is looking directly at her and the look on his face makes her stomach somersault.

'Is he a friend of Rick's?' Tristan asks.

'Don't know,' Cara says, 'Tania seems well acquainted, so I guess so.'

'And who's that other big guy with his paws all over Mo?'

'Oh, Trist, you're not getting all protective over your li'l sis, are you?' Cara sits up.

'No, but he'd better not be leading her a merry dance,' Tristan says protectively.

'She's quite capable of looking after herself, you know!'

'Yeah, but I can't help feeling responsible for her. And for you, Beth and Sky, come to that.'

Cara smiles. He's such a good mate. 'I know, Trist, and Christo would love you for that,' she says, planting a kiss on his cheek.

On the other side of the fire, Oliver catches his breath. Even though Cara and the man are obviously close, something tells him they are not together either. So, who *is* she with? He breathes out slowly, steadying himself.

Surely she's not on her own?

The mellow sounds of Phil Collins' 'In The Air Tonight' fill the cool night air and the beat of the drum tap-taps on Oliver's heart, prodding him to take action.

'Hey, Ollie, Morwenna and her brother are in a band,' Tas says, pointing in the direction of Tristan and Cara. 'I said we'd check them out while we're in Cornwall.'

'That guy's your brother?' Oliver exclaims loudly, and both Tas and Morwenna look at him with startled expressions.

'Ye-es,' Morwenna says slowly. 'Why?'

God! My nerves are all over the place.

Thinking on his feet, Oliver says, 'He doesn't look like you.'

'Oh, I don't know, I can see a resemblance,' says Tas, looking over at Tristan and then scrutinising Morwenna. 'Personally, though, I prefer Morwenna's luscious, auburn locks.' Twisting a strand of her hair gently round his finger, Tas gazes at her with smouldering eyes.

Morwenna's face flushes scarlet.

'Jane not coming tonight?' Tania asks, looking across the men at Morwenna.

'Yeah, later,' Morwenna replies. 'In fact, isn't that her now? My brother's a different person since they've been together.'

As one, they turn. Oliver watches the sandy-haired man rise to his feet and, opening his arms wide, walk towards his girlfriend. Ben instantly moves closer to Cara and puts his arm around her. Oliver grimaces. If nothing else, he's got to save her from the attentions of that young man.

'Oh, Gawd, I just lurve this song,' Tania shrieks as James Blunt's 'You're Beautiful' wafts across the sand. 'It's so hauntingly sad but I bloody love it.'

Oliver listens to the lyrics and it's as if the singer is giving him a sign. He's got to do something. Tania says something to him but he can't hear a word. Her overt attention is making him feel claustrophobic and he needs to be free of her. He looks across at Cara. If he doesn't act now he never will. Oliver rises to his feet. With wildly pounding heart, he closes the divide.

Thwarted mid-sentence, Tania stares open-mouthed as he sets off across the beach.

Sitting on the log next to Tristan, Jane talks animatedly to her boyfriend and Cara. It's only Ben who observes the actor approaching. Suddenly Oliver stands in front of them. As Cara looks up, a hush descends.

'Cara, would you do me the honour of this dance?' Oliver formally asks, holding out his hand.

Glancing from Oliver to Cara, Jane squeezes Tristan's knee. Sarah, sitting with her boyfriend, Rob, realises she's gawping, and Martha's eyes are out on stalks.

With the café's fairy lights and the glow of the bonfire behind him, Oliver appears shrouded in a million twinkling stars. He looks so appealing, but should she say no? Cara dismisses the thought.

'I would be delighted to,' she says, amazed at how polite they are being.

As she places her hand in his, a surge of electricity courses through them both but Oliver doesn't let go. Holding on tightly, he leads Cara to join the other people dancing on the sand. He turns to face her and suddenly she's in his arms. It feels so natural. He knew it would. Holding her close, certain that she must feel his leaping heart, Oliver deeply inhales her scent.

This is so surreal, thinks Cara. Just wait 'til Mum hears about this!

Aware that her friends are watching, Cara feels stiff and awkward but, as Oliver takes the lead, soon they find their rhythm.

He certainly knows how to dance! Must be all that acting training.

Suddenly Tas and Morwenna are beside them.

'Not interrupting anything, are we?' asks Tas with a grin.

Oliver laughs and Morwenna raises a tentative eyebrow. Before Cara has a chance to respond, Tas puts Morwenna into a dramatic spin and whisks her away across the sand. It's all Morwenna can do to hold on tightly to this bear of a man.

Oliver smiles at Cara. The look in his eyes is soft and gentle and for a moment she forgets the rest of the world.

For Oliver, Cara is like a dream; one he has always had but never able to recall. He wonders how long they can stay locked together like this. It's heady stuff. He's uncertain what to say, but there doesn't seem the need to put thoughts into words. As they dance together in the moonlight, Oliver lets the music wash over him.

Tania, still smarting over Oliver's abrupt exit, sips her lager and looks out across the beach. She's jealous, but also fascinated by the light that surrounds the couple and thinks she must have had way too much to drink.

'How you doin', Tan?' Rick sits beside his lover.

'OK,' she says, without averting her gaze from Oliver and Cara.

'Well, would you look at that!' Rick raises his fingers to his mouth to wolf-whistle but stops himself. Something about Oliver and Cara is so intimate and private, there's simply no room for the world to interfere. 'We give good parties, don't we, Tan?' he says, putting his arm around her.

'Mmm,' she says, not trusting herself to speak. Instead, she lays her head against his shoulder and tries to block out the lyrics, but it's no good. There's no denying what's happening out there beyond the firelight. This song is for the beautiful couple dancing on the sand.

Oliver feels a shiver course through Cara's body. Holding her firmly but gently, as if she is the most fragile and precious thing in the world, he can't believe how each song sends him a message. He wants this moment to last forever. And he *so* wants to kiss her; to experience her. But if he starts now he knows he will never stop. Instead, as the music comes to an end, tenderly he brushes his lips against her forehead.

'Cara,' he whispers, and he knows her name has been on his lips all of his life.

Chapter Eighteen

Cara's legs have turned to jelly and what the hell is her stomach doing? For crying out loud! Despite the music having stopped, Oliver still holds her. Frantically, she tries to think of something intelligent to say, but the emotions coursing through her have rendered her speechless.

'So, what do you say to a dip in the sea?' Tas bellows, approaching out of the darkness with his arm firmly around Morwenna's waist.

'You've got to be joking,' Morwenna exclaims. 'The sea will be freezing! Give it a month or two, then maybe…'

'Baby, never fear, I'd soon warm you up!' he says and Morwenna laughs nervously. 'But I will definitely hold you to that.' Tas turns his attentions to Oliver and Cara. 'What are you two doing now?'

Good question. 'What are we doing now?' Oliver asks quietly.

Cara takes a deep breath. 'Well, I have a full day tomorrow so I should be getting home.'

Overwhelmed by crushing disappointment, Oliver knows he can't let her disappear so quickly; not when he's only just found her.

'Is home far? Did you come by car?'

Cara laughs. 'No, I came by foot! I live at the end of the beach.'

Another who enjoys the freedom of this fabulous cove.

And then Oliver recalls the cheeky lad with the Labrador and the adorable young girl. His eyes open wide. 'Are you Cara Penhaligon?' he asks incredulously.

'You've got me.' She smiles up at him.

Oh, how I wish I had!

'But I have one of your paintings!' he exclaims.

'Yes, I know. *The Minack.*'

'And you didn't say anything?'

Cara shakes her head. Seeing a small frown furrow his brow, swiftly she adds, 'I've had other things on my mind tonight.'

Could she possibly mean him? Could he affect her as much as she does him?

Could I do that to her?

Deep in his belly the bubbling excitement builds.

'I met your family earlier,' he says. 'Beth, Sky and your mother, although I've met her before. Oh, and not forgetting Barnaby.' Warmth fills his soul.

Cara smiles. 'I know that too!'

'Cara Penhaligon,' Oliver says in a mock stern voice, 'you have had me at a disadvantage from the start.'

'The start of what?' Cara asks.

Oliver can hardly speak. She's hit the nail on the head. There's nothing that can be started. He rakes a hand through his hair. He can't just let her disappear into the night and walk out of his life, but what other option does he have?

'Allow me to walk you to your door at least.'

Graciously Cara accepts his offer. Glancing towards the café, she sees Tristan and Jane striding across the sand towards them. Behind them, Ben looks sulkily in her direction.

'Mo, we're making tracks. See you tomorrow around one,' Tristan says pointedly to his sister. The look on his face makes Cara want to laugh.

Morwenna nods.

Glancing at Tas's hand on his sister's waist, Tristan frowns. He looks over at Cara and Oliver, and is startled to meet Cara's steady gaze. She raises an eyebrow.

'Can't help it,' he says, smiling sheepishly.

Now she laughs. As Cara walks towards her friends by the fire, Oliver's eyes follow her.

'Blimey, Cara!' exclaims Martha, breathless with excitement. 'Dancing with Oliver Foxley, you lucky, lucky…' Casting around for a suitable word, she eventually settles on, '…friend!'

Cara smiles, embarrassed.

'Yeah, a bit of a smooth mover, isn't he?' says Ben moodily, glaring in Oliver's direction.

'Oh, Ben, it was only a few dances,' Cara says.

'Yeah, but I wanted to have the last dance with you.'

Cara smiles apologetically. Picking up her cardigan from the log, she throws it around her shoulders.

'Do me a favour, Cara,' says Tristan, as he and Jane approach. 'Keep an eye on Mo, will you? You know what she's like when she fancies someone and I think she's got the hots for that guy.' He jerks his head in Tas's direction.

'Tristan, Mo can look after herself but, OK, I will keep an eye out.'

'And keep an eye out for yourself too,' he says.

'Now you're being ridiculous, Trist. They're just walking us back to The Lookout. Nothing's going to happen.'

Jane steps forward and hugs Cara. 'Enjoy, sweet girl, but maintain perspective.'

Cara groans. 'Not you too! Three dances and you think I've lost all reasoning.'

'I'm just saying…' Turning her palms up to the sky, Jane pulls a face and raises her eyebrows.

Cara studies Tristan's girlfriend for a moment. Both women are acutely aware of the good-looking actor standing only a few yards away. He has powerful magnetism.

'Thanks, guys,' Cara calls out across the sand to Rick and Tania, still sitting on the log on the far side of the fire. 'It was a great evening.'

'Glad you had a good time,' Rick says, saluting her with his beer bottle. 'There will be many more, won't there, Tan?'

'Yeah,' Tania mumbles, her eyes glued to Oliver.

Cara turns back, her stomach double-somersaulting when she sees the look in Oliver's eyes. Perhaps Tristan *is* right.

'Goodbyes over?' asks Tas, steering Morwenna into the darkness, but not before she's looked over her shoulder and pulled an amazed face at Cara. Oliver and Cara fall into step behind them.

'It's a beautiful night,' says Oliver, wishing he could be as natural with Cara as Tas is with Morwenna. He wants to put his arm around her so badly.

Cara glances up at the sky. 'Yes, it is, but we get quite a few like this.'

'No pollution,' Oliver comments. He has not felt this nervous or awkward since a teenager. So far their conversations have, at best, been stilted but his feelings are overflowing. 'How long have you lived in the cove?'

She steals a glance. He is so ruggedly good-looking in the moonlight. Unaccustomedly, Cara feels shy.

'Well, Beth's just turned nine. We moved in a year before she was born, so ten years… give or take.'

So there is a 'we'. Of course there is! He knew she couldn't be on her own.

Despite the cool night air, Oliver's skin is hot and clammy. Her partner – or husband – obviously couldn't make the party for some reason and that eager young man must have seized the opportunity to get close in his absence. Well, he can certainly understand that! Drawing deeply on his training as an actor, Oliver focuses his mind to override his emotions. When he speaks his voice sounds remarkably normal.

'I have a nine-year-old. Jamie.'

'Is he here with you now?'

'No. The family is in Surrey. It's just me here for the summer.'

Just you… for the summer.

'Perhaps they'll visit when it gets warmer,' she suggests.

'Maybe,' he says doubtfully.

Cara steals another glance. He sounds so adrift.

Is that it, then? For God's sake, speak to her.

'Samantha's seventeen and at the stage when spending time with her old man is no longer considered cool. Charlie's fifteen and has a girlfriend so I don't think he'll be easily prised away. I only recently found out he's been dating for over a year,' he says incredulously. 'And Sebastian's eleven and very self-sufficient. He loves football and as long as he can kick a ball around he doesn't mind where he is.'

But Jamie, thinks Oliver, would like it here, and his heart swells at the thought of his quiet, sensitive, youngest child.

'They sound a great family,' Cara says. Oliver nods briefly, his lips twitching into a small smile. 'I'm sure, in the future, your daughter will want to spend time in your company again.'

She wonders what his wife's like. Gorgeous, no doubt. Unsuccessfully, Cara tries to recall any media photos of his family.

They walk on in silence, listening to the sound of waves breaking some distance away.

Oliver welcomes the peace and tranquillity, allowing it to calm his racing heart. 'You are very lucky to live here,' he says with feeling.

'Well, I think so,' Cara says, wondering at his wistfulness. 'But you must have travelled all over the world and experienced many beautiful places.'

'I have, that's true, but there's something particularly magical about this place. It's so free.'

So, he feels it too! Who'd have thought that someone with all his worldly experience would be so attuned to the cove's unique atmosphere? Not only great-looking, but also sensitive and deep…

From some distance ahead they hear Morwenna squeal. Suddenly, emerging out of the darkness, she rushes past laughing. Tas is only a few yards behind.

'Just bagging myself a fair Cornish maid,' he says, as he passes by.

Oliver grins, but quickly the grin fades. How he wishes he could do just that. They hear Morwenna shriek and then burst into giggles. Cara chuckles. Tristan would be beside himself if he could hear his sister now.

Oliver glances at Cara. He loves the sound of her laughter, which contradicts the haunting sadness in her eyes. He has never met anyone so desirable. Everything about her is perfect to him: her lovely oval face with its small straight nose; her beautifully shaped pale lips just waiting to be kissed; her long blonde hair falling over her shoulders and glistening in the moonlight. And it's obvious her clothes disguise a neat figure. Desire stirs.

'That's my place,' Cara says, pointing to a light suspended halfway up the cliff face. 'There are steps just round the corner.'

Oliver's senses, already strained to breaking point, tip over into panic mode. Surely it's not going to end here?

They walk on in silence. A few yards further on, wooden steps, little more than a ladder, rise up the rock face.

'Stairway to heaven,' Oliver whispers.

'Sorry, what did you say?'

'Not important.' He shakes his head and smiles at her.

Cara looks beyond him to the sea. In the moonlight, at the water's edge, Morwenna and Tas are locked in a passionate embrace. Yes, Tristan would be well panicked by now. Perhaps she should try and slow things down. She turns towards Rick's Beach Hut. The main lights have been switched off but the fairy lights are still on and a healthy glow emanates from the embers of the fire. She breathes in the salt air. Oh, how she loves this cove. It fills her soul and gives her solace.

'Anyone for coffee?' she calls out in Morwenna and Tas's direction, and Oliver raises his eyes to the night sky, silently thanking God.

As Cara climbs, Oliver follows, his breath hitching in his throat as he savours the rise and fall of her neat buttocks.

'Only twenty-eight steps,' she calls out over her shoulder.

'No wonder you're all so fit in Cornwall.'

Cara laughs, acknowledging the compliment. 'Well, you must be doing something right in Surrey.'

Oliver stops and looks up at her disappearing figure. He, too, smiles at the compliment but almost immediately the smile freezes on his face. What the hell is he doing? He feels like some love-struck teenager, not knowing what to do or how to react, and his thoughts turn to his eldest son and his girlfriend dilemma. Deanna, Samantha, Charlie, Sebastian and Jamie are his life. What is he thinking?

Cara reaches the top step and glances down. Seeing Oliver's disquiet envelop him like a grey cloud, she wonders at this handsome man whose public image is so powerful and self-assured, yet the person he has presented her with appears troubled and full of doubt.

'Are you intending to finish the climb?' she asks.

Oliver looks up to see Cara watching him. Highlighted from behind by The Lookout's porch light, she appears shrouded in a golden glow. The look on her face is thoughtful and full of concern, and she simply takes his breath away.

'Yes,' he whispers.

As Oliver emerges onto the top step, a black and white cat suddenly appears round the corner of the bungalow. Calling a greeting, it trots towards Cara with its tail bolt upright.

'Hello, Basil. What have you been up to tonight?' She bends to stroke it. Rising off its front paws, the cat pushes its head into the palm of her hand. 'This is another family member,' she says to Oliver, 'or have you two already met?'

Oliver shakes his head, bemused. Has he arrived in some enchanted land?

Cara regards him for a moment and then opens the stable door. 'Welcome to The Lookout,' she says before disappearing inside.

Oliver inhales deeply, the sea air tickling his senses, and takes a long look at this magical world in which he finds himself. From the light of the moon he can see that The Lookout is a modest bungalow with a couple of gables and obvious extensions. It's a hotchpotch affair. To one end, a flat-roofed two-storey extension has been added. In fact, the bungalow looks like a child's Lego building with several afterthoughts. Nevertheless, it has charm and is not the least ostentatious. Behind the building he can sense the dark bulk of the cliffs rising high above its roofline. Turning his attention to the beach, he looks for Tas and Morwenna but they are nowhere to be seen. The moon casts its silvery light upon the ocean, scything a path across the surface, and Oliver listens to the waves gently breaking on the shore. Apart from that, all is silent. As the peace and tranquillity of the cove seduce him, Oliver knows that now he's brought Cara safely to her door he *must* walk away.

But she has left the door open…

Entering a porch full of children's paraphernalia, he smiles. This is so familiar. He walks through to a simply furnished living room, its walls and wood panelling painted white. Even the exposed floorboards are whitewashed. Against the far wall is a wood-burning stove set on a slate hearth, and to one side is a dusky blue sofa with blue and white striped scatter cushions. A matching armchair is positioned against the opposite wall. A dining table and chairs fill a bay window, from which Oliver imagines there must be fantastic views along the cove. The room is simple, clean and totally authentic, without a whiff of an interior designer's staged idea of beachside living.

This is the real deal.

Glancing through an opening into a galley kitchen, he sees Cara at the sink, filling a kettle.

She looks over her shoulder. 'How do you take your coffee?'

'White please. No sugar.'

'Make yourself comfortable,' she says, turning back to the sink.

Fighting an overwhelming urge to seize the kettle from her and take her in his arms, Oliver moves further into the living room. The art on the walls is obviously Cara's and displayed on the far wall, dominating the room, is a full-sized electric-blue surfboard. On it – painted Andy Warhol style – are the faces of a stunning, younger Cara and a golden, open-faced man. His heart races at the sight of a teenage Cara and this glimpse into her past, but it's the young man that demands his attention. The face looking down at him is natural, sunny and full of character; an adult version of Sky.

This has got to be the missing husband/partner. Will he walk in at any moment? Perhaps Cara is just friendly and thinks nothing of inviting strangers back to their place for coffee. Maybe that's how this golden, free-spirited couple live.

All at once Oliver feels trapped. His life has always seemed relatively free and certainly smoothly run – largely due to his wife's efficient nature – but recently it has felt neither quite so smooth nor free. He is still standing in the middle of the room staring at the surfboard when Cara emerges from the kitchen.

'Ah, you've spotted the board,' she says, then cringes. What a ridiculous thing to say! How could he possibly not?

'It's stunning,' he says. But what he really wants to say is that she is stunning... in every way.

'Thank you. It was one of the pieces I did for my degree.'

'Where did you study?' he asks.

'Oh, I didn't go far. Falmouth.'

Everything you could ever want is here in this county.

'It was a great time,' she says, and Oliver detects a wistfulness.

'And the young man? With that face he must be Sky's father.'

'Yes, Christo,' she says gazing up at the familiar face. She swallows the lump forming in her throat, refusing to give in to the emotion.

So, your name is Christo. Why aren't you here with your beautiful wife tonight? Perhaps you're a fisherman? You look the outdoor type. Maybe you are at sea now and will return in the early hours after you've landed your catch? Oliver is stunned at the level of jealousy consuming him and shocked by the anger that swiftly follows. *Why the hell are you not here?*

If Christo had been present this evening he would never have had the chance to dance with Cara. He would have had to simply appreciate her from afar. If Christo had been here tonight he wouldn't, now, be battling with all these raging feelings and emotions.

For God's sake, why did you leave her alone tonight?

A sound at the door interrupts his thoughts and, together, Cara and Oliver turn. Entwined in each other's arms, Morwenna and Tas navigate their way from the hallway into the living room.

'Coffee, you two?' Cara asks, shooting her friend a meaningful look.

Morwenna extracts herself from Tas and joins Cara in the kitchen.

'Mo, steady on,' Cara whispers, as she spoons coffee into four mugs.

'Don't think I can!' Morwenna's face is flushed, her eyes shining.

'You've only just met him.' Cara frowns as she pours hot water from the kettle onto the granules.

'I know.' Morwenna hugs herself, a huge smile splitting her face.

'Well, try,' Cara says, picking up two mugs. 'Bring the others, will you?' She walks into the living room.

Taken aback by Cara's clipped tone, Morwenna strokes the cat, now lying in its favourite spot amongst the pot plants. Opening one eye, sleepily it considers her.

'Hey, Basil, did you know it's so much easier being a cat?'

From the living room, Tas's playful voice rings out loud and clear. 'Morwenna, baby, I'm getting lonely in here!'

'Got to go!' she whispers conspiratorially to Basil, as she picks up the two remaining mugs.

Sitting in the armchair, Tas pats his knee as Morwenna enters the room. Giggling nervously and avoiding eye contact with Cara, she sets the mugs on the floor and sits on his lap. Immediately, he wraps his arms around her and gently nuzzles the back of her neck.

Sitting on the sofa at the furthest end from Oliver, Cara is acutely aware that their body language is in sharp contrast. She attempts to relax. After all, this is her place, but it seems so surreal having a famous actor in her home. She blows on her coffee and takes a sip.

'I love your paintings, Cara,' Oliver says.

Taken by surprise, she swallows a large mouthful and chokes, the hot liquid burning her throat. Gasping for air, she places her mug on the floor.

Swiftly Oliver closes the gap. 'Sorry, I didn't mean to startle you,' he says, gently patting her back, 'but I do love them.'

Cara turns to look at him, half-choking. 'Thanks,' she gasps. 'I think I'm OK now.'

Reluctantly Oliver removes his hand. He feels so alive. Something about this woman fires him up. He doesn't know what it is – apart from her obvious assets. Something else is at play here.

'Have you always painted?' he asks.

'Forever. My parents gave me some watercolours one Christmas, I think I was about four at the time. Apparently, I created numerous abstracts, which obviously meant something to me but I'm not sure anyone else understood!' Cara laughs.

'Well, no such trouble now. Each of these paintings is beautiful.'

Cara stares at him in astonishment. What a compliment!

'Well, thank you, Oliver Foxley.'

Mesmerised by the emerald green and golden lights dancing in her dark brown eyes, Oliver holds Cara's gaze for a long heartbeat. A darker line defines each iris. There are pools of hidden depths in those eyes and Oliver fears that if he holds her gaze a second longer he will dive straight in and never want to resurface.

'You must have heard that before?' he says, averting his gaze.

'Well, yes. People have shown their appreciation over the years, but…' Flustered, she lets the sentence peter out. For some reason it's important he value her work, but if she voiced that how odd would it sound? She turns away.

God, how he wants to take her in his arms! Oliver shifts on the sofa, wondering when Christo will appear.

'Where's Barnaby?' he asks, spying a dog basket in the corner of the room.

'With my parents, along with the children. They're staying the night as an Easter treat. I'm picking them up tomorrow.' She glances at her watch. 'Or rather today.'

Easter! Oliver makes a mental note to phone Deanna.

'Do they live far?'

'No. On the edge of a village with outstanding views over Mounts Bay.'

'Ah yes, St Michael's Mount. We visited last autumn. A fascinating place.'

'Do you know Cornwall well?' Cara asks.

'Not well. Perhaps you would suggest some places I should see while I'm here. I'd like to get to know the county better.'

Cara laughs. 'Where to begin?'

Oh, how he loves her laugh. It's so spirited and carefree, belying the raw pain that fills her eyes. Why are her eyes so sad? Is it just her look? If so, her children haven't inherited it.

Oliver glances at his watch. It's past two. Aware that Cara has a full day ahead of her, reluctantly he decides it's time to leave. He glances at his friend. Morwenna's head rests on Tas's shoulder, her eyes closed. If only he could hold Cara like that.

'Tas, we should make tracks,' he says.

Tas nods and whispers in Morwenna's ear.

'So soon?' she says, opening her eyes.

'Hey, baby, don't you fret. We'll see each other again. In any case, you've promised me a midnight swim. I'm going to hold you to that!'

Morwenna smiles and gets to her feet.

Oliver, too, rises and collects the empty mugs. Out of practice at seeing a man clearing up in her

273

home, Cara watches as he moves round the room. His easy, athletic movements speak to something deep within and, involuntarily, a shiver runs through her body.

'I can give you a lift back to the car park,' Morwenna says to Tas, 'as long as you don't mind slumming it.'

'Baby, I'd slum it anywhere with you.'

Cara smiles to herself. Tas is *so* full on.

'You haven't seen the inside of Doris yet,' warns Morwenna.

'Doris?'

'Yes. Doris is a Daewoo.'

'Ah well, that explains it,' Tas teases, his eyes glinting mischievously.

As Oliver re-enters the living room he glances at Cara. He doesn't want to leave not knowing when, or if, he will see her again, but what can he do?

'Mo, just chill a bit,' whispers Cara, hugging her friend.

'What's a girl to do?' Morwenna says, and winks.

Cara shrugs. She's done all she can. Morwenna is her own woman.

As Tas steps forward, wrapping Cara in an enormous hug, he almost unbalances her. Cara laughs.

'Thank you for the coffee, oh, fairest of maidens. I hope we see you at one of our performances in the not too distant future.' He turns his attention to Oliver. 'Mr Fox, Doris awaits.'

Oliver drags his eyes away from Cara. 'Who?'

Tas grins at his friend. 'Doris is a Daewoo!'

'What?' Oliver says, confused.

'Step this way, my man, and all will be revealed,' says Tas, following Morwenna from the room.

Oliver deliberates. Would it be OK to hug Cara? Of course it would. It's a courteous thing to do.

But before he gets the chance, Cara says, 'I'll see you off at the door.' She smiles at him.

Parked in front of the bungalow next to Cara's vehicle is Morwenna's car. Through the porch windows they watch as Morwenna opens the doors for Tas to inspect its interior.

'That,' says Cara, 'is Doris.'

Oliver laughs. 'Ah, now all is clear!'

As a silence falls between them Cara thinks, you're nothing like I thought you would be.

'Thank you for your charming company tonight, Cara,' Oliver says softly.

She glances up at him and catches her breath. There's that look again. She could so easily get lost in that look if she weren't careful.

'You're welcome. Yours wasn't so bad either!' she replies flippantly, and then cringes. She didn't mean to say it like that. She doesn't feel flippant at all.

Cara bites her lip, her head in a spin. Truthfully, she isn't sure what his company has been like. At best, their conversations have been stilted; stop-start ever since she tried to make him have that lobster. But, putting aside her awareness of his public image, something about Oliver speaks to her on a deeper level. Maybe that's why she's being so impertinent. Some form of safety mechanism.

'Sorry, I didn't mean to be rude,' she says, looking away.

'You're not being rude, Cara.' Placing his fingertips lightly under her chin, Oliver brings her exquisite face back to his. Looking deep into her eyes, he says, 'I think you are enchanting.'

Oh, how he'd love to kiss those pale lips! But Oliver simply smiles and turns away.

As the car sets off down the track, he wills himself not to look back at Cara standing at the open stable door, but he is powerless to resist. His heart leaps when he sees that she, too, appears unable to let him simply drive away and the eyes that observe him, though still full of sorrow, now ask a question.

Chapter Nineteen

Oliver tosses and turns, a vision of Cara filling his head, and there's an itch he cannot scratch. He switches on the bedside lamp. It's dark outside. The hour before dawn. If he were a smoker he would have a cigarette. Briefly, he wonders if Tania has left any lying about. Throwing back the bed covers, he makes his way to the en-suite and stares at himself in the mirror. In the glare of the bathroom light he appears flushed and there's a dazzled look on his face. Grabbing the sides of the basin, he closes his eyes.

Yes, that would be right. She has dazzled me.

Glancing up at his reflection again, Oliver looks himself squarely in the face. Is this his mid-life crisis? Did he subconsciously choose Tas's Cornish summer tour over that sure-fire blockbuster to specifically put himself in this responsibility-free zone? God knows he's experienced an inexplicable excitement every time he's thought about this forthcoming stint in Cornwall. Is this what happens to middle-aged men in long-term relationships when they suddenly find themselves in the presence of a beautiful free spirit? Oliver groans. But why does she have such sad eyes? They are so full of hurt. Like a bolt from the blue, he realises he just wants to kiss away her pain and make her happy.

And I could make you so very happy, Cara.

Running the cold tap, Oliver splashes water on his face. Perhaps the shock will knock some sense into him.

Why the hell wasn't her husband with her?

He's still angry about that. Perhaps Christo wasn't fishing at all. Maybe he's gone off with someone else. That would explain Cara being on her own and also the hurt. But the young face on the surfboard was not that of a shallow man; it was the face of someone who would recognise her worth.

Why are you so sad, Cara?

Oliver stares at his reflection again. The dazzled look is still there.

'Shit!'

He walks to the door and switches off the bathroom light. Though exhausted, he knows sleep will evade him. Dressing quickly, he grabs his fleece from the back of the door and makes his way down the hall. As he passes Tas's room, deep snores resonate from within. No doubt his friend is enjoying some very pleasant dreams. Oliver opens the front door.

The early morning air is cool and damp, and hits him like a smack in the face. Zipping up his jacket and thrusting his hands deep into his pockets, Oliver makes his way up the drive. He stops at the granite entrance pillars and glances back at the farmhouse. No signs of life at this early hour. As he heads down the track, the pre-dawn light is a murky grey.

Just like the 'grey mist'.

Oliver stops in amazement, realising his constant companion is conspicuous by its absence. He considers this new phenomenon carefully.

The lane is deeply rutted and bordered by stone hedges with the occasional wizened tree. Presently, coming to the end, Oliver sees two five-barred gates leading into separate fields. Tyre tracks in the mud make him smile. Rick is right. Secluded and well out of the way, it makes a perfect spot for lovers' trysts.

Away to the east, a pale, milky haze lightens the sky and Oliver watches as dawn approaches. Breathing in deeply, filling his lungs, he can smell the sea; somewhere, not too far away, he can hear the muffled sound of waves crashing against rock. Opening the right-hand gate and keeping to the edge of the field, he comes to a set of granite steps built into the Cornish hedge. He climbs over. Following a narrow path through gorse and with the sound of the waves growing louder, he emerges out onto the cliff path. Oliver follows it for a hundred yards then takes a track leading onto a rocky promontory. There's no one about. His only companions are the gulls swooping above the cliffs. A cool breeze whips up and Oliver gazes out over an ocean as vast as the sky. There's a big swell today and he looks down at the waves pounding against the rocks far below, sending spumes of spray skywards towards the lone figure standing on the cliff above.

It would be so easy to lose yourself in the elements if you weren't careful.

Oliver steps away from the edge. Selecting a flattish rock, he sits cross-legged and prepares to meditate. At first it's hard to clear his mind – Cara insists on filling it – but as dawn arrives on the Lizard he, at last, finds the meditative state that brings him some form of inner peace.

*

Looking out of the window, Carol watches Cara climb out of her car. There's something about her daughter that makes Carol observe her closely. As Cara opens her arms wide, Sky hurtles headlong into her embrace. The next minute they enter the cottage together, with Sky enthusiastically relaying what he's been doing during the previous twenty-four hours.

'Goodness, Sky. You've packed in as much as if you'd been staying with Grandma and Grandpa for at least a week!' Cara says. Sky grins from ear to ear. 'Hope he hasn't worn you out, Mum.'

'Never! Our grandchildren keep us young, darling.' Carol gives her daughter a hug. 'How was your evening?'

'Good. It was quite a party and the weather was kind, though it turned chilly later.'

Yes, there's a definite shift, thinks Carol. Could it have anything to do with that 'friend' patiently wooing her?

'What did you eat?' Carol asks, wondering how she can bring the conversation around to this line of questioning without appearing too obvious.

'Oh, lobster, crab, steak, spare ribs. Rick had three barbeques on the go and he and Tania put on a good spread. Yes, it was a great evening.'

Carol has the distinct impression her daughter is confirming the fact to herself. Interesting…

'Hi, Mum,' Bethany says, appearing on the stairs.

'Hello, my sweet.' In an instant Cara closes the divide. Lifting Bethany from the step and sweeping her into a hug, she buries her nose in her daughter's clean, blonde hair. Deeply she inhales her scent.

'Mum!' cries Bethany.

'Sorry, Beth, but I've missed you,' she says, placing the young girl on the ground.

'Where's my lovely daughter?' Ken emerges from the kitchen, an apron tied around his waist.

'So, let me guess.' Cara sniffs the air. 'Roast pork?'

'With a twist. Found this great Jamie Oliver recipe on the Internet.' Ken kisses her on the cheek.

With the giving of Easter Eggs, the morning passes in a flurry and lunch is almost over before the conversation turns once more to the party.

'So, how's Tristan these days?' asks Ken.

'Happy. He has a new girlfriend,' Cara says enthusiastically.

'Another young surf chick?'

'No, Dad, not this time. Jane is a school teacher at Truro High.'

Ken's eyebrows shoot skywards. 'That's a first!'

Cara nods. 'She's great company. I like her a lot and Tristan seems a man reborn. I hope they go the distance.'

'It will do him the world of good,' comments Carol.

'And what about that lively sister of his?' asks Ken.

Cara laughs. 'I think Mo's about to cause Tristan a few headaches!'

'Oh, why's that?' asks Carol.

'Well, she met someone last night. Trist asked me to keep an eye on her, but she seems pretty unstoppable.' He told her to look out for herself as well…

Carol sees Cara smile to herself. Definitely interesting!

'Whoever it is needs to be a strong character,' comments Ken.

'I don't think that's going to be a problem.' Cara laughs again. 'Tas is larger than life!'

'That's an unusual name. Is it a nickname?' Ken asks, spooning a second helping of apple tart and ice cream into Sky's empty bowl. He raises a questioning eyebrow at his granddaughter. Bethany nods and passes her bowl.

'I don't know,' says Cara.

'Tasmanian Devil,' says Sky, listening to the adults' banter. Carol stares at her grandson.

'That's right, Sky,' Cara says. 'There is an animal called a Tasmanian Devil but I don't think that's his name.'

'What does he look like?' asks Carol.

'Let's see. Approximately six feet, dark mop of hair, big face, twinkling eyes. A bear of a man.'

It can only be him, thinks Carol. That grandson of hers is as bright as a button.

'And, Mum, you'll never guess what – Sheila will be beside herself – I danced with no other than—' pausing for effect, Cara is unable to contain her smile '—Oliver Foxley!'

Surprised at the lack of response, she glances across the table and is struck by the thoughtful look on her mother's face.

'Oliver Foxley, no less,' Carol says, trying to quell the fear in her heart.

'Yes, and you were right, he *is* better-looking in the flesh.' She blushes as a vision of what Oliver might look like in the flesh unwittingly comes to her. 'He's not a bit how I thought he would be,' she continues swiftly.

'How did you think he would be?' Carol asks carefully.

'Oh, you know, all self-assured, starry and remote, but he wasn't like that at all.' Recalling the look in the blue eyes that watched her all evening and the way he held her as they danced, Cara feels the unmistakable onset of butterflies.

'How was he, then?' Carol asks, noticing her daughter's high colour.

'Well, that's an interesting one.' Cara frowns. 'Kind of lost and adrift...'

Carol recalls Oliver's attractive wife and her strength of character that filled the gallery, and something troublesome nags at her.

'I doubt that a man with his status and money is lost and adrift,' comments Ken.

'Oh, Ken, there's so much more than status and money to make people feel they belong,' Carol says.

'I know. All I'm saying is it sure goes a long way in keeping the wolf from the door.'

Carol considers her husband's comment. He's right, of course. Oliver's life is on a completely different level from theirs but what if he's not happy? What then? Her gaze slides across the table to her daughter. Someone like Cara would be sweet temptation to an unsettled man; so lovely, talented, free-spirited and, seemingly, carefree.

'He may not have any money worries,' Cara continues, 'but I get the impression that all is not as his public image would suggest.'

'Who knows what goes on behind closed doors?' Ken smiles kindly at his daughter. 'We all put on a front for others and, to some extent, we are all actors. But Oliver Foxley, well, he's a consummate actor and unlikely to ever show his true feelings.'

Cara nods, but deep down she's not so sure. The man she met last night wasn't acting.

Silence falls around the table, only broken by Bethany's small voice. 'I like him.'

'Me too,' pipes up Sky. 'He thinks Barnaby has very good eye to mouth cordnashun... or something.'

Cara smiles. Yes, she thinks she likes him too.

Sometimes it takes the innocence of childhood to see through the tangled web we adults weave, thinks Carol.

'Co-ordination, Sky,' Ken gently corrects his grandson. 'Good boy for remembering that difficult word. And he's right. Barnaby does, indeed, have very good eye to mouth co-ordination.'

Lying quietly in the corner of the room, the Labrador thumps his tail at the sound of his name.

*

Oliver finishes his call to Deanna and looks out of the window. Sprouting from the top of the stone wall on the far side of the lawn are three trees, gnarled and twisted.

Stunted. Never given the opportunity to grow into something strong and true.

'You ready, Mr Fox?' Tas calls across the room.

'Coming.' Oliver turns and follows his friend outside, closing the heavy oak door behind him. 'No Tania today?'

'Hangover. No surprise there!' Tas says, unlocking the doors to the Jeep.

Oliver climbs in. A movement in one of the upstairs windows makes him glance at the farmhouse. He's sure it was Tania... watching. As Tas reverses the car into the lane, Oliver wonders whether she really is suffering from a hangover. It crosses his mind that she might not be joining them for lunch because of him. Women! He loves them, but their demands can be so complicated at times.

His early morning meditation put meeting Cara into some kind of perspective. However, the ensuing phone call with Deanna has left him troubled, even though their conversation was perfectly civil. Discussing the family's plans for the day, Deanna informed him of the Easter presents she'd bought for their children. Then, almost as an afterthought, she enquired about his first performance. Reluctant to finish the call, feeling they needed more connection, he continued to chat about nothing in particular but each conversation left him wanting more.

In the end he asked, 'Is there anything you want to say to me, Dee?'

'That's an odd thing to say, Ollie. What sort of thing do you think I would want to say?'

He was shocked then. Had he really voiced his thoughts?

'Oh, I don't know. Just something more?'

'Well, let me think,' she said, as if humouring one of her children. 'There's some post for you when you get back. By the way, Ollie, when are you coming home?'

'I thought I'd head back after tomorrow's performance. Don't bother about supper for me. I'll grab something on the way. I should be home around ten.'

'OK.' A brief silence followed before Deanna said, 'I'll see you tomorrow night, then.'

Late morning, Easter Sunday, and there are more cars on the road. Soon, the Jeep turns down the lane leading to the cove and the traffic drops away. It's another clear day and the sun, though weak, rides high in a cloudless, pale blue sky. As Tas negotiates the last bend and pulls into the café's car park, a flat-calm sea sparkles in welcome. Several families have already set up for a day on the beach, their windbreaks and tents turning the yellow sand into a kaleidoscope of colour. The car park is almost full and Tas expertly navigates the large Jeep into one of the remaining spaces.

'Seems like Rick's got a good business here,' Oliver comments as they walk towards the entrance.

'Hard work, though. Look what time he got home last night and here he is again!'

'But seasonal.'

'Yeah, guess so.' Tas pushes open the door to the café. Immediately, they are engulfed by the busy atmosphere, the noise dipping momentarily as faces turn towards them.

'You never fail, Mr Fox!' Tas grins at his friend. Oliver smiles in resignation.

Three young waitresses move amongst the diners. Rick is behind the bar, talking to one of his assistants. He nods to the two men as they approach.

'You've made it, then,' he says. 'I've reserved a table for you on the decking. Bit more private out there.'

They make their way through the packed café, Tas counting the number of double-takes as Oliver moves through the crowd. He often does this when he's in the actor's company; it's a game he likes to play.

The table is in relative seclusion with a good view of the beach and as Oliver pulls out a chair, he looks towards the far end of the cove. In the far distance, he can see Cara's bungalow perched high on the cliff and his heartbeat quickens at the thought of catching a glimpse of her. He scans the area but there's no sign, and then he remembers she is collecting her children today. If they linger over lunch maybe he will see her when she returns.

Rick arrives with the menus and talks them through the specials. Still to regain his appetite, Oliver realises the last good meal he had was the previous day's breakfast. He decides on a pan-roasted lobster with salad, and smiles, thinking that Cara would finally approve of his choice.

'How about a nice, chilled bottle of white?' Tas suggests.

'Sounds good,' agrees Oliver. 'What would you recommend, Rick?'

'Well, the Chardonnays are always good with lobster, as are the Pinots. I stock a very good Helfrich Pinot Gris Alsace 2008.'

They order a bottle.

Oliver closes his eyes and lets his mind drift. It feels good with the sun on his face. Despite the earlier unsatisfactory conversation with Deanna, he is somewhat soothed.

'It is him, isn't it?' The unmistakable Essex accent cuts through his thoughts. 'Go on, Trace, ask for 'is autograph.'

Oliver takes a deep breath before opening his eyes. Time to be 'on show' again.

The girl has bleached blonde hair and looks in her mid-twenties. She's skinny and wears tight jeans, a tiny T-shirt, bejewelled flip-flops and full-on make-up; the orange foundation smeared thickly over her face.

Why do they do that? She's probably quite pretty without all that muck on her face.

Oliver closes his eyes again, his thumb and forefinger pinching the bridge of his nose.

Perhaps she will go away if I don't acknowledge her.

But the girl persists.

'Excuse me,' she says boldly. 'You are who we think you are, aren't you?'

'Depends who you think he is,' says Tas.

The bleached blonde coolly surveys the man sitting opposite Oliver.

Reluctantly Oliver opens his eyes. She has a pen and postcard at the ready.

'Can I 'ave your autograph?'

'Of course,' he says, slipping seamlessly into his public persona. 'Would you like me to mention anyone in particular?'

'Yeah, me!'

'And you are…?'

The girl giggles. 'Trace. Oh, and Debs, my friend over there,' she adds, as an afterthought.

Oliver glances in the direction of the girl standing on the edge of the decking. A blush spreads across her face. The antithesis of her friend – brunette and plump – she, too, wears the obligatory tight jeans, though, in her case, these are stretched to breaking point. A T-shirt barely contains her ample bosom. Oliver smiles at her.

Big mistake!

As she rushes towards him, he notices Tas unreservedly eyeing her up.

'We love your films,' she says, excitedly. 'You're so great in all of them.'

'Glad you like them,' Oliver says, accepting the pen and postcard from the bottle blonde. A Cornish piskie sitting on a rock stares out at him. In the background, golden sands and an azure sea beckon.

It could be anywhere in the world but the postcard says, 'Greetings from Kennack Sands'. He turns the postcard over and scribbles a message to Trace and her friend before handing the postcard back.

'Oh thanks. That's so great!' gushes Debs.

For a moment he thinks she's going to kiss him but, fortunately, Rick arrives with the wine.

'Hey, girls,' he says, accurately summing up the situation, 'give the guy a break!'

'Oh yeah, sorry.' Trace has the decency to look sheepish. The girls examine the postcard and, giggling, jump down onto the sand.

'Don't you ever get the urge to sign it George Clooney?' asks Rick. Oliver snorts. 'What did you write?'

'To Trace and Debs. Enjoying the view!'

Tas and Rick burst out laughing.

'Well, it's true. It is a great view,' says Oliver with a smirk. Then, more seriously, 'From here I can see right along the cove.'

'It takes some beating, that's for sure,' Rick agrees.

Spinning round in his seat, Tas takes the opportunity to ogle Deb's large bottom. 'What's the name of that rock offshore?' he asks.

'Anvil Rock. Bet you can't guess why,' Rick says with a laugh. He pours a small amount of wine into Oliver's glass.

'Yeah, 'spose it does look anvil-shaped,' agrees Tas. 'Just need some sweaty, muscular, giant blacksmith standing up to his knees in the ocean, like some mighty Poseidon.'

Oliver swills the wine around his mouth. It has a honeyed, floral bouquet and he can detect rich notes of peach, apricot, tropical fruits and spices. It will go very nicely with his lobster. He nods at Rick.

'Is that Cara's place at the far end?' asks Tas.

'Yeah,' Rick says, pouring wine. 'Noticed you two mingling with the local talent last night.'

'That Morwenna, she's a big-hearted girl,' comments Tas appreciatively.

'She's a great character,' says Rick, placing the bottle on the table. 'And as for Cara, well…'

Detecting a softness in the Australian's voice, Oliver shields his eyes against the sun and glances up at the man. There's a faraway look on Rick's face as he stares at the bungalow perched on the cliff.

'Still can't come to terms with it,' Rick says, shaking his head. 'None of us can. It sent shockwaves through the community.'

'Come to terms with what?' asks Tas, taking a gulp of wine.

Blood pounds loudly in Oliver's head. Carefully, he places his glass on the table. 'What happened?' he asks slowly.

Rick pulls out a chair. Turning it round, he sits astride it.

'It was a couple of years ago. They were a great couple, so sunny natured. Christo was a brilliant guy to be around. A full-on lover of life and a gifted surfer, too. Never far from the water.' Rick pauses before continuing. 'Anyway, they were always in here with that little family of theirs. When I first arrived and opened the café they went out of their way to make me feel real welcome. It was Christo and Cara who suggested live music here. It was a great idea. In fact, Morwenna and Tristan were gigging here that Saturday night and everyone was in high spirits. It was a brilliant evening and Christo seemed fine. The first I knew something was wrong was when the air ambulance landed on the beach early the next morning and whisked him away to Treliske. We never saw him again.'

'Blimey! What happened?' asks Tas.

'Brain tumour. Aggressive type. Poor guy was dead within two weeks, leaving that lovely girl to bring up their young family on her own.'

An iron fist tightens around Oliver's heart.

No wonder you have such sorrow in your eyes.

He fights an overwhelming urge to abandon lunch and go and find her right now, to hold her safe in his arms, to comfort and soothe her and tell her everything will be all right. That he will make everything all right.

'What a shit deal,' says Tas.

'Yeah, definitely. But she's one helluva girl,' says Rick with feeling. 'So strong. Christo would be mighty proud of the way she's bringing up those kids and how she's coped with everything. Never shown any signs of caving in, at least not in public, but each time I see her I just want to scoop her up and take care of her. I mean, she's so damn gorgeous.'

Not just me, then.

'And she's a talented artist too,' continues Rick. 'Hasn't lost that.'

One of the young waitresses approaches. 'Lobster with orange and basil,' she announces, breaking the subdued atmosphere around the table.

Oliver nods and the girl places the plate in front of him before turning to Tas.

'And that must be my Mediterranean chicken with chorizo?' says Tas, winking at her. She hands him his plate, smiling widely.

'I'll catch you later,' Rick says, rising from the chair. 'Melanie, here, will look after you but let me know if there's anything else you want.'

Chapter Twenty

Apart from the hall light, the house is in darkness. Oliver turns the key quietly in the lock. The distant sound of a television carries along the hallway. Dropping his bag at the base of the stairs, he tosses his keys into the bowl on the hallway table and makes his way towards the TV room. Deanna is curled up on the couch, her eyes closed. Oliver hesitates. He studies her for a moment, then walks across the room and kisses her gently on the forehead.

'Hello, sleepyhead.'

Deanna opens her eyes and sits up. 'I must have dropped off. What time is it?'

'Midnight. You needn't have waited up.'

'I thought you'd be home earlier. Was the traffic bad?'

'Easter Monday and one long queue out of Cornwall.'

'Poor you. Do you want a drink?'

Would that help? He has spent a second night tossing and turning, thinking of Cara.

'Perhaps a whisky.'

Deanna rises from the couch and kisses her husband lightly on the lips. 'It's good to have you back, Ollie.'

'It's good to be back,' he says automatically.

He watches her leave the room before sinking onto the couch. He's home, so why does he feel so detached? He takes a long look around, observing the room as if for the first time. It's stylish and perfectly colour co-ordinated. Everything matches; from the curtains to the cushions, to the subtle coloured paintwork a few shades lighter than the carpet. Even the numerous photo frames adorning the mantelpiece are in perfect harmony. A set designer's dream of an affluent, middle-class home; in sharp contrast to The Lookout's simple, white-panelled living room. With sudden shocking insight, Oliver realises this is definitely Deanna's territory. Although there are signs of the children, very little of his character is evident.

Deanna returns with a tumbler of whisky, the ice cubes clinking against the side of the glass as she places it on a side table. Picking up the remote control, she switches off the television and sits in the chair opposite her husband.

'So how was the performance this afternoon?' she asks.

'Good. A full audience.'

'And the cast? Have you worked with any of them before?'

'No. They're a mixed bunch but we seem to get along OK,' Oliver says.

'Tas always likes to shake things up,' she says, stifling a yawn. 'Well, I'm off to bed. Don't be long, Ollie. You look tired.'

Exhausted, more like!

'I just want to check a couple of things,' Oliver responds. 'I'll try not to disturb you.'

As Deanna walks to the door, she says over her shoulder, 'There's post for you in the study, but I'm sure it can wait until morning.'

Oliver stretches out his legs. Locking his fingers behind his head, he leans back and surveys the room again. The only thing giving away that he lives here is his image in several of the photos. Picking up the glass, he drains the whisky in one and swiftly exits the room. As soon as he enters his study he feels at home. This is his domain; masculine, but not overtly so. Looking critically around the space, he sees the only evidence of his wife is her choice of carpet and window dressing. He remembers how she demanded strong-coloured tartan curtains to pick out the dark blue of the carpet. As it was of little consequence to him what fabric hung at the windows he readily accommodated her wishes, but now he wonders if he rolled over too easily.

Is this how we've rubbed along all these years?

He glances up at Cara's painting above the mantelpiece and feels a strange yearning for something he can't put his finger on; something unknown. He stares at the canvas for several minutes, absorbing Cara's brushstrokes, and some of the passion with which she painted *The Minack* rubs off. But now she isn't just some random artist. She has a face, a voice and a body... all beautiful. Cara Penhaligon is all woman to him. Oliver shakes his head.

What's happening to me? Could it be...?

He simply cannot let that happen.

Neatly stacked on his desk are several unopened envelopes and Oliver debates whether to leave them until the morning, as Deanna suggested.

No, why should I unquestioningly follow her lead?

The thought takes him by surprise. Why is he casting Deanna in the role of villainess? She has done nothing wrong. He tries to convince himself that the journey, on top of two sleepless nights, has rendered him exhausted and feeling less than charitable. Oliver picks up the envelopes and rifles through them. Mainly bills... but what's this? Instantly, he recognises the handwriting. Why didn't he take Deanna's advice and leave the post until morning? Now he's *got* to open it. There's no chance of sleep, knowing it's sitting on his desk.

Oliver opens the top drawer and extracts a letter opener. Sliding the blade beneath the flap, he opens the envelope in one clean sweep. With mounting apprehension, he removes a sheet of blue notepaper. Her manic characters leap off the page, effectively shattering the calm of his study.

Oliver, YOU PROMISED, but you haven't kept your promise.

PHONE ME or I WILL HAVE TO INTRODUCE MYSELF to that attractive wife of yours.

Next time I will knock on the door (not just deliver to your letterbox) and won't your WIFE AND I HAVE A LOT TO TALK ABOUT! I expect your call.

My undying love, Sylvie xxxx

Oliver's mouth turns dry. He picks up the envelope again. No stamp. So she did hand deliver it!
'Fuck!'
Running a hand through his hair, once again he wonders how secure the house is. Changing the number of the landline has achieved nothing. She knows where he lives! How? Did she find out on Holy Isle? Oliver walks from room to room, checking the windows and making sure all external doors are locked. She's gone to the next level now. There's no denying it, she's deranged and who knows what she's

capable of? With everything else going on he has not given Sylvie any thought since her phone call. How easily she has slipped his mind.

I should have phoned. If she speaks to Deanna, God only knows where that will lead!

Oliver glances at his watch. It's way past midnight. Too late to phone her now, although she's probably awake plotting her next move. The thought makes him break into a cold sweat.

What the hell am I going to do?

He can't involve the police. What would that do to his reputation? And if the press ever got a whiff of what went on at the retreat, well… it didn't bear thinking about. They would crucify him and drag his family through the mud. No, he is just going to have to handle this himself. He will phone her tomorrow and play her at her own game.

Satisfied the house is secure, Oliver picks up his bag and silently makes his way upstairs. He walks past the children's closed doors to the master bedroom at the far end but, before entering, turns and looks down the hall. Again, he is struck by how little of him is here. Has he been absent that long? As Oliver opens the bedroom door, a feeling of disconnectedness threatens to overwhelm him. He places his bag on the floor and makes his way to the en-suite. Switching on the bathroom light, he closes the door quietly behind him and walks to the basins.

Averting his gaze from the mirror, unwilling to see what his reflection might reveal, he quickly washes and cleans his teeth. Then, discarding his clothes in the laundry basket, he walks from the room and climbs into bed.

For a long while Oliver stares up at the ceiling, unseeing. He's far away in a simply furnished bungalow perched high on a cliff, and Cara's light fills his soul. Though desperate for sleep, he knows a third sleepless night beckons.

Turning onto his side, he reaches for his wife. 'Dee,' he whispers, hoping that by making love to her he will reconnect.

'Not now, Ollie,' Deanna mumbles, as she surfaces from deep sleep and feels her husband's growing need.

Oliver freezes. He feels so far removed from this life. He turns away and, after what seems like hours, falls into a fitful sleep where he is visited by Cara's golden light, Deanna's cool strength and Sylvie's dark energy.

*

It's mid-morning when Oliver eventually comes to. The bed beside him is empty; the sheets cold. He feels exhausted and a raging headache instantly takes hold. Light floods in through a gap in the curtains but he just wants to block out the day. As the 'grey mist' claims its victim once again, Oliver acknowledges his old adversary.

'So where have you been these past few days?' he growls.

Suddenly his eyes fly open, recalling the previous evening's unwanted discovery.

Shit! Sylvie!

He's got to deal with her... and the sooner, the better.

He will call her, but before he does he will go for a run. He can't afford to be anything less than 'on the ball' and, maybe, fresh air will clear his headache. Oliver throws back the covers and quickly gets dressed.

Pausing at the top of the stairs he listens for a moment, the sounds of family giving him some sense of belonging. He descends the stairs and stops at the open door to the TV room. His youngest sons are engrossed in the latest Xbox game. Fiercely competitive, Sebastian sits forward, completely absorbed.

'Hello, boys,' says Oliver.

Jamie looks up and smiles.

'Hi, Dad,' says Sebastian, allowing Oliver's presence to draw him away from the action for a nanosecond.

'How long are you here?' asks Jamie.

'Three days.'

'Will you come cycling with me?'

'Sure,' agrees Oliver.

'Oh, come on, Jamie, concentrate!' Sebastian's irritated voice cuts into their conversation. Pulling a wry face, Jamie returns to the battle.

'Hi, Dad. Good to see you.' His eldest son stands in the kitchen doorway, a half-eaten slice of toast in his hand.

'Hi, Charlie. What are you up to today?'

'Off to Nathan's and I'm late. Said I'd meet him at ten thirty.'

Oliver's eyes follow his son as he walks down the hallway. The lad is almost as tall as he is and each day he matures that little bit more. Suddenly, a vision of life at home without Samantha and Charlie hits Oliver squarely between the eyes, leaving him feeling even more adrift. He enters the kitchen.

'Hi, Sammy.' He kisses his daughter affectionately on the cheek.

'Hi, Dad.' Her lips brush his cheek in return but, immediately, she returns to her magazine.

'I've put a wash on for you, Ollie,' says Deanna, appearing at the utility-room door. 'Do you want a cooked breakfast?'

'No, just toast. Thought I'd go for a run.' He pops two slices of bread into the toaster.

'Dad, will you persuade Mum for me?' asks Samantha.

'Persuade Mum of what?' Oliver glances at his daughter. She is so like a young Deanna and his heart swells with love and pride.

'Oh, Sammy is being ridiculous,' says Deanna in a no-nonsense voice. 'She thinks she wants a tattoo!'

'I don't think I want one, I *know* I want one!' Samantha says indignantly. 'All the girls at school are having them. What do you think, Dad?'

'There's no point asking him,' says Deanna dismissively. 'You know he lets you do whatever you want.'

Samantha smiles sweetly at Oliver.

'Not anything, Deanna,' Oliver says, bristling. 'There has to be a valid reason for Sammy's actions.' He turns his attention to his daughter. 'Where do you want one? Not your tummy, I hope. Think how it will stretch when you're pregnant.'

'Da-ad!' Samantha exclaims, embarrassed.

'I don't know why you're even humouring her. It's simply not going to happen,' Deanna says with finality.

Samantha groans.

Oliver stares at his wife. Whatever happened to open discussion? Ignoring Deanna, he asks again, 'Where, Sammy?'

Samantha studies Oliver thoughtfully. 'Well, Rosie's got one at the top of her back, which looks really cool.'

'Not cool when you're wearing a low-backed evening dress,' comments Deanna.

'And when am I ever likely to wear one of those?' snaps Samantha.

'Maybe not often now,' Oliver says gently, 'but in a year or two I'm sure you will have every reason to. Then, you might curse the day you had it done. Why not consider somewhere less obvious?'

'Oliver, don't encourage her.' Deanna's reprimanding voice rings out strong and clear.

Startled, Samantha looks at her parents. Closing the magazine, she gets up from the table and says, 'I think I'll give it a bit more thought.' Quickly she makes her exit.

Oliver and Deanna stare at each other, neither saying a word. The air crackles with tension and both jump as the toaster pops.

'Don't encourage her,' Deanna says, turning away to stack the dishwasher.

Oliver is rankled. It's as if he's viewing everything through different eyes today. 'You can't tell a seventeen-year-old not to do something and simply expect her to comply,' he says, extracting butter from the fridge.

'Do you think I don't know that?'

'Well, obviously not, judging by your handling of the situation.'

Deanna straightens up. 'Oliver, I have been handling the situation for years for *all* your children while you've been away playing at life.'

Oliver puts down the butter knife and stares at his wife's back. 'Is that what you think I do, Deanna?' he says, his voice dangerously low. 'Play at life?'

Hearing his tone, Deanna turns towards him and her heart stalls. 'Well, not exactly play…'

'Please enlighten me. What exactly do you think it is I do for you and this family?'

'Oh, Ollie, I know what you do for *our* family,' she says. 'It's just… at times I feel it's only me bringing up the children.'

Controlling his anger, Oliver considers his wife's words. She is so independent. Most of the time she treats him as merely an extension of those children he has given her, so, yes, she probably doesn't see him as sharing the responsibility. And then he thinks of Cara bringing up her children single-handedly not through choice, and his anger spills over. How dare Deanna complain about bringing up a family on her own? His commitment to his children is total. He has supported them all – including her – from the start.

'Deanna, have you any idea how many times I've not wanted to be away from you all?' Oliver seethes with anger but keeps his voice steady. 'However, in order to keep this family going to your exacting standards I have had to earn a certain level of money, which has entailed, as you well know, work that takes me away.'

Deanna blinks rapidly. Her exacting standards?

'Well, do you?' Oliver demands.

Deanna falters, witnessing a side to her husband she has rarely seen, and then only on screen.

'Ollie, of course I do. It's just sometimes I feel the weight of responsibility.'

'And you think I don't?' He's not going to let it go that easily.

'Well, you can escape into acting,' she says, flinching at the emotion that passes across his face. Digging deep, she finds the iron will that always carries her through and has never failed her yet. In a strong, clear voice she says, 'I don't have the luxury of dipping in and out of family life.'

Oliver glares at his wife, the silence weighing heavily between them. In a couple of sentences she has diminished his career to some escapist dream, suggested his responsibility as a parent is lacking and his time away from the family something over which he has a choice.

'Is this what you've always thought or is this something that has just occurred to you?' His voice is as cold as ice.

Deanna catches her breath as a frisson of fear courses through her body. Turning away, she looks out over the lawns and down to the lake. There's that flash again. What is it?

'Deanna, do *not* turn away from me.' Oliver's angry voice makes her turn back and the look on his face shocks her to the core. 'This is something we need to talk about.'

This is an Oliver she does not know. How should she handle this man?

'Ollie, I just find it overwhelming at times,' she says, hitting just the right vulnerable tone.

Despite his anger, Oliver's resolve weakens. It must be hard at times and what she says is true. Because of his career, he has been absent on many occasions during their marriage.

Deanna watches the hard set of her husband's jaw soften and lets out a silent breath. That was tricky. Now all she has to do is cement the slight advantage she has. Conscious that she refused his advances last night, she takes a step towards Oliver and kisses him deeply.

'You don't have to go running just yet, do you?' she says, looking up at him with big doe-eyes.

Coolly, Oliver considers his attractive wife. He still has an urgent need to exorcise the intense emotions swirling around his body ever since first setting eyes on Cara, and it wouldn't hurt to remind Deanna just how good her situation is.

'No, Deanna, I don't.'

*

One hour later, Oliver swings his legs out of bed for the second time that morning. He's still smarting from Deanna's accusations; nevertheless, the sex has gone some way to exonerate the deep hurt her words have inflicted. And that torturous itch has been scratched.

Deanna props herself on her elbows and watches her husband walk naked to the en-suite. He looks mighty fine and she cannot believe the lovemaking that has just taken place. It hasn't been this good for a while. In fact, it stirred memories of the incredible excitement they experienced when first together. She feels dazed and stunningly replete, and a satisfied smile settles on her lips. She knows her words angered him but maybe, in some perverse way, those very words aroused in him the drama that Oliver finds so lacking in his day-to-day existence. Rolling onto her back, Deanna stretches contentedly and presses her thighs together. She can still feel him there. Uncharacteristically, she does not immediately focus on her rigorous daily schedule but, instead, thinks back over their years together.

Her husband is a complex man. She doesn't fully understand him, but she has lived with him long enough to recognise his demons. At first, during the early days of their relationship, when Oliver could no longer hide his black moods from her, she was bewildered and believed it to be something she had caused. It took her a while to recognise the role she would have to play but once she understood what was needed, as with all things she undertakes, Deanna became a master at it. Concentrating hard on perfecting her strength and independence, she conveniently and neatly packaged his days locked away with only his dark thoughts for company as the 'grey mist'. When the children came along, as soon as they were old enough to understand, she explained their father's depression was an additional and necessary element to his character that enabled him to be a successful actor, and not something for them to be unduly concerned about. And it was true. From the very start of his chosen profession Oliver was an exceptional actor, capable of plumbing depths of emotion that few actors could even contemplate. Deanna knows this is due, in no small part, to his subtle understanding of the human psyche. They ingrained into the children that the 'grey mist' was a family secret; one to be kept hidden from their friends and the wider world.

Where the press were concerned, his mental instability proved tricky when they started clamouring for more information about Oliver Foxley, the rising star. She remembers an occasion when he appeared in that controversial West End musical and first came to the critics' attention. The press soon discovered where they lived and they were hounded by photographers outside their flat for days on end. She had to pretend that Oliver wasn't there while he remained hidden in the spare room. Getting him to and from the theatre was a feat of precision engineering! Eventually, the paparazzi gave up and lost interest in that particular story.

Over the intervening years they faced a number of obstacles that could have been their undoing but, working together, they pulled it off, discovering successful strategies by which to present their lives in an acceptable way to Oliver's adoring fans. She smiles smugly, knowing they managed to fool the press, too. Not one reporter is aware of Oliver's mental health struggles. However, the toll on her husband is extreme. Exhausted from the energy necessary to maintain a happy and professional façade in public, he continues to retreat from the world for days at a time. Deanna prides herself on her inner strength, knowing that if she were made of lesser stuff she would not have been able to cope.

Emerging from the en-suite, Oliver is surprised to find Deanna still lying on the bed. Post-sex, her hair is dishevelled and there's a wanton look on her face. He hasn't seen her looking this relaxed for a long time, in fact, not since the very first heady days of their relationship. Meeting her gaze, he smiles slowly, his eyes trailing over her body, taking in the small but perfectly formed breasts, her flat stomach and long, elegant legs. He walks to the bed and kisses his wife hard on the mouth. Immediately she responds.

'Deanna, I *am* going for that run,' Oliver says, resisting.

'Maybe later, then?' she suggests, her eyes full of promise.

He laughs softly. 'Yes, later.' Tenderly, he cups her face in his hand. 'You know, wife, you are one attractive woman.'

'And you, husband,' she says, without missing a beat, 'are one fine specimen of a man.'

He dresses quickly and walks to the door. Glancing back, Oliver briefly considers abandoning his run to spend more time with this unusually accommodating version of his wife. Then he remembers Sylvie.

'Hold that thought,' he says, exiting the room.

As he passes Samantha's closed door he hears his daughter chatting on her mobile. When he reaches the TV room Sebastian and Jamie are still in combat, but this time both boys are so engrossed in the game that neither looks up as he walks by. Oliver enters his study. Pulling open the top drawer of the desk, he extracts his mobile phone and National Trust card, and then slips out of the French doors onto the stone terrace. He breathes in deeply. It's different air here. Suddenly he longs to smell the sea. Oliver squints up at the sky. Thick cloud cover, but a weak sun is trying to break through. He glances across the manicured lawns down to the woods. It doesn't feel the same, knowing Sylvie has been here. She could be lurking anywhere. Other than getting a guard dog, which Deanna won't entertain, what else can he do to make his family less vulnerable? He could employ a security guard but Deanna would think that totally unnecessary and, anyway, it would only make her question why he was going to such lengths. No, he will just have to deal with Sylvie himself. Keep her sweet. Fingering the phone in his pocket, Oliver steps down onto the lawn. He will go to the tower. There's good reception there.

Sylvie focuses her binoculars on Oliver. He's wearing a tracksuit and she wonders if he's going to the building located behind the house. She has already checked it out – a large oak-framed affair housing a gym, sauna and swimming pool. But Oliver strides across the lawn directly towards her. Even though camouflaged behind a large rhododendron, Sylvie shrinks further into its foliage. He's getting so close and she's about to turn away when Oliver suddenly changes direction and heads towards a gate in the far corner of the garden. Quickly scanning the house to see if anyone else is about to join him, Sylvie makes her way as silently as possible through the trees, keeping Oliver in sight. There's something very relaxed about him as he athletically covers the ground and Sylvie clicks her tongue in annoyance. Why should he be so content and at ease with the world when she is so desperate for him? Coming to an uneven section of ground, she has to concentrate on several roots that threaten to trip her and when she looks up again, Oliver is nowhere to be seen. Sylvie lets out a small angry sound. Cutting through the woods, she heads up an incline and is about to emerge from the cover of the trees when she spots him not far ahead, stepping up onto the track. Again, Sylvie shrinks back.

Oliver can't shake off the feeling he's being watched. A run will do him good. He peers in both directions but there's not a soul about. He looks deeper into the forest bordering both sides of the track. The trees grow tightly packed, daylight barely penetrating the canopy, and an eerie stillness pervades the air. So many places to hide. The hairs on Oliver's neck stand erect. All at once there's movement and the sound of snapping branches.

With his senses already on high alert, Oliver attempts to still his racing heart.

Without warning, ten yards ahead, a roe deer leaps out of the undergrowth and onto the track; an older buck with three-point antlers. It turns and stares at the man standing stock still in the middle of the path. Oliver holds his breath. It's magnificent! Shafts of sunlight filter through the trees and alight along its back, turning the reddish body to a burnished gold. Ears pricked, the deer assesses with intelligent eyes the level of threat the human poses. For a brief heartbeat, time stands still as man and beast face each other – the hunter and the prey – and an acknowledgement of the strength and magnificence of the other passes between them. Then the moment is gone. With a flick of its ear the buck turns and leaps away into the foliage on the other side of the track. Oliver lets out a long, silent breath.

Footpaths and bridleways crisscross this particular area of the Surrey Hills. Oliver decides to run a ten-mile circular woodland route, hoping that by the time he reaches the tower – approximately the halfway point – his body will be flooded with endorphins, which will help him handle Sylvie more effectively. Setting off at a comfortable jog, he heads in a northerly direction away from the house.

As Oliver disappears round the bend, Sylvie cautiously steps up onto the track. Spooked by the sudden appearance of the deer, she wonders what else is lurking in the woods. Is it safe to continue sleeping in the car? Turning to her present predicament, she considers what she should do. She can't possibly keep up with him. She turns in the opposite direction and walks back to her car, deep in thought and mulling over her options. She is beyond frustrated at his lack of contact. If he doesn't phone soon she *will* take it to the next level. That smug wife of his needs to have that self-satisfied look wiped right off her face.

Sylvie climbs in her car. From the passenger footwell, she picks up a carrier bag and takes out a sandwich and a carton of juice. She will eat her lunch and wait for Oliver to return. Then she will confront him.

Oliver works up a sweat, the blood coursing through his veins and his heart pounding as he steadily increases his pace along the sandy heathland tracks. How lucky they are to have this National-Trust-owned, historic estate of arboretums and rhododendron woods right on the doorstep. Without slowing, Oliver picks up another track and heads west, following a bridle path leading to the high, sandy, open heath of Duke's Warren. The track takes him through a level landscape of heather, bracken, bilberry, gorse, pine and birch. When reaching steeper parts, he tests his stamina and stretches his muscles to the limit. This is good. Apart from meditation, strenuous exercise is what keeps the 'grey mist' in check.

Presently, the trees start to thin. As he approaches the summit of Leith Hill, Oliver puts in a burst of speed, making short work of the final, sharp incline. Ahead of him, crowning the highest point in south-east England and completely dominating the area, stands the sixty-five-feet-high Georgian folly built in the style of a gothic tower from the Middle Ages. Catching his breath, Oliver walks to its base. The sweeping views from the treeless summit never fail to amaze. Across a landscape of outstanding natural beauty, fourteen counties can be seen. The spectacular views made it a popular spot for Victorian picnics, with large numbers of day-trippers ferried by horse and carriage to feast around the tower. Known as Prospect House, and erected in 1765 by the eccentric Richard Hull of Leith Hill Place, whose body rests beneath it, the tower was built to increase the height of Leith Hill to over a thousand feet above sea level.

Two chattering horse riders suddenly appear and circle the tower before heading along a path through the woods. Some distance away to the west, a man and a woman emerge from the pine trees along the Greensand Way, and two accompanying cocker spaniels busily work their way through the foliage.

Oliver enters the tower. Showing his National Trust card to the attendant, he climbs the narrow, internal, spiral stairway. Seventy-four steps later, he emerges out onto the top. Good. He is alone. When he makes this call he doesn't want any distractions.

The clouds have cleared and Oliver absorbs the spectacular, panoramic views. Stalling for time, he looks through the fixed telescope and pans the vista, circling 360 degrees. To the north is Heathrow Airport, the Wembley Arch, the London Eye, St Paul's Cathedral and Canary Wharf and he smiles tenderly as he remembers Jamie's excitement at spying the clock face of Big Ben in Westminster for the first time. Panning around to the east, he spies the Reigate masts and, working in a southerly direction, the Sussex Weald, the South Downs and, through the Shoreham Gap, a glimpse of the English Channel. But what holds his attention the most is the fascinating sight of aircraft slowly rising above the skyline far below at nearby Gatwick Airport.

He can't put it off any longer. Taking out his mobile, Oliver taps the phone against his forehead and takes a deep breath.

When her mobile rings, Sylvie is noisily sucking orange juice through a straw, planning her next move. The sound is so unexpected that she chokes, spluttering juice down her front.

'Yes,' she says angrily, brushing the liquid off her sweatshirt.

'Sylvie?'

She catches her breath. There's no mistaking that voice. 'You got my note.'

'I did,' Oliver replies. 'Why are you coming to the house? I said I would phone.'

'But you haven't.'

'I've been busy but I keep my promises. You can trust me.'

Can she trust him? He's keeping her on a very long leash and she wants it a lot shorter. 'I miss you,' she says.

Silently, Oliver groans. 'Sylvie, you don't know me to miss.'

'Oh, but I do, Oliver. Better than you think.'

There's something deeply threatening to her words.

'I told you I was working away,' he says. 'You're lucky I'm here to have received your note.' Maybe, if she thinks he won't be around it will dissuade her from visiting the house again. 'I'm away for many months.'

Silence.

'Sylvie, are you still there? Did you hear what I said?'

'Yes.'

'I promise I will phone from time to time, but I am very busy,' Oliver says.

'I want to see you.'

'That's not possible, Sylvie.'

'Why?'

'Because I'm not going to be here,' Oliver says evenly, keeping the exasperation from his voice.

'Where will you be?'

'Around. Travelling,' he says vaguely.

'No!' Her mind goes into a tailspin. She can't lose him now. She has to know where he is. Sylvie starts to rock, banging her head against the steering wheel.

Startled by the intensity of her shout, Oliver removes the phone from his ear. Beads of perspiration prick his forehead. It is very quiet at the top of the tower and in the distance he can hear the roar of a plane's engines on the runway.

Replacing the mobile to his ear, he says firmly, 'Yes, Sylvie.'

'I need to see you.' Sylvie stops rocking and stares out of the window, her face set in an ugly mask. 'If I don't see you I will go to the house.'

Fuck!

'Sylvie. As I said, there's no time.' Oliver fights rising panic. 'I'm not around.'

'When will you be around?'

He planned to return to Surrey between performances but, if Sylvie is going to stalk him each time he's back, maybe it would be better for the family if he stayed away. That way she won't be hanging round the house, and if she's not around the house she may forget her threat. 'Not until the autumn.'

'What are you doing that's taking you away for so long?' Sylvie asks. 'Are you filming?'

Oliver relaxes a little at the more normal line of questioning. 'No, it's a play.'

'Where?'

'As I said, around.'

Sylvie frowns. It's obvious he's not going to tell her, but the Internet will.

Oliver waits for a response but none is forthcoming. Once again, he focuses on the magnificent view. This is what he wants in life: something spectacular and dramatic. Not the sordid little game of some unhinged female holding him over a barrel. How has Sylvie managed to infiltrate his life? He's experienced the attention of ardent fans before but never to this extent. If he lets her down gently maybe she will eventually give up, but he knows it's unlikely.

'I promise to phone you, but you do understand that meeting up is simply not possible at this time.'

Sylvie starts rocking again. She will just have to follow him. Best go and fill up with petrol.

'OK.'

Oliver watches as another plane takes off in the distance, powering its way through the clear blue sky. What he'd give to be on board flying out of this situation.

'I'll say goodbye, then.' Oliver ends the call with disquiet. He thinks she has understood, but perhaps he should return to Cornwall today.

No, damn it! Why should she manipulate me? What is it about these women who have me dancing to their merry tunes?

Stunned, Oliver realises he has cast Deanna in the same light as Sylvie; but there's nothing remotely similar about the two women. In the far recesses of his mind a thought occurs and carefully he examines it. Grimly, he acknowledges that however Deanna dresses it up she does manipulate him. Even their lovemaking this morning was instigated by her. When he needed her last night she simply rebuked him. And then he remembers her cruel words that shattered his sense of self-worth and effectively stripped him of his place within the family. Bile rises as Oliver's anger takes hold once again.

What do they say about love? That love and hate are intimately linked within the human brain and there really is a fine line.

He shakes his head sadly. Maybe it would be a good idea to cut short his stay in Surrey.

Taking one last look at the stunning view, Oliver makes the decision to go cycling with Jamie that afternoon and head back to Cornwall early the following morning.

Chapter Twenty-One

Squeezing liquid soap into the stream of water, Cara watches the bubbles form. It's mesmerising the way they expand and take over the surface of the bath water and her artist's eye studies the shapes formed between. She's so engrossed that she doesn't hear the sound of knocking.

'Mum! There's a man at the door.' Sky stands in the bathroom doorway.

'What? Oh!' Cara turns off the taps. Checking the water temperature, she says, 'Undress and hop in, Sky. I'll be back in a minute.'

The boy peels off his clothes in one swift action and Cara laughs. 'Well, that's one way!'

Sky grins and clambers over the side of the bath.

As Cara walks into the living room, through the bay window she sees Bethany at the stable door talking to Greg.

'Hope I'm not disturbing anything,' Greg says, as Cara enters the porch behind her daughter. 'I thought you'd like to learn my latest thoughts with the entries for Threadneedle.'

Excitement grabs at her. This is for real!

Greg steps into the porch. Unzipping his jacket, he hangs it on a coat hook and follows Cara and

Bethany into the living room. They can hear Sky singing at the top of his voice.

'I won't be a minute,' Cara says to Greg. 'Have a seat.'

Picking up a jumper lying on the arm of the sofa, she cringes at how messy the bungalow is but then pulls herself up short. Too bad. If he just rocks up without warning, what can he expect? She walks to the bathroom and deposits the jumper in the linen basket.

'You OK in here for a bit, Sky?' The boy stops singing and nods. 'Just shout when you're ready to get out.'

'OK.' Gathering bubbles into mountains, Sky blows them across the surface of the bathwater like clouds before a big wind.

Cara walks back to the living room. 'Can I get you a drink, Greg?'

'No, thanks,' he replies. 'I only called by on the off-chance you'd be here. I can't stay too long.' She sits down in the chair opposite him. 'You'll be pleased to know that several paintings were of a good enough standard.' A muscle twitches in his cheek at the little white lie; *all* passed his critical assessment. 'I've selected the maximum number to put forward to the selectors: *Lanyon Quoit at Night, The Cove at Sunset, Porthcurno Early Morning, Rainbow over*

Rinsey Head; Herons on the Helford and Marazion Moon.'

Cara studies Greg. He doesn't look comfortable and seems out of place.

'What do you think?' Greg asks, almost as an afterthought.

'Well, OK. Yes, I suppose.' She winces. How flaky she must sound to him. 'I mean, I was pretty pleased with the way they turned out.'

'Pretty pleased?' Greg repeats incredulously. 'As I've said before, Cara, you are one cool customer.'

Cara frowns. She's still unsure what he means.

The low afternoon light plays tricks and as the shadows fall across Greg's face, he appears to Cara both attractive and dangerous. She can well imagine him as a pirate with a gold earring in one ear; ruthless with women and, yet, at the same time, sophisticated, charming and welcome in the highest echelons of society. He really confuses her.

'So, what I propose is this,' Greg says authoritatively. 'We go through the registration now and submit your work online for pre-selection. You will, of course, have to ensure the canvases are unavailable until we know the outcome of the prize.'

'Register now?'

'No time like the present.'

Cara thinks quickly. To do the online registration will mean using the computer – in her bedroom.

Does she want him in there? It was difficult enough allowing him in her studio.

'Is there a problem, Cara?'

'No problem.'

Greg looks at his watch.

'The computer is through here,' says Cara, 'but you'll have to excuse the mess. I wasn't expecting visitors.'

As Greg follows Cara from the room, Bethany glances up from her Kindle and thoughtfully observes the American.

Sky's singing carries along the hallway and Cara pauses. Opening the bathroom door a fraction, she puts her head round the corner. 'Do you want more hot water, Sky?'

The boy turns in the bath, bubbles piled high upon his head, and nods. Cara enters the room, pushing the door to behind her. Smoothly, Greg puts out a foot, successfully preventing the door from fully closing, and silently observes the domestic scene unfold.

'Have you washed behind your ears?' Cara asks, leaning over the bath and turning on the hot tap.

'Yes.' Innocent brown eyes look up at her.

'Sk-y-y?' She draws out his name into a question.

'Maybe not a lot.'

Squeezing shower gel onto a sponge, she sets about washing her son. As Greg watches this small, intimate act, he swallows hard.

'There you go.' Cara turns off the tap and kisses Sky on the nose. 'I'll come and dry you in ten minutes.'

Quickly, Greg steps away from the door. As Cara emerges into the hallway, he smiles at her. Without saying a word, he follows her to her bedroom, instantly noticing the unmade bed, the clothes strewn over a chair and a couple of towels dumped on the floor. Wet, no doubt!

Cara's eyes critically sweep the room. Inwardly, she groans. Rushing to the bed, she pulls the duvet straight.

'Don't worry on my behalf,' he says smoothly.

'I had no idea anyone would be coming in here,' she says apologetically.

'As I said, don't worry.' Greg maintains a smoothness honed over many years. 'Now, let's log on.' He inclines his head towards the computer perched on a small table by the French doors.

The computer takes an age to fire up and Cara is very aware of him standing behind her. Feeling panicked, she wonders if he has this effect on her because of his superior knowledge of art. She's hugely flattered that someone like him should see merit in her creativity. She also has great respect for him as a first-rate art critic.

At last the screen flickers into life. Lightly resting his hand on Cara's shoulder, Greg instructs her to sign on to the Threadneedle Prize website. Twenty minutes later she has completed the registration.

'Well, that wasn't too painful, was it?' Greg says, his fingers still lingering on her collarbone.

Cara logs out. Swivelling in the chair, she dislodges his hand.

'Now all we have to do is await the decision,' he says, checking his watch. His wife will be wondering where he is.

On the way back to the living room, Cara looks in on her son.

Sky stands in the centre of the bathroom wrapped in a large towel. 'The water went cold,' he explains.

'Sorry. It took longer than I thought,' she says. 'Don't forget to pull out the plug.'

'Goodbye, Sky,' says Greg behind her. 'Perhaps we can walk the dogs together one day?'

Sky nods enthusiastically. 'Barnaby would like that.'

'Milo too.' Greg smiles at the lad before following Cara into the living room.

'Beth, it's not good for you to read in the dark,' Cara says, switching on the light.

Still studiously reading at the table, Bethany looks up in surprise. 'Sorry, Mum. I didn't notice.'

'What are you reading?' Greg asks.

'Harry Potter.'

He tries to recall anything about the wizard but fails miserably. 'Good, is it?'

'Yes.' The young girl looks at him with intelligent, kind eyes, waiting for him to say something more. Greg remains silent. 'It's the *Order of the Phoenix*.'

'Ah,' he says, floundering.

'I'll get your jacket,' says Cara, swiftly turning away to hide the smile on her face. Greg seems as thrown by her daughter as Cara is by him.

'Goodbye, Beth,' Greg says, quickly following Cara out into the hallway.

When they step out onto the track, the tide is almost fully in.

'Hope summer arrives soon,' Cara says, rubbing her arms against the early evening chill.

'I have to return to the States soon,' says Greg. 'However, when your paintings are selected I will fly back to guide you. Now all we have to do is let the selectors come to the right decision.'

Excitement snatches at Cara again and she smiles.

Suddenly Greg crushes her to his chest. Taking a step back, he looks at her with a gaze so intense that Cara is the first to break eye contact. It's the same look he gave her that day she met him at Rick's, which is doubly disconcerting now that she's met Marietta.

'Now, I really must be going,' he says. Leaning forward, he kisses her lightly on the lips.

Chapter Twenty-Two

Sylvie watches the car nose its way out of the drive. She waits until it disappears round the corner before taking her foot off the clutch. As long as Oliver keeps to the speed limit it shouldn't be too difficult to follow him. Two things make the car easy to pick out. Not only is it a cool Mercedes cabriolet roadster in a distinctive shade of metallic blue, but also it has a personalised number plate – D3 ANA. Sylvie holds back as the Mercedes turns onto the parish road, then she follows. Half an hour later they join the mid-morning motorway traffic. The Mercedes is five cars ahead. Sylvie maintains her distance; her mind focused and her jaw set.

Sliding his hands to a comfortable position on the steering wheel, Oliver enjoys the sensuous feel of the leather. The car is capable of nought to sixty in just over five seconds with a top speed of one hundred and fifty-five miles per hour. His right foot hovers lightly on the accelerator. How he'd love to floor it and leave all this traffic behind. He knows his present to Deanna was extravagant but if ever there's a birthday to celebrate it's a girl's fortieth. They pored over the specifications, not skimping on accessories, and by the time his wife had chosen all the extras it had cost him just shy of fifty thousand pounds. But it's worth every penny. The SLK is a joy to drive. He glances around the cockpit, appreciating the intuitive design that puts everything at his fingertips. Even the sports steering wheel, featuring multi-function buttons, allows him to operate many controls without taking his hands off.

Oliver checks the mirrors before indicating right and pulling out into the fast lane. Feeling the power, he can't resist. As the car accelerates away he watches the speedometer's red needle glide past eighty and on towards ninety. His smile broadens as the sports car whizzes past the traffic in the middle lane. The road in front is empty, but flashing lights and blaring horns grab his attention. Glancing in the rear-view mirror, he watches incredulously as a dark blue car swerves dangerously across the traffic from the inside to outside lane, narrowly missing the rear of one vehicle and the bonnet of another.

Bloody idiot! No doubt it fancies bullying me out of the way.

Oliver eases back to the speed limit. The dark blue car stays in the outside lane, matching his speed but keeping its distance. Checking the side mirror, Oliver joins the traffic in the middle lane, aware that the dark blue car does likewise. However, with no further incidents, he soon relaxes back into the ergonomic seat. The black leather upholstery with the contrasting silver inserts adds a stylish touch to the all-black interior and he's pleased they chose this instead of standard cloth.

Deanna certainly knows how to make something stand out head and shoulders above the crowd.

But, this time, the thought does not bring a warm, contented glow and Oliver scowls as the familiar, pervasive 'grey mist' threatens to descend. How can it creep up on him out of nowhere? After all these years he'd hoped to have discovered some inner alarm alerting him to its insidious presence, but he can fall asleep happy and wake the next morning plunged in despair. Age has taught him nothing.

'Count your blessings, Oliver. This will bring you to the light,' his psychotherapist's voice resounds in his head.

He abandoned therapy several years ago, believing he was finally mastering his depression, but the depth of recent mood swings has caused great concern. Perhaps he should book further sessions.

Oliver glances at the clock on the console. If the traffic remains at this level he should be on the Lizard by mid-afternoon. His mind wanders to the previous afternoon and his cycle ride with Jamie around the Surrey Hills. It was good spending quality time with his son, doing something physical. On their return to Hunter's Moon, he even managed to persuade himself he had everything under control and that Sylvie didn't pose a serious threat. Oliver shifts in his seat.

To the west, a warm, welcoming glow lights the far horizon. Good, because the clouds above him threaten ominously. Suddenly the heavens open. In a gathering spiral, the 'grey mist' descends, swirling around him and seeping into every pore. As it claims him in its vice-like grip, Oliver surrenders to his old foe. Switching on the windscreen wipers, he selects maximum setting and powers on towards the beckoning light.

*

Rain lashes the windscreen and Sylvie curses. She watches in dismay as the Mercedes pulls smoothly away and curses again. The wipers have an erratic momentum of their own. As the blades slide across the wet glass, a long sliver of rubber on the driver's side flaps madly with each sweep. In one, sudden, frantic motion the offending section breaks free, flying away into the slipstream and leaving an arc of rubber smeared across the windscreen in the centre of her eye-line.

'Shit! Shit! Shit!' Sylvie shouts, slamming her hand against the steering wheel. 'Bloody weather!'

The traffic closes in around her in a menacing fashion and she takes her foot off the accelerator. At once, the car stops its whining rattle and rapidly loses speed, causing the car behind to swerve into the outside lane to avoid a collision. Horn blaring, it overtakes, and Sylvie watches dispassionately as the middle-aged man at the wheel glares at her through the torrential rain. A sarcastic smile curls her lips as she raises her middle finger.

Passing a road sign alerting drivers to services half a mile ahead, she decides to stop for coffee and let the worst of the storm pass. There's no way she will catch up with Oliver now. She can only hope he's going back to that farmhouse on the cliffs. As her pent-up frustrations spill over, Sylvie screams at the darkening skies.

The windscreen wipers continue their seamless dance, slipping and sliding over the wet surface of the glass in perfect symmetry, like a pair of well-rehearsed skaters executing impeccable turns, unfazed by the drama taking place in the driver's seat.

Chapter Twenty-Three

'I'm just hanging up the washing,' Cara calls to her children. It's a fine, blustery day; perfect for drying.

Grappling with the washing basket, she opens the porch door and steps out into the world. Immediately the wind whips at her long hair. Turning to get it out of her face, she glances along the track and does a double-take. Walking towards her, with an uncertain smile on his face, is Oliver.

'Hello,' he says.

'Hi,' she responds. Having not seen him since the beach party, she has successfully accepted their previous meeting as simply an amazing and ridiculously surreal experience. 'What blows you this way?' she asks, breaking a silence that threatens to develop into awkwardness.

You! he wants to shout.

'I had a few hours to kill and wondered how you were.'

Ignoring the butterflies in her stomach preparing for flight, Cara wonders why.

'Looks like you've been busy.' Oliver nods to the overflowing basket. 'Here, let me help.' He takes a step towards her.

Hastily Cara steps back. 'Oh, no, I wouldn't dream of it! Go in and make yourself comfortable. I'll only be a few minutes.' The last thing she needs is this world-famous actor pegging out her smalls! 'The children are inside,' she adds.

He watches as Cara disappears around the side of the bungalow. She's as lovely as he remembers, if not more so. Since their first meeting, it's been hard to get her out of his mind. Oliver steps over the threshold into Cara's world.

As he enters the living room, Bethany looks up from her Kindle and smiles.

'Hey, Oliver! Have you come for lunch?' asks Sky excitedly.

Oliver laughs. 'If I'm asked, I guess.'

'Oh, stay for lunch,' Bethany pleads.

'Watch this,' commands Sky. 'I've taught Barnaby a new trick.' Grabbing Oliver's hand, he pulls him onto the sofa next to his sister.

Glancing down at the young girl shyly observing him, Oliver asks, 'What are you reading?'

'Harry Potter, the *Order of the Phoenix*. Have you read it?'

'I have,' he says.

'You have?' she exclaims, her eyes opening wide.

'Yes, I read it with my son, Jamie.'

Her face breaks into a smile.

'Look, Oliver!' shouts Sky.

Alert to the boy's every action, the Labrador sits attentively.

'Roll over,' Sky commands, making a circular motion with his hand. The dog obediently lies down, rolls over and then sits, eagerly awaiting the next instruction. Sky laughs and pats the Labrador's head. 'Good boy, Barnaby!'

'Well done,' says Oliver, aware that Bethany has closed the gap between them.

'How old is your son,' she asks.

'Jamie? He's nine.'

'The same age as me,' says Bethany.

Oliver smiles. Jamie would like her, if they ever met. But how could that ever occur?

'I have two other sons and a daughter as well. Charlie, Sebastian and Samantha.' His heart softens as he thinks of his children, all so different but each contributing to the whole.

'BLP is nine. BLP is nine,' chants Sky, circling the dog.

'Shut up,' Bethany cries, her body suddenly rigid; her face frozen.

Oliver frowns. *What's happening here?*

'BLP is nine, Beautiful Little Princess is nine!'

Bethany jumps to her feet. 'SHUT UP SKY!'

'Hey, what's going on?' Cara stands in the doorway, the empty washing basket in her hand. She glances from Bethany to Sky and then at Oliver. What must he think?

'Mum, make him stop, please,' Bethany pleads.

Sky continues chanting, but more quietly now.

'Sky, stop calling Beth by that name and stop circling Barnaby. Just look how excited you've made him.' She glances at Oliver again. 'Sorry.'

Oliver shakes his head and gives a bewildered smile.

On the verge of tears, Bethany says to her brother, 'You horrible, stupid, fat pig.'

'Oh, Beth! That's not helping, is it?' Walking to her daughter, Cara hugs her, while making an angry face at her son. 'I'm sorry you had to witness this,' she says to Oliver.

'I don't actually know what I've just witnessed,' Oliver says.

'BLP are Beth's initials,' pipes up Sky, grinning. 'Beautiful Little Princess.'

'Mum!' wails Bethany.

'Let's all take a deep breath,' suggests Cara, glancing up at the surfboard on the living-room wall.

'But that's wonderful, Beth, and perfect for you,' Oliver says. 'What is your middle name?'

The young girl blinks at him, the threatened tears stemmed.

'Lowena,' Sky sings out his sister's name.

'What a lovely name,' Oliver says, and Cara watches as her daughter's face is transformed with a small smile.

'Lowena is old Cornish for joy or happiness,' Bethany proudly informs him.

'And what's your middle name, Sky?' Oliver turns his attention to the boy.

'Fat. Stupid Fat Pig,' Bethany says angrily and Cara groans.

Ignoring his sister, Sky says, 'Felix.'

'Latin for happy or lucky,' adds Cara, as if to herself.

'And what about you, Cara? Do you have a middle name?' Oliver asks.

'Yes, but I don't think it has any particular meaning. Justine. My mother tells me she gave me that name because in her youth she used to hang out with the Moody Blues and had a thing for Justin Hayward!' She laughs.

Oliver smiles. 'Well, my initials are OTF, and they don't stand for Old Tragic Fool. See if you can guess what my middle name is.'

There's something about the way he says it that gives Cara pause. Is he being funny? She doesn't think so. But why would he say that? Why would he see himself in that light?

'Tree,' offers Sky.

'Er, no…'

'Timothy,' suggests Bethany quietly.

Oliver shakes his head.

'Trumpet.' Sky warms to the challenge.

'Wrong again.'

'Thomas?' asks Bethany.

'Tractor!' Sky giggles.

Cara laughs. How absurd!

She watches in fascination as Oliver successfully turns the potentially explosive situation into a fun game. Both her children appear entranced.

Aware of her gaze, Oliver looks up and smiles. He had no idea what he was doing earlier, coming to find her like that, but he was powerless to keep away. He was racked with indecision but it has, nevertheless, turned out well. This is just what he needed.

'Do you know, Cara?' he asks.

She tries to recall if she's ever seen his full name in print. She shakes her head.

'Tobias,' he says, 'and it, too, has a meaning. In Hebrew, Tobias means God is good.'

'Tobias,' says Bethany, 'I like that. Tobias... Toby.' She plays with the name, a serious look on her face.

'Yes, Toby is the shortened version,' Oliver says.

Cara smiles. She likes the name too. Glancing up at the clock on the kitchen wall, she asks, 'Would you like to stay for lunch, Oliver?'

'Please stay,' says Bethany.

Sky grins conspiratorially at the actor.

*

The afternoon slips towards evening and Oliver reluctantly drags himself away. He's performing tonight, but he'd much rather spend the evening with this little family.

As Cara opens the stable door and steps outside, a strong breeze catches her hair. She holds it out of her face. A lone windsurfer skims across the water, jumping the waves and moving briskly from one side of the cove to the other.

Oliver stands beside Cara as they watch in silence. He longs to move closer. It's not just that she's so lovely. He feels a connection so strong and is drawn to her in a way he has never known before.

'So, now you've experienced an afternoon at home with the Penhaligons,' Cara says, groaning inwardly. How pompous that must sound!

An afternoon? I'd like it to be a lifetime!

The thought takes Oliver by surprise and he glances down at her. 'Much like an afternoon with the Foxleys.'

She laughs. 'You must miss your children, being here without them.'

Oliver nods slowly. His children, yes. Instantly he feels guilt at the omission of his wife.

'What was all that about earlier with Beth and Sky?'

Looking down at her feet, Cara kicks a small stone lying on the track. When she meets his gaze, sadness pools deeply in her eyes. 'Christo used to call Beth his "Beautiful Little Princess".'

'I heard what happened,' Oliver says softly. 'I'm so very sorry, Cara.' He wants to hold her so badly and soothe away her pain.

Biting her lip, she blinks rapidly.

'Will you do something for me?' he asks. It's unimaginable to think he may not see her again. 'Will you show me *your* Cornwall, if you have the time?'

Please have time!

Oh, so that's the reason he's here! thinks Cara.

'Well, I have some commissions to finish and I work several days at the gallery.' Cara considers Oliver for a long moment. 'But I'm sure I could make the time.' She smiles. 'Yes, I'd like to show you *my* Cornwall.'

Oliver lets out a long, silent breath.

'Thank you,' he says, gently squeezing her arm. 'And now I really must be going. Tas will skin me alive if I'm late.'

'Oh yes, you're at Nancegollan village hall tonight, aren't you? Mum and Sheila are going.'

Nancegollan! How he loves these Cornish names.

'Is that so? I'll be sure to make a fuss of them!' Oliver's eyes twinkle and a mischievous smile spreads across his face.

'Please don't. They may never recover,' Cara says, her smile matching his.

Oliver laughs, carefree for the first time in years. As he gazes into Cara's dark brown eyes a sense of well-being settles deep within his soul.

'Thank you, Cara, for sharing your lovely family with me this afternoon.'

He walks away from her but after a few yards turns back. She still stands at the door watching him and his heartbeat quickens. Something about her takes him to a different place entirely; a place he intuitively knows exists but has never visited.

Cara raises her hand and gives a small wave. A smile tugs at the corners of her mouth. But it's her eyes that hold him spellbound. Her sadness is lifting and a glimpse of something else is taking its place.

Chapter Twenty-Four

Deanna sits in the orangery nursing a mug of steaming coffee. She watches elongating shadows move across the freshly mown lawns leading down to the lake and the forest beyond. All afternoon the weather has been fair and the gardener has taken the opportunity to create perfectly symmetrical stripes in the grass. This is how she likes her world: orderly, with everything in its place. She glances around at the large exotic plants reaching up to the glazed roof and the citrus trees that thrive in this space. The vision appeals to her critical eye. Late afternoon light enters the room, creating a unique atmosphere unlike any other room in the house and she recalls how fulfilled and absorbed she was while researching and sourcing this particular building. Hunter's Moon was originally built in the eighteenth century and she wanted something that reflected the symbols of prestige and wealth that stood in the grounds of fashionable and period residences during that time. With its distinguished classical architectural features, the orangery she eventually selected is a carefully designed traditional build that blends perfectly with the main lodge house, its wooden doors and windows finished in a fashionably stylish blue/grey Farrow and Ball paint.

Deanna sips her coffee. Although unable to pursue a career in theatre, which was always her intention, since her marriage to Oliver she has been able to indulge many of her ideas and desires, unhindered. This has gone some way towards appeasing her dissatisfaction at not being the career woman she always thought she would be. She thinks back to the first time Oliver won an award. Of course he was the star, fêted by all and sundry, but she shared the red-carpet experience and was at his side throughout. She clearly remembers his acceptance speech. He thanked her for being his 'rock' and for being with him from the tiniest flicker of fame, and she relished the spotlight briefly landing upon her. However, the feeling was quickly extinguished when he posed for photographs with that hideously self-satisfied actress, Heather McMullen, his co-star in the film that propelled their lives into the stratosphere. A Dame now, for goodness sake!

By the time Oliver attended the marketing events associated with the release of the film, they were living in the UK once more and she'd given birth to Samantha. Although her body quickly returned to her pre-baby figure, she was dissatisfied with it and set about studiously attaining a previously unknown level of fitness. They briefly returned to Los Angeles for the Awards' Ceremony, which was thrillingly exciting, but she was uncomfortable with her choice of dress. It didn't help when Heather made her appearance, looking every inch the mega-star that she was. The award-winning actress politely enquired how the baby was before pushing Deanna out of the way and, hooking arms with Oliver, posing in front of the cameras. Heather also made sure that any reporter in earshot would hear her say that although Deanna might be Oliver's 'rock' it was she who had recognised his incredible gift as soon as he'd stepped onto the set, and that she was his biggest fan. Smiling sweetly at Deanna, Heather added that, while his wife was preoccupied bringing the first little Foxley into the world, she was the one to nurture and encourage the star's rising talent. Even now, so many years on, Deanna is sickened by the woman's public disdain for her. After all, it is *she* who is Oliver's wife! Oh, yes, the former Deanna Harrington has lived through a lot to become the Deanna Foxley of today.

'Mum, what's for tea?' Sebastian asks from the entrance to the orangery.

Deanna takes one last look across the immaculate lawns. Putting aside her musings, she turns to her son and smiles. 'Your favourite.'

*

As the actors take their final bow, Sylvie turns up her collar and pulls her hat firmly over her ears. She watches as Oliver extricates himself from the line-up and approaches two women in the front row. A pretty, older woman immediately springs to her feet and Oliver hugs her. Recognising her as the woman from the beach café, Sylvie narrows her eyes.

'This is my friend Sheila,' Carol says, attempting to keep her voice steady.

'Nice to meet you, Sheila,' Oliver says, only too aware of the effect he is having on both women.

'I've met you before,' says Sheila excitedly, 'last autumn, when you signed autographs outside Cara's gallery.'

Thinking back to that day, Oliver cannot recall Carol's smaller, plumper friend. 'I'm sorry, I don't remember.'

'We can't forget *you*!' exclaims Sheila. 'But then, it's not every day of the week an actor of note struts his stuff in little old Porthleven.' She roars with laughter and Oliver recoils at her full-on energy.

Carol smiles. What her friend lacks in height is more than compensated in character.

'I hope you enjoyed the play,' Oliver says.

'Oh, yes,' Sheila squeals. 'I had no idea you had such a wonderful singing voice.'

'It's not often I get to use it. It's a fairly well-hidden secret.'

'Do you have many of those?' she asks cheekily.

'Sheila!' Carol reprimands, shocked.

'Well, you don't often get the chance to ask such a direct question, do you?' Sheila says, ignoring Carol's tone.

Oliver pales, grappling with an uninvited image of Sylvie riding him hard and shouting out his name. Even now, he feels so dirty. Inwardly he groans. He'd managed to put her out of his mind fairly effectively until this plump little woman came along.

'Not many,' he says politely.

Carol can see he's visibly shaken. Trust Sheila…

Tas approaches and Oliver happily relinquishes the responsibility of conversation to his friend. Glancing around, he watches an elderly couple navigate their way along a row of seats but it's the person hovering at the back of the hall that grabs his attention. He can't tell if it's a man or a woman, but the intensity coming from the figure is nauseatingly familiar.

Don't be so dramatic! How could she possibly be here in Nancegollan, of all places?

He turns away, but has to look again… just to be sure. The figure is no longer there and he wonders if he simply imagined it. However, a sense of disquiet lingers.

'Oh, yes,' Sheila twitters on. 'We've planned a night out with more of the girls for the next performance, haven't we, Carol?'

Carol nods, embarrassed. She steals a glance at Oliver. He appears distracted, scanning the back of the hall.

'Are you enjoying your time in Cornwall, Oliver?' she asks.

'I'm loving it,' he says, dragging his attention back to the two women. 'You are all so lucky to live here.'

'Yes, we are,' she says with feeling.

'Were you born here?'

Carol laughs. 'Goodness no! London born and bred, me. I came to Cornwall for a party and stayed.'

I came to Cornwall for Cara and stayed.

Catching Carol's eye a fraction longer than necessary, Oliver quickly asks, 'What did you do in London?'

'It was the Swinging Sixties and I was a model,' she says, flattered that he should ask.

'That's easy to understand,' he says.

Carol blushes. 'I was fairly successful at it, too,' she adds proudly. 'It was at the time of Twiggy and Jean Shrimpton. In fact, I worked on a number of assignments in which they featured as the top models.'

Oliver looks at Carol with interest. He remembers Cara telling him how her mother used to hang out with the Moody Blues and had a 'thing' for Justin Hayward.

There's more to this woman than meets the eye.

'Do you miss any of that?' he asks, knowing the answer already.

'No-o-o!' Carol says, expressively. 'I can't deny it, I partied like the rest. It was a time when you could do anything, go anywhere, be anybody you wanted to be, but we got our fingers burned along the way. It was only when I met Ken that I discovered what real life was all about.'

'Well, I envy you.'

Carol smiles politely.

'Guess we'd better hit the road, Mr Fox,' Tas says, wrapping up his conversation with the effervescent Sheila and glancing meaningfully at Oliver. 'Bye, ladies.'

'Hope we see you again soon,' says Oliver, smiling at the two women. He turns to follow his friend.

'Oh my God, Carol,' Sheila says excitedly, 'he's *so* dreamy!'

'Yes, Oliver is very disarming,' Carol says, wondering what she could possibly have that he would envy.

*

As the men leave the building, Oliver quickly scans the area.

'You OK?' Tas asks.

'Thought I recognised someone earlier but I must have been mistaken.'

'What, a stalker?' Tas laughs.

'Yes.'

Tas's laugh stalls in his throat. 'Are you serious?'

'Yes.'

'Christ, Ollie. How long has this been going on?'

'Since the beginning of the year.'

Tas considers the actor for a moment. 'Male or female?'

'Female.'

'What's she been doing?'

Damn! He hadn't meant to say anything.

'Pretty harmless stuff. Leaving notes on the car and I thought I saw her a couple of times. She has phoned home, though.' He recalls she didn't want Tas to visit her; that would make his friend laugh.

'Have you reported it to the police?' Tas asks, climbing into the Jeep.

'No. I can handle it.'

'Does Deanna know?'

'God, no! I don't want her spooked.'

'But if this woman's got your home phone number she more than likely knows where you live!'

Oliver nods slowly. 'You've got to go to the police, Ollie. Where's your head at?'

'Tas, I can handle it. She's harmless.' But there's no denying his disquiet. Extracting the mobile from his jacket pocket, Oliver phones home. 'Hello, darling. How's everything?' He makes sure his voice sounds casual.

'Great! I've got some girlfriends round for an impromptu party. You know, while the cat's away…'

Oliver hears laughter in the background. 'That's good, Dee. Glad you're having fun.' He pauses. 'Everything OK with the kids?'

'Yes, everything's fine, Ollie,' Deanna says. 'What's this about?'

'Just checking in. You know me.'

'Yes, I do, and this is not like you.'

What if he just told her everything that happened on Holy Isle, that Sylvie is unhinged and a possible danger to the family? What would she make of that? She wouldn't understand. She'd blame him.

'Everything OK with the house?'

'Well, the roof's still on, if that's what you mean?' Deanna says, exasperatedly.

'No, I don't mean that, Deanna,' Oliver says, his voice strained. 'Have you noticed anything unusual?'

'Yes, a herd of zebra wandered through earlier,' she says sarcastically. 'Oh, and then a lion appeared out of the forest, its eyes shining brightly…' She falters as she remembers the flashes coming from the edge of the woods. 'What's this all about, Ollie?'

'Nothing. I don't like being away from the family. Just keep your eyes open.'

'Now you're beginning to freak me out.'

Bloody Sylvie! Not for the first time, Oliver feels the tightrope he walks with his wife.

'There's nothing to worry about,' he says.

Negotiating a left-hand bend, Tas glances at his friend and raises an eyebrow.

'Enjoy your party.' Oliver finishes the call and sinks into the passenger seat. 'That went well!'

'Don't you think you should get some security installed?' Tas suggests. 'Who knows what nutters are out there?'

'We've got a burglar alarm.'

'Security, Ollie… like guards!'

Oliver snorts. 'Deanna would have a fit. She'd hate to live like that.'

'Deanna will have a fit if anything happens to you or the kids,' Tas responds.

'I considered a guard dog but you know how she is about animals.'

Navigating through the granite entrance pillars, Tas parks in front of the farmhouse and switches off the engine. Turning to Oliver, he considers his friend. 'It doesn't matter what Deanna feels about animals,' he says seriously. 'I agree that place of yours is tucked away and off the beaten track but what if some unhinged, fanatical idiot finds out where you live? You're a sitting duck. You've got to get some security in place.'

Oliver nods. If Sylvie is in Cornwall at least she's not causing problems in Surrey. But if she's not in Cornwall, where is she? And what trouble could she be stirring? Perhaps he should phone her.

'You're right, Tas. I'll organise it, whether Deanna likes it or not.'

*

Sitting on the bed in the B&B's prettily decorated room, Sylvie sucks the end of a felt-tip pen as she stares at the leaflet in her hand. What a stroke of luck she stopped off in Truro on her way to the Lizard. After losing Oliver in the torrential storm, she continued her journey praying he'd be staying at the farmhouse again. If not, trying to track him down would be like finding a needle in a haystack and she'd probably have to abandon her plan and return to London.

Feeling exhausted, her nerves in shreds, she parked in one of the outlying car parks at the head of the Fal River and wandered through the city's maze of cobbled alleyways, oblivious to the beautiful buildings and elegant Georgian architecture around her. Eventually she found herself in Boscawen Street, hungry and unable to recall when she'd last had a good meal. She was debating where to eat when a poster in the tourist office window caught her eye. *Sorrows in the Sand*, the headline screamed, and under this was an image of Oliver and a red-headed woman, together with a list of dates and venues for the Tasmanian Devil Theatre Company's summer tour. Without hesitation she entered the office and picked up half a dozen leaflets.

Sylvie congratulates herself on being so thorough in tracking Oliver. Having already gleaned some information from the Internet, she now has a complete list of his performances. No longer does she have to sleep in the car keeping watch on his whereabouts; she can treat herself to a decent night's sleep. Sylvie grins. Her boss has asked some difficult questions about the number of sick days she's been taking and she was beginning to run out of plausible explanations. Now she can return to her job knowing that every Friday night she will leave work and travel to Cornwall, safe in the absolute knowledge that each weekend she will be with her lover.

Removing the felt-tip pen from her mouth, Sylvie carefully draws a heart around Oliver's face. Then, drawing a box around the redhead at his side, she starts to fill it in. As Sylvie's emotions consume her, the pen scratches ever more manically across the paper until the red-headed actress is completely obliterated. She throws her head back and laughs, then rocks forwards and backwards on the bed, its springs groaning as her frantic movements grow ever more violent.

'Now I've got you, Oliver Foxley! You can't escape me that easily.'

Chapter Twenty-Five

Cara and Oliver step off the coast path and onto a narrow track leading through heather and gorse. Little more than an animal track, few people would think to follow it. The gorse is a vibrant yellow, its flower heads popping as they noisily burst open, and a smell of coconut gently wafts on the breeze. The sea sparkles as if a thousand glittering diamonds have been carelessly scattered across its surface, and cotton-wool clouds dot a clear blue sky. Thrift and sea campion carpet the cliffs in pink and white flowers and butterflies flit from one wildflower to the next, feeding on the nectar. July in Cornwall. Not for the first time Oliver believes he has arrived in some magical, faraway land.

Arriving at a rocky promontory almost at the cliff's edge, Cara glances back at him. 'It's just round here.' Carefully she walks around the rock face.

Oliver follows and stops in amazement. The view is breathtaking. Immediately in front is the sweep of the cove with The Lookout's roof below, maybe thirty yards away. His eyes skim over the half-dozen assorted properties skirting the cove to the far end of the beach where he can see Rick's Beach Hut and the car park. But it's what lies beyond that is so awesome. Stretching away into the distance, spread out like an enormous 3D map, is the impressive Loe Bar dividing the sea from a freshwater lake and, at its far end, Porthleven's most recognisable building, the Bickford-Smith Institute with its seventy feet tower, next to the pier and harbour entrance. Beyond this, the south coast of Cornwall spans from Praa Sands and Prussia Cove, across a shimmering Mounts Bay – where the tip of iconic St Michael's Mount can clearly be seen rising out of the water – sweeping on past Penzance and Newlyn to the cliffs at Porthcurno. In the far distance is Gwennap Head.

Oliver breathes in deeply, feeling relaxed yet energised. For as long as he can remember this balance is what he has strived to achieve. It has taken various techniques and teachings, and not inconsiderable funds, to find it; yet, here it is happening effortlessly in these natural surroundings.

'Beautiful, isn't it?' Cara says, turning to him.

Oliver nods. 'You've brought me to the edge of the world.'

Cara smiles. 'It never fails to hit the spot. Whenever I feel desperate I come up here.'

Dragging his eyes away from the spectacular view, Oliver considers her for a long moment. God knows, he's felt desperate during his lifetime and understands only too well how debilitating that feeling can be. With everything that has happened to

Cara he empathises with the overpowering desperation she must have felt, and his heart goes out to her. Someone like Cara should never have to experience such desolation... ever.

'We often spot seals and pods of dolphin from here and, sometimes, basking sharks too.' She turns back to the view. 'There's a huge variety of seabirds – gannets, guillemots, oystercatchers, cormorants, kittiwakes, fulmars, shags and, if we're lucky, a peregrine falcon or two. And, of course, one of England's rarest breeding birds has recently returned to these cliffs – the chough.'

Oliver's face softens. He loves spending time with her. During the past few weeks Cara has proudly shown him *her* Cornwall, sharing her knowledge and highlighting things the casual tourist would seldom discover. She is so passionate about this land of hers that he could listen to her lovely voice forever. Despite his best endeavours, he has fallen under her spell and there is absolutely nothing he can do about it.

'If you look in this direction...' Cara turns 180 degrees. The breeze snatches at her hair and she holds it out of her face.

Oliver doesn't turn.

Glancing inquisitively at him, she catches her breath. It's not the first time she's caught him gazing at her in that way. In fact, he's looked at her like that on every occasion they've been together, but he has never made a move. Placing her hands on his shoulders, she turns him to face the opposite direction.

'Beyond that point is Dollar Cove,' she says, indicating to the far headland. 'Have you heard of it?'

'Vaguely, I think.' Although her touch was light, it has set his pulse racing.

'Its official name is Jangye Ryn, but the beach has derived its name from folklore. A Portuguese treasure ship sank offshore in 1526, and in 1783 a ship carrying silver dollars was also wrecked nearby.'

'I like its folklore name,' he says. 'Have any Pieces of Eight ever turned up?'

She smiles. 'Despite plenty of searches, I've not heard of any significant finds.'

'This coastline must be littered with wrecks,' Oliver says, gazing out over the calm bay.

'Hundreds. There's a hidden reef offshore which has caught out many ships over the centuries.'

Sitting on the flat rock where she has sat a thousand times before, Cara stretches out her legs and leans back against the cliff face. Oliver sits beside her.

'It's not safe to swim at Dollar Cove due to the strong rip currents at low water,' she says. 'You need to be really careful. We've done it, but only when it's calm and a very high tide.'

Instantly, Oliver has a vision of Cara in the waters of a calm, flat sea. Oh, what he'd give to experience that with her.

'There's hardly ever anyone on the beach,' Cara continues, diverting his thoughts. 'There are no facilities and families tend to go to the next cove because it has a lifeguard service during the summer months.' She closes her eyes, feeling the warmth of the sun on her face. 'You're more likely to find geologists at Dollar Cove because of the rock formations.'

'What's the name of the next cove?' Oliver asks, taking the opportunity to gaze unobserved at her lovely face.

'Church Cove we locals call it, but it's sometimes referred to as Gunwalloe Church Cove because there's another Church Cove on the eastern side of the Lizard.' She opens her eyes and laughs at his expression. 'Well, you did ask!'

'That's true.' He smiles.

She grins at him. 'Continuing your education… the fifteenth-century church of St Winwaloe nestles into the cliff on the northern side of the cove. It's unusual because it has a small, squat bell tower, which is detached from the rest of the church.'

'Interesting.'

'And there are a number of caves in the cove as well. The National Trust own both Church Cove and

Dollar Cove. Oh, and Mullion Golf Course, which is mainly former sand dunes, overlooks it.'

'Ever thought of working for the local tourist board?' Oliver teases.

'I'll bear it in mind,' she answers. 'If my painting of the cove doesn't come together soon I may well have to seek alternative employment!'

'Don't worry, Cara, it will happen,' says Oliver kindly. 'I find that if I'm having trouble learning lines and the scene doesn't feel right, if I concentrate on another section of the script and then revisit the difficult part, more often than not it falls into place.'

Plucking a leaf from a clump of sea pinks growing at the side of the rock, Cara laces it through her fingers as she considers Oliver's advice. 'I have never understood how you actors remember all those words.'

He laughs. 'It comes with practice. If you start at an early enough age it becomes the norm.'

'Did you always know you were destined to be an actor?'

He ponders her question, thinking back to his first, tentative steps when he discovered – to his utter amazement and not inconsiderable relief – that while portraying another person's emotions the greyness in his soul left him in peace.

'Not sure I knew I was *destined* to be an actor, but from my early teens I was often selected to play the main character in school productions.'

She wonders about Oliver the boy. Was he always easy on the eye or did he have to grow into the handsome man now sitting beside her? She still can't believe it. Who would have thought she'd be sitting here with this world-famous actor in her special spot above her beloved cove!

'Did you go straight to drama school?' she asks.

Oliver glances at Cara. It would be so easy to slip into the 'tried and tested' format and give the bland PR answers he is so accustomed to churning out, never showing the real person behind the mask. But, for Cara…

'Yes,' he says. 'I wasn't particularly interested in anything else, apart from sport. I found words comforted me and brought me to life.'

'Comforted you?' Cara frowns. Why would he need comforting?

Unaccustomed to exposing his vulnerability, Oliver momentarily spins into panic before realising that he longs to show Cara the real Oliver Foxley.

'Yes, comfort,' he says, looking deep into her eyes. Once again, he experiences the sensation of being drawn in, diving deeper and deeper into their hidden depths and never wanting to come up for air. 'I had a difficult childhood and acting was my only escape.'

Cara's face softens with compassion. From the very first moment she met him, instinctively she knew Oliver's public image was not that of the private man. She is humbled by his offering of a glimpse of his true self.

'How was it difficult?' she asks gently.

It is so refreshing to talk like this and Oliver finds himself falling ever deeper into the abyss. He should be backing away.

'I am the youngest of four boys. My brothers are all very outgoing and confident. It was only me who didn't inherit those characteristics. I was introspective and thoughtful. Overlooked. My father was a successful academic and my mother didn't have time for me, or just wasn't interested.' It still hurts, even after all these years. Suddenly feeling insecure and not wishing to ruin whatever it is they have between them, Oliver asks, 'Do you really want to know about this, Cara?'

She nods.

He hasn't spoken in this way to anyone for a very long time. In fact, has he ever spoken to anyone like this, apart from his therapist? Even then, he was selective about what information he imparted. This is how he yearns to speak with Deanna. Oliver closes his eyes and tilts his head up to the sky, enjoying the warmth of the afternoon sun. The only sounds are the waves breaking way below on the sand and the cry of the gulls, snatched away on the breeze. This is bliss, being here with Cara…

'Go on,' she encourages.

Oliver opens his eyes and stares out to sea, transported to his confusing teenage years; remembering how it was. 'From late childhood I have suffered with depression, only no one really knew much about the condition back then. It was considered an impediment and a flaw, one to be brushed under the carpet and ignored.' As he speaks, he realises this is exactly how Deanna deals with his mental imbalance. 'I used to try and talk to my mother about it. I believed she, of all people, would understand, but she would simply change the subject or turn away from me, which just made me even more introspective. It wasn't until I was in my early twenties and living in the States that I sought help and understood the problem is a treatable, clinical disorder.' He hesitates before turning to Cara and looking her straight in the eye.

Cara's heart goes out to him. 'Are you on medication?' she asks softly.

Oliver nods. 'Have been for years. For some reason, though, since being in Cornwall I haven't needed such a high dose. Must be the magic of the place.' He smiles.

'Your public image gives none of this away.'

'I'm not an actor for nothing,' he says grimly. 'For a while I was in therapy and I've thoroughly researched the illness. I also meditate when I can and manage to keep it under control, more or less.' Oliver sighs. 'Anyway, I'm sure you don't want to hear about all this doom and gloom on such a beautiful day.'

Cara observes him thoughtfully. 'You are describing a soul's journey, Oliver. How can that possibly be doom and gloom? You have learnt and are continuing to learn as you move through your life.'

Oliver stares at Cara in amazement. She understands! An old head on young shoulders.

'Is that how you view your life?' he asks carefully.

Sadness clouds her beautiful eyes and he curses himself for bringing it back.

'Yes, at least I try to. When Christo died I hated the world,' she says, her voice distorting. 'It was all so sudden. One minute he was there and then he wasn't. All I wanted to do was curl up in a ball and join him. But I had two little people to care for and dying simply wasn't an option. I decided that God had given Christo to me from a very young age for a reason: so that we could fully experience each other in the time we had together.'

Her words move Oliver beyond any dramatic script he has ever read.

'Christo and I were just three when we met. We were together from then on and hardly ever apart.' The look in her eyes softens as she remembers her husband as a toddler with his mop of blond hair and cheeky face, so like Sky. She takes a deep breath before continuing. 'We went through school together and when all our friends swapped partners and experimented, neither of us was interested in anyone else. We were happy with each other and married young. So, you see, I was lucky to have Christo in my life for twenty-seven years. Longer than many marriages.' She smiles sadly at Oliver. 'Anyway, eventually I came to realise that nothing could bring me peace but myself.'

Oliver is humbled, his condition seemingly nothing by comparison. He wants to hug her and tell her that he will never let life hurt her ever again.

'You have great wisdom, Cara.'

She shakes her head. 'No, but I am learning from life that the darkest times can bring us to the brightest places and that the most painful struggles can grant us the most necessary growth.' Shyly, she glances at Oliver. 'And, sometimes, the most heartbreaking losses can make room for the most wonderful people.' Oliver's heart leaps. 'I'm also learning that what seems like a curse can actually be a blessing and what seems like the end of the road is actually just the discovery that we are meant to travel down a different path. No matter how difficult things seem there is always hope, and no matter how powerless we feel or how horrible things are, we can't give up. We have to keep going. Even when it's scary and when all of our strength seems gone, we have to keep picking ourselves up and move forward, because whatever we're battling in the moment will pass and we will make it through. We've made it this far. We can make it through whatever comes next.'

For a man with so many words to his vocabulary, Oliver is momentarily speechless. Cara is not only stunning on the outside but also incredibly beautiful on the inside; blessed with a wise and deep spiritual understanding. Something buried within his psyche shifts as he realises his life has been one huge jigsaw puzzle with the pieces never quite falling into place, constantly yo-yoing between episodes of lightness and innocence, darkness and despair. But now, by coincidence, fate or sheer blind luck, he has met Cara, and it's patently clear that the two of them, on some level, belong together. As lovers – a thrill of excitement courses through him – or as friends, or as something entirely different. They just work and he has never felt so alive, even though they are heading into uncharted waters.

Cara watches the waves break on the beach below, cleansing the sands as they retreat to the ocean. Like life, each day she can wipe the slate clean and start over again. She thinks back to the first moment she met Oliver and felt the intense energy radiating from him as he stood behind her in the queue. Even though he recoiled when she turned to face him, some inner sense told her this was someone with whom she would just click. Yes, she was in awe of him because of his public image, and she felt awkward because of the emotions he stirred but, instinctively, she knew there was something more to this man other than just his incredible good looks. He is so honest with her, which can't be easy in his position, and it's such a relief not having to pretend to be anyone or anything with him. There's no denying how comfortable she now feels with him. It's as if she's known him all her life. Cara gazes at Oliver with a softness that has eluded her for a very long time.

'Cara,' Oliver whispers, desire flooding his body. He leans towards her.

But suddenly she's on her feet, looking at her watch. 'Oh no! Look at the time. Greg's coming at three.' She scans the cove and spots the Marsdens' red hatchback making its way up the track. 'I'd forgotten, Oliver, I'm sorry. I've got an appointment with Greg. I have to go.'

On the cusp of something profound, Greg – whoever he is – has shattered the moment. Oliver curses under his breath. Rising to his feet, he follows Cara's swiftly disappearing figure.

As she reaches the path high above The Lookout's rooftop, Cara stops and looks down. Oliver follows her gaze. A stylish man climbs out of the car, immaculately turned out in corduroys and moleskin shirt.

'Hi, Greg,' calls Cara.

The man turns, shields his eyes and squints up at her. He smiles but as his gaze takes in Oliver standing beside her, a fleeting emotion registers upon his face.

Turning away, Cara hurries along the path and Oliver lengthens his stride to keep up with her. Twenty yards further on, they descend a set of roughly hewn steps between two properties.

'Greg's come about the Threadneedle Prize,' Cara breathlessly explains, as they emerge onto the main track.

Oliver smiles at the excitement in her voice. He's not sure if it's the sun dazzling him but an energetic golden aura surrounds Cara, making her appear even lovelier, if that were possible. As they walk towards The Lookout, Oliver searches his memory for any snippets concerning the Threadneedle Prize. He thinks his wife may have visited the exhibition one year with a friend. Did she go to the Mall Galleries?

Deanna! What the hell am I doing?

Cara looks across the track and smiles at Oliver, her eyes shining with excitement.

Greg watches their approach. 'Good afternoon, Cara,' he says in his smooth American accent. Thrown by Oliver's presence, he doesn't kiss her on the lips but, instead, on both cheeks.

'Hi, Greg. This is Oliver.'

Oliver accepts Greg's perfectly manicured handshake.

'Oliver,' says Greg imperiously. 'I assume you are who I think you are?'

'He is,' says Cara, frowning at his tone.

'And what brings you to the cove?'

Oliver wants to say *Cara.* Instead, he says, 'An easterly wind.'

As Greg falters, Oliver considers him with interest. It's usually emotional women who react to him in this way.

'Let's go inside,' suggests Cara, pushing open the stable door. Immediately, Barnaby bounds out to greet them.

Neatly stepping aside, avoiding any contact with the dog, Greg enters the hallway behind her. Oliver affectionately rubs the Labrador's head.

'Anyone for coffee or tea?' asks Cara.

'Earl Grey, if you have any,' says Greg, 'with lemon.'

Walking into the kitchen, Cara spies a lone lemon sitting in the fruit bowl. What a stroke of luck! 'And you, Oliver?' she calls over her shoulder.

'Coffee, please, Cara. As it comes.'

She smiles and busies herself in the kitchen while Oliver and Greg make small talk. When she enters the living room she's immediately struck by the difference in the men's body language: Oliver sits at ease on the sofa, while Greg perches stylishly in the opposite armchair. She hands each man a mug. Did she imagine it or did Greg just tut? Cara joins Oliver on the sofa and listens to their discussion.

Haughtily, Greg quizzes Oliver over his most recent film and his character's motivation. There's nothing defensive in Oliver's answer; it's just the perfect PR spiel. He has handled trickier men before, but Greg intrigues him.

'What brings you to the cove, Greg?' Oliver asks, thinking it's time for a change of subject.

'My wife.' Sadness creeps into Greg's eyes. 'She's unwell.'

'I'm sorry to hear that,' says Oliver genuinely.

'It was suggested a change of air would assist her recovery.'

'How is Marietta?' enquires Cara softly.

'Not so good today.' Greg doesn't elaborate. Putting his wife's illness to one side, he says, 'I've had some encouraging news regarding your application.'

Eagerly, Cara sits forward.

'I shouldn't tell you this before the end of the pre-selection process, but three of the paintings we submitted have gained approval,' Greg says.

Unable to mask her excitement, Cara's eyes light up.

'They are *The Cove at Sunset, Porthcurno Early Morning* and *Lanyon Quoit at Night.* However, there's one in particular that stands out for the selectors. Can you guess which?'

Cara considers her paintings. She has no idea which one the selectors would have chosen but if she doesn't come up with an answer, no doubt, Greg will again think her flaky.

'*Lanyon Quoit,*' she says, guessing wildly.

Greg shakes his head slowly.

'Well, it's fifty-fifty now! Either *The Cove at Sunset* or *Porthcurno Early Morning,*' she says with some amusement.

Unable to resist playing with her, Greg prolongs the moment.

Oliver observes the man. *Patronising fool!*

'The latter,' Greg eventually says.

Cara breaks into a smile. She painted the beach at Porthcurno with an early morning pink light, the Logan Rock in the background appearing through a fine mist. It came together effortlessly.

'As you know, there's a hefty first prize of twenty thousand pounds,' Greg says, 'but visitors can vote for their own favourite quite independently of the judges. This means the prize winner could win an additional ten thousand pounds.'

Cara's smile broadens. That would really make a difference. They could all have a long overdue holiday, her parents included.

Sitting beside her, Oliver feels her excitement. *If anyone deserves to win, it's Cara. But what is Greg's agenda? What is he getting out of this?*

There's something about the man that is just too smooth and polished. Oliver doesn't trust him an inch.

'What do you think of that, Cara?' Greg asks, aware of Oliver's scrutiny.

'Fantastic, if I can pull it off!'

'If you are selected, I will return to the UK and guide you,' Greg says importantly.

Oliver clenches his jaw.

A flurry of excitement at the door makes them all turn. Appearing in the doorway, Sky dumps his school bag on the floor and grins when he sees Oliver. 'Have you come to tea?'

Oliver smiles at the lad. 'Sadly no, I have a performance tonight.' Crestfallen, Sky walks over to Barnaby. 'But I'm sure I can stay for another hour.'

'Yippee!' Sky says, sitting on the floor beside his dog. He strokes Barnaby's ears.

Bethany enters the room and glances shyly at Greg, offering him a small smile as she joins Oliver and Cara on the sofa. Sitting between them, she snuggles up to the actor.

Cara's eyes widen in surprise. It's unlike her daughter to be so forward! She is such a good barometer of people and she, too, obviously feels comfortable in his presence. Over the top of Bethany's head, Cara smiles at Oliver.

As he glances down at the young girl, Oliver's heart melts. This little family is becoming so precious to him. And then he thinks of his family in Surrey and immediately attempts to stem the strong emotions threatening to blindside him. What the hell is he doing playing at happy families in Cornwall? Yes, things are not so great with Deanna at the moment, but he made his bed many years ago.

Greg clears his throat. 'Well, I must go.' He rises from the armchair and Cara gets to her feet. 'It's been nice meeting you, Oliver.'

'You too,' responds Oliver, remaining seated.

'Bye, children.'

Bethany compresses her lips into a smile.

Greg turns his attention to Sky. 'Don't forget our dog walk, young man.'

Sky grins. 'I won't. Barnaby likes Milo.'

Greg quickly follows Cara out of the bungalow. As soon as they are outside he catches hold of her elbow and turns her to face him. 'Cara, how do you know Oliver Foxley?'

'We met at Rick's beach party,' she says innocently. 'Why?'

'Are you two having an affair?' Greg asks urgently.

'Oh no, he's just a friend.' She laughs a little too loudly, unable to stem the blush.

'I never thought I'd appreciate Marietta's interest in that actor,' says Greg with a tinge of bitterness, 'but you do know that he and his wife are reported to have one of the strongest marriages in the business?'

'He's a friend, Greg,' Cara says, looking him straight in the eye.

'I'm just looking out for you, Cara, that's all. I wouldn't want to see you get hurt.'

Through the bay window Oliver observes Greg talking to Cara. She seems ill at ease and he wonders what's being said. He frowns as the American leans forward and kisses Cara lightly on the mouth.

How very familiar!

'He's always doing that,' comments Bethany quietly beside him.

At once Oliver is on red alert. What is it about Greg that puts him on edge? The man is obviously educated and has done well for himself, but there's

something unnaturally taut about him, as if his sophisticated manner is a well-polished act.

Maybe he's just tense because of his wife's illness?

Oliver's frown deepens. Greg seems pleasant enough, if a little self-important, but there's something about him that doesn't quite stack up. And what game does he think he's playing with Cara?

As Greg opens the driver's door to the Marsdens' hatchback, he notices Oliver watching. Nodding once, he makes sure the actor sees his small, satisfied smile before climbing into the car.

Chapter Twenty-Six

'A burglar alarm I can live with but high fencing, electric gates, CCTV plus a security guard and that frightful dog...' Deanna shudders. 'You've imprisoned us in a gilded cage!'

Oliver gazes at the ocean, calm and serene; the antithesis of his wife's current mood. Having pulled into a lay-by to answer his mobile, he now faces Deanna's wrath. As the sun dips behind St Michael's Mount, a stunning sunset bathes the bay in a blood-red glow.

If this were a painting it would be hard to accept as real.

Oliver's mind wanders fondly to Cara but his wife's sharp tone brings him back to the present.

'What's happened to make you do this?'

It's a fair question, but he can't give her the true answer. 'The way the world is.'

'No, Oliver, that's not good enough. We've lived here perfectly happily for nearly eighteen years. It's not you that has to live under lock and key. What have you done?'

'Don't be so dramatic, Dee.'

'I am not being dramatic.' Deanna seethes. 'You are free to come and go as you please but we have to live here. Your celebrity has made us prisoners in our own home.'

'*My* celebrity, Deanna, is what's given you that home,' he says evenly.

But Deanna is on a roll. 'If you've done something to jeopardise the safety of my family I will never forgive you.'

'*Our* family.' Oliver's voice is dangerously low.

'Our family?' Deanna screams, her customary coolness escaping her. 'You're never here! You're always swanning around the globe and only coming home when you feel like it.'

Oliver holds the phone away from his ear. That old chestnut. Why does it always come back to her accusing him of not pulling his weight where the family is concerned? It's below the belt, and she knows it. He can hear her breathing heavily, steadying her fury. Oliver remains silent and watches a fishing boat travelling across the mirror-like sea. A dozen seagulls follow in its wake.

So serene. Like a painting come to life. Again, his mind wanders to Cara.

'Have you finished?' he asks.

'Aargh!' Deanna shrieks. 'You are *so* frustrating!'

'Look, what's a guard dog? You won't have to come into contact with it.'

'That's not the point. It's what it represents. The psychological aspect, as you of all people should know.'

Oliver squeezes his eyes shut. For the first time in several weeks, the 'grey mist' engulfs him. Has she pushed him over the edge on purpose? When he speaks again it is little more than a growl. 'Deanna, get used to it. The world has changed and we have to change with it if we are to remain safe.'

'Oh, that's just fine for you to say. You don't have to live in jail!'

'You knew what you were getting into when you married me. If you didn't want the trappings and restrictions celebrity brings then you should have married someone out of the public eye.'

Hearing the underlying message, Deanna softens her voice. 'But you have no idea what it's like living this way. How I feel…' She lets the sentence hang.

Oliver sighs. It's been a couple of weeks since he was last in Surrey, going over the plans with the security firm. Perhaps he should return soon to assess if Deanna is being unreasonable. Though, with the threat of Sylvie hanging over them, what option does he have but to install extra security?

'Dee,' he says more gently. 'I'll come back for a couple of days next week and we'll talk about it then.'

Deanna smiles. She still knows how to push his buttons. 'The security guard and dog must go.'

'They remain,' Oliver says.

'Oliver, they will go,' she says defiantly.

'Deanna, they will not.'

'But *you* don't have to live like this!' Deanna feels like screaming. 'Oh, don't bother coming back. There's no point you being here anyway. You only get in the way.'

'Well, I wouldn't want to do that,' he says sarcastically.

Once again, Oliver feels his role within the family is inconsequential. She's got his children and that's all Deanna is interested in. Perfectly independent.

'Anyway, Sammy's going to Rosie's parents' villa for the summer and I'm taking the boys to Ma and Pa's for a few weeks.'

'When did you decide this?' Oliver asks.

'Oh, Sammy was asked months back,' Deanna says airily.

Oliver frowns. Why hasn't Deanna discussed it with him? Obviously, his daughter is of an age when she can make up her own mind but it would have been nice to be included in the family's plans.

'And I decided to decamp to Norfolk the day the security guard arrived.' Unflinchingly, Deanna delivers this last piece of news.

Oliver grits his teeth. She certainly knows how to pack a punch. He watches a car pass by on the lonely road.

'It will be good for the boys to spend time with their grandparents,' he says, 'but your reasons for visiting, Deanna, are totally ridiculous.'

'How would you possibly know? As I've said before, you come and go as you please. It's us who are forced to live with the consequences of your actions and decisions.' Deanna feels her trademark strength and full mastery return. 'Frankly, I'm sick of it, Oliver. Don't come back any time soon until you've thought about that.'

'If that's what you want.'

There's an edge to his voice and Deanna hesitates, experiencing a tremor of foreboding. She is on the verge of softening him up again when Oliver disconnects.

*

Sylvie can't believe her luck. Having taken a couple of days off work to make a long weekend, she is on her way to the farmhouse to check Oliver's whereabouts when she passes him parked in a lay-by, speaking on his mobile. She stops in a farmer's gateway nearby and waits. Ten minutes later Oliver drives by. Dipping her head, Sylvie surreptitiously watches as the Mercedes disappears round the bend before pulling out into the road, ensuring enough

385

distance between the two cars not to draw attention. She's getting good at this.

*

Oliver's mood is black. Not only does his wife know how to bury the knife up to the hilt but also to twist it... slowly. As he grapples with his old adversary once more, his anger turns inwards. How disappointed he is in himself. He thought he had mastered his depression, but that was just an egotistical illusion. The 'grey mist' – conspicuous by its absence for most of the time he's been in Cornwall – is here again, in all its forceful glory.

Does he want to go to the gig tonight? He could simply return to the farmhouse; no one will be around. Rick and Tania are running the event and Tas will be there enjoying himself. He could ride out the storm without bothering anybody. But Oliver doesn't want to be on his own this evening. As dusk descends, he drives straight past the turning to the farmhouse. Aware of headlights following, he thinks nothing of it. Cars on the coast road only have a limited number of destinations. Indicating right, he takes the lane leading to the cove.

Oliver parks the Mercedes and gets out. Apart from the sound of breaking waves some distance away and the gentle strum of guitars, all is quiet.

Breathing in the sea air, he attempts to lighten his sombre mood. He glances along the track and the light from The Lookout blinks like a beacon. How he'd love to be going there right now, but he doesn't want Cara to experience his vile mood. And, anyway, he can't just turn up like that. There has to be a reason. Oliver walks towards Rick's Beach Hut, the 'grey mist' hanging heavily upon him.

Sylvie holds back and stops on the bend. She plunges the car into darkness and waits until Oliver enters the café before switching on the headlights again. Parking as far away from the Mercedes as possible, she considers her options. Excited at being so close, she's also frustrated she can't get nearer, but coming across him so unexpectedly must surely be a sign! This is her chance to meet him again, and who knows where that may lead?

Switching on the internal light, Sylvie pulls out a scarf from the glove compartment. Tying it around her head Bohemian-style, she pinches her cheeks to bring some colour to her pale face. It's a shame her make-up bag is at the B&B, however, she does have a plum-coloured lipstick in her handbag. Applying it carefully, she rolls her lips together and pouts at her image in the mirror.

'Not bad.'

Sylvie flicks off the light and gets out of the car. All is quiet, apart from the sound of the ocean and muffled laughter coming from the café. It's dark, except for the lights shining from some of the properties along the cliff. Suddenly, headlights appear on the road behind her and, instinctively, she cowers back into the shadows. A car pulls into the car park and she turns away, pretending to search for something in her bag. Two guys get out and walk to the entrance. As they enter, Sylvie hears a party in full swing. When the door closes again, all is quiet.

What if it's a private party?

Desperation drives her on. As she nears the café, she sees a notice pinned to the door.

Celtic Folk Rock

with
The Corringtons

7p.m. until Late
Come on in!

It's an open invitation. Seeing this as yet another sign, Sylvie slips in unnoticed and stands at the back of the café. It's crowded and there's a buzz of excitement in the air. She scans the room. No sign of Oliver. She heads towards the bar and instantly recognises the tall blonde serving at the far end. It's the bitch who so openly flaunted herself with her lover. Sylvie's eyes narrow to slits.

'What would you like?' A man's voice shakes her out of her dark thoughts.

'Cider.' She says the first thing that comes into her head.

'Which one? We've got Bulmers, Strongbow and Cornish Rattler.'

'Cornish Rattler,' she says, liking the sound of the name.

'Good choice. Guaranteed to tickle your taste buds.' The barman smiles at her and then turns away.

Sylvie glances around again. Oliver is still nowhere to be seen.

'Here you go.' Placing a glass on the counter in front of her, the man yells along the bar, 'Hey, Tan, we're almost out of the Rattler Pear!'

Paying for her drink, Sylvie turns away. Oliver must be in another part of the café. Pushing her way through the crowd, she spots him standing at the side of the decking talking to the driver of the big black Jeep. She hangs back.

'You all right, Ollie? You seem distracted,' Tas asks.

Oliver takes a swig of beer. 'It's Deanna. She's not happy.'

'What, you being so far away?'

'No, that doesn't upset her,' Oliver says with a hollow laugh. 'She's unhappy about the new security measures.'

'She'd be a lot unhappier if some rabid fan got in and ran amok around the place,' Tas says.

'Yeah, well, I didn't go into specifics. Just said it was precautionary. Anyway, she's well pissed off and is decamping the family to her parents' for the summer.'

'Possibly a good move?' suggests Tas.

'Maybe…'

Changing the subject, Tas says, 'Think we're in for a treat tonight.' He nods towards the three musicians standing under the sailcloth at the far end of the decking.

Tristan stops strumming his guitar. Unhappy with the sound, he tightens a couple of strings and, cocking his head, strums again. He nods. 'Welcome to this intimate little gathering,' he says into the microphone and an expectant hush descends. 'Let's get the evening started and make some sweet music.'

Looking towards his sister, he counts them in, and then they're away into the first song of the set.

Morwenna lightly grasps the microphone and closes her eyes, acutely aware of Tas standing only a few rows away. She's seen him a few times since the beach party but, deep down, she knows he'll be moving on once the play comes to a close. And that's

OK, she tells herself. His character is overpowering and it's difficult not to be intimidated by his knowledge and worldliness. Taking a deep breath, she starts to sing. Her voice is rich and full-bodied; her nerves have not let her down. Daring to open her eyes, she sees Tas smiling broadly at her.

'See what I mean?' Tas says, turning to Oliver. 'They've definitely got something. That Morwenna has a fabulous voice, every bit as clear and pure as Andrea Corr's.'

Oliver agrees. The Corringtons make a good sound. He tries to let the music soothe his troubled soul but Deanna has deeply rattled him and his mood is hard to shift. He glances around. Will Cara come to support her friends?

Standing on the far side of the decking, Sylvie has not taken her eyes off Oliver since first spotting him in the crowd. As his eyes graze over her, she waits for his acknowledgement but her presence doesn't register. Oliver continues to scan the crowd. Sylvie's jaw drops.

She's not here!

Bitter disappointment consumes him and Oliver is left in no doubt. How much longer can he curb his feelings? Raising the beer bottle to his lips, he turns his attention back to the musicians.

'Thank you,' says Morwenna, as the audience applaud their opening number.

Tristan carefully places his guitar on its stand and walks to a set of keyboards, as the backing vocalist, and multi-instrumentalist, selects a bodhran from the collection of instruments at his feet. Fingering a tin whistle, Morwenna counts them into the next song – a haunting acoustic.

Oliver looks around again and his heart leaps straight into his mouth. Cara stands in the archway leading from the café out to the decking. As she turns in his direction her eyes light up and she breaks into a smile. She says something to her female companion before making her way through the crowd towards him.

'Hi, Oliver,' Cara says, as she reaches him. 'Enjoying the music?'

'Greatly.'

Tas looks over his shoulder and nods at Cara before turning back to watch Morwenna.

'This is Tristan's girlfriend, Jane.' Cara makes the introduction.

'Hi. You were at the beach party,' Oliver says with a smile.

'Hello again,' Jane says, flattered he should remember.

'I didn't know you'd be here,' Cara says softly as she turns to face the stage. 'I'm glad you are.' She smiles up at him; a beautiful golden smile.

With hammering heart, Oliver senses the 'grey mist' retreating fast. In amazement, he realises that Cara can do what no therapist has ever achieved. No longer does he feel alone or adrift. He feels found.

As Cara listens to the music, she remembers how she and Christo encouraged The Corringtons from their earliest days, when they were just friends jamming together on a wet Sunday afternoon at The Lookout, with Christo accompanying on guitar. She thought she'd be filled with melancholy hearing them again tonight and considered not coming. The memories of the last time she saw them performing at the café and the following, hateful, life-changing day are still too raw. But Cara doesn't feel melancholic. In fact, she feels as if life is just about to take a turn for the better and, deep down, she knows it has everything to do with the man standing closely beside her. She senses Christo watching over her and is sure he gives his blessing.

Sylvie stares at Oliver and Cara, her mind turning to ever more malicious thoughts as she sees the way he is with her. Who is this girl? He should be with *her* – he promised! As Cara turns to speak to Oliver, Sylvie watches him lean in closely to hear her more clearly above the music. She sees their eyes lock. No! She can't stand it. He promised he would phone, but he hasn't. It's just lies. And what of that bitch behind the bar? She was all over him the last time she saw them together. So, he thinks he can have all these other women but not keep his promise to her. This won't do! He belongs to her.

Sylvie walks to the bar and orders another Cornish Rattler, this time from Tania. As Tania walks to the cooler cabinet Sylvie's eyes travel up and down her body, finding fault. She's not so attractive close up. Although she has legs that go on forever, this woman is not someone *her* Oliver would fall for. She flaunts herself too much and flirts with every man she comes into contact with. Is that why Oliver is paying so much attention to that other blonde?

When Tania returns to the skinny woman at the bar, she's surprised to find her breasts being ogled. Pouring cider into a glass, she places it on the counter.

'Seen anything you like?'

Slowly Sylvie raises her eyes. 'Not a lot.'

Tania reels, shocked at the vindictive look on the woman's face. 'Hey! Who the fuck do you think you are?'

There's a touch of madness to Sylvie's laugh and Tania shivers.

Placing her money on the counter, Sylvie picks up the glass and moves away, but then turns back. 'You will never have him, slut,' she hisses. 'He belongs to me. And if you insist on trying to get him I can't be held responsible for my actions. Hands off. He's forbidden territory.' She glares at Tania. 'And as for that ridiculous dance…'

She puts her glass down and takes a couple of steps back. Raising her hands high above her head, Sylvie starts to erotically sway, dipping and rising, not once breaking eye contact. 'Just let it happen…' she says, mimicking the Australian's husky whisper.

Tania's eyes open wide and her jaw drops.

Dismissively, Sylvie runs her eyes over Tania's body one more time. 'I've warned you,' she growls. 'Hands off!' Grabbing the glass, she turns away.

Shocked, Tania holds onto the bar to steady herself.

Sylvie pushes her way through the crowd, once again taking up position on the far side of the decking. As she takes a gulp of cider, she looks across the sea of people in Oliver's direction and chokes.

With one foot propped against the archway, Cara gazes up at Oliver standing in front of her, his right arm outstretched over her shoulder and the palm of his hand flat against the wall for support. Their bodies are almost touching. The look on Oliver's face is tender as he talks to her. They appear oblivious to the other people in the room, and there is something very private and intimate about the way they are with each other.

As Sylvie's jealousy spills over, something evil and twisted slithers up from the depths of her stomach, infecting her like a virus. Voices in her head tell her to destroy all that is good and beautiful, and there's no denying it: the woman with Oliver is stunning. Her beauty transcends her looks, going much deeper in a way that Sylvie has never witnessed before. Suddenly she has a powerful vision of Cara shrouded in a pure golden light, alone on a barren bank, standing beneath a gnarled and twisted tree above a dark and foreboding bog. Her light shines out across the mire, highlighting something thrashing about in the darkness. A twisted, moaning figure crawls its way out of the blackness of the bog. Cloaked in misery and sadness, it clambers up the bank towards the beautiful, golden woman. To Sylvie's horror, she realises the twisted figure is her. The glass slips from her grasp, its contents spewing out across the decking.

'Shit!'

With trembling hand, she retrieves the empty glass. What the hell was that? She glances over at Oliver again. He looks so happy, smiling down at Cara, his face relaxed and eyes alight. Even Sylvie cannot deny the look of love.

'Shit! Shit! Shit!'

A few people turn to look at the strange, skinny woman in the corner. Quickly, they move away.

Beside herself with frustration, Sylvie feels like screaming. She wants to tear Oliver away from that beautiful bitch. He is so near and, still, yet so far. Why is he being so unkind? She knows he likes to play hard to get, but she needs and wants him *now*! Sylvie considers how best to remind Oliver that he belongs to her.

*

Two hours later, Morwenna speaks into her microphone. 'Sadly, that was our last song.' She laughs at the collective groan.

'More!' the audience shout. Morwenna confers with her brother.

'Thanks very much, guys,' says Tristan, grabbing his microphone, 'but haven't you all got homes to go to?'

Further shouts and encouragement and the audience stamp their feet.

'OK, one more,' he says. 'We don't want to wreck Rick's deck… and try saying that when you've had a few!' He laughs and then grows sombre. 'This song is in memory of a truly fantastic and special friend who was not only very supportive of us but also a massive Coldplay fan.'

Tristan looks across at Cara with compassion, and a sea of faces turns in her direction. As if only now becoming aware of their body language, Cara pushes herself away from Oliver and, abruptly, he is brought back to earth from an amazing dream. Cara smiles sadly as she listens to the familiar music. This was Christo's favourite Coldplay song. She bites down hard on her lip, refusing to give into the emotions the music stirs.

Feeling Cara's distress, Oliver yearns to soothe away her pain. He hears the lyrics and it's as if Tristan sings directly to him. He has always felt lost and incomplete but, tonight, he knows the missing piece to the frustrating puzzle of his life has been found.

A big, fat tear slides down Cara's face and brusquely she brushes it away. In an instant Jane is at her side. Putting her arm around Cara, Jane sways with her to the music, effectively deflecting any inquisitive stares. Just a couple of friends enjoying the song.

Oliver feels useless. It should be him holding Cara, kissing away her tears and making everything OK. It's what he wants to do more than anything.

Sylvie watches like a hawk. Seeing Cara's sadness and the pain it causes Oliver, she sneers and her bleak heart rejoices.

As the music finally comes to an end and the crowd reluctantly starts to leave, Oliver turns to Cara. 'What are you doing now?'

'I've got to get back. My parents are babysitting.'

'I'll walk you home.'

She nods and offers a watery smile. Turning to Jane, Cara says, 'Thanks, Jane. You're such a good friend.'

Jane gives her a hug and kisses her on the cheek.

Eventually extricating themselves from their friends, Oliver and Cara exit onto the boardwalk. Sylvie holds back, keeping to the shadows. A thick blanket of silence hangs over the cove, only broken by an occasional shout of farewell as people leave the café. Cara switches on her torch as they walk across the car park onto the track. Oliver glances up at the night sky. The moon is almost full and the sky is awash with stars.

These Cornish skies are amazing! It's never like this in Surrey.

Deanna enters his consciousness, but it's a bittersweet thought and he pushes it to one side. Looking across at Cara, Oliver knows he's in danger of not turning back. In the darkness he finds her hand.

As Sylvie follows, her jealousy eats away at her. Where are they going? The track looks as if it disappears over the edge of the cliff!

They are only yards from The Lookout when Oliver stops and turns Cara to face him. Without speaking, she moves into his loving embrace as if it's the most natural thing in the world. As he covers her mouth with a kiss of such tenderness, Cara feels the deep-rooted sadness leave her body and tentative hope take its place.

Sylvie stops and stares. Filled with hatred for this woman who dares steal her man, she is also transfixed by the glow that surrounds the couple. Despite her venomous thoughts, she feels calm serenity reach out to her.

Oliver's insides have contracted and the 'grey mist' has scuttled to the furthest recesses of his being. Cara is warm and soft and yielding, and he wishes the kiss could go on forever. Gently he pulls away and gazes down at her. Cara's eyes are closed; her face tilted up to his. When he doesn't kiss her again she opens her eyes. With a sudden thrill, Oliver sees his feelings reflected back at him.

'Cara,' he whispers, his voice thick with emotion, and he watches the deeply etched sadness in her beautiful eyes disappear.

'Oliver,' she says breathlessly.

It would be so easy to make love to her here and now. He dare not kiss her again.

'Let me deliver you to your door,' he says gallantly, and she laughs. Oh, how he loves hearing her laughter.

Finding each other's hands once again, Oliver and Cara walk slowly towards the light shining from The Lookout's porch.

Hanging back in the gloom, Sylvie watches as they enter the last bungalow along the track.

*

Ken glances at his wife. 'What's troubling you, Carol?'

Headlights appear in the distance over the brow of the hill and his attention diverts back to the dark road ahead.

'Our daughter.'

'What do you mean?'

Carol sighs. 'Didn't you see how she looked tonight?'

'Yes, happy for the first time in many months.' Ken glances at his wife again. 'Surely, you can't deny her that?'

'Of course not, Ken! I, as much as you, want her to be happy.'

'Then what?'

Carol sighs again. 'What do you suppose is making her so happy?'

Ken considers her question. 'I suspect it has rather a lot to do with that charming actor I met tonight.'

'I fear it does.'

Indicating right, he turns off the main road. 'Why fear?'

'Where have you been these past two decades?' Carol asks, exasperatedly.

'With you, my love,' Ken answers calmly, 'and a wonderful life it is too.'

Carol smiles, despite her concerns. Then slowly she says, 'Oliver Foxley is married, and the wife that I met is a formidable woman.'

*

Oliver stands in the darkness, thankful the others have yet to return to the farmhouse. He has a lot to sort out. Standing at the open French doors, he looks across the lawn to the Cornish stone hedge and the heathland beyond. The moon casts a silvery glow over the surroundings. It could be any century, so unspoiled and unchanged is the landscape. Glancing up at the man in the moon, he wonders if Cara also looks up at him, suspended in the same sky only two miles further along the coast. The thought warms his heart, momentarily affording some peace to his troubled soul. He tries to distinguish the individual stars making up the Milky Way arcing across the night sky. How many other people in the world are looking up at the galaxy at this precise moment in his predicament? He loves Deanna – of course he does – despite the current dysfunctional nature of their relationship. They have built a life together and created a family, and she has been beside him from the very first flicker of his fame. But, there is something about Cara that speaks to him on a level he and his wife have failed to reach. He has never felt anything close to what he feels for Cara.

As he relives their kiss, there is the sweetest taste on his lips. He shouldn't have done that, but he was powerless and it seemed such a natural thing to do. There was nothing awkward about it. Oliver groans. He has to stop this right now, for all their sakes. He saw the way Cara looked at him. It made his heart stop and his stomach turn inside out, and he wanted her in a way he had never wanted anyone before. But what he feels for her, and what he hopes she feels for him, has nowhere to go. He punches the doorframe, but there's no avoiding it: Oliver Foxley is in love for the very first time.

'Why?' he cries into the night air. 'Why bring her to me now?' An eerie screech carries on the wind and Oliver shivers.

A movement to his right makes him turn and he watches as the pale, ghostly shape of an owl glides across the lawn on buoyant wingbeats towards the heathland. A silent predator of the night world. He stands at the open door a while longer until he hears tyres crunching on the gravel. Closing the French doors, he quickly makes his way to his room before the others enter the house.

Bethany is sound asleep and Cara quietly closes the bedroom door. Checking on Sky, she finds him awake. Barnaby, curled up at the foot of the bed, looks up inquisitively as she enters the room and thumps his tail on the duvet.

'Did you have a good evening with Grandma and Grandpa?' Cara asks, sitting next to Barnaby.

'Yes.' Sky breaks into a smile. 'Grandpa and I had two bowls of ice cream.'

'Did you, now?' says Cara, stringing out the last word.

'Promise not to tell Grandma? I don't want to get him into trouble.'

'It'll be our secret,' Cara says, smiling at her son. She brushes his fringe out of his eyes. 'It's late, Sky. You should be asleep.'

Turning onto his side, the young boy pulls a well-loved teddy into his arms.

'Goodnight, sweet Sky. Pleasant dreams.' She kisses him on the forehead and calls to Barnaby. Reluctantly, the dog gets off the bed.

She's at the door when Sky calls out. 'Was Oliver with you tonight?'

Unprepared for the question, she breaks into a smile. 'Yes, he was.'

'I like him. Can he take me to school one day?'

'Oh, I don't know about that. He's a busy man.' And he has a family of his own, she thinks. But, seeing the disappointment on her son's face, she adds, 'I tell you what, I'll ask him to supper one evening. That would be fun, wouldn't it?'

The boy nods.

'Goodnight, Sky.' She blows him a kiss and pulls the door to, leaving it ajar a couple of inches.

As Cara walks to her bedroom, she contemplates all that has happened during the evening. Oliver Foxley kissed her! It seemed so right. There was nothing ungainly about it, no embarrassing smashing of teeth or bruising of lips. It was just lovely. And it stirred feelings she never thought to experience again. Briefly, she wonders if he is simply playing with her, flirting with the idea of a summer fling to pass the time while he is in Cornwall, but instantly she rejects the thought. Oliver is not shallow or flippant and he has never portrayed himself to be anything other than caring and thoughtful, especially where she is concerned. Butterflies in the pit of her stomach take flight. And he has never cowered from exposing his raw, vulnerable side to her. No, Oliver is something real, something worth keeping and someone she would be prepared to love because of his flaws, not in spite of them.

Aware that she is close to falling in love, Cara reaches for the cherished photo displayed on her bedside cabinet. In a voice filled with emotion, she whispers, 'Christo, there will always be a place in my heart for you.'

Chapter Twenty-Seven

Oliver straightens up from a deep bow. It has been a particularly good show and another full house. It's always encouraging when matinees prove as popular as evening performances. As the season has progressed, the members of the Tasmanian Devil Theatre Company have become like family; their delivery ever smoother.

'Coming for a drink, Mr Fox?' Tas approaches Oliver.

'Can't. I have a supper date with a small boy.'

Tas cocks his head, a questioning look on his face.

'Sky Penhaligon.' Oliver enlightens his friend.

'Ah, that cheeky little chap!' Tas chuckles. 'Sure it's not with his mother?' He raises an eyebrow as a fleeting emotion passes across Oliver's face. 'I see…'

'You see nothing, Tas. There's nothing to see,' Oliver says more harshly than intended.

'Hey!' Tas stares at his friend. 'It's none of my business.'

'No.'

'But, Ollie, Cornwall gets under the skin – I warned you about that before you joined the company – and you're a long way from home. Just don't get carried away with it all.' Slapping his leading man on the back, Tas moves away to talk to another cast member.

Oliver walks to the side of the stage and picks up his jacket before making his way to the exit. It's bright and sunny when he emerges out into the car park of Helston's Old Cattle Market. He presses the key fob in his hand and the Mercedes' doors unlock.

'Oliver!'

The blood in his veins turns to ice as he turns in the direction of her voice.

Leaning against the bonnet of her car, Sylvie drinks in his beauty. 'You are very naughty! You haven't phoned.'

'What are you doing here?' Oliver asks in a shocked whisper. He can see the madness dancing just beneath the surface of her wild eyes as she walks towards him.

'You promised to call but you haven't, so I thought I'd come to you.'

'Sylvie, you can't just turn up like this!'

'Why not? I'm a big girl now,' she says, swaying from side to side like a child; her eyes wide and innocent.

Oliver looks around. A few cast members, making their way to their cars, glance in his direction and call out goodbye. He waits for them to pass before grabbing Sylvie roughly by the wrist and dragging her towards her car. Her wrist is thin; it would so easily snap. Oliver eases his hold.

'Sylvie, this has got to stop.'

'Why? If I want to see the play you can't stop me.'

That's true.

'Where are you staying?' he asks.

Thinking about her room at the B&B, Sylvie wonders if he will come back with her. 'Just outside Mullion.'

A bit too close for comfort.

'I told you I was busy for several months.'

'Yes, I know.' She smiles up at him. 'That's why I came to you!'

How the hell is he going to get rid of her? Oliver rakes a hand through his hair.

'But you're not busy now,' she says coquettishly.

'Actually, I am.'

She pouts. 'Why won't you see me? You said you'd phone but you haven't kept your word, Oliver.'

If he leaves for Cara's now, Sylvie is bound to follow. The last thing he wants is to put that little family in jeopardy.

'Everything OK here?' Tas asks, approaching.

Sylvie glances warily at the driver of the big black Jeep.

'Tas, this is Sylvie, a *big* fan of the play,' Oliver says. 'In fact, she's come all the way from London to see it, but sadly she has to go back.'

Sylvie stares at Oliver. What's he saying? He's sending her away? No! He can't be so cruel.

Something in Oliver's tone warns Tas this is no ardent fan. Looking behind Sylvie, he recognises the dark blue car. This must be Oliver's stalker.

'Well, that's a shame,' Tas says lightly. 'Seeing as you've come such a long way I think you deserve some special merchandise to take back with you.' Before Sylvie has a chance to react, Tas marches her towards the hall.

'Hey, get off me!' she protests, as he forcefully steers her through the door.

Oliver climbs into the Mercedes and quickly heads towards the Lizard. He can't stop Sylvie seeing the play and, no doubt, she will follow him for the rest of the tour. Twenty minutes later he pulls up outside The Lookout and parks alongside Cara's car. It's a glorious late afternoon and several families are on the beach. A number of sailing dinghies tack across the bay and a couple of kayakers paddle in the shallows.

'Oliver!' Sky appears at the open car window.

'Hello, young man,' says Oliver. 'What have you been up to?'

'Barnaby and me, we've been on the beach doing the cordnashun game,' Sky informs him. Oliver's brow furrows. 'You know… the game with the Frisbee.'

'Aha!' says Oliver, climbing out of the car. 'He was excellent, I recall.'

Bethany watches shyly from the stable door.

'Hello, Beth,' Oliver says and smiles. She smiles in return. As soon as he reaches the porch, Bethany finds his hand and leads him into the living room. Oliver's heart squeezes.

In the kitchen, Cara puts the finishing touches to a fish pie and almost drops it at the sight of Bethany leading Oliver by the hand. Sky chatters excitedly. Her children are so natural with him. The perfect family. She grows hot at the thought.

'Hello, Oliver,' she says, carefully placing the pie in the oven. 'We're so pleased you could come to supper.'

'Thank you for the invite,' he says, and Sky beams.

'How was the matinee?' she asks.

Oliver angrily pushes away a vision of Sylvie in the car park. *Nothing* is going to spoil his evening with this lovely family.

'Good. Packed.'

'Were my mother and Sheila there again?' Cara laughs. She knows they have been to a number of performances.

'They gave this one a miss,' Oliver says with a smile. Bethany still holds his hand.

'Beth, why don't you let go of Oliver?' Cara suggests gently. 'He's not going anywhere for a while!'

Reluctantly, Bethany drops his hand and glances up at him shyly. Oliver winks.

'Now, what can I get you? Tea, coffee or something stronger?'

*

Four hours later, once Bethany and Sky have gone to bed after demanding Oliver read them a story, he and Cara sit quietly on the boat seat overlooking the cove. The sun dips towards the horizon but there are still several people on the beach, making the most of the long summer's day. Following the shock of seeing Sylvie, it has been a wonderfully uncomplicated evening and Oliver feels mellow as he drinks his beer.

'Thank you, Cara,' he says, thanking her for so much more than just supper. Cara smiles and sips her wine. 'This is so special.' His gaze casts over the cove.

'I never tire of the view. It's ever changing,' Cara says, remembering how she and Christo spent ages trying out various locations to find the best spot for the seat.

Looking in the direction of the café, Oliver can make out Tania on the boardwalk lighting up a cigarette. 'It's a good vantage point.'

'You can see everything that happens from here.'

'Is that why it's called The Lookout?'

Cara shakes her head. 'No. Christo gave it that name because when things get tough I like to look out across the Atlantic towards Puerto Rico and wonder what all those people four thousand miles away are doing.' There's a faraway look in her eyes as she speaks. 'When his grandfather lived here it was simply called The Bungalow.' She pulls herself back to the present. 'I wouldn't want to live anywhere else, though. I'm happy here.'

Oliver gazes at her. Despite all that has happened to her she does look happy. The sadness has lifted from her eyes. 'I'm glad you're happy, Cara.'

She looks at him in surprise, then smiles. 'It's this place, Oliver. There's magic in the air.'

'I thought that the very first time I was here,' he says, looking directly at her. A wave of excitement courses through him as he remembers the powerful impact she had on him when he first set eyes on her.

'I'm glad you feel it too,' she says. 'Most people just see a ramshackle bungalow clinging to an unkempt patch of cliff in an out-of-the-way cove. I suppose, if I ever find myself settled in a loving relationship I will attempt to tame the land and create a colourful garden. Perhaps I'll enclose it in a white picket fence! But, for the present, I have more pressing considerations.'

He's looking at her in that special way of his, and Cara wishes he would kiss her again. If only he were free…

They watch the sun sink slowly below the horizon, putting on a final display before plunging the cove into darkness. Suddenly the discordant sounds of a ringtone shatter the peace and tranquillity. Oliver stands and extracts the mobile from his pocket.

'Hello,' he says and then frowns. Immediately he strides across the rough garden towards the cliff edge.

Rising to her feet, Cara switches on the outside light. She returns to the seat and hears a heated discussion taking place. Who has called at this hour? Is it his wife? It must be important. She's about to give him some privacy and go inside when Oliver looks over at her with an apologetic smile. He turns away again, says something further and then slips the mobile back into his pocket. He doesn't immediately return but stands a while longer looking out across the, now, inky black ocean. Cara recognises his deflated stance. She's been there herself, and in that very spot too. Eventually he turns and there's a deeply troubled look on his face. When he joins her once more on the boat seat he doesn't say anything, but just takes her hand.

'What is it, Oliver?' she asks softly.

Lacing his fingers through hers, Oliver notices how well her hand fits his. He feels as if he could share all his concerns with her, but is that fair? And would his troubles turn her away? Perhaps that's what should happen, seeing as his feelings for her have nowhere to go. He wonders if he's brave enough to risk losing whatever it is they have between them. Making his mind up, Oliver takes a deep breath and starts to speak. He tells her about his visit to Holy Isle, holding nothing back, and, as he talks, the weight of the world lifts from his shoulders.

'... and then, this afternoon, Sylvie was waiting for me outside the Old Cattle Market. She's demanding I see her again before she goes back to London, otherwise she will tell Deanna everything.'

Cara considers what Oliver has just shared with her. How awful it must be to have people treat you as public property, but how could he let things get so out of hand? He must have been in a very dark place to allow this woman to enter his room and take advantage of him. Fleetingly, Cara wonders if there's more to this story but she swiftly dismisses the thought. Oliver has never flinched from showing himself to her in all his colours. How exhausting it must be for him to always consider how he comes across in case the things he says, or does, are twisted. The stress must be enormous! No wonder he seems so at ease in her humble abode and happy to participate in simple, family pleasures.

'Oliver, why don't you tell your wife?' she asks softly. 'Then this Sylvie won't have a hold over you.'

Oliver shakes his head. 'Deanna wouldn't understand. I can't talk to her like this…' His voice trails away, and Cara's heart goes out to the man who has just laid himself bare.

'Well, then, why don't you just deny it? Say Sylvie has an overactive imagination, which is true. After all, it's only her word against yours. Surely your wife would believe you?'

Oliver looks at Cara and smiles sadly. It is so easy to talk to her. She has not held him in judgement.

'She wouldn't, not after all the extra security I've put in place.' His eyes are full of tenderness. 'Thank you for listening.'

'Always.'

Unseeing, he turns and stares out to sea, her hand still in his. A frown furrows his brow. If only he could talk to Deanna like this. When did they lose their connection?

Cara studies his profile. Who would have thought Oliver Foxley had such troubles? How trusting to be so honest with her.

'You need to go to the police, Oliver. She can't be allowed to blackmail you and get away with it.' Oliver shakes his head. 'But why not?'

'Going to the police is only one step away from the press getting hold of the story. Even the faintest whiff of a scandal will stick like glue… for years. The repercussions for my family are enormous. No, I can't go to the police.'

Falling silent, they listen to the soothing sounds of the ocean, and Oliver places his arm around Cara's shoulder, drawing her to him. He smiles as she rests her head on his shoulder. Everything happens so naturally with Cara. He could sit here forever. Suddenly he has a vision of them in their dotage, sitting on the boat seat and looking out over the sea, still happy in each other's company. How can that ever be?

And what the hell is he going to do about Sylvie?

'Oliver.'

'Hmm?'

'Are you busy next Friday evening?'

'No, why?'

'The children's paternal grandparents are picking them up from school. They're having Beth and Sky for the weekend.' Cara stills her racing heart. 'I wondered if you'd like to come for dinner,' she says uncertainly. 'Just you and me.'

Just the two of us, alone!

As a thrill courses through Oliver's body, Cara feels a muscle spasm involuntarily in his arm.

'I can think of nothing I'd rather do,' Oliver says, gently twisting a strand of her long blonde hair between his fingers.

Lifting her head, Cara glances up at him. There's no mistaking the longing in his eyes.

Chapter Twenty-Eight

Tania looks up as Oliver enters the kitchen. 'Good morning.'

'Morning,' he growls in response.

'Want some coffee? I've just made some.' She points at the cafetière.

'Thanks. I need to be alert this morning,' he says grimly. He pours himself a black coffee.

Biting into her buttered toast, Tania considers her guest. He looks pale and drawn.

Oliver pulls out a chair, its legs scraping noisily over the flagstone floor. The sound is alarmingly jarring in the quiet of the kitchen and he winces. Sitting, he runs a hand through his hair. He's had a terrible night. It was so hard leaving Cara, but he fought his desire and returned to the farmhouse only to spend the rest of the night tossing and turning, finding no peace. He tried to meditate, but his body was hot-wired and his mind kept wandering to Sylvie and how to handle her this morning. Lifting his gaze, Oliver sees Tania studying him.

'Haven't seen you for a while,' she says. 'Everything OK, Ollie?'

He grimaces but says nothing. She joins him at the table.

'What are you doing up so early?' Oliver asks.

'I've got some deliveries at the café to take care of,' she says. 'By the way, I had a strange encounter at The Corrington gig. I served a very odd woman. She was scarily weird!'

The hairs on the back of Oliver's neck stand erect. 'What did she look like?' he demands.

'Approximately mid to late thirties. Small, skinny, mousy-haired, wild-eyed! Definitely a bit unhinged.'

Sylvie was at the café!

'She threatened me and told me I would never have you, as if I ever needed reminding of that!' Tania says wistfully. 'But more than that, she said you belonged to her and that you were forbidden territory. What did she mean by that? Who is she?'

Oliver groans.

This is getting totally out of hand!

'My most ardent fan who just so happens to dwell in cloud cuckoo land.'

Tania stares at Oliver. His face is deathly white and there are dark circles beneath his sunken eyes.

'Do you want some painkillers?' she asks. Oliver shakes his head. Tania hesitates before continuing, 'Ollie, I think she's been to the farmhouse.'

'Why do you say that?' Oliver asks sharply.

'Well, she commented on something she could only know about if she'd been here.' Tania doesn't elaborate. 'Do you think she's dangerous?'

If Sylvie knows where I'm staying and she's been to the café, what else does she know? Does she know where Cara lives? Oliver breaks out into a cold sweat.

'Do you, Ollie?' Tania asks.

'Do I what?'

'Think she's dangerous?'

Oliver feels the onset of panic. How can he protect both his family and Cara's at the same time? There's little comfort knowing that if Sylvie is in one place she can't be in the other. Perhaps he should do what Cara suggests and go to the police. Maybe the press interest could be contained.

Fuck! If only I could discuss it with Deanna. Together we could work it out.

For what seems like the millionth time during his marriage, Oliver grapples with the familiar disconnectedness.

'You really don't look well,' says Tania with concern.

'I'm fine.' Abruptly, Oliver rises to his feet. He has got to sort this out. 'I don't think she's dangerous, Tan, but it wouldn't hurt to be vigilant,' he says in a serious voice.

*

Sitting on the outside decking overlooking Gyllyngvase Beach, Sylvie wraps her cardigan tightly around her body against the cool onshore breeze. It's early, but already several families have claimed their patch of beach for the glorious summer day predicted by the weather forecasters. She looks repeatedly towards the entrance. He promised to meet her for breakfast and she congratulates herself on the way she manipulated this latest contact. It wasn't the invitation she hoped for – he didn't volunteer it – but at least he agreed to meet her. She glances at her watch again. Where is he? The café is popular and she's had to fend off a number of people wanting to sit at her table. He's not going to stand her up, is he? Suddenly a figure appears at the top of the slope. Even though he's tried to disguise himself by wearing a baseball cap and sunglasses, she would know him anywhere.

Oliver kicks himself for agreeing to meet Sylvie but, sick of her threats, he is determined to sort this out once and for all. The café is full, thank goodness! The more people about, the better, though he hopes there aren't too many cameras. Oliver peers through the glass entrance door, but she's not inside. He walks onto the decked verandah and sees her sitting at the first table overlooking the beach. She waves enthusiastically. Reluctantly, he approaches.

Sylvie jumps to her feet. Rushing towards him, she throws her arms around his neck and tries to kiss him. Averting his face, Oliver pushes her away.

'Sylvie, sit down!' he says in exasperation. He sits opposite and glances across the sand.

Sparkling in the sunshine, the sea is a wonderful shade of blue, and the air is filled with the sounds of happy families. It's too beautiful a day to be anything less than joyful, but Oliver feels only despondency and gloom.

'Can I get you anything?' asks a pretty, young waitress.

'Coffee, please, black.' He smiles and the girl returns his smile. Oliver watches as she disappears inside the café. Turning his attention to Sylvie, he removes his sunglasses and observes her dispassionately. 'So, Sylvie,' he says in a flat voice, 'what are we going to do?'

Sylvie stares at him, rocking slightly. Having seen the loving way he looks at Cara, she doesn't like the coldness in the eyes that meet hers. Folding her arms on the table to still her movements, she says, 'You haven't phoned.'

'I told you, I'm busy,' Oliver says impatiently. 'I also told you I would phone you from time to time, Sylvie. Time to time…'

'But you haven't.'

Oliver groans. He *so* doesn't want this.

'And as you haven't phoned me, I thought I'd come to you instead!' Sylvie says, as if cleverly providing the perfect solution to a perplexing conundrum.

'But why, Sylvie? What in God's name makes you think I want you to come to me?'

The waitress arrives with his coffee. Setting it down on the table, she flashes him a dazzling smile before moving on to the next table. Sylvie scowls. How dare that little tart smile at her man, as if she weren't even there?

Noticing Sylvie's look of hatred directed at the waitress, Oliver snaps her attention back to him. 'Sylvie, answer me.'

Her eyes grow large. Why is he talking to her so harshly? Of course he wants her to come to him. She is his lover!

'Because you love me.'

Oliver gives a hollow laugh. 'How wrong you are. Listen to me.' Slowly he accentuates each word. 'I_ do_ not_ love_ you!'

'But you loved me in Scotland.'

Feeling sick at the memory, Oliver sips his coffee. It's hot and scalds his mouth but he welcomes the pain, distracting him from the unwelcome vision of Sylvie writhing on top of him. He looks at her again with eyes of steel.

'What do you not understand, Sylvie? I have never loved you and never will. I love my wife and family and that's all there is to it.'

Sylvie rocks to and fro, blinking rapidly and chewing her cheeks. This is not the romantic breakfast date she envisaged. Suddenly she grows perfectly still. Relaxing her jaw, she looks challengingly across the table at Oliver.

'If you love your wife and family so much, what were you doing with that blonde from the cliff bungalow?' Sylvie spits out the words.

Dear God, she does know where Cara lives!

Oliver turns pale and his blood runs cold. How dare this woman stalk him and threaten all those he cares for?

'Yes, I saw you, smooching up to her and kissing her. What would your wifey think of that, Oliver?'

'Sylvie,' he growls menacingly, 'it has nothing to do with you how I conduct my life or what my wife thinks.'

Sylvie hesitates, thrown by his tone. Quickly she changes tack. 'But I love you so much, Oliver,' she says in a girly voice. 'Why are you being so cruel?'

Oliver watches as tears run down her face. 'Are you on medication?' he asks more gently.

She shakes her head and then nods.

'Is there anyone you can talk to?' He remembers the woman with her on Holy Isle. 'Your aunt, perhaps?'

Wiping her face with the back of her hand, Sylvie nods. This is good. He's looking at her in a much more kindly way now. Keep the tears falling.

'Why don't you phone her? Maybe your medication needs adjusting. If so, you will feel so much better. It will help you see life from a different perspective.'

Sylvie bites her lip and Oliver glances at his watch. He's had enough of this. Putting on his sunglasses, he wedges a fiver under the saucer.

Sylvie looks on in alarm. 'Don't go, Oliver,' she pleads.

'I have to.'

'No!' she shouts.

As he rises from the table, so does Sylvie. With a desperate lunge she grabs him around his waist and falls to her knees. 'I'd do anything for you!'

'Don't do this, Sylvie,' he says, shaking her off. 'Don't demean yourself.'

Sylvie falls prostrate to the floor. Several tables now watch the unfolding drama with interest.

'I love you,' she sobs.

'Rubbish, Sylvie. Get some help,' Oliver growls, as he walks briskly away.

'But I do, Oliver. I love you,' she screams.

He doesn't look back.

Sylvie watches him as he climbs the slope and disappears down the road. Turning to collect her handbag, she glares at the people inquisitively staring.

'What are you dumb suckers looking at?' she shouts.

No sign of tears now…

Chapter Twenty-Nine

As Oliver lowers the window, a blast of warm air hits him squarely in the face. The cove is cloaked in peaceful serenity and the tide gently laps the shoreline. A low hum of voices, interspersed with sudden laughter, wafts over from the decking; people enjoying a Friday night out. He sits a while longer, breathing in the unique atmosphere. During the last week he's barely slept. He should be feeling dreadful, yet he feels more alive and invigorated than ever. Starting the engine, he noses the car out of the car park and heads towards The Lookout. He has never felt so nervous. He's like a schoolboy on his first date.

Cara looks round the room one more time and tells herself not to panic. Just breathe. She glances up at the surfboard on the wall and gazes at Christo's characterful face.

'I know, I know,' she whispers, 'but it's just a meal. Nothing's going to happen. How can it?'

No longer can she ignore her growing feelings for Oliver. He has lifted her from deep despair and she will always be grateful to him for that. However, she cannot forget or discount the fact that he has a wife and children waiting for him in Surrey. She will not be the catalyst for tearing that precious achievement apart.

Headlights sweep the track before she hears his car. Despite her assurances to Christo, the butterflies lift and swirl. She breathes in deeply, trying to instil some calm, knowing she has no one else but herself to blame. *She* asked him. Smoothing down her dress, Cara walks to the porch door, her nerves jittering and those damned butterflies refusing to settle. She feels as giddy as a schoolgirl with a heavy crush. As she reaches for the handle her hand trembles. It's just a meal, she tells herself again.

With one last deep breath she opens the door.

Oliver grabs the bottle of wine from the passenger seat. He considered champagne but somehow it didn't feel appropriate. Eventually he settled on a good red wine. Climbing out of the Mercedes, he turns towards The Lookout and his heart misses a beat. Bathed in a glorious golden light, Cara is simply beautiful.

'Hi,' he says, walking towards her and hoping his voice doesn't give away his nervousness.

'Hi yourself,' she says, wondering whether she should kiss him on the cheek in welcome.

But, before Cara has a chance to decide, Oliver wraps her in a passionate embrace. He meant it to be a light-hearted hug but, as if it has a life of its own, his mouth immediately seeks hers. As the kiss deepens, it turns into something else. Eventually they prise themselves apart and stare at each other in amazement. Nerves settled; eyes shining. No longer is Oliver lost and adrift in the wilderness. He has come home.

'Hello, you,' he whispers tenderly, as if to a lover rediscovered after many years apart.

Cara smiles. Without saying a word she leads him inside.

*

Whoa! This feels weird. Oliver glances down. To his surprise, he's wearing a wetsuit and sitting astride a brightly coloured surfboard. The top of his head prickles under the heat of a merciless sun. Unbalanced, he repositions his body and tries to relax, offering no resistance to the swell. In the distance he can hear the sounds of a day on the beach: breaking surf, shouts, laughter, babies crying and dogs barking. As the swell effortlessly lifts his board Oliver grips the rails, aware of a deep, vast ocean beneath.

Sudden laughter and Oliver turns. Clear blue eyes dance in merriment as they consider him. The young man with the memorably characterful face is deeply tanned, his blond hair sea-wet dark.

'OK, man?' Christo asks, paddling his surfboard alongside.

'Think so,' says Oliver as another swell rocks his board and threatens to unbalance him.

'Imagine the ocean is a beguiling woman,' says Christo, grinning. 'Don't resist, just go with the flow.' He laughs again.

Something about Christo is so alive; a young man embracing every experience to come his way. His energy is infectious.

Oliver paddles his board sideways to the beach. They are some way offshore. To their right is Anvil Rock and directly in front is The Lookout, perched high on the cliffs. Other surfers are in the sea, either sitting and waiting, or standing and riding the waves, but Christo and he are alone in this section of water. As Oliver's eyes become accustomed to the light, figures on the beach take shape and he sees a young Cara looking in their direction, shielding her eyes against the sun. She waves and Christo waves back. Oliver's heart skips a beat. She is aged about twenty, her long blonde hair reaches to her waist and her bikini-clad body is lithe and naturally sun-kissed. She is stunning – as he knew she would be – untouched by any stain of future tragedy.

'You've noticed the wife, then,' says Christo good-naturedly, his eyes dancing with laughter. 'She's an angel. Don't know what I did to deserve her. She's the best thing that ever happened to me.' His voice is full of pride.

Dragging his eyes away from Cara, Oliver sees the look of love on the young man's face.

'Besides the surf, that is,' adds Christo with a grin.

Oliver gives a small smile.

How did I get out here on the ocean with Christo? And what the hell am I doing on a surfboard?

'OK, man, ready to catch waves?' Effortlessly, Christo turns his board to face the ocean. 'Just remember, duck-dive any breaking wave over two feet. That way, all the progress you've made paddling out won't be lost by being washed backwards by the wave. Simple!'

Lying flat on his board, Christo pushes himself up and arches his back, chest up. With a steady stroke he paddles across the plate-glass sea towards the rhythmic, big peaks on the horizon.

Do I know how to do this?

Oliver turns back to look at Cara one more time and his heart leaps. The young Cara stands on the beach watching him, but the look she gives him comes straight from the mature woman he knows today… and it promises him the world. Slowly she smiles.

'Come on, Oliver!' shouts Christo. 'It's now or never. Take on the forces of Mother Nature for the thrill of your life.'

Because the tide is full, the current is very strong. Keeping Christo in his sights, Oliver paddles past Anvil Rock, battling through the waves to the line-up. When the first wave comes he turns and, with head down, pulls water hard, paddling his board as fast he can. As he starts to accelerate down the face of the wave, Oliver rises to his feet and balances himself. Gritting his teeth in determined concentration, he maintains speed to outrun it; the explosion at his heels. And he makes it. He gets away! After that there's no stopping him. Together, actor and surfer catch wave after wave, making it down the face of each before it hits the curve, trips and topples over, crashing down on them.

The sun, still strong, dips rapidly towards the horizon, gifting the remaining people on the sands a magnificent fiery sunset. He and Christo have been out there for hours and every muscle in Oliver's body aches, yet he feels invigorated and full of life. He has survived! Together, they carry their boards up the beach, exhausted yet never more alive.

'Wow, man, you sure know how to surf,' Christo says. 'It'll be Mavericks for you next!'

Oliver laughs. 'It's one of the most exciting things I've ever done.'

Planting his board in the sand, Christo unzips his wetsuit. 'Yeah, it's one hell of a thrill, that's for sure. But you're wrong.' He glances sideways at Oliver.

'One of the most exciting things you'll ever do is waiting for you up there.' He jerks his head towards The Lookout and Oliver's eyes open wide. 'But I tell you, man, don't play with her heart.' Christo's voice is deadly serious. 'If you can't follow through don't even start…'

*

Oliver's eyes flicker open. A pre-dawn light fills the room and for a brief moment he wonders where he is. And then it all comes flooding back. Rolling onto his side, he sees her sleeping peacefully beside him. Throughout the night they have found solace in each other's touch; the one fixing the other.

Oliver props himself on one elbow, careful not to disturb her, and gazes at Cara in wonder. She looks so young, just like the girl in his dream, without a care in the world. He, too, feels as if he hasn't a care in the world, though he knows he should have every care. For the first time in his life Oliver feels whole, all the missing pieces of the frustrating jigsaw finally having found their rightful place. Reaching out, he draws Cara gently to him. He so wants to make love to her again but, for now, he will let her sleep. As he curves his body protectively around her sleeping form, Oliver hears Christo's warning ring in his ears. Silently, he promises he will follow through.

Cara snuggles into Oliver's warm embrace and a smile settles on her lips. Later, when she thinks back to this moment, she is never sure whether it was just her imagination or if she did hear him whisper, 'Thank you for showing up, beautiful girl of my dreams.'

*

The sound of waves and a scratching, tapping noise drag Oliver from a deep, healing sleep. He doesn't want to wake – he's warm and peaceful where he is – but the noise increases. Slowly he opens his eyes. Shafts of sunlight filter through the wooden slatted blinds and a pair of calico curtains billow in a gentle breeze. The sound comes from the roof. Looking up to the vaulted ceiling, he follows the tapping as it works its way along the roofline. An animal of some sort – is it a rat? A shrill, raucous cry identifies it as a gull. Unseen, the bird rises off the ridge tiles and hovers briefly on an air pocket before swooping out over the cliffs towards the shoreline in search of breakfast. Sounds of beachside living. How he'd love to wake to this every morning.

Clasping his hands behind his head, Oliver looks around. It's a simple, understated room. Even though she makes a living from the use of vibrant colour, everything in Cara's bedroom is painted white, even the A-frames. He loves this paradox in her. His hand reaches out to her side of the bed – the sheets are cold – and it occurs to him he might be in the middle of another dream. The surfing dream with Christo seemed real enough. Maybe he will wake to find he's in bed at the farmhouse, or in Surrey with Deanna. This last thought makes him pause…

The alarm clock displays 06:15. By rights, he should be exhausted but he feels super-energised. Throughout the night they made love and his staying power amazed him, but with Cara it all seems as natural as breathing. Eventually they fell asleep, entwined in each other's arms.

Oliver gets out of bed and retrieves his clothes from a heap on the floor, smiling wryly as he recalls how he couldn't get out of them quickly enough last night. He pulls on his jeans and shirt, and walks down the hallway, calling for Cara. All is silent. As he makes his way through the living room to the kitchen, Oliver notices her car parked alongside the Mercedes. Taking a glass from a cupboard, he fills it with cold water and takes a sip.

'Morning, Basil.'

From its favourite position amongst the pot plants on the window sill, the cat blinks at him, stretches and then resumes its slumbers.

Where is she?

Oliver peers through the kitchen window, but there's no sign of Cara. Perhaps she's painting in her studio and hasn't heard him? He climbs the wooden stairs and stops at the door, respectful of her inner sanctum. The room is a wonderful space for an artist's studio. Light floods in on three sides from windows with commanding views over the cove. Propped against the walls are numerous canvases, but it's the one on the easel that catches his eye. On it is an outline of the hidden view she shared with him when they were on the cusp of something profound, only for Greg to break the moment. Was that only four weeks ago? Time has taken on a different dimension in Cornwall; his Surrey life is but a vague recollection. The work in progress promises to be achingly beautiful, but it causes an odd sensation. It makes him want to cry. Oliver frowns.

Must be a reaction to the enormity of what we've started.

He descends the wooden stairs. As he enters the living room, a note propped against a vase on the dining table catches his eye.

Help yourself to tea or coffee. If you want something a little more adventurous

follow the footprints in the sand…

He smiles. As with her paintings, Cara's handwriting is distinctively creative.

Oliver decides not to bother with shoes. Closing the porch door behind him, he gingerly crosses the stony track onto grass and heads towards the steps leading down to the beach. The sky is a cloudless, cornflower blue and the warmth of the early morning sun caresses his skin. A gentle summer breeze ruffles his hair. He pauses at the top of the steps and looks along the full expanse of the cove. There's not a soul about. The sands are pristine, washed clean by the last full tide, and a flock of seagulls zealously guard the water's edge eyeing up the next meal. Glancing to his left, Oliver sees footprints leading across the sand before disappearing around a rocky promontory. He descends the steps and follows her trail.

The tide is out, allowing him access to a further stretch of sand usually cut off by the sea. Here, the cliffs tower high above a natural and wild cove with no human habitation in sight. At the far end is Cara. Oblivious to his presence, she walks with head bent, her white jeans rolled up to her knees. Occasionally she stoops to pick up a shell or some other object of interest and Oliver's heart swells. He loves that she should still finds things of interest, even though she's lived here for years and has probably beachcombed every inch. Her blonde hair glistens in the sunlight and he is simply dazzled by her.

A beautiful, guardian angel of silver and gold.

The thought surprises him but, as he watches, Cara's radiance intensifies as if, indeed, she is an angel come to earth. He knows their night of passion was born of the deepest love and the highest faith, for he felt her within; soul-bound complete, entwined forever in pure serenity...

How poetic and so early in the morning too!

The discordant screech of a gull from high on the cliffs makes Cara look up. Catching sight of Oliver, she waves. It was one hell of a night! She left him sleeping, needing time alone to assimilate all that occurred. He looks different this morning, she thinks. Still devastatingly good-looking, of course, but there's an additional element to his countenance. What is it? She smiles as the answer comes to her. He looks free.

'Fancy a swim?' she calls along the lonely beach.

'What, now?'

'No time like the present,' she says with a laugh.

Unzipping her jeans, she steps out of them and then peels off her T-shirt. Lastly, she removes her knickers. Vulnerable and naked, Cara glances at Oliver, but there's nothing vulnerable about the look she gives him. It's the same one from his dream, promising him the world. Turning, she runs into the sea. As she dives beneath the waves, her neat buttocks rise briefly out of the water enticing him in. Oliver's breath hitches in his throat. Surfacing a few yards further out, Cara shakes her long wet hair out of her face and turns to face him. With the sun behind her, she rises out of the ocean and, with arms outstretched, raises her hands high above her head, the water cascading through her open fingers giving the impression of wings.

Indeed! A beautiful, guardian angel of silver and gold.

'Come on in, Oliver,' she says, a smile lighting her face. 'It's as warm as a bath.'

Oliver glances up at the cliffs and along the beach. This would be a prime opportunity for unsolicited photographs to end up in the papers. Unbuttoning his shirt, he takes it off and places it on the sand. Then, checking the beach and cliff top again, he removes his jeans. Oliver stands naked on the sand.

Even though she's just spent the most glorious night with this man, Cara breathes in sharply. He's in great shape: no spare flesh; muscles well defined; and there's an outline of a six-pack. She savours his physique.

Oliver walks towards the sea, the wet sand oozing between his toes. It's a glorious feeling to be unfettered by any trappings. Entering the water, he winces and sees her playful grin.

'Just you wait 'til I get you,' he threatens with a smile.

Cara lets out a little shriek, at the same time giving him a wide-eyed look.

He wades in deeper. The cold water chills his skin as it works its way up his legs. Suddenly he dives beneath the waves and, resurfacing in a sea of bubbles, sets off towards her in an overarm crawl, his muscles glistening as he powers through the sea. Soon, he is beside her.

'Nothing like a bracing swim to start the day,' she says casually.

'Warm bath, you said!' Oliver gives her a mock stern look.

'Well, to a cold-blooded creature it probably is,' she says mischievously, 'though you proved last night to be anything but…'

Reaching out, Oliver pulls Cara through the water towards him. Gently, he lifts her out of the sea. He watches, mesmerised, as the water runs in rivulets from her shoulders across her soft, rounded breasts, teasing her nipples erect. He has never seen anyone so exquisite and he cannot speak. He doesn't need to; the look in his eyes says it all. Despite the cold, he feels himself stir.

Putting her arms around his neck, Cara wraps her legs round his waist. Feeling safe in his arms, so strong and powerful, she allows herself to believe that, together, they can face the world.

Oliver braces himself against the rhythmic swell of the sea. Cupping her buttocks in the palms of his hands, he draws her into a loving kiss. As their passion grows, any concern about water temperature is soon forgotten.

Pulling back briefly, Oliver gazes at Cara, spellbound. In a voice he hardly recognises as his own, he whispers, 'Cara, you have saved me. You are my one, my all.'

*

High on the cliff, amongst the heather and wildflowers, Sylvie grinds her teeth together in fury.

'Bastard! You are mine.'

She holds the camera steady and, focusing on Oliver's face, takes the photograph. She has never seen him look so passionate or enraptured, not in any of the numerous love scenes she's examined time and again. She thought she knew his complete range of emotions, but this is something new. She scowls and clicks away. Then she zooms in on Cara's face. She wants to hate her but there's something about this woman that confuses her. It's as if Cara pours oil onto Sylvie's troubled waters, easing and soothing away her pain. Lying low on the cliff, careful not to be seen, Sylvie is transfixed by the luminous glow that surrounds the couple. She watches them making love in the sea, oblivious to anything but each other, and quickly lowers her head when they finally emerge from the water. As Oliver glances up at the cliff top again Sylvie ducks, then watches as they gather their clothes and walk hand in hand, naked, along the beach.

Rising to her knees, Sylvie keeps her finger on the shutter button until Oliver and Cara disappear around the rocky promontory into the main cove. Only then does she howl into the wind, her misery and sadness becoming unbearable. She remembers her excitement at finding herself in his presence on Holy Isle. But last weekend he was so cruel, telling her he didn't love her and never had, although she knows that's a lie – he loved her in Scotland. If it weren't for this woman turning his head he would love her again. Beyond frustration, Sylvie raises the camera high above her head, ready to smash it against a rock. She hesitates. Slowly, a look of pure maliciousness replaces the one of despair. If she can't be with him then neither will this golden woman. She will see to that.

*

Approaching the rocky outcrop, Oliver glances cautiously along the empty beach of the main cove and hears Cara's carefree, light-hearted laugh.

'Can't help it,' he says, holding his clothes in front of him to afford some dignity. 'You never know who may be snooping.'

She considers the constraints of his life, so different from her own. 'It's so early, Oliver. I doubt there will be anyone on the beach for at least an hour.'

She turns and smiles up at him. It's only then he notices the small but vibrantly coloured hummingbird tattoo on her left ankle.

'Cara, you are full of surprises,' he says in wonder.

She glances down. 'Oh, that. One wild summer when I was sixteen. Seemed a good idea at the time. I still like it, though.'

Oliver nods. He loves it.

'What time do you have to go?' she asks.

'I can stay until three.'

'That gives us around seven hours,' says Cara, doing a quick calculation. 'What would you like to do?'

Oliver gazes at the golden girl with the hummingbird tattoo walking naked beside him, at ease in her own skin and making no attempt to cover her beautiful body.

'That's easy,' he says without hesitation. 'You!'

Chapter Thirty

Deanna stares out of the windscreen. She can't put her finger on it but her conversation with Oliver the previous evening has left her feeling out of sorts. Her husband sounded distracted, as if on autopilot.

'Postie's here,' calls Sebastian from the back seat.

'Hmm?'

'The postman, Mum!'

Deanna looks towards the electric gates. On the other side – in the real world – the postman climbs out of his van.

'Go and intercept him before he puts the post in the box, Seb.'

Her son opens the car door. Yelling instructions at the postman, he sets off at a run up the gravelled drive.

Nothing shy and retiring about that one, thinks Deanna. She glances in the rear-view mirror. Where is Charlie? He knows she wants to get away early to miss the traffic. She catches sight of Jamie watching his brother out of the window.

'Are you looking forward to seeing Granny and Grumps?'

Jamie nods and meets his mother's gaze in the mirror. He's so quiet, her youngest. She never really knows what he's thinking. He looks pale and she wonders if he's going down with something.

'Are you OK, Jamie?'

'Yes, but…' The boy purses his lips and looks away.

'But what?' she asks softly.

'I miss Dad,' he mumbles. 'I wish he was here.'

'I wish your dad was here too,' Deanna says, colouring slightly as she remembers telling him not to come back as he would only be in the way. Nagging disquiet gnaws at her. Turning in her seat, she reassures her son. 'Now that we're spending August in Norfolk the time will fly by and your dad will be home again before you know it. You can phone him once we arrive, if you like.'

Through the rear window she sees Charlie carrying a huge suitcase out of the house. Deanna smiles at Jamie and gets out of the car. 'What have you got in there?' she asks, walking towards her eldest son. 'We're only away for a month.'

'Just covering all eventualities,' Charlie says, smiling engagingly.

'Well, put it in the boot. You know I'm keen to miss the traffic.'

She continues to the house and punches in the burglar-alarm code, although she doubts it will be necessary with all the security. Closing the front door behind her, she walks back to the car just as Sebastian skids to a halt in a flurry of gravel, armed with the post.

'Sebastian, don't do that! It makes such a mess.' Giving her son a stern look, Deanna stomps on the skid marks. The boy shrugs and climbs in the car next to Jamie.

'OK, we'd better get going if we're to make Fakenham in time for lunch,' Deanna says, getting in the car. 'You know what the Dartford Tunnel can be like.'

Charlie closes the boot and climbs in the passenger seat.

From his seat in the back, Sebastian waves the post at his mother through the gap between the front seats.

'Put it in the glove compartment, Charlie,' Deanna instructs. 'I'll look at it once we've arrived. Everyone strapped in?'

She drives the Range Rover towards the opening gates. Braking at the entrance, Deanna checks the track before sweeping out of the drive. The electric gates close smoothly behind her. At last, she's escaped the gilded prison Oliver has created.

Looking quietly out of the window, Jamie is the only one who notices the dark blue car with his initials on its number plate parked at the entrance to the National Trust car park. He hasn't seen it for several weeks and wonders where it's been.

*

Mission accomplished! Sylvie congratulates herself.

Arriving at the start of the week with package in hand, she expected to hand-deliver it to that smug wife of Oliver's, only to find that a pair of tall gates now prevented her from accessing his property. She walked the fence line looking for a place to enter, but the newly erected fence is impenetrable. When the Doberman picked up her scent and started barking at her from the far perimeter of Oliver's grounds, she was fearful, but the guard held onto the dog. Thwarted, she scurried back to her car and resorted to Plan B, posting the package that same afternoon.

She arrived early this morning, parked the car and waited. Keeping her binoculars trained on the electric gates, Sylvie observed the postman arrive and pass a bundle of envelopes to a boy, her package included. As she watched the boy run back to the Range Rover, mounting excitement consumed her. Now that self-satisfied cow will get her comeuppance! A malicious smile cracked her face but it was soon wiped off when Deanna ignored the post. Instead, the tall lad sitting in the passenger seat took it from the boy and stowed it away in the glove compartment.

No! She wanted to witness Deanna's reaction.

Nevertheless, as the Range Rover sweeps out of the drive, Sylvie hugs herself with glee. Her package was successfully delivered. Even though she won't have the satisfaction of seeing the look of shock on Deanna's face when she opens the envelope, Sylvie knows it won't be long before all hell breaks loose. All she has to do now is return to Cornwall and keep watch. She can hardly wait for the fallout. Raising the binoculars one final time, Sylvie scans the grounds and sees the guard walking the fence line with his dog. It's odd that Oliver's property is so inaccessible. She used to be able to nip through the post-and-rail fencing, but now there's a high, welded mesh fence surrounding the estate. She frowns. Has he done this on her account? She breaks into contemptuous laughter. Serves him right. If he's not going to play ball, then she's going to make his life as uncomfortable as possible.

Chapter Thirty-One

It's another glorious August day and the sun rides high in a cloudless sky. Porthleven bustles with tourists and the restaurants are packed. Carol loves days like this and she should be full of joy, but her thoughts weigh heavily upon her. She must choose her words very carefully. The door to The Art Shack is open and she sees Cara at the till talking to a young couple. As she enters the gallery, Carol smiles at her daughter and waits for the couple to leave before shutting the door and turning the sign to 'closed'.

'Mum, what are you doing?' asks Cara.

'I want to have a quiet word with you, my darling girl,' Carol says. With hammering heart, she approaches her daughter.

Cara frowns.

'Would you like coffee?' Carol asks, stalling for time. She walks round to the back of the counter.

'Mum, stop procrastinating. Whatever 'quiet word' you are planning to have you might as well start now.'

Carol pulls up a stool and takes Cara's hands in hers. Where on earth does she start?

'Mum, what's wrong? You're worrying me. Is it Dad?'

'No, it's not your father.' Carol takes a deep breath. 'It's you, Cara. We are worried about you.'

Cara laughs, the tension releasing. 'Don't worry about me. I'm just fine.'

Carol scrutinises her daughter. It's true, she looks positively blooming. That's the problem.

'Cara, please listen to your mother for a moment. You know your father and I want only the very best for you. We want to see you happy again.'

'I am,' Cara says.

'I know, darling.' Carol hesitates. 'But it's the source of your happiness that worries us.' She watches myriad emotions sweep across her daughter's face.

Swiftly, Cara extracts her hands and climbs off the stool. Walking away, she gathers her thoughts before turning to face her mother. 'Oliver means the world to me.'

Carol nods. 'I can understand that but, darling, he's not available.'

Cara studies her mother. Is this going to be a lecture on right and wrong? No one can dictate to her on that! The day Christo died, right and wrong died too. She knows from bitter experience that life is fleeting and if anything wonderful, exquisite and out of the ordinary comes along it should be grabbed with both hands. There's no grand prize for being good or strong, or loyal or loving. Life is just what it is.

'Mum, please don't think badly of me. It's not as simple as that. It's not that black and white.'

'Oh, Cara, I'm not judging you. You are an adult and can make up your own mind. You've faced more heartbreak than most and I know you won't take things on lightly. I'm just concerned you run the risk of having your heart broken again.'

Cara considers her mother's words. Yes, she has fallen for Oliver big time, but he's fallen for her too – hook, line and sinker. Neither of them knows what the future may hold but, for this moment in time, they are happy. Besides, to live in the moment is how she survives.

Cara walks over to her mother and hugs her. 'When Christo died, something died in me too,' she says softly. 'I didn't ever believe I'd find it again.' She takes a deep breath. 'But life continued, though it was a poorer version of the life that went before. I seemed to be forever waiting for that something to return. Only it didn't.'

Carol bites her lip. Cara has always seemed so resilient and has never expressed her thoughts since that fateful day. She seems so far away... With heart fit to breaking, Carol waits patiently for her daughter to continue.

Cara glances around the gallery. It's her space filled with her style and yet, many times over the past two years, she's been merely the understudy standing in for the real Cara Penhaligon, currently unavailable. She turns back to Carol.

'When I first met Oliver I had no expectations, but he kept coming back. As we spent time together we discovered our keys fitted each other's locks and, at last, I feel safe enough to let my truest self step forward.' Cara wonders if her mother will think she has lost the plot, but the look on Carol's face encourages her to continue. 'I can be completely and honestly who I am with Oliver and we love each other for who we are, not for who we pretend to be. I truly believe that each of us unveils the best part of the other.'

'Cara,' Carol whispers, 'you are describing soul mates!'

Cara nods. 'I believe I am. But I also know how cruel life can be and, so, I will not hold him to anything. I will let life take its own course and allow the connection be what it is. It may only last five weeks, five months or five years… or it may last a lifetime. Who knows? But I will let it manifest itself the way it is meant to. I know that our meeting is no chance encounter. This relationship has a destiny. If it stays or if it leaves, I am thankful for having been loved by him. And, anyway, life is too short to be anything but happy. Falling down is part of life. Getting back up is living.'

Carol blinks back tears. Her daughter never fails to amaze her with insights and understanding that go far beyond her own. It's obvious she's in love with Oliver, and Carol has always seen the way he is with Cara, but still she can't shake off that vision of Deanna and her all-encompassing strength. How will they cope with that?

Cara smiles at her mother. Gently, she squeezes her hand. 'I believe that Oliver's soul has come into my life for reasons I do not yet fully understand, but I am prepared to simply let it be who and what it is meant to be.'

Chapter Thirty-Two

Cornwall basks in the hottest day of the year with temperatures hitting 32°C and the Met Office issues a 'level three' heatwave warning. There's not a cloud in the sky and the winds are light, offering little relief from the incessant heat. It must be more refreshing down on the sand close to the sea, but up here on the cliffs it's scorching. Even the gulls seem lethargic, sitting silently on the granite outcrops and expending little energy, simply extending their wings to catch any hint of a breeze.

Sylvie angrily wipes perspiration from her forehead, her lank hair sticking to her skin. Through her binoculars, she watches the beach way below. They're playing happy families and she can't bear his obvious happiness. Why are they still together? The package was delivered two weeks ago. His wife should have reacted by now! Sylvie's mind is in torment, finding no answers and giving no rest. They look the ideal family. It's like watching a sickeningly perfect commercial for the latest holiday resort: great-looking parents and healthy, cheerful kids playing in the surf with their dog. Any advertiser would kill for this dream team. It's nauseating.

'Bastard! I hate you.' As she utters the words she knows it's not true.

Letting the binoculars drop on their strap around her neck, she stands with feet apart and raises her long cotton skirt above her knees. Her bare arms blister under the heat of an unforgiving sun. It's as if she's melting. She should have brought sunscreen. A sudden burst of laughter makes her turn. Two teenage boys walk the cliff path and she scowls at them, raising her skirt even higher and exposing her knickers.

'Seen enough?'

The lads stare at the strange woman standing close to the cliff edge.

'Be careful,' one calls out. 'There have been rock falls in this area.'

'What the fuck's it got to do with you?' Sylvie shouts. 'Piss off!'

The boys continue walking towards the cove, but before disappearing round the corner they glance back. Sylvie still watches. Turning her back to them, she hitches up her skirt around her waist and bends over, wiggling her bottom at them.

Nasty little boys!

Cackling, she straightens up and shakes out her long, floaty skirt; a wild, gypsy girl once more. Now, where is Oliver? Raising her binoculars, she scans the beach. Oh, how sickeningly cutesy. He's in the sea with the blond boy, throwing a Frisbee for the dog. Where's the golden woman gone? Sylvie scrambles along the cliff edge. Ah, there she is.

Observing mother and daughter investigating one of the many rock pools along this stretch of beach, Sylvie watches Cara pick something up and place it in the palm of Bethany's hand. It looks like a starfish. She watches the young girl study it closely before running across the sand to show it to Oliver.

Filled with hatred and jealousy, Sylvie knows she's witnessing a happy and carefree day on the beach; an experience she has never had. Something dark and twisted stirs within her cold heart. Lurking, creeping and slithering, slowly it infects her like a virus that can't be cured. Standing, a forlorn figure on the cliff top, she listens to the clamouring voices telling her to smash and rip apart this little family. She has lived her whole adult life with the possibility of Oliver. Without him, she has nothing. Feeling as if she is slowly dying, Sylvie casts expletives at the figures on the beach below, her misery growing more unbearable. As evil wins, becoming part of her, filling and controlling her, Sylvie loses her mind. Even God can't save her now.

Turning her face to the sun suspended high in the cloudless sky, she cannot feel its warmth. She looks out over the azure sea, sparkling and dazzling, and watches a container ship silently traversing the far horizon. It's so peaceful and serene, but she will smash it. She will swoop over the figures on the sand below and peck out the eyes of that golden woman and her children in front of him. She will destroy Oliver.

Sylvie takes a few paces back and then runs towards the edge of the cliff. As heather and granite give way to air, she spreads her arms wide. But Sylvie doesn't fly. Instead, she plummets towards the pristine sands eagerly rushing up to greet her.

*

Uncharacteristically, Barnaby growls and Cara turns towards the dog. His hackles are raised and she follows his intense stare.

'Oh my God!' Her hands fly up to her mouth.

At the sound of her cry, Oliver turns sharply. Hearing a thud, he looks towards the cliffs. A pile of rags lies at their base, but from the look of horror on Cara's face he already suspects what it is. Oliver runs from the surf across the sand with the Labrador in hot pursuit.

'Barnaby, here!' Cara calls urgently. The dog halts and immediately trots back to his mistress. 'Beth, you and Sky stay here. Don't move!' she says, more harshly than intended. 'And keep hold of Barnaby.'

Cara runs across the beach. As she approaches the stricken figure she can see it's a woman. Oliver kneels beside her, holding her hand. He looks up with concern and guilt in his eyes.

'It's Sylvie,' he says in a shocked whisper.

Cara looks down at the moaning woman on the sand. Her eyes have rolled back into their sockets and her right leg sticks out at an unnatural angle, the foot twisted beneath; bone protruding.

'I'll get help,' she says. Calling to her children, Cara sets off at a run towards the main cove with Barnaby keeping pace.

Oliver brushes Sylvie's hair out of her face with the lightest touch. 'Sylvie, what have you done?' His tone is compassionate and full of concern. Sylvie groans, eyelids flickering. 'Just lie still. Help will be here soon.'

Sylvie's eyes fly open and she grimaces. What's she doing lying here? She should be soaring. She has no feeling below her pelvis but the pain in her back is acute. And then Oliver swims into focus. What's he doing? He's holding her hand and whispering sweet nothings in her ear. Is she dreaming? The pain is unbearable. She gasps and lets out a moan, the sound of a wounded animal.

Oliver pales. 'Don't try to move.'

'I'm cold,' she croaks, shivering violently as shock sets in.

Wearing only swimming trunks, Oliver has nothing to cover her with. He lies down beside her and wraps her in his arms, giving his warmth.

'Oliver…'

'Shhh, Sylvie. Just try to keep still.'

The sand is cold in the shadow of the cliff but he will not leave. As the minutes pass by, Sylvie slips into unconsciousness.

'Sylvie, come back,' Oliver calls.

Presently, Cara arrives with a blanket. 'The air ambulance is on its way.'

'Where are Beth and Sky?' Oliver asks, carefully extracting himself from Sylvie and rising to his knees.

'Janine's looking after them,' Cara says, gently placing the blanket over the stricken woman. Sylvie moans deliriously.

A sudden shout and Oliver turns to see a group of people approaching from around the rocky outcrop. Rick is amongst them. The jungle drums are working well.

'Is there anything we can do?' Rick calls out.

'Just make sure everyone keeps back so the air ambulance can land safely,' Oliver says.

Rick nods and turns to the growing crowd alerted to an incident in the next cove.

'Oliver?' Sylvie calls out weakly.

'Sylvie, I'm here,' he says, turning back to her.

Her eyes snap open, full of pain. She stares at him in bewilderment. Then her eyes focus on Cara, shrouded in a beautiful, golden light. Is she an angel?

Cara takes Sylvie's hand in hers and Oliver looks on in awe, as a healing light transfers itself to the broken woman lying on the sand.

As warmth travels up Sylvie's arm into her chest and down her spine, the agony in her eyes decreases. 'Oliver,' she croaks, 'I love you.'

'I know and it's OK.'

Hearing the distant sound of rotating blades, Oliver watches as the red helicopter swoops in from Porthleven Beach on its approach to the hidden cove. As it manoeuvres into position to land, the noise intensifies and the downdraft forces the crowd to stand back.

'Love me, Oliver, please,' Sylvie begs.

Cara glances at Oliver, her heart aching with the tragedy of it all.

Tenderly, Oliver takes Sylvie's free hand in his. 'I love you,' he says, the lump in his throat distorting his voice.

Sylvie smiles. Suddenly, her face is transformed.

As the paramedics approach across the sand, Sylvie's eyes cloud over and a trickle of blood escapes from the corner of her mouth, dripping onto the sand and staining it red. Her limp, battered body is lifeless – an empty husk at the base of the cliff – but at last her spirit is free.

*

'What a sorry state of affairs,' says Rick to no one in particular. 'Do you two want a drink?'

'No, thanks, Rick.' Cara says. 'I'd better get back to the kids.'

Rick nods. 'Probably just as well if you both disappear. Looks like the press have arrived.'

Oliver glances sharply in the direction of the café. A car emblazoned with the local radio signage pulls into the car park. 'Thanks for your help,' he says, pale with shock.

Did Sylvie slip, or did she jump? He knows it's no coincidence her being here. She was stalking him again. When the paramedics asked if they knew the woman he considered keeping quiet, but his hard-working conscience demanded he be honest. He explained she was an acquaintance. When they enquired if she had any family he told them of the aunt who could be contacted via the monks on Holy Isle. They didn't ask anything further, just took his and Cara's contact details so they could be called upon to give evidence at the inquest.

Cara's hand is warm and soft and gives him some comfort. As Rick bids them farewell, Oliver follows her up the cliff steps. As they emerge onto the grass in front of The Lookout, Cara stumbles. With lightning-quick reflexes, Oliver catches her.

'Cara?' His voice is full of concern.

She clings to him and buries her head against his chest. Closing her eyes, Cara swallows hard but she cannot stem the tears. She cries for Sylvie and her unrequited love; for Christo at leaving them way too soon; and for the uncertainty of her relationship with Oliver.

'My beautiful girl,' Oliver says softly. 'Let it all out.' He rocks her gently and, lovingly, strokes her long, blonde hair.

As they stand together in the muggy evening air, Oliver looks out over the cove. Several people are still on the beach, making the most of the stunning summer's day, and he can see Rick and Tania standing on the decking. Marvelling at the tranquil scene before him, he wonders how many other tragedies this deceptively peaceful cove has witnessed over the centuries.

Eventually, Cara lifts her head and peers up at him. Her face is blotched and red.

'Let's get you inside,' Oliver says quietly.

With his arm around her waist, he walks her towards the porch but she stumbles again. As soon as the door is open, he sweeps her into his arms and carries her to her bedroom. Carefully, he lays her on her bed. Immediately, she curls up into a ball.

'Can I get you anything?' Oliver asks, worry deeply etched upon his face.

She shakes her head. She just wants to drift away and block out the world.

'Let's get you into bed, then.'

He persuades her to sit up and, like a child, Cara allows him to undress her; all the fight in her extinguished. Oliver lies down beside her. Tenderly, he cradles her in his arms. The minutes tick by and he watches the last golden rays of sun streaming through the wooden slatted blinds turn to the greyness of dusk.

'I'm just going to get Beth and Sky,' he whispers in her ear.

Unsure whether she's heard him, he raises his head. She's asleep; her tears streaked dry upon her face. Careful not to disturb her, Oliver gets out of bed. He looks down at this beautiful woman who has so unexpectedly come into his life and his heart overflows with love and compassion. He pulls the sheet gently over her body. Tas's summer tour is rapidly coming to an end but he cannot imagine life without her. Exiting her bedroom, he walks through the silent bungalow and switches on the porch light before heading along the track to Janine's house, deep in thought.

'Oliver, come in.' Janine opens her front door and steps aside. The hallway is crammed full of jackets, boots, buckets and spades. 'Is Cara OK? It must have been a huge shock for her, what with the air ambulance being called out,' she whispers.

'It's taken its toll,' he says, 'but she's sleeping now.'

'You know, Beth and Sky can stay here. The twins love having them for a sleepover.'

'Are you sure, Janine?'

'Of course!' She leads the way to the lounge. 'Hey, kids, what do you say to a sleepover?'

The children look up from colouring in a large paper tablecloth spread out over the floor. In unison, the twins shout, 'Yes!'

Perhaps it would be best for Beth and Sky to stay the night with Janine's family. It may help block out the memories of the day.

'Bobkin will be hungry,' says Bethany. 'Will you feed him for me, please?'

'Of course, Beth.' Oliver smiles at the young girl.

'And don't forget Barnaby and Basil,' calls Sky. 'They will be hungry too.'

'Thanks, Janine. I am indebted to you,' Oliver says, relieved at the normality of it all.

'Not at all,' she responds, placing a reassuring hand on his arm. 'Beth and Sky are no trouble and

Molls and Mills love having them to stay. Anyway, I'd do anything for Cara, as I know you would too.'

It's true. He'd give his life.

Calling to Barnaby, Oliver walks slowly back to The Lookout. The tide is on the turn and in the deepening dusk a couple walk hand in hand along the shoreline.

Of all the places I've travelled in the world, none is more beautiful than this.

He stops and looks back at Rick's Beach Hut. Yes, he can understand why the Australian is happy to settle here. As the cove weaves its magic there's no escaping the unquestionable truth staring him in the face: He wants to be here with Cara and her children. Oliver sighs and walks on. Apart from the porch light, The Lookout is in darkness. He checks on Cara and finds her sleeping soundly: The sleep of a thousand sleeps. Having fed all the animals, finally he pours himself a large glass of wine and, taking a deep slug, phones his wife. When she answers, her voice is that of a stranger's.

'Hi, Dee. How's everything?'

'Good. The folks are well and the boys are having a great time. How's it with you?'

Where does he start?

'Fine. Full houses most nights. Can't believe it's the home stretch. We'll be at the Minack soon.' He doesn't want to think about it. 'When are you returning to Surrey?'

'Oh, we'll stay in Norfolk until the boys go back to school. It's so much nicer here.'

Oliver flinches. Did she really have to say that? She's made it perfectly clear she doesn't like the changes at Hunter's Moon. The security measures are probably unnecessary now but as they're in place they may as well stay, though he will concede on the guard and his dog.

'Deanna, a woman died today.'

'Oh?'

'She died in front of me.'

Silence.

'Dee, did you hear what I said?'

'Yes. That's tough. Did you know her?'

How can I even start to explain?

'Not really.'

'Well, then. It's sad for her family but you'll recover from the shock, Ollie. Life goes on.'

For some...

It has been absent for weeks, but now Oliver feels the 'grey mist' descending and he soon finishes the call. He sits listening to the silence, the only sound Barnaby's contented snores from the corner of the room. Eventually, he switches off the light and walks to Cara's bedroom. The wooden blinds are folded back and she stands naked at the open French doors, bathed in moonlight.

'It's so hot,' she says, turning as he enters. 'I wanted to sleep with the doors open and listen to the ocean.'

He smiles. 'Are you feeling better?'

She nods. 'Where are the children?'

'Sleepover at Janine's. I checked earlier. I don't think they understand what happened today.'

'Are you OK, Oliver?'

He grimaces. 'It's a shock and I know it's my fault. Sylvie wouldn't have been on the cliffs if I hadn't been here.'

'You can't blame yourself for Sylvie's actions. If it wasn't today it would have been some other time,' Cara says, walking towards him. She takes his hands. 'Stay with me tonight?' she whispers.

He nods.

Without speaking, she helps him out of his clothes and leads him to her bed. Lying down beside him, Cara turns to face Oliver. The actor's rugged good looks are further accentuated by the moon's silvery light but she hardly notices, seeing only his essence; not the shell. She kisses him tenderly and, soon, they are far away from the shocks of the day. Later, lying together in each other's arms, two halves of a whole, they listen to the waves breaking gently on the shore. Through the open French doors they gaze at the moon casting its light in the ink-black sky, and a meteor shower gifts them a display of streaking lights.

'Perfect,' Oliver murmurs.

Cara smiles. It is.

'You know, Cara,' Oliver whispers, 'I've been homesick for so long, for a place I was not sure even existed. A place where my heart would be full and my soul understood.' Gently he kisses her beneath her ear. 'Thank you for being that place.' Trailing a hand over the contours of her body, Oliver breathes in her scent and knows he is home. 'I love you, Cara Justine Penhaligon,' he says with certainty.

Fighting back tears, Cara wonders if this declaration of love has been brought on due to the shared tragedy they have lived through today. But as she turns and looks deep into his eyes she knows it is true.

'And I love you, Oliver Tobias Foxley,' she says softly. 'But you know what else?'

He shakes his head.

And then Cara utters the three little words he's been yearning to hear all his life.

'I… get… you.'

Chapter Thirty-Three

Indicating left, Deanna turns into the driveway of the lovely, old house that used to be her home. She remembers a happy and secure childhood growing up here with her sister but, having lived longer with Oliver than she did in Norfolk, the memories belong to a different person. Someone she now hardly recognises.

Switching off the engine, she turns to her son. 'Are you feeling OK, Jamie?'

The boy nods, his face ashen and his eyes like saucers.

'You just have to do what the doctor said and your wrist will soon be on the mend.'

Jamie looks down at his arm. It feels odd immobilised in the plaster cast, but he can still move his fingers.

'As long as you remember to do the exercises, your fracture will heal properly,' Deanna says encouragingly. 'Thank goodness it's your left wrist. At least you will still be able to write and do things with your right hand.'

'I wish Dad was here.'

Deanna smiles at her son. 'Not long now, Jamie. Only another couple of weeks and he'll be home.'

She's about to get out of the car when she remembers the post in the glove compartment. Leaning across, Deanna pulls out the various envelopes. A letter from her sister, bills – she reminds herself to check them later – and a couple of clothing magazines. But what's this? A large, hard-backed, brown envelope addressed to Mrs Foxley. She turns it over. No sender's label.

'You go in, Jamie. I won't be long.'

As Deanna watches her son walk carefully along the stone path towards his grandparents' house, she inserts her finger beneath the flap of the envelope and works it open. Extracting the contents, she sees a dozen photographs printed on A4 photographic paper. Sylvie's bold, angry writing jumps off the yellow Post-it note stuck to the top one.

Just what is Oliver Foxley getting up to in Cornwall?

A well-wisher.

As Deanna removes the note, the blood drains from her face. The photograph is of Oliver and a woman embracing in the sea. At first, she wonders if it's something to do with the play but when she looks at the next photograph bile rises in her throat and her blood runs cold. It's a close-up of Oliver gazing in wonder at the woman in his arms. She has never seen that emotion on her husband's face, not in any theatre production or any of his many films; and he has never gazed at her like that. She forces herself to look at the rest of the photographs, hoping they will prove to be stills but knowing they are not. Who is this blonde beauty? She's stunning! And is it trick photography? In every image she appears shrouded in a golden light.

As innumerable emotions threaten to strangle her, Deanna stares at the young woman and then her eyes alight upon her husband's face. She remembers how devastated she felt when she first suspected there was something more than just a professional relationship between him and that appalling actress, Heather McMullen. But these photographs speak of something much more.

The final photograph is of Oliver and Cara walking hand in hand along the beach, naked. They look so at ease in each other's company in the natural surroundings, it's as if they belong together. Vehemently, Deanna rejects the idea. How could he do this to her? She's worked so hard to create this life of theirs and, yet, here he is leading one all of his own. Perhaps he's always had a life of his own. Deanna pushes away this thought too, but it won't let her off the hook that easily. Just how many affairs has her husband had over the years? Apart from the hurt, how dare he make such a fool of her?

She looks at the Post-it note again. Some well-wisher…

Deanna stares out of the window. Oliver has sounded so odd these past few weeks and now she knows why. She studies the photographs again, lingering too long over the close-up of Oliver and Cara in the sea, obviously in the throes of making love. She has never seen that rapturous look on his face before. Her life, as she knows it, is unravelling. What's she going to do?

She's got to act fast.

Chapter Thirty-Four

The Minack Theatre: the theatre under the stars. A spectacularly perched, terraced amphitheatre on the cliffs above Porthcurno, hewn out of granite rocks above a sheer drop into the Atlantic and the brainchild of one woman whose back-breaking, lifetime's work was its creation. From 1931, Rowena Cade worked tirelessly in all weathers each winter into her mid-eighties to create her vision for the enjoyment of future generations, always working on a shoestring and using the skills of just two men – her gardener, Billy Rawlings, and his mate, Charles Thomas Angove. Granite was cut by hand from a pile of tumbled boulders, stones were inched into place and terraces in-filled with earth, small stones and pebbles were shovelled down from the higher ledges, and sand was fetched in bags on Rowena's back from Porthcurno beach way below. When she died in 1983, just short of her ninetieth birthday, Rowena Cade was still thinking of the future and left elaborate sketches suggesting how the theatre might be covered on days when it rains; plans which have yet to be implemented.

Oliver waits patiently in the wings for the backstage crew to change the set. It's the final scene.

All summer long, *Sorrows in the Sand* has been a sell-out success and he can't believe they've already arrived at the last night. Glancing out over the theatre's dramatic backdrop, he watches the moon shine its light across the bay, casting a magical silvery path across the ocean. Leading where? Oliver smiles.

Puerto Rico. Four thousand miles away...

It is a truly spectacular setting and the weather has been kind for each of the Tasmanian Devil Theatre Company's performances. The theatre is packed, the audience not only touched by the magic that is the Minack Theatre but also by the leading man's delivery. It's not every day an award-winning, world-famous actor is so accessible and they have not been short-changed; Oliver has given his all.

He turns and looks across the stage. She's sitting in the second row with her family and friends. As with the very first time he saw her, his stomach tightens. Will the excitement she stirs in him ever diminish? He doubts it. He knows he has difficult decisions ahead but he has made up his mind.

'Almost there,' Jodie, his red-headed love interest, whispers.

Oliver nods. Patiently, they wait to make their entrance.

What about Deanna? He frowns. Yes, it's going to be tough and he's steeling himself for the battle ahead, but Deanna is strong and independent and her life revolves around her children. She's made it patently clear he hardly exists for her. She will cope. No doubt she will screw him over financially, but he doesn't really care if it means he and Cara will be together. And, anyway, he can always make money. His agent has already presented him with a good script and, this time, he has accepted the movie without hesitation. He glances at Cara again. The love of his life…

'Here we go,' says Jodie, putting her arm round his waist. Together, they walk out of the shadows and onto the stage.

*

Cara glances along the row. Her parents are here with their friends, and Tristan, Jane, Morwenna and the rest of the gang have also come along for Oliver's final performance. Ben, too, with his new girlfriend: a sweet-faced girl from St Just. Sky and Beth are staying with their friends, the twins. Cara feels safe and secure, surrounded by family and friends, and a delicious warmth spreads deep within her. She knows it's love – and after she'd given up hope of ever feeling anything again – but it still catches her by surprise. Who would have thought? It truly is a beautiful world.

As Oliver and Jodie step into the spotlight, Cara turns her attention to the stage and senses Christo smiling down at her.

Presently, drawing back from his final embrace with Jodie, Oliver turns to the audience and delivers his last line. 'There comes a point in life when you have to just write your sorrows in the sand and let the tide gently wash them away...'

As the lights dim, the audience holds a collective breath before erupting into enthusiastic applause.

'That was a great performance you put in tonight, Jodie,' Oliver says to the actress, as they join hands. She smiles. Forming a line with the rest of the troupe, they bow to the appreciative audience before departing the stage.

'Well, that was just wonderful! What *are* we going to do now, Carol?' says Sheila, neatly folding her blanket and handing it to her husband.

'Face reality, I suppose.'

'You poor girls,' says Barry good-naturedly. 'How are you going to cope stuck with little old Ken and me?'

'Oh, I expect we'll find a way!' says Carol with a laugh. Sheila pulls a face.

'Are you waiting for Oliver?' Tristan calls along the row to Cara.

'Yes.'

'OK. We'll catch you tomorrow. Twelve thirty?'

Cara nods. They've planned a get-together at Rick's Beach Hut with all the friends to celebrate the end of the season. It's a bittersweet occasion, as Oliver returns to Surrey the following day. She knows it will be excruciatingly hard for him but he's going to tell Deanna of his decision. Cara frowns. Deep down in the pit of her stomach there's that feeling again. Why does she feel as if she's clenching onto a handful of sand which, bit by bit, is slipping through her straining fingers?

'See you tomorrow,' Jane mouths and, standing behind her, Morwenna waves. They turn and follow Tristan, joining the crocodile of people wending its way up the granite steps to the car park.

Carol hugs her daughter. She was always such a naturally beautiful girl but there's an additional glow to her these days. It's lovely seeing her so obviously happy, though Carol can't help but feel a twinge of panic.

'Enjoy the rest of the weekend and I'll see you on Monday,' she says. 'Don't hurry in.'

'Thanks, Mum. Bye, Dad.' Cara kisses Ken on the cheek.

From the aisle Sheila calls out, 'Look after that gorgeous hunk of yours and don't do anything I wouldn't do!'

'Don't you be leading my daughter astray,' admonishes Carol.

Sheila laughs. 'Too late for that, I fear!'

Standing behind his wife, Barry rolls his eyes and smiles kindly at Cara. She watches as they join the queue, before making her way to the front of the stage. A few cast members are trickling back on. Cara stands for several minutes looking out over the sea. The Milky Way stretches across a pollution-free sky and she follows the trajectory of a shooting star, remembering the last time she saw a meteor shower. It was the first time Oliver admitted his love for her, though he's told her several times since. Oh, how she loves this county! She never wants to leave. And then she sees him.

Chatting to one of his fellow actors, Oliver emerges onto the stage and sees her waiting for him… achingly beautiful.

Deanna stands in the darkness, observing. Her husband looks different. In all the years she's known him he's grappled with his inner demons and, yet, here he is happy and relaxed, as if he hasn't a care in the world. With a sudden rush of emotion she realises her husband looks whole.

She watches as Oliver and his companion move aside, allowing other actors onto the stage. At last they say goodbye and as the other man walks away, Oliver looks across the stage with a loving expression on his face. Deanna follows his gaze and her heart lurches to a stop. The young woman is even more stunning than in the photographs. How can she possibly compete? Momentarily, she falters as deep instinct tells her these two souls belong together. For the first time in her life she is unsure, without direction, but she refuses to allow the feeling to gain momentum. Digging deep and as her inbuilt strength kicks in, Deanna steps forward.

'Hello, Ollie,' she says lightly.

Unsuccessfully, Oliver attempts to mask his shock. He can't find his voice. This is not how it's meant to play out. Cara is waiting for him. He tries to look beyond Deanna, but she blocks him.

'The play went well,' she says, ignoring the look on his face. 'You must be very happy with that performance.'

Speech still evades him and he knows he has turned pale. He has got to sort this out. Deanna watches as her husband fights to master his emotions.

'Deanna!' His voice is a strangled cry. 'What are you doing here?'

'I thought I'd surprise you.'

On a scale of one to ten the surprise is off the scale!

'I've booked a hotel for us tonight,' she says.

Oliver blinks. This can't be happening. He's going home with Cara. Home…

'Deanna, there's something I have to tell you.'

The urgency in his voice makes Deanna's heart pound with fear. Pulling Jamie out of the shadows, she positions their youngest child to face his dad. Oliver reels at the extra shock and then his heart softens, swiftly followed by concern as he notices the plaster cast on his son's arm. He holds out his arms and the boy runs to him. Tenderly, Oliver hugs his son. Looking over Jamie's head, he catches the look in Deanna's eyes. She knew she held the trump card all along.

'I've missed you, Dad,' says Jamie, hugging his father extra hard.

'What happened, Jamie?'

'I fractured my wrist falling out of a tree at Granny and Grumps'. The doctor says I have to wear the cast for up to six weeks.' The boy pulls a face. 'I'll have to go back to school with it on. It's ever so itchy.'

Why the hell didn't Deanna tell him their son broke his wrist? Anger surges through Oliver and then turns inwards. Where has *he* been for Jamie when his son needed him? He feels age-old depression laughing at him: *'Holiday time over!'* Still holding Jamie, he looks at his wife again. As the 'grey mist' descends, Oliver knows she has won.

From her position at the front of the stage, Cara sees shock register on Oliver's face as a slim, attractive, dark-haired woman steps between them, effectively blocking her view. She watches as a young boy is brought out from the shadows and Oliver dips down to hug him. With sinking heart and a growing lump in her throat – and before Oliver fully understands the unfolding drama and the decision he *must* make – Cara already knows the outcome. Although prepared to leave his wife, Oliver will not abandon his son.

As Deanna glances in Cara's direction, her look is complex: subservient, yet laced with an apology. But there's also a strength that tells Cara in no uncertain terms that she, the mother of Oliver's children, will not allow her life to be stripped away from her.

As the seconds pass, Deanna steels herself. She will not be the first to break eye contact. Deep down she acknowledges how inadequate she is compared to Cara, but she will not give her rival the satisfaction of understanding this. Ultimately, Deanna's look turns to one of triumph.

Blinking back tears, and with a breaking heart, Cara wraps Oliver in a virtual, loving hug and wishes him well in life. Quickly she turns away and lets the darkness swallow her.

Feeling a surge of love coming in his direction, Oliver straightens up. His wife wears a triumphant look and, immediately, he turns in Cara's direction. She's not there. Frantically he searches the rows of fast-emptying seats, but she is nowhere to be seen. Cara has simply vanished into the night.

Epilogue

Eleven months later

Forty… Forty-one… Forty-two… Oliver powers through the water, clocking up the lengths, his body still fizzing from last night's dream. It's the same dream he's had for the past five nights, only it doesn't seem like a dream at all. Wickedly, his mind plays tricks, coaxing him into believing it is real, only for him to wake overwhelmed with disappointment when facing his reality. Pale by comparison.

Smooth as silk, the water seductively caresses his body. The music and lights are low and in the womb-like environment he has created, despite the demons inside his head, Oliver feels cocooned. It's early; the family has yet to stir. He couldn't just lie there next to Deanna waiting for the day to begin; he had to do something. Silently he made his way through the sleeping household to the handsome, oak-framed building situated behind the house.

Although hugely expensive, the leisure complex was money well spent, incorporating a swimming pool, gym and sauna. All the family use it and the children are competent swimmers, even Jamie.

Initially, the boy was wary of the strange atmosphere and the reflections the water made on the ceiling and walls but, refusing to be any less than his siblings, he rose to the challenge and eventually overcame his fears. As Oliver surges on towards his goal he thinks about his quiet, sensitive, youngest son. Jamie is the reason he is still here. He refuses to let the sacrifice he has made diminish his love for the boy.

Following the final performance at the Minack, they stayed for one night only at that old haunt of Sir Alfred Munnings in Lamorna Cove, but Oliver hardly noticed his surroundings. He barely conversed, so complex were his emotions where Deanna was concerned. The only suggestion of normality was his interaction with his son. After returning to Surrey he was equally remote, indulging in long runs over the North Downs or punishing himself with gruelling workouts in the gym. Of course, Deanna confronted him with the photographs and he could not deny the accusations hurled at him. They were true. He was in love with Cara. For the sake of the children they continued to operate as a couple, although they moved into separate rooms. However, as the weeks lengthened into months, they regained some semblance of their former life and he recently moved back into the marital bed.

But the recurring dream brings it all back, and Oliver wonders if he will ever fully recover from the previous summer. How many times has he been on the point of phoning Cara to offer up some sort of explanation, but what could he say that she isn't already aware of? Unable to resist, he checked to see who won the Threadneedle Prize, and it was no surprise to learn that her incredible talent had been recognised. He was so proud of his beautiful, golden girl and immediately wrote to tell her so, only for the letter to be torn up in frustration and never posted. Why would she want to hear from him? He abandoned her. Neither had he kept his promise to Christo – he hadn't followed through.

Oliver ups his pace, creating waves that slap angrily against the sides of the tiled pool. Cutting through the water in a powerful overarm crawl, he completes another ten lengths before entering the meditative zone and dares to revisit his dream.

Alone in the Cornish landscape, Oliver walks the cliff path and the closer he gets to the cove, the more laboured his breathing becomes. He knows this path so well. Every twist and turn, rock and secret crevice, and every grassy hillock where they lay on their backs, holding hands and watching the sun go down, not daring to think about the future, simply content in each other's company.

Just over the horizon he knows The Lookout's roof will appear. His stomach is in knots. Will she be there? What will he say? Will they even acknowledge each other? How can they not? He stops and looks out over the ocean. Breathing in the salty sea air, he attempts to quieten his clamouring heart. Standing sentinel on the cliff edge amongst the sea pinks, a seagull eyes him suspiciously. Suddenly, with a raucous cry, it takes to the air, the sound piercing the quiet of the hot, still afternoon. His palms are moist with perspiration and he wipes them on his trousers. He feels paralysed and cannot take another step. This is where Sylvie jumped – or slipped – and a wave of nausea sweeps over him as he relives the shock of that afternoon, the sickening thud and her last, gasping breath. He still feels guilty, although he knows he was powerless to save her. If it hadn't been the fall that claimed her it would have been something else. He shudders and closes his mind to that terrible time, not daring to consider what else she would have conjured up to inflict upon his wife and children, let alone that other most precious of families.

Oliver resumes his journey and reaches the bend with heart in mouth. Shockingly, a couple of hundred yards ahead, Deanna strides purposefully along the path. What's she doing here? He thought he was alone. Holding back, he nervously glances down at The Lookout. There's the shed where Bethany's rabbit lives, and the upended boat that Christo turned into a seat where they would sit and gaze up at the Milky Way. Now, when he looks up at the same galaxy from his Surrey home it comforts him to think that she, too, might be looking up at the night sky and be thinking of him.

The bungalow is neat and well-kept, startlingly white from a recent coat of paint, and a low fence bounds a carefully tended lawn edged with diamond and sapphire encrusted flowers. He smiles. He always knew this was a magical land. But the smile freezes on his face as he remembers her telling him that if ever she found herself settled in a loving relationship she would tame the cliff around the bungalow and create a colourful garden enclosed by a white picket fence. The stab of jealousy is deep. Suddenly a door opens and he watches as Cara emerges, her long blonde hair tied back in a ponytail. The sound of breaking waves on the sand and the cry of the gulls on the wind seem accentuated to his heightened senses. He holds his breath, unable to contain the emotions surging through him.

Shielding her eyes from the sun, she looks up. 'Oliver, how nice to see you again,' she says, as if he's an old family friend and no passion has ever passed between them. 'You must be parched walking the coast path in this heat. Why don't you come down and join us for a drink?'

'Thank you. I'd love to, but how do I get down?' he answers politely.

'Don't you remember?' she asks in surprise.

He shakes his head.

'Well, if you find the way I'll be waiting for you.' She smiles up at him.

Oliver's heart misses a beat. After all he *hasn't* done for her she is waiting for him. He can see his wife far ahead on the coast path but he won't be following her. He will find a way to reach his beautiful, golden girl.

With mounting excitement he sets off down the path and, twenty yards on, discovers the roughly hewn steps leading down beside Janine's house. Emerging onto the track, he stops and glances back at Rick's Beach Hut but, to his surprise, the beach is bare; as if the café never existed. In panic, he turns towards The Lookout. Will this also have vanished? But Cara is there, standing in front of her bungalow, wearing a T-shirt and white jeans rolled up to her knees, the iridescent hummingbird tattoo shimmering on her left ankle. Her skin is sun-kissed and her hair glistens in the afternoon sun. She is as lovely as he remembers and, deep in his belly, he feels the unmistakable stirrings of desire. Without hesitation, he starts to close the gap.

'Ollie!' Deanna's voice rings out harshly above the sound of the waves. He turns. His wife stands a short distance beyond Janine's house, her figure threateningly black against the brilliant blue sky. 'Where are you going?' she asks curiously.

How did she get there? When he last saw her, she was way in the distance on the upper path. Disappointment grabs at his throat and he turns urgently to Cara. She is shrouded in her unique golden glow and her eyes promise him the world.

'I'm sorry, Deanna,' he says, turning back to his wife. 'I'm going home.'

'Home? What are you talking about? You said there was a café up ahead, but I can't see one.'

'Nothing's the same any more. Everything has changed.'

'Nothing has changed,' Deanna says, her right foot tapping impatiently. 'It's as it always has been and always will be.'

As the 'grey mist' descends, obliterating the warmth of the sun on this brilliant day, he turns once again to Cara.

'We are waiting, Oliver,' she says, smiling encouragingly and opening her arms wide. 'We *all* are.'

It's the way she says 'all'. What does she mean? But this is it – his chance to put things right.

'I'm coming,' he says, walking unhesitatingly towards her. 'Wild horses wouldn't keep me away.'

'That's not home, Ollie,' Deanna's no-nonsense voice rings out loud and clear, 'and you know it.'

But she's too late. Cara is in his arms. Immediately, his mouth finds hers and she's every bit as soft and warm as he remembers. As their tender kiss turns to passion, Cara's healing, golden light fills his body and the splinters of ice that have worked their way into his heart melt away. His old adversary stands back, admitting defeat.

And one hundred… Oliver stops swimming. Breathing heavily and holding onto the edge of the pool with one hand, brusquely he clears the water from his eyes.

I am not crying!

He has completed his marathon in the deep end. Effortlessly, he pulls himself out of the water and stands for a moment looking out through the plate-glass windows, across the immaculate lawn leading down to the lake by the trees. It's the start of a beautiful summer's day, not unlike the one in his dream. Quickly, he showers and gets dressed. He's about to switch off the lights when his eldest son appears with two of his school friends.

'Morning, Dad,' says Charlie. 'Gary and Nathan have come over to use the pool.'

He chats briefly with Charlie and his friends and then walks out into the sunshine. He's halfway to the house when his son calls after him.

'Hey, Dad, I forgot to say, there's a package for you in your study.'

'OK. Remember to switch everything off when you've finished.'

Charlie nods and turns back inside. Oliver carries on towards the house, wondering if the package is the script his agent has promised to send him.

'I'm dropping Sammy at Rosie's and then I'm taking Sebastian and Jamie to football,' Deanna informs him as he enters the kitchen. 'I've got rehearsals until four so you won't forget to collect the boys, will you?'

'Err... no!'

Deanna's face twitches; the smallest of smiles. Her eyes do not meet his. And then she's gone. As stage manager for the local amateur dramatics group, she has finally found an outlet for her theatrical frustrations.

Oliver pours himself a mug of coffee and wanders through to his study. Propped against his desk is a large package wrapped in brown paper and 'Fragile' tape. Instantly he recognises her distinctively creative handwriting. With pounding heart, he puts the mug down on the desk and, as if in slow motion, opens the top drawer. Taking out a pair of scissors, he very carefully cuts the tape. Even though his heart races, he feels detached and cushioned from his emotions, as if his higher self offers up some protection. As he peels back the paper, an envelope falls out and he places this on the desk.

Slowly the canvas reveals itself. It's the work in progress that was propped on her easel. Even then it held the promise of being achingly beautiful, but now, finished, it is exceptional. It's the hidden view from the cliffs beyond The Lookout; encompassing the south coast of Cornwall from the cove, past Loe Bar to Praa Sands and Prussia Cove, across a shimmering Mounts Bay with the tip of iconic St Michael's Mount rising out of the water, sweeping on past Penzance and Newlyn to the cliffs at Porthcurno and, in the far distance, Gwennap Head.

No longer can he hold back. Remembering how, when he first viewed the painting, it made him want to cry, Oliver gives vent to his emotions. For the second time that morning he wipes away tears.

In the bottom left-hand corner Cara has painted the roof of The Lookout and, at the far end of the curve of sand, Rick's Beach Hut. The cove is where he goes when he's lonely. It is etched upon his heart; as is she. He will never forget her. How can he? She is a part of him! Even now he can sense her lightness of spirit and her beautiful, golden glow that so effectively banishes the 'grey mist' from the very darkest recesses of his being. He hears her carefree laugh, which offers up so much hope and promise, and Oliver swallows hard, his chest tightening. And isn't that a bark and a young boy's shout? He yearns to see Sky chasing after his dog along the beach and playing in the surf at the water's edge. A vision of Bethany with her shy but all-knowing look comes to him and he recalls how she told him, in that quiet and serious way of hers, that the cormorants in her mother's painting of the Minack flapped their wings when no one was looking. If he looks hard enough will *they* all come to life? With a lump in his throat Oliver scans the cove for the little family that so completely captured his heart, hoping that Cara will somehow manifest. His craving for her never fades. But the beach is empty. There is no golden girl. The only sign of life is half a dozen gulls hanging in the air, greedily eyeing the sands below as the tide gently ebbs and flows.

Oliver swallows his disappointment. During that summer he knows Cara gave to him without strings; she did not keep track of what he owed her. She gave because she was genuine and chose to do so without any ulterior motive, and because she knew what it was like to be without. She showed him what it was to be emotionally smart and the love they shared was so deep, strong and complex that he doubts he ever truly loved before. She understood and connected with him in every way and on every level, and he knows he has had something in his life that few people ever experience – the perfect love with his soul mate. This is the reason he was guided to reject the sure-fire box office hit and, instead, accept Tas's low-key summer tour. During that summer he discovered someone who bestowed a great sense of peace, calm and happiness that no therapy ever achieved, and she reminded him to be all that much more aware of the beauty in life. Their perfect love is the most significant and satisfying thing he will experience in his lifetime, and he will always be thankful for having received such a gift.

Lovingly, Oliver commits to memory the sensations of the cove: the smell of the sea; the sound of the ocean; the cry of the gulls. Wherever his travels take him in the world, this sound will always transport him back to that glorious Cornish summer when Cara shined her healing, golden light and effectively banished the greyness from his soul.

Picking up the canvas, Oliver props it on the armchair. He will hang it later alongside her painting of the Minack. Turning back to his desk, he picks up the envelope and hesitates, deep intuition advising him to be strong. With trembling fingers, he extracts her letter.

Dear Oliver,

I have been meaning to write to you for a long time but the words I wanted to convey have been hard to find. However, write I must, regardless how inadequate my words may prove to be.

This painting I created for you. From the very first brushstroke it was always yours. Do you remember when I showed you this view for the first time you said I had taken you to the edge of the world? Well, it was you *who took* me *to the very edge of the world. I will never forget our summer together and I want to thank you with all my heart for enabling me to feel once again. I also want you to know that I completely understand why it is impossible for us to be together. I accept your decision and respect you for it.*

Oliver blinks rapidly as Cara's words swim out of focus.

This painting, entitled On the Cusp, *(I know you will understand why) is my gift to you for the glorious summer, which will stay with me forever. When I am old and grey I will look back at our time together and be thankful for having been loved by you.*

When we first met I knew our meeting was no chance encounter, but I was never really sure of the destiny of our relationship. I believed your soul had come into my life for reasons I did not fully understand but I was prepared to simply let it be who and what it was meant to be. Now all is clear, and I want to thank you for bestowing the greatest gift of all.

On May 22nd at 6.23 a.m., our son was born, weighing 7lbs 10oz. He is a beautiful, healthy and joyful baby and we all love him dearly. I have named him Tobias Oliver. I don't expect anything from you. I know that you have a family of your own and I will never come to you for financial support. And please, rest assured, the press will never learn that you are the father of this most precious of gifts.

Awash with emotion, Oliver wants to howl at the universe.

Included with the letter is a photograph of a baby wrapped in a fleece. Is this what his dream means when she says they are *all* waiting for him? Oliver's index finger lingers over the image of the baby in the already treasured photograph. She is right. He *is* beautiful, and the most precious of gifts – a son born of the deepest love and the highest faith. He turns the photograph over. Written on the back is a single word… Toby.

Feeling as if he's been punched in the stomach and his heart has stopped beating, Oliver turns his attention back to Cara's letter.

As some very wise person once said, 'In the end just three things matter: How well we have lived; how well we have loved; how well we have learned to let go...'

We hope you enjoyed this book!

Kate Ryder's next book is coming in summer 2018.

More addictive fiction from Aria:

Find out more
http://headofzeus.com/books/isbn/978178854154
1

Find out more
http://headofzeus.com/books/isbn/978178854021
6

Find out more
http://headofzeus.com/books/isbn/978178669489
8

Acknowledgments

Firstly, a big thank you to Caroline Ridding for believing in this book. I will never forget having to re-read your email three times before realising it didn't contain a refusal! Also, to Lucy Gilmour and the rest of the wonderful team at Aria for guiding me through the publishing process and bringing this novel to life.

Special thanks must also go to the talented Rachael Mia Allen, who shared deep insights and expressed so eloquently what it is to be an artist.

To The Romantic Novelists' Association and their invaluable New Writers' Scheme, whose guidance and critiquing encouraged me not to give up.

Also, in memory of the indomitable spirit that was Rowena Cade. We are so fortunate she had the foresight to create the 'theatre under the star's' perched on the cliffs above Porthcurno for future generations to enjoy, and for providing me with the perfect stage on which to weave the penultimate chapter.

And, last but not least, to my husband for graciously understanding the many hours I spent living a different life with my characters and who, unfailingly, kept me supplied with coffee!

About Kate Ryder

KATE RYDER has worked in a number of industries including publishing, mainly as a proofreader/copy editor and writer for a national newspaper, magazines and publishing houses. A member of the New Writers Scheme with the Romantic Novelists Association, in 2013 she published her debut novel, '*The Forgotten Promise*, a timeslip romance and mysterious ghost story, which was shortlisted for Choc Lit's 2016 "Search for a Star" and also honoured with a Chill with a Book "Book of the Month" Award. Kate lives in a renovated 200-year-old sawmill in the beautiful Tamar Valley with her husband

Find me on Twitter
https://twitter.com/KateRyder_Books
Find me on Facebook
https://www.facebook.com/kateryder.author
Visit my website
http://www.kateryder.me/

Become an Aria Addict

Aria is the new digital-first fiction imprint from Head of Zeus.

It's Aria's ambition to discover and publish tomorrow's superstars, targeting fiction addicts and readers keen to discover new and exciting authors.

Aria will publish a variety of genres under the commercial fiction umbrella such as women's fiction, crime, thrillers, historical fiction, saga and erotica.

So, whether you're a budding writer looking for a publisher or an avid reader looking for something to escape with – Aria will have something for you.

Get in touch: aria@headofzeus.com

Become an Aria Addict
http://ariafiction.com/newsletter/subscribe
Find us on Twitter
https://twitter.com/Aria_Fiction
Find us on Facebook
http://www.facebook.com/ariafiction
Find us on BookGrail

http://www.bookgrail.com/store/aria/

Addictive Fiction

First published in the United Kingdom in 2018 by
Aria, an imprint of Head of Zeus Ltd

9 7 5 3 1 2 4 6 8

A CIP catalogue record for this book is available
from the British Library.

ISBN (E) 9781788541091

Aria
c/o Head of Zeus

First Floor East
5–8 Hardwick Street
London EC1R 4RG

www.ariafiction.com

Printed in Great Britain
by Amazon

74039546R00292